BROKEN SOULS

PATRICIA GIBNEY

Published by Bookouture in 2019

An imprint of StoryFire Ltd.
Carmelite House
50 Victoria Embankment
London EC4Y 0DZ

www.bookouture.com

ISBN: 978-1-83888-080-4
eBook ISBN: 978-1-83888-079-8

To Marie Brennan
For everything

*

The four-year-old boy tore off the paper and pushed the sweet into his mouth. The toffee stuck to his baby teeth. He tried to extract it with a finger. The toffee stuck to his fingers and he began to cry.

The slap of the ruler across his knuckles caught him by surprise and momentarily stopped his whimpering. But once he felt the pain shoot up his hand, he screamed.

'I want to go home!'

'Shut up. Not another word. You're upsetting the other children. Look around you. You're a mean little boy, and if you don't stop, I'll stand you outside the door in the rain. You know there are bad people out there and the bad people come to take away naughty little children. Do you want that to happen to you?'

He sniffed away his tears and bit his lip, feeling the toffee still stuck to his front tooth.

'I asked you a question. Answer me.' Another crack of the ruler, this time on the desk.

'No.' He nodded vigorously. He did not want to feel that ruler on his hand or anywhere else again. He would be a good boy.

'Put that wrapper in the bin and open your spelling book.'

He had no idea which one was his spelling book.

'Come up here!'

Making his way to the front of the classroom, he tried fruitlessly to tear the sweet wrapper from his hand.

'It's stuck.' With the piece of paper sticking fast to his throbbing fingers, he faced the teacher.

The ruler came down hard and sharp on his hand once more.

'Get back to your seat.'

His first day at school was turning out to be even worse than life at home. As he walked back to his desk, he felt the warmth trickle down his leg and settle inside his white ankle sock. The ruler would surely visit him again many times, today and in days to come. He didn't think he wanted to wait around for that. But where else could he go?

He spent the morning sitting in his wet shorts; he didn't even go out to the playground when the other children left for their break. He stayed at his desk, opened his lunch box and munched on the bruised banana. The teacher sat at her desk at the head of the classroom, her eyes blinking with every movement of his jaw.

'Come here,' she said when the other children returned.

He looked up fearfully and the banana lodged in his throat.

Not wanting to feel the timber of the ruler again, he put down the fruit and made his way forward. When he reached her desk, barely able to see over the edge, she leaned forward and grabbed his hair. He shrieked when he saw the long-bladed scissors in her hand.

'Your hair is much too long. You can hardly see out through it. You need a trim.'

He tried to say no, but the words stuck to the roof of his mouth like the toffee had stuck to his fingers. He loved his hair. Shoulder length. It reminded him of the photo of his mother. He had her hair.

The teacher waved the scissors in front of him before tugging his fringe. She looked at him triumphantly, a lock of his hair clasped in her hand.

'Now I can see your horrible little face.'

Silently, he wished for the day to end.

NOVEMBER

Is there ever a good day to die?

The man didn't think so as he silently answered his own question. The sky was a greyish blue. Murky. The clouds on the horizon forewarned of a touch of rain to come. Otherwise, the day wasn't too bad.

He moved slowly into the forest of trees that skirted the narrow road around the lake. He wanted to see the lake before he did what he had to do. It was late evening and he was sure the fishermen would have departed. Not that there were many fish to be caught in November, he thought wryly.

The forest floor foliage was green and lush, and smelly. The branches above his head, winter bare. Broken twigs and ferns crunched beneath his feet. Had someone walked this exact same way recently? His brain was crowded with so many unanswered questions, it was like a bubble waiting to be pricked with a spike. And he knew that there was no one in the world to care; to really care for him. He was totally alone. Desolate as the branches, at peace with himself. Almost.

A knotted branch tangled in his hair as he delved further through the dense forest to where it was dark and more than a little bit damp. He paused and listened to the sounds of animals he could not see scurrying through the long grass. I'm not afraid any more, he thought. Not afraid of any living thing.

He crouched down and, virtually crawling, scrabbled his way through thorns and briars. The sound of water reached his ears. The trumpet of winter swans pierced the air.

Pausing once again, he listened. Followed the sound.

Reaching a clearing, he found the source of the water. Not the lake, but a stone mound spewing a fresh spring from a crevice between the rocks. He leaned over. Scooped some water into his mouth and relished the taste. He made up his mind. He was going to fight back.

That was when he heard another sound.

As he turned his head, a hand circled his mouth and another clenched tightly on his throat. His last thought was: it is a good day to die.

DECEMBER

CHAPTER ONE

Wednesday

Ragmullin in December presented itself as a beautiful place. From a distance.

Lottie stared out through the window at the early-morning sky. No hint of blue, just flat grey. Even the snow looked like gunmetal. The snowman her son Sean had built for her fifteen-month-old grandson Louis, stood rock solid in the garden.

It was too early to go to work. She forced herself to load the washing machine and then the dishwasher. Moving to the hall, she listened at the foot of the stairs. No sound came from above, so she returned to the kitchen and switched on the kettle.

Tea, rather than coffee, was her choice of drink at the moment. Too much coffee gave her the jitters. Waiting for the kettle to boil, she absently folded a stack of clean clothes, separating them into bundles for her three children. The girls were officially adults now. A few weeks ago, they'd celebrated Chloe's eighteenth birthday. The party had been organised by twenty-one-year-old Katie and fifteen-year-old Sean. Sean was already taller than Lottie and possessed the same startling blue eyes as his father had. She was momentarily catapulted back to a time before Adam had died. Five years ago. Cancer. Too young. Too quick. Too hard to believe. Too long grieving until Mark Boyd had proposed to her. She'd dithered for a while, unsure what to do, but she knew she loved him. The night of Chloe's party, she'd said yes to him, though they had yet to sort out the details, like setting a date and telling people. So far, it was their secret. Her choice.

The kettle purred. She fetched a mug and popped a slice of out-of-date bread into the toaster. Added bread to the whiteboard list attached to the refrigerator. Hopefully Katie would run to the shops later. Some hope, she told herself, and snapped a quick photo of the list in case she had to do it herself after work.

When the toaster popped, she took out the bread and chewed. It was dry. The tea tasted like sawdust. Feck it. She decided to stop on the way for a McDonald's coffee, jitters be damned.

Pulling on her jacket, she tied a bobbin around her straggly hair and shoved it under her hood. As she left the house, she wondered what kind of humour Boyd would be in today.

*

Mark Boyd tightened the knot on his tie and appraised the effect in his tiny bathroom mirror. He wasn't impressed with the image reflected back at him. His tightly cut hair was now more salt than pepper and his eyes betrayed last night's heavy drinking. Sunken hollows emphasised his cheekbones. At his age, he knew he shouldn't have sagging skin around his throat. He should get out on his bike for a cycle. But the weather was too cold and icy for cycling, he thought, ignoring the fact that he had a turbo bike folded up in the corner of his kitchenette. No, he needed to deal with the tangible issues in his life. For that he had requested a half-day off work. He hoped Lottie approved it, otherwise he'd have to go AWOL.

In the living area of his one-bedroom apartment he heard his friend Larry Kirby snoring loudly, his torso sprawled across the couch and feet plonked on the overflowing coffee table. Beer cans and bottles littered all available space. Boyd felt his bones creak and his skin prickle. He hated mess. Quickly he gathered up the cans and bottles, placing them in a sack for recycling.

Kirby stirred. Struggled to sit upright. 'Where the hell am I?' He glanced around, bleary-eyed, and ran a hand through his mop of busy hair. 'Oh, Boyd, it's you. That was some session last night. Where's McKeown?'

Boyd shrugged and thought for a moment. They'd abandoned Sam McKeown, the newest member of their team, in Cafferty's Pub when they'd left at … shit, he had no idea what time it'd been.

'God only knows where he ended up.' He placed the recycling sack on the floor beside his turbo bike. 'Fancy a coffee? There's a clean towel in the airing cupboard if you want to take a shower.' He found a packet of paracetamol and swallowed two.

Kirby sniffed his armpits. 'Don't suppose you have a shirt I could wear?'

Boyd smirked. Kirby was twice his width. 'What do you think?'

'I'll have that coffee, so.'

As Boyd busied himself making the coffee, Kirby said, 'Are you okay?'

'Despite a thundering hangover, I'm grand.'

'You were pretty intense last night. All maudlin and depressed.'

'I'm always like that, according to you.' Boyd wondered what he'd been saying towards the latter part of the night.

Kirby yawned loudly. 'Every second word out of your mouth was Lottie this and Lottie that. God, I don't know what McKeown must have thought of you.'

Boyd brought two mugs of coffee to the living area and sat down opposite Kirby. 'Was I that bad?'

'Worse.'

'Shit.'

'Why don't you put a ring on her finger? Anyone with one eye can see you two are meant for each other.'

Boyd felt the blush work its way up his cheeks. He'd been thrilled when Lottie had agreed to marry him, but they'd decided – no, he thought, *she'd* decided to tell no one yet, as it was too awkward with them both working in the same garda station. But all that was before everything else. He said, 'I don't know what to do.'

'I still have an engagement ring if you want it.' Kirby laughed, then grimaced.

'I can buy my own, thank you very much. When and if I need one.' Boyd closed his eyes and ran a hand over his throbbing forehead. The paracetamol was taking its time to do the job.

'Suit yourself.' Kirby put his mug down on the table. Clutching his hands between his knees, he stared glassy-eyed. 'I've no use for it now that Gilly's … you know …'

'I know, it's bloody tough. Give yourself time to grieve.' Boyd thought of Garda Gilly O'Donoghue, who had been murdered during the summer. Gilly was the first woman Larry Kirby had fallen for since his divorce years previously.

'That's what everyone says.' With creaking knees and a raspy cough from too many cigars, Kirby stood. 'Jesus, I stink. I'll see you at the office. What the hell time is it now?'

'Half past six.'

'Ah, for Christ's sake. Why'd you wake me at such an ungodly hour? I've time for a snooze before work. I'm off. See you later.'

As Boyd sipped his coffee, he spied a whiskey bottle lying on its side under the couch. He got down on his knees and picked it up; shook his head and went to fetch his Dyson.

CHAPTER TWO

The pigs were making an unmerciful noise in the sheds. Wind rattled the windows violently as another blizzard spun snow diagonally across the yard.

Beth Clarke took a mug from the cupboard and turned on the tap. Nothing. She tried again. Still nothing.

'Dad!' She shouted into the living room, where her father was furiously banging the keys of an old-fashioned calculator. 'What's wrong with the water?'

'Frozen pipes, no doubt.' His voice sounded faint against the thump of his fingers.

'What are you going to do about it?' She clattered the mug into the sink and checked to see if there was enough water in the kettle for him to make his tea later. Probably. Just.

'For pity's sake,' he growled.

She turned round to find him standing in the doorway, one hand holding a calculator and the other clutching a sheaf of pages bleeding handwritten figures into crooked columns. He was dressed in yesterday's clothes.

'Were you up all night?'

'Yeah, more's the pity. I can't balance this VAT return. Don't suppose you could put this lot onto your laptop, could you?' His voice cut in two with a cough and he doubled over, wheezing.

'You suppose correctly.' Bending down, Beth picked up her rucksack from beneath the table and hauled it onto her back. She smoothed her black skinny jeans down to her ankles and tied up a lace on her shiny red boots. 'I'm off to work.

'Work? Surely they won't be expecting you in this weather.'

'I've to attend the switching-on of the Christmas lights this afternoon. First, though, I have to visit the festive markets in town.' She felt a rush of excitement. She loved writing features for the local newspaper.

'You can't drive that road in this weather. It's nearly fifteen kilometres.'

'As if I didn't know,' she said under her breath.

'Give me a minute to throw on a coat. I'll drop you into town.'

'I'll be fine.' She picked up her black puffa jacket from the back of a chair and dragged it on before realising she'd put it on over her rucksack. 'Damn.'

As she rearranged herself, she heard the pad of her father's bare feet trek to his makeshift office in the corner of the living room. He's a lost cause, she thought.

Opening the back door, she was immediately assaulted by the high-pitched squeal of the pigs.

'Don't forget to feed the stock,' she shouted, her words sucked from her mouth by the wind.

Carefully she made her way across the yard to her Volkswagen Golf. Bright blue. Her mother had bought it not long before she'd hightailed it off to somewhere it never snowed. Five years ago, when Beth was just nineteen. She paused. She'd heard that her mother had returned to Ragmullin, but she had no desire to seek her out.

The car door was frozen stiff. She breathed on the handle, hoping to defrost the lock. No such luck. She'd have to use the last drop of water from the kettle. Perhaps, when her father found it impossible to make himself a mug of tea, he might motivate himself to fix a few things around the farm.

God, but she hated living in the village of Ballydoon.

She firmly believed it was the absolute arsehole of nowhere.

*

It was a full seven minutes before Christy heard Beth drive slowly away down the frozen road.

'That girl definitely has a streak of her mother in her,' he mumbled to himself, and he didn't think it was a good streak either. His wife – or ex-wife if he wanted to be pedantic – had always carried a devilish look in her eye, and did whatever she wanted whenever the whim took hold of her. He prayed to God that Beth wouldn't leave him too.

A glance at the ledger told him there wasn't a hope in hell of balancing the figures. Trying to keep the farm going was proving too much for him. He'd closed down the garage in the village, even though that hadn't been of his own free will. He cursed the deal he'd done, but it had been necessary. He still couldn't manage. Throwing down the invoices, he went to the kitchen to make breakfast.

He shook the kettle. Empty. He turned on the tap. Nothing. The pipes had frozen in the night.

'Blast it all to hell and back,' he said.

Fetching a carton from the fridge, he poured milk into a glass. Gulping down the cool liquid, he scanned the yard through the window. The pigs were unusually loud this morning. Feeling the weight of the world settling on his fifty-six-year-old shoulders, Christy Clarke tugged on his wellingtons, dragged his coat from the hook on the back of the door and went to investigate the frozen pipes.

'Shut up, you fuckers,' he yelled at the pigs as he passed the shed door.

*

The stairs got her every time. Not the number of them; there were twenty-one. No, it was their narrowness and lack of depth. Her toes stubbed every second step, and on a couple of occasions, while perfectly sober, she'd climbed the last three on her hands and knees. Today, because the lift was out of order yet again, she took them slowly, the weight of her life settling into the soles of her feet.

At her apartment, Cara Dunne inserted her key in the lock. Inside, she leaned against the door and watched her breath hang in the air. She slipped off her damp shoes and shook out her coat before hanging it up, then walked past the bathroom to the open-plan living area. It was bright on one side and dark on the other, where there was no window; just a green wall with one drab painting.

Putting her hat on the radiator, she found it was freezing. Damn. She checked the thermostat; it was on the highest setting. Something wasn't working. What a day for it to happen.

She sat in her armchair and switched on her phone to locate the caretaker's number. She couldn't remember his name. Mills or Wills or something like that. Her brain was dulled from the pain she'd suffered in the last few months. Most of that pain, she had to admit, was in her heart, but it metamorphosed into her physiology like a metastatic cancer, racking her with spasms without warning. She'd taken time off work. She was due to return next week. But she couldn't. Not yet. Nothing had been resolved. And he was still out there, laughing his head off and telling lies about her. Another pain shot up her chest and she tried to control her breathing.

Her eye was drawn to the old brown suitcase nestled on the shelf beneath the television. A suitcase of someone else's memories. A suitcase that had travelled everywhere with her in the years since she'd headed to Dublin to study to become a teacher. A suitcase battered and broken. Like herself. Gosh, she thought, I'm such a cliché.

She made her way into the bedroom, stripped off her damp jeans and placed them on the radiator. Cold. Ah, the caretaker.

Opening the wardrobe, she caught sight of the dress. Hanging under clear plastic at the end of the rail. Mocking her. A dress she would never wear. Why had she kept it? She had no idea of anything any more. He had stolen every last original thought from her brain and then abandoned her with a laugh. She felt acid lodge in her throat and thought she might throw up. But she swallowed it back down, like she'd have to swallow her pride and face her friends and colleagues. One day. Soon. Or never?

She shrugged away the thought and took out the hanger with the plastic-covered dress. She would try it on one last time, then it was headed for eBay.

A creak. Somewhere in the apartment.

She paused with the gown weighing heavy on her arm. What had she heard? She listened. Nothing. Must be the radiators.

'I'm really going mad now,' she said aloud.

She laid out the gown on the bed and whipped off her shirt. She undid the zipper on the cover and lifted out the diamond-studded satin garment. Her eyes filled with tears for a day that would never arrive. Holding out the dress, she stepped into it. The cool material sheathed her body like a second skin as she gently tugged it up to her shoulders, breathing in as she stretched to pull up the side zip.

There it was again. The creak. A door. Opening.

She'd locked the front door, hadn't she? Apart from her bedroom, the only other door in the open-plan apartment was the bathroom. In the wardrobe mirror she watched her face turn pale and her mouth open, an unuttered yell lodged in her throat.

With the dress hampering her feet, she crept into the living room.

'Anyone here?' she said, hoping no one answered her.

Nothing. No one.

She looked in the small kitchen. Empty.

Another creak, and the bathroom door opened.

She backed up against the cold radiator.

There was someone in her apartment.

CHAPTER THREE

Lottie sat with a screen of spreadsheets in front of her, driving herself demented. End-of-year budget returns were imminent. She hadn't even completed the November performance sheets. She hated figures. Hated reports and files and computers. But she also knew this was an integral part of her job as detective inspector in the town of Ragmullin. A point hammered home constantly by Acting Superintendent David McMahon.

'Concentrate,' she said, hoping that her own voice would drum motivation and conviction into her brain.

'Talking to yourself again?' Detective Sergeant Mark Boyd stood at the door to her cubbyhole office.

'Good morning.' She pushed the keyboard away from her. 'You look like you were on the beer last night.'

'You should see the state of Kirby.' Boyd lounged against the door frame.

She had to admit he didn't look too bad, but she was astute enough to recognise the dark circles under his eyes. 'What happened to him?'

'Nothing that the hair of the dog won't cure.'

She looked out over Boyd's shoulder to the main office. 'He's not in yet. Surely he didn't find a pub open at this hour of the morning?'

Kirby's workspace overflowed with paper, files and food wrappers, but there was no sign of the man himself. Detective Maria Lynch was on maternity leave until January at the earliest, so Detective Sam McKeown had been transferred from Athlone. The big man with the shaved head was sitting at his desk, banging away on his keyboard. Lottie liked Sam, even though she had yet to make it her business to find out more about him. Hopefully he could remain part of the team when Maria returned to work.

'I'd say he's on his way,' Boyd said. 'He left my place this morning before I did.'

'It *was* a big session, so.' A twinge of jealousy crept into Lottie's voice. They hadn't asked her out with them. But why should they? She was the boss and maybe they wanted a boys' night out. It rankled all the same.

'Why the sour puss?' Boyd folded his arms and leaned one foot back against the wall.

'Must be from looking at you standing there doing nothing.'

'Ha! It's because we didn't ask you out with us, isn't it?'

'No, it's not!' But she grinned. Boyd could always read her mind, and while it was uncanny, it was a little unsettling.

'We went to Cafferty's to watch a match, and you know how it is, one pint led to another and then another.'

'I remember the days well,' she said, recalling the years after Adam's death when she'd drowned herself in alcohol. It had taken time, but now she was alcohol-free. Almost. She just needed to hold herself together. To care for her family and protect them.

'What have we on today?' he said.

'November reports are overdue.'

'I've dispatched mine.' His face creased smugly.

'Of course you have.' If she had half of Boyd's organisational skills, she'd be chief superintendent by now.

'Do you want a hand?' He unfolded his arms and moved towards her desk.

'No thanks.'

'I'd have them finished in half the time. Let me help you.'

'I can manage, thank you very much.' She hadn't meant to sound so sharp, but some days she couldn't help herself. She was about to say something else when the phone rang.

After she'd finished with the call, she stood and pulled on her jacket.

'Get your coat,' she said.

'Where are we going?'

'There's been another suicide.'

'Why are we needed?'

'This is the second in three weeks, Boyd. Maybe something is going on.'

'Something is going on in that daft brain of yours. You're making up conspiracy theories now.'

'Don't worry about it. I'll bring McKeown.' She picked up her bag and slung it over her shoulder.

'Okay, okay,' Boyd said. 'I'll go with you.'

'Fine. But you better quit with the smart comments.'

She pushed out past him and caught sight of the glint in his eye as her hand brushed his. She'd felt it and he felt it too. That sudden thrill of physical contact. No matter that it was fleeting and unintentional. It was there. And she had to admit, she loved it.

*

Kirby shoved his kitbag under the desk and attempted to dampen down his unruly hair with shaking fingers. The shower in the locker room only spouted out cold water, and even that hadn't done much to stem the ache gripping his head and the churning of his insides. He looked at McKeown to see if he'd heard the rumbles coming from his stomach. But McKeown had his head down and seemed not to have heard anything. Good.

He rested one foot on the bag, and as pain shot through the other, he hoped his overindulgence last night had not reignited his gout. It was a blasted pain in the neck, he thought; or rather, in his foot.

'Where's the boss?' He waited as McKeown raised his head to peer over the computer. Jesus, he looked fresh, and here was Kirby himself looking like something out of date that you would shove in a bin.

'Gone out.'

'I gathered that. Where?'

'Heard mention of a suicide.'

'Didn't you work a suicide a few weeks ago?' Kirby scrunched his eyes, trying to recall the case.

'I did. Nothing suspicious.'

'Who is it this time?'

McKeown stopped what he was doing and stood. Leaning over Kirby's desk, he said, 'I don't know who it is because I wasn't informed, and for your information, I've enough reports piled up to high heaven to keep me more than busy without getting involved in stuff I'm not wanted in.'

He sat back down. Kirby revised his opinion. His colleague, like himself, was in the throes of a hangover.

CHAPTER FOUR

The apartment blocks at Hill Point had been constructed during what was widely called the Celtic Tiger boom years. The project had been an exciting one for the midland town of Ragmullin. But once the complex had been built, despite the fact that it offered multiple housing units, it was evident that Ragmullin could have done without the blot on the landscape. The saving grace was that it was the only high-rise building in the town. If you didn't count the twin-spired 1930s cathedral casting its shadow downwards and outwards, visible no matter where you stood.

The block they were looking for was easy to find, with two squad cars and an ambulance parked haphazardly outside.

Boyd parked the car. Lottie jumped out and walked on ahead. Inside she found the lift out of order and had to take the concrete stairs to the third floor.

In the narrow corridor, two redundant paramedics lounged against a wall, a folded-up trolley between them. A uniformed guard stood outside the apartment door.

'Good morning, Garda Thornton. Bring me up to date,' Lottie said once she got her breath back. She pulled on protective gloves and booties.

'Good morning, Inspector.' He didn't need to consult his notes; he was what Lottie termed an old hand on the job. 'The next-door neighbour on the left-hand side there reported the incident. I sent her back to her own flat with an officer. I had a look inside and something looks off.'

'Off?'

'Once you go in, you'll see for yourself.'

'Have you called SOCOs?'

'I thought you should assess it first. Everyone and their mother has been through there at this stage. It might be a straightforward suicide, but … I don't know. The deceased is called Cara Dunne. Her body is in the bathroom.'

'Has a doctor attended?'

'Been and gone.'

'Did you interview him?'

'Yes. He says the woman is dead.'

Lottie waited until Boyd arrived. He was out of breath, which was unusual for him as he was a fitness freak. While he pulled on gloves, she pushed the door inwards. From her initial glance, she could see it was a small apartment. A navy coat was hanging on a hook in the narrow hallway. She ran her hand over the garment. Damp.

She moved inside. Putting off the inevitable, she walked past the bathroom containing the body and stood on a square of brown carpet that designated an open-plan living area with a kitchenette to the right. She pushed open the nearest door and peered in. A compact bedroom. Bed neatly made up. A cotton nightdress was folded on the pillow. Bedside cabinet and wardrobe. Venetian blinds shaded the window. A pair of jeans was lying over the radiator. A red shirt looked like it had been flung on the bed. Plastic, used for protecting clothing, was crumpled up on the floor.

She walked back to the bathroom. The door was slightly ajar. She pushed it with the tip of her finger. It moved only a little. She squinted in through the slit. White ceramic bath with a corroded shower head. Toilet and sink. The cream tiles on the floor were wet. Other than that, nothing seemed out of place. But … the smell. She recoiled at the acidic odour of urine.

'I can't see the body,' she said.

'Behind the door,' Boyd told her.

She eased around the half-open door. Stepped into the small space. As she turned, she stopped. Her hand flew to her mouth and she felt her knees weaken. A gasp escaped through her fingers.

Behind the door hung the body of a woman with a black leather belt wrenched tight around her neck. Her mouth was open, as were her eyes, pinpricks of blood dotting the whites. Her throat was scratched intermittently where the belt had cut into her skin. Her arms dangled by her sides; her hands were clenched in death. Lottie had seen death do unimaginable things to the human body, but this was grotesque. She shook herself to remain professional.

Guessing the age of a dead woman was not easy. To her trained eye, however, Cara Dunne looked to be in her mid to late thirties.

A dress of white satin, studded with diamonds that sparkled under the light, draped the hanging figure like a shroud. It reached her ankles, where bare feet peeked out. From the puddle on the floor, it was evident that Cara Dunne had wet herself in her dying throes.

Lottie dragged her gaze back to the dress. A wedding dress. New. Unworn. Until now. A price label hung from a zipper just under the victim's arm. She wanted to touch the dress, to feel the smoothness of the material between her fingers, but she didn't move a muscle, just allowed her senses to formulate what might have happened in this small, non-descript bathroom, with its black mould creeping along the tiles above the bath.

The smell of death was so strong in the small room that Lottie tasted it on her tongue. She studied Cara Dunne's face. Smooth skin, no wrinkles. Was that from death, or had the woman's skin always been like that? Her hair was blonde, short and straight. As Lottie's eyes travelled upwards, she noticed that the other end of the belt was tied tightly to a chrome valve protruding from the wall above the door to the right. A six-inch-high three-legged stool lay on its side in the corner behind the door.

A question burned a line through Lottie's brain. Could this woman have hanged herself? On first impression, it appeared likely. Had she been jilted? Or had she changed her mind and decided this was the only way out of a wedding? Lottie had a suspicion that all was not as the image projected. Garda Thornton was right. Something was off.

A knock on the door and Boyd said, 'Can I come in?'

'There's no room in here. Wait until I come out. Call SOCOs. Ask for Jim McGlynn.'

She squeezed back out into the hallway. While Boyd made the call, she glanced around the living room again, searching for signs of a disturbance, but couldn't see a thing out of place. A hat lay on the radiator as if it had been placed there to dry. She put her hand to the radiator, found it to be cold, and noticed a distinct chill in the air. A rug was draped over the back of the chair, and on the seat, she found a mobile phone. Without lifting it, she pressed the home button. No pin was required. The screen had an app for contacts, and icons for phone calls and texts. Nothing else. Lottie thought this a little odd. Everyone she knew had numerous apps. Even her mother used Gmail on her phone.

The only other furniture was a television on a stand, under which rested an ancient brown suitcase. In the kitchenette, everything was neat and tidy. No dishes in the sink or on the draining board. The fridge was well stocked. The carton of milk was in date, as was the tray of chicken fillets.

'I can't see a suicide note,' she said. 'I'm going to have another look in the bedroom.'

Boyd followed her.

On the bedside cabinet there was a black leather-covered book that looked like a bible. When she opened it, Lottie found that it was a prayer book. The pages were like feathers, soft and light to the touch, and she felt there was something soothing in turning them. She replaced the book and opened the drawer. It held a vial of sleeping pills and a packet of paracetamol. If Cara had wanted to kill herself, why hadn't she taken the pills? Much easier.

She moved to the wardrobe with its open door. The smell of lavender wafted in the air. Hanging on a rail were jeans, shirts and blouses. A pair of black Nike trainers were on the floor. The plastic covering must have held the wedding dress, she thought.

Kneeling down, Boyd lifted the bedspread from the steel-legged bed and searched beneath it. 'Nothing under here.'

Back in the living room, Lottie opened the side glass panel of the window. The room was immediately filled with the noise of life. Down below, the canal was frozen. A train eased out of the station with loud screeches. A canal boat was docked by the bridge and a car horn blew somewhere to her right, and she could hear the distinct sound of builders at work somewhere close by. She breathed in the freshness of the morning.

'If I'd wanted to kill myself, and if I didn't want to take an overdose, I'd have jumped out the window. What do you think?' She turned to Boyd.

'You don't like heights,' he said, folding his arms, 'so you wouldn't do that.'

'I'm not afraid of heights.'

'I'm speaking hypothetically. I thought that was what you were doing.'

'This apartment is three floors up … Oh, it doesn't matter.' She closed the window and turned to Boyd. 'Did you phone McGlynn?'

'He's on his way.' He yawned and unfolded his arms. 'Do we need the state pathologist?'

Lottie thought for a moment. Did they need Jane Dore? Everything presented itself as a suicide, but the lack of a note bothered her, as did the scratches on Cara's neck. 'Call her assistant. If my gut is wrong, I'll deal with the aftermath.'

'The door wasn't damaged. Did she let someone in?'

'If she did, then maybe she knew the person who killed her.'

Boyd sighed. 'That's if she *was* killed.'

Lottie shook her head and walked out past him. 'I'm going to have a word with the neighbour. See if you can find anything that points to suspicious death – and try to get rid of that hangover, it's making you sluggish. Okay?'

She left him there, his mouth hanging open, in the small cramped hall with a dead woman hanging in a wedding dress behind the door.

CHAPTER FIVE

The office was as stuffy as it usually was, but Beth wasn't allowed to turn off the radiator. Her boss, chief news editor Nick Downes, was sitting with a scarf around his neck and his coat on his shoulders. That man was never warm, she thought.

Writing up her report on the official opening of the Christmas markets had taken her five minutes. She'd have to make up stuff to fill the four columns for the front page. Unless Ryan had taken a decent photograph, she was fecked. What else could she write? Distracted, she glanced at her phone. She'd better remember to bring a couple of bottles of water home, in case her dad hadn't got the frozen pipes sorted.

As she was about to make a note, a text came up on her phone. She read it, then looked around for Ryan. She caught the photographer's eye as he walked in the door.

'Keep your coat on and grab your camera,' she said.

'Why?'

'We have a job.' She turned to her editor. 'Nick, we have a possible suicide. Okay to take a look and maybe grab a few photos?'

Nick swivelled his chair around, sucking loudly on the end of a pen, his beard swallowing up thin lips. 'I don't think it's in the spirit of Christmas to be infringing on the privacy of a suicide victim's family, do you?'

Beth stood in the middle of the cramped office, the sleeves of her jacket halfway up her arms, her bag between her legs. 'What?'

'You heard me. Have a little compassion.'

What the hell was he on about? 'This is the second one in three weeks. There might be something fishy going on.'

'Second what?'

Belligerent was a word she often used to describe her father, and now her editor was earning the same distinction.

'Second suicide,' she explained.

'You caused enough of a stir with your report on the one a few weeks ago. I should never have okayed it,' Nick said. 'And who told you there's been another one?'

Zipping up her jacket, keeping out of his eyeline, Beth bit back the expletive-ridden retort she wanted to shout and considered her position. She was on a six-month rolling contract. She needed the work and couldn't afford to mess it up by angering her boss. But she couldn't say it was an anonymous text.

'I saw it on Twitter,' she lied.

'Show me.'

She scrolled through her phone. 'Oh, it's been taken down.'

'What do you mean, taken down?'

He was a dinosaur.

'Sometimes the Twitter administrators delete inappropriate content. You know, if a complaint is made.'

'Aha! You see. And you wanted to spread *inappropriate content* on the front page of our next edition. Take off your coat and sit down. Finish the Christmas markets article. That's what our readers want. A feel-good story on the front page. Don't forget, later on you have to cover the switching-on of the lights.'

Beth did as she was told.

'Are we leaving or not?' Ryan said, looping the strap of his camera bag over his shoulder.

'Shut up and sit down,' Beth and Nick said in unison.

*

Trying to keep his annoyance invisible, Ryan Slevin shoved his rolled-up jacket under the desk and nudged the mouse to activate his computer. After linking his camera to the console, he waited and watched the screen as the Christmas market photographs he'd taken earlier loaded.

Chewing on his lip, he considered the images, deciding he would need to use Photoshop to make them newsworthy. Most were shady and dark, snapped underneath the canopies hanging over the huts lined along the street. He kept scrolling. At least he had captured a few with kids in them. Kids sold newspapers, Nick always said. Ryan hoped he could spell the names. Most of them had been on their way to the library. Without parental permission, he was winging it. Their teacher had said it was okay, so what the heck. Kids sold newspapers.

He felt a shadow at his shoulder while he worked. Then it flittered over his desk and clouded the screen.

'Watching kiddie porn, are you, Ryan?'

He automatically hit the screen saver before looking up at Beth, with her wide smile, twinkling eyes and long, glossy black hair.

'Feck off,' he said.

'I need a fairly large photo, or maybe four or five in a montage, to cover four columns on the front page.' She sat on the edge of his desk. He felt like she was violating his personal space.

'Why?'

'Because I've feck all to write about. Anyway, kids sell—'

'Newspapers.' He laughed. 'Leave it with me.' As she moved back to her desk, he added, 'Have you written the piece already?'

'What's to write? Some dude dressed up as Santa Claus singing Rudolph out of tune and pressing a dummy switch to light up the stalls. In the morning. For Christ's sake.'

'It was kind of dark.' He knew his argument was lame.

'Nice wide smiles on happy faces, Ryan. That's all we need to keep the boss happy.'

He un-snoozed the screen and scrolled once again. That was when he saw it. In the photograph. He clicked the mouse, zoomed in. It couldn't be. Could it?

'Shit.'

'What?' Beth said.

'Nothing.'

'Don't mess them up.'

'I've been here a damn sight longer than you, so don't be giving me orders.' He was only half joking as he returned his gaze to the screen.

Tapping his foot nervously on the floor, he wondered about the image he'd taken, and a shiver raced down his spine.

CHAPTER SIX

Eve Clarke's apartment was in stark contrast to Cara Dunne's. Deep hues of primary-coloured paint and bright furniture gave it an air of modernism. Eve poured two mugs of coffee from a carafe. The aroma distilled a smell Lottie recognised as an undercurrent of alcohol and cigarettes. She sat on a bright yellow chair with red cushions and took the offered cup.

'It's just awful about Cara,' Eve said as she sat opposite.

The coffee was good. Lottie felt it warm up her toes. Eve was staring at her, eyes wide behind gold-rimmed spectacles. Her black denim jeans were pressed, her white shirt immaculate, with two buttons open at the neck showing a circle of wrinkles. She was stick thin, perhaps in her mid fifties. Her hands were the giveaway. A ravine of liver spots speckled the skin.

'Did you know her well?'

'Only to say hello.' Eve's face was closed. No sign of tears for her dead neighbour.

'But you became suspicious that something had happened to her. Why was that?'

'The walls in these apartments are paper thin. If my neighbour's baby cries, on the other side, I can hear it. That's the Cullens. I never hear a peep from Cara's. Not even the television.'

'So what alerted you?'

'Raised voices, followed by nothing for about ten minutes. Then the door banged.'

'Was it unusual for her to have visitors?'

'In recent months, yes.'

'And you're at home all day, every day?'

Eve blushed. 'I used to work, but then my marriage broke down. I went abroad for a number of years. Since returning to Ragmullin, I haven't been able to get a job.'

'How long have you been living here?' Lottie cast a glance around the uncluttered apartment.

'Just under a year.'

'And Cara has been living next door all that time?'

'She was there before I arrived.'

'You live alone?' Lottie thought the apartment lacked the appearance of anyone actually inhabiting it. Though on further thought, the stale smell countered that argument.

'Yes.'

'Can you tell me what Cara was like?'

'Inspector, is this really necessary? I just found her body. I didn't do anything to her.'

'I need all the information I can get at the initial stages of an investigation.'

'Investigation? You think she was killed, then?'

'I didn't say that. Has Cara any family?'

'I don't know.'

'Right.' Lottie felt like this conversation was getting her nowhere. She placed her mug on the coffee table. 'Had you ever been in her apartment before this morning?'

'Never.'

'How did you gain entry, then?'

'She called to my door a few weeks after I moved in. Asked if I would hold her spare key in case she got locked out. I agreed. After that, we only ever spoke in the hallway when we bumped into each other.'

'Let me get this straight. You heard voices and a door banging, so you went to investigate. What did you do exactly?'

'I knocked on her door. There was no answer. I thought maybe she had gone out. I came back here, and that's when it struck me that I'd heard two voices shouting. It seemed odd, you know, when normally I hear nothing.'

'What happened then?'

'I got my keys, went next door again. When I still got no reply, I said to myself that I had nothing to lose. I opened the door, called her name. Then I saw her coat hanging in the hallway. In this weather, no one goes out without a coat. I noticed the bathroom door slightly open. I thought, what if she'd fallen in the shower? I decided to have a quick look. That's when ... you know ...' She breathed out a long sigh after her speech.

Lottie thought it sounded rehearsed. As if Eve had spent the last hour reciting it in front of a mirror. For now, she let it pass. 'What did you do next?'

'I ran back here, got my phone and called 999.'

'Did you check if she was dead?'

Eve's features folded inwards. 'I remembered there's a doctor's surgery on the ground floor. I ran down the three flights of stairs and got him to come up. He checked her and said to wait for the ambulance and guards.'

More DNA and fingerprints, Lottie thought. That was if it turned into a murder investigation.

'Okay,' she said, keeping her voice neutral.

'Did I do something wrong?'

'There's no right or wrong. You did the correct thing in getting the doctor before the emergency services arrived.'

Eve exhaled, and a crease appeared on her forehead. 'She looked dead. She is dead, isn't she?'

'She is.'

'Oh, thank God.' Eva blushed. 'I don't mean thank God she's dead, just that I didn't leave a dying woman hanging there.'

'I know what you mean.' Lottie stood. 'Did Cara have a job?'

'She was a teacher, as far as I know.'

'Which school?'

'I've no idea. Like I said, I didn't really know her.'

'One other thing. Her coat and hat were damp. Do you know where she might have been earlier this morning?'

'Mass, probably. I think she went every morning.'

'She was religious?'

Eve put down her mug and stood to lead Lottie to the door. 'You're not aware, then, are you?'

'Aware of what?'

'Cara was engaged to be married, but the last I heard it was all off. Since then, she's not been to work, and she's gone to Mass every day. I think she was praying for him to come back.'

'Who?'

'Her ex-fiancé.'

'Who was he?'

Eve hesitated. 'I've no idea.'

'Are you sure?'

The woman looked uncomfortable as she nodded.

And Lottie knew she was lying.

*

Out in the corridor, Lottie was confronted by an irate-looking Jim McGlynn.

'In my opinion, it's a waste of time calling out SOCOs to suicides. We've enough to be doing.' He was suitably attired for the job in hand. Above his face mask, a pair of emerald eyes bored holes into Lottie's.

Ignoring his gripe, she said, 'Have you had a look yet?'

'I've only just arrived. Will you give me a chance?'

'I want to see the belt around Cara's neck when you have it examined.' Standing to one side, she let him pass just as another man came from the stairs.

He put out his hand. 'You must be Detective Inspector Lottie Parker.'

'I am.' She shook his hand. 'And you are …?'

'Tim Jones. Assistant to the state pathologist. I believe you have a suspicious death for me to have a gander at.'

After checking his ID, Lottie indicated the open door to the apartment. 'Cara Dunne. Hanged with a belt tied to a valve over the bathroom door. After assessing the scene, I'm not sure she could have done it herself. We need your expert opinion.'

'Let me at her,' Jones said, and followed McGlynn into the apartment.

Lottie caught Boyd's eye where he stood by the emergency exit door at the opposite end of the hallway. He shrugged his shoulders.

'Inappropriate turn of phrase,' she said, joining him.

'Nothing I haven't heard from you before,' he smirked.

She pointed at the door. 'Have you been out there?'

'Waiting for you.' He pushed down on the steel bar and the door swung open. Concrete steps led both up and down. 'I tend to agree with you, though.'

'In what respect?' Lottie followed him up the steps.

'That the death looks suspicious. If you take into account the victim's short stature and the fact that that stool was low, it doesn't tally. I think someone murdered her.' He pushed through another door out onto the roof, making sure to leave the door ajar.

Lottie leaned on the iron railing and looked out over the frosty canal and railway tracks. A train shunted into the station; mist stilled the air in its wake. 'She was a teacher. We need to find out where she taught and talk to her colleagues, and find her friends.'

'Right.'

'She had an engagement broken off recently.'

'Interesting. Places in a new light the fact that she was dressed in a wedding dress.'

'And puts the ex-fiancé in the frame.'

Lottie took her hands from the railing, pulled off the latex gloves and blew on her palms, trying to inject heat into her fingers. She noted a rusted steel ladder leading down the side of the building from the roof. The deluge of snow had covered any footprints there might have been.

'Does the neighbour know who the fiancé is?' Boyd thrust his own hands deep into his pockets as the wind swirled snow around them.

'No. Says she didn't know Cara Dunne very well.'

'But she was able to gain entry to the apartment.'

Lottie sighed. 'She had a spare key for emergencies. Let herself in because she heard raised voices. We need to interview the doctor from the ground floor.'

'I'll do it.'

'And get his DNA and fingerprints for elimination.'

'Sure thing,' Boyd said.

She studied the hard line of his jaw. 'Is everything all right?'

'What do you mean?'

'You seem distant.'

He laughed. 'I'm just tired after last night.'

'Right.' She moved off the roof and back to the open door. 'If Cara was murdered, this emergency exit could have been used as a means of escape by her attacker.'

'There is no way back into the building from the rooftop unless the door is left open, so he either came in the front door or he lives in the block.'

'Or someone let him in the emergency door and left it propped open.'

'I'll tell SOCOs to take prints,' Boyd said, 'and I'll get door-to-door enquiries started.' He went on ahead of her.

Lottie stepped from the cold air into the relative warmth of the corridor, but she couldn't stop the shivers on her skin. Something was up with Boyd, and she felt it was more than hangover grumpiness.

'The body can be removed to the mortuary.' Tim Jones was pulling off his forensic suit and balling it into a brown evidence bag. Garda Tom Thornton noted the details on the bag with a Sharpie pen and sealed it up.

'Can you tell us anything, Dr Jones? Foul play?' Lottie said, glad to talk about work and not feelings.

'It looks suspicious.'

'In what way?'

'Many ways, but for one I don't know how a woman of such slight build could have got the belt tightly secured to that valve so high up on the wall. Even standing on the stool she isn't tall enough, and she would need more upper-body strength.'

'Anything else?' Lottie said.

'She has scratches on her neck. I need to get her on the table.'

'Time of death?' She pushed for more information.

'I'd say in the last six hours. Can't be more specific at the moment.'

'Will Jane Dore be doing the post-mortem?' Lottie said.

'I'm sure she will, if I deem the death suspicious.' Jones headed off towards the stairs.

'Well, I was right,' Boyd said.

'About what?'

'There's no way that woman could have hanged herself.'

'Stranger things have happened.' But Lottie agreed with him. 'I didn't notice any other wedding paraphernalia in the apartment, apart from the dress. You interview the doctor, and then we need to find out more about Ms Cara Dunne.'

CHAPTER SEVEN

Fiona Heffernan finished her rounds on the ward and hurried along the long corridor to the locker room in the oldest part of the abbey. She felt the excitement building and it was beginning to erode some of her fear. Tomorrow her life would change for ever. Tomorrow would be the first day of the rest of her life. Tomorrow she would be free.

She did a little dance on the cold stone floor in her bare feet before slipping off her navy cotton trousers and pulling her white tunic up over her head. She hung up the trousers on a wire hanger and folded the tunic onto the floor of the locker. A line of goose bumps prickled up her skin and the tiny dark hairs on her arms stood to attention as she grabbed a towel and glanced over her shoulder. Despite the fact that there was no one around, she had an uncomfortable feeling of being watched. The fear returned full blast like an Arctic storm bumping along her skin.

Holding the fluffy white towel to her chest, she stepped around the row of battered lockers and took a look. Empty. The shower units were to her right. Two cramped stalls with old shower heads that dripped continuously. She walked on her tiptoes. The change in the sound of the dripping of water from one of the shower heads made her jump. The plastic curtain had long since disintegrated and the white tiles were rusted to yellow ochre. Thrusting her hand inside, she tried to turn the tap in an attempt to halt the dribble of water. It wouldn't budge. She did likewise in the other shower stall. No result.

It was polar cold in the room, and Fiona felt there were more inviting things in life than a cold shower at the end of a shift. She decided to have it later.

Setting her lips in a firm line of determination, she was about to get dressed when a flash of white caught the corner of her eye. She froze, her body on high alert. With the towel still clutched tightly, hiding her underwear, she listened.

There it was again. A flutter and a flash of white to the right where her steel locker stood in a line of five. She jumped when the wind rattled the one window in the room, the six panes of frosted glass shuddering in their frames, snow beating a pattern with the wind.

Holding her breath, trying not to sniff the fusty air, she took a step forward. 'Hello? Is there someone there?' she said lamely.

Another step.

'Hello? Who's there? Hello?'

She reached the end of the lockers and waited by the edge of the final one. She held her breath, hands shaking uncontrollably, tremors convulsing her body, and stuck her head around the side of the narrow cabinet. There was no one there.

She breathed a sigh of relief.

That was when she felt the soft whisper of air on the nape of her neck.

*

As Boyd idled the car in the line of traffic on the bridge, Lottie looked out of the window. Sections of the water on the canal were frozen solid. Moorhens dipped their heads among the reeds, skidding on the ice, searching in vain for food. She noticed an old-fashioned canal barge tied up to a stack of rubber tyres on the shore.

'Do you think anyone lives on that?' she said.

Boyd puffed on an e-cigarette and shrugged his shoulders. 'Haven't a clue. Maybe you want to investigate that too.'

'No need to be a smartarse. We have enough work as it is.' She turned her attention to a man with a sleeping bag wrapped around his shoulders, weaving through the stalled traffic. The unlit Christmas lights trailed across the width of Main Street ahead. The traffic began to move. Slowly.

'Fancy a bag of chips?' Boyd said, nodding towards the Malloca Café.

'That's a great idea. Look, a parking space. No, over there.'

With a grunt, Boyd swung the car into the tiny space and switched off the engine.

'Plenty of vinegar,' she said.

'Right so.' He got out of the car and waited to cross the road.

Lottie knocked on the window. 'You better bring a couple of bags for Kirby and McKeown. Add curry sauce. Good for a hangover.'

She smiled to herself as Boyd grumbled loudly, making his way between the cars in the traffic jam. She rested her head against the glass. The street looked so dull with the Christmas lights off. That was when she remembered she was supposed to be bringing her grandson to see the official switching-on ceremony later that afternoon. Shit! The day was getting away from her. It had taken ages to seal off Cara Dunne's apartment and organise uniforms to do the door-to-door legwork, and then Boyd had had to interview and fingerprint the doctor, who only confirmed what Eve Clarke had said. Cara Dunne was dead when he'd seen her, but not long dead.

She slammed the heel of her hand against her forehead. Cara's post-mortem would probably be held around five, and she needed to be there for it. But she also wanted to be with her grandson Louis, Katie's son. Dilemma time. Maybe Boyd could attend the post-mortem. Then she remembered that he'd asked for time off. Well, that was a no, now that they were dealing with a suspicious death. She wondered why he needed it. He rarely took leave out of the blue, but he'd been taking a lot recently.

As she watched him struggle back across the road with a large brown bag in his hand, her phone vibrated in her pocket. Acting Superintendent McMahon. Shit, she still hadn't finished the November report.

*

Opening her eyes, Fiona shook her head and discovered it was a mistake to try moving. A bolt of pain careened through her brain like a meteor shower. She blinked away a kaleidoscope of stars.

Her hand touched something soft and cold. Snow? Shivering uncontrollably, she realised she was lying flat on her back. As she shifted slightly, something wet slithered down her face. She could taste it at the edge of her lips. Blood.

She blinked again. Beneath heavy eyelids, she squinted up at the dark sky pulsing with a cloud of snow. She was outside. But how? She recalled the locker room and someone behind her. A fuzzy recollection was trying to make itself known to her. Something being pulled roughly over her head. Soft material against her frozen skin. Someone dragging her. Through the door. Up the steps. Out onto the roof. The roof!

She tried to move her hand. It wouldn't budge. Her fingers felt like they were solid blocks of ice, and she wondered why she was covered in white. Snow? No, it was heavier.

Something black was at the side of her head. It moved, leaving a footprint in its wake. A boot appeared on the other side. She felt the roughness of gloved hands grabbing her under her armpits, pinching her skin. Her body being raised until she was standing.

But she wasn't standing. She was being held upright. Her head thumped with a horrid pain and she couldn't fathom out what was happening to her. There was somewhere she was supposed to be, someone she was meant to call. But where? Who?

She could see the landscape stretching out before her. The afternoon sun dipped like a shadow on the horizon, which was almost entirely blotted out by the falling snow. Trees swayed in the wind. And in the distance, almost hidden by the blizzard, were the statues. Fiona knew exactly where she was, and she knew in that instant that she would end her thirty-four-year-old life on the ground below her.

She tried to open her lips, to speak a word of protest, to beg for mercy, because in this moment of surreal clarity, she knew where she was supposed to be. Being dragged to the edge of a precipice was not on her agenda for today. No, she had had different plans in mind. And they were all disintegrating into the minute particles of black nothingness where she was headed. To the life beyond.

She couldn't speak or cry out.

She lost focus and swayed.

She was doomed.

CHAPTER EIGHT

After they'd finished their chips, Lottie set Kirby and McKeown the job of digging up background information on Cara Dunne, in particular to find out who her fiancé was and where he lived and worked. She needed to interview him and eliminate him from the investigation – or not.

Her gut was telling her she was dealing with a murder, even though she'd have to wait for confirmation from the post-mortem results. The smell of vinegar reached her from her fingers, even after washing them and scrubbing vigorously with the baby wipes she'd found in her handbag.

'Can I have a word?' Boyd entered the office and closed the door behind him.

'Sure. Sit down.'

'Those few hours off that I requested. I really do have to leave at four thirty. Is that okay?'

She glanced at the clock on the wall. 'Boyd, for goodness' sake. I want you to liaise with the SOCOs and the state pathologist. Until we know for sure what happened to Cara Dunne, we need to treat this as a live investigation.'

'I know all that.' He sat down and leaned his elbows on her desk, one hand under his chin. 'But I need to head home to Galway. I rarely ask for time off, you know that, and—'

'What's going on in Galway? You were there last week for a day as well.' Shit, she thought. Boyd's business was his own, but she still felt he was keeping a secret from her. Friends didn't keep secrets from each other, did they? And she and Boyd were more than friends.

'It's my mother,' he said, shifting uneasily on the chair. 'She has an appointment and she asked me to attend with her.'

'Can't Grace go with her?' Lottie had met Boyd's sister and liked the girl.

'You know what Grace is like, so no, she can't.'

Lottie bristled at the inherent rebuke in his tone. With an audible sigh, she said, 'What about Cara's post-mortem?'

'It's not even scheduled yet.'

'How do you know?'

'Because I rang to find out. Tim Jones said it could be morning before Jane Dore arrives from Dublin.'

'Right so. I suppose there's no point in keeping you here if you're working half-heartedly.'

'Jesus, Lottie, don't take it personally.' He stood.

'I'm not. I'm under pressure. All this work we have, Boyd, not to mention the November performance reports, and you want to hightail to Galway. McMahon is on my back. God give me strength.'

'I offered to help this morning, but you said you had it under control.'

She couldn't argue with that, because it was true. Her thick-headed stubbornness was biting her on the arse.

When she looked up, Boyd had returned to the main office and was switching off his computer while dragging on his coat. She felt a deep sense of loneliness settle in her chest. He was keeping her out of something. What and why? She had no idea.

Then her desk phone rang.

*

Trevor Toner entered the theatre and hurriedly pulled on his dance shoes, wrapping a velour towel around his neck. He stood and watched the stage for a moment. The dance routine wasn't going to plan.

'No, no, no,' he shouted, moving towards the stage. 'Take it from the top. Five, six, seven, eight …'

Glancing at Shelly, his assistant, he sat down beside her and wondered why he bothered. The show was due to open next week, and rehearsals seemed to be catapulting him backwards instead of forwards. He waited as the young dance troupe prepared to restart, then signalled for the music. Shelly tapped the iPhone attached to the speakers and Wham! belted out 'Wake Me Up Before You Go-Go'. He supposed his charges had never heard of George Michael, let alone Wham!, but that shouldn't hinder their performance of a simple routine, even though they appeared to have dead legs today.

Looking on in despair as the six teenagers and two little girls jumped at the wrong time, he buried his face in the towel.

'What's up?' Shelly slid closer to him.

'It's a disaster,' Trevor wailed, unable to keep the hysteria out of his voice. 'It'll never be ready in time.'

'It's always ready in time. What happened to "it'll be all right on the night"?'

'I know, I know.' He turned to her. 'But look at the state of them.'

'Stop panicking.' She unwound her ponytail and let her hair hang loose around her shoulders. 'I need a break and you need to calm down.' She placed a hand on his arm, letting it linger there, before adding, 'I'll fetch us some water.'

Her flirtations were lost on him. She still didn't get it, he thought as she skipped out of the door.

Jumping up onto the stage, he said, 'This is the last time I'm showing you the routine, okay?' He gesticulated wildly. 'Stand down there and watch me and learn. Otherwise I'm leaving and this show can die on its feet.'

The mean-guy routine didn't come naturally to him in public. He knew he looked like a mannequin let loose in a shop window as he took a deep breath, waiting for the beat to kick in and the music to wend its way into his veins. He glanced at his toes to make sure he was ready. When he looked up again, he noticed a shadow on the balcony. Someone moved through the front row before letting the seat down and sitting. Maybe it was a talent scout, Trevor thought irrationally. Not at his stage of life, surely. Thirty-six was too old for Broadway.

Nevertheless, he was going to give this his best shot. He needed to demonstrate to the kids, plus whoever was watching, just how to dance.

CHAPTER NINE

The atmosphere had an eerie stillness to it. Like the calm before a full-blown storm. The drive through the village of Ballydoon had brought Lottie back in time. One street. Two pubs. A solitary shop that looked like it sold everything from a bale of briquettes to a cappuccino in a cardboard cup. A signpost told her there was a school up to the left, past the church with a cemetery across the road. A green area was bare other than an ancient water pump, painted blue, which looked out of place in the centre.

A garage with dirt and grime on its plate-glass window screamed that it had been closed for some time. The petrol pumps were defunct. The whole village seemed to be dying on bandaged feet, crying out for redemption.

Ballydoon Abbey stood at the end of a roadway lined with trees. Branches, heavy with snow, hung low across the treacherous avenue.

Lottie looked up at the abbey roof and noticed smoke hanging in the air as it struggled to rise from a chimney stack. Her day so far had been filled with death and spreadsheets. She wasn't sure which was worse. At least she'd succeeded in getting Boyd to delay his departure for an hour or so because she wanted him at the scene for initial observations.

At the inner cordon, her eyes were drawn towards the prostrate figure. She noticed the long dress clothing the body. It was whiter than the slushy snow on which the woman lay. It couldn't be another victim in a wedding dress, could it? Shit, she thought.

From where she stood, she saw very little blood. The young woman was lying on her stomach, face sideways, and Lottie wondered why brain matter had not spattered across the virgin snow. Had she been dead before she fell?

As she pulled on her protective clothing, she glanced up at the building again. It stood three storeys tall above her, though in other places it was only two storeys. A small chapel was attached to the side, its slated roof thick with the fresh fall of snow, unblemished by the prints of birds nestled tightly on a weathervane. Light spilled from the windows and a lamp over a doorway cast a yellow hue on the macabre proceedings beneath it. The distinct smell of fried food reached her nose, carried on the crest of a breeze, and she wondered if the kitchen was close by. She hoped the smell might dilute the death odour.

Jim McGlynn, SOCO leader, had arrived before her. He was busy shouting orders at his team, and his eyes tracked her, almost daring her to impinge on his crime scene.

'Is it another suicide, Jim?' Her expelled breath stilled like a reluctant fog in the air. He had done well to get here so quickly, and hopefully he'd left a competent team at Hill Point. She knew the importance of forensics in establishing whether a crime had been committed and building evidence against an accused. That was if they got to that stage.

McGlynn looked at her as if to say *do you think I'm a magician?* But he remained silent.

Boyd joined her, zipping up his white clothing, and scrunched his eyes at the body. 'Is she wearing a wedding dress?'

Lottie gave him the same stare McGlynn had thrown her way. She addressed the SOCO team leader. 'Can you turn her over, please?'

'Detective Inspector Parker, I'm trying to do my job.'

'If it's a suicide, what's the big deal?'

McGlynn leaned back on his haunches, checking the victim's bare arm. 'If it is suicide, it's the third suspected case in three weeks, and the second one in this area alone.'

'It *is* suicide, then?' Lottie jumped on his statement. She recalled the recent death at Lough Doon Forest, less than three kilometres from the village.

'I didn't say that. And you and I both know that Ms Dunne's death looked very suspicious.'

She watched as McGlynn instructed an assistant to take photographs of the body *in situ* and another to video their actions and movements.

'What are you photographing?' she said.

'Her arms.'

'I can see that, but I can't see the relevance.' A bitter east wind momentarily lifted the material of the victim's dress, before it rested back on the flesh.

'There might be signs of a struggle,' he muttered.

'And are there?'

'You have no patience whatsoever.'

'I know.'

She inched closer. The young woman's arms were outstretched. The silk of the sleeveless wedding dress billowed slightly once again. Her legs were bare. No shoes or tights. Her jet-black hair made a stark contrast to the side of her white face that was visible. 'Was she dead on impact or beforehand?'

McGlynn hunched over the body. 'God give me patience with you.' He sighed a long breath into the wind. 'Nothing evident from examination by sight, but the pathologist will be able to determine cause of death. Look at that, though.'

Lottie leaned over and noticed a large gash on the forehead. 'Pre-mortem trauma?'

McGlynn glared at her. 'If that's what you call sustaining a head wound shortly before death, then yes.'

'Did she fall or was she hit with something?'

'I'm not a—'

'Magician. Okay.' She glanced over at the small crowd who'd gathered in the snow outside the cordon. 'Who found the body?'

'How would I know?' McGlynn grunted.

Lottie and Boyd headed to the garda sergeant who was struggling to keep the stragglers behind a taut crime-scene tape. 'Who was first on scene?'

He checked his notebook. 'A nurse. Alan Hughes.'

'A nurse?'

'This is a nursing home.'

'I know that.'

Lottie glanced back at McGlynn, who was now working under a hastily erected tripod with a halogen light. Some of his crew were trying unsuccessfully to raise a tent over the body. It was looking more like a crime scene. Second death in the space of a few hours, both women in wedding dresses. Too much of a coincidence, Lottie thought as she scanned the crowd. She was surprised to see her friend Father Joe Burke standing amongst them. What was he doing here? Before she could approach him, a man stepped forward. Hair hidden beneath a black beanie hat, a rough beard lining his jaw, and from what she could see, his eyes were as dark as his hat.

'I'm Alan Hughes.' His voice was gruff and hoarse. 'I found her.'

'Are you okay?' Lottie asked.

'Flu.' He sneezed into a paper tissue.

Lottie turned to her uniformed colleague. 'Take everyone's details and note down whatever information you can gather. Where they were. When they last saw the dead woman. You know the score. And make sure no one contaminates the scene. Nobody is to leave until all are interviewed. Boyd, you stay with McGlynn and see what you can find out. I'm going to have a quick word with Mr Hughes in the car.'

She stripped off the white protective gear, shoving it into a proffered paper bag before dipping out under the tape. She led Hughes towards the unmarked garda car. She could have brought him inside the abbey, but she thought he might talk more freely away from it. Sometimes having a demarcation from the scene helped witnesses to open up. When he was seated in the passenger seat, she sat in on the other side.

He was visibly shivering as he tore off his hat. His hair was tightly cut, peppered with grey strands, and his hands were big; more like a farmer than a nurse, she thought. He twisted round on the seat and she caught a glint in his eyes. Fear, or sadness? Sometimes she found those emotions hard to tell apart.

'Mr Hughes … Can I call you Alan?'

'Yes.'

'Alan, tell me everything. From the beginning.'

'What do you want to know?'

Oh God, Lottie groaned silently. 'Do you know the young woman's name?'

'The dead woman?'

'Yes.'

'She's Fiona Heffernan,' he said. 'I worked with her.'

'She's a nurse?'

'She *was* a nurse.'

'Did she quit?'

'No. She fucking flung herself from the roof.'

Lottie tapped her knuckles against the steering wheel. 'Was Fiona working today?'

'Yes. Her shift was eight thirty till three.'

'Where did she live?'

'I don't know that.'

'Was she local to the village?'

'I don't know!' His voice rose an octave, losing the gruff, hard-man timbre.

'Do you have any idea what she did after her shift?'

'Look, Inspector, I don't mean to be rude, but I'd only just arrived for work. I'm on the afternoon shift. I parked my car and was heading inside when I saw her. Lying there like a snow angel.' He stifled a sob.

'That's a good description.' Lottie glanced through the window, over his shoulder, scanning up along the building to the roof and back down to the body. 'Do you have any idea why Ms Heffernan would be wearing a wedding dress?'

'Not really.' He shrugged. 'Not today, anyway.'

Lottie frowned. 'Not today? What do you mean by that?'

'I'll tell you what I mean. Fiona wasn't due to get married until tomorrow.'

After she'd arranged for Alan Hughes to be swabbed and taken to the station for fingerprinting and a formal interview, she sought out Father Joe. He was shivering in a heavy parka jacket, the hood tight around his face. She'd recognise him anywhere.

'What brings you here?' she said.

'Afternoon visitation. Administering to the sick is part of my priestly duties, you know.'

'But this is not your parish,' she said, massaging her hands furiously to keep the blood flowing.

'Father Curran couldn't make it today, so he asked me. He's the local parish priest, by the way.'

'Okay. How are you doing?'

'I'm fine. Keeping busy.'

She smiled, remembering all he'd endured two years ago. 'Did you know the dead woman?'

'I haven't seen the body, so I can't swear on a stack of bibles.'

'Her name was Fiona Heffernan. She was a nurse.' Lottie could have sworn his face paled. 'You knew her?'

'Not Fiona? That's terrible. Met her on my rounds a few times.' He looked up at the roof and down to the ground, and shook his head.

'How often do you visit the sick out here?'

'Not often. I think this is my third or fourth time. I only do it when Father Curran asks me to fill in for him. You should have a chat with him. He lives in the parochial house beside the church, in the village.'

'Right. Thanks.' She spied Kirby getting out of his car. 'I'd better get inside and start my investigation. Chat soon.'

He smiled; the smile she remembered that lit up his eyes.

'Lottie?' he said, grabbing her sleeve as she turned away. 'You can talk to me any time about anything. You know that.'

She nodded and pulled her hood up to hide the blush she felt flaring on her cheeks. Maybe she should talk to him about her engagement to Boyd. Or maybe not. She wouldn't be having a church wedding anyway, Boyd being divorced. There'd be no white dress for her, she thought as she walked away.

CHAPTER TEN

The Railway Hotel was not where Steve O'Carroll had envisaged he'd be following his career. It gave him a chip the size of a four-by-four plank weighing down on his narrow shoulders. His mother had had hopes for him to reach the heights of a different kind of bar. He had studied at King's Inn, in Dublin, but failed his final-year exams. Not his fault. No way. But he couldn't explain the true reason to anyone. No one would have believed that Steve O'Carroll had suffered a breakdown. And now? He found himself giving orders to an imbecile behind the bar in Ragmullin's Railway Hotel.

'What are you doing? I told you already: the white wine goes in the fridge, not the red. Why don't you listen to me? How long have you worked here?'

'Two weeks.' The barman had a squint in one eye that made him appear to be constantly winking. Steve had had enough of winks, nods and nudges to last him a lifetime.

'What's your name again?'

'Benny.'

'Are you colour blind, Benny? If you can't learn the difference between red and white wine, you're in the wrong career. Hurry up. We've a wedding reception tomorrow and you have another crate to unload and shelves to stock. I want a full inventory in an hour. Got it?'

'Got it.'

Steve leaned his elbows on the bar and put his head in his hands. Why was life such a bitch? Not to mention the one real bitch. But he wasn't going to think of her. He had enough on his plate with the reception tomorrow. A small one, but his standards were high. He knew that five-star TripAdvisor reviews would bring in more customers. And maybe get him his ticket out of this shit town, once and for all.

Lowering his hands, he watched Benny take bottles from the crate to stock the refrigerator. It was hard to find anyone with experience, and Benny's CV had read well. Maybe he should have checked out the references before hiring him.

As he turned to make sure the white linen tablecloths had been delivered from the launderette, he saw a garda walk in the door with a tall man, his head glistening with snowflakes, hair shaved so tight that Steve wondered what number blade he used. His own brown hair was tied in a neat ponytail at the back of his neck. He felt it added an air of mystery. Not something one expected to find on the head of a hotel assistant manager. Even if it was only the Railway Hotel.

As the man approached, shaking his jacket free from his shoulders, Steve decided that if he ever cut his own hair, he was going to shave it off entirely. He liked the look. Mean and lean.

He smiled, straightened his shoulders and patted down his lapels, hoping no flecks of dandruff were visible. 'Can I help you, gentlemen?'

'I'd like to speak to Steve O'Carroll.'

'That's me.' He indicated a small table under the window with four chairs around it. 'Have a seat.'

'We'll stand, if you don't mind.'

Instantly, Steve felt his nerves prickle. 'How can I help you?'

The bald guy checked his phone, then stared back at him. 'You were engaged to Cara Dunne, is that right?'

'Sure was. It's all over now. Thank God.'

'Why do you say that?'

Steve didn't like the tone. 'Why are you here?' he asked warily.

'I'm afraid I have to inform you that the body of Cara Dunne was found this morning at her home.'

'Cara? Dead?' Steve bit his lip. He wanted to sit down, but remained standing. 'Are you having me on?'

'I don't make a habit of playing practical jokes on people I've never met before.'

'But … I don't understand. She's dead? How? What happened?'

'I'm not at liberty to say at the moment. But I'd like to ask you a few questions. Maybe we should sit down after all.'

*

As he moved towards the table under the window, McKeown kept his eyes firmly on Steve O'Carroll. O'Carroll in turn kept his chin pointed upwards with a touch of arrogance. He carried his wiry frame with ease, gleaming hair tied in a ponytail. It looked a little odd with the black suit, white shirt and blue tie. There was another thing McKeown had noticed. From the moment he'd broken the news that Cara Dunne was dead, O'Carroll had shown little emotion. This was going to take some skill, and McKeown was confident he was the man for the job.

He flung his damp jacket over the back of a chair, then took a breath and released it through his nose. He'd had to wait until the school was on lunch hour to get talking to the teachers, and then only two or three of them remembered Cara Dunne's ex-fiancé's name. That didn't say much for Steve O'Carroll, or perhaps they'd just been in shock.

'Can you tell me where you were this morning? Say from seven a.m. to ten p.m.?'

'Hold on a minute. You've just told me Cara is dead. You haven't told me how or when, and then you ask me where I've been.'

'Mr O'Carroll. Steve.' McKeown sat, stretched his long legs out to the side and placed his hands on the table. 'Tell me what you were doing this morning.'

'I will, once you tell me what's happened to Cara.'

'Her body was found at her apartment earlier on today. Looks suspicious.'

'Looks or is?'

'You don't seem too concerned about her death.' This cat-and-mouse shit did McKeown's head in. He fought the urge to grab O'Carroll by the shirt collar and yank his ponytail. Instead, he stared at him, slit-eyed. It did the job.

O'Carroll sighed. 'Cara and I split up three months ago. I may as well tell you now, because you'll hear it from her teacher pals, it wasn't mutual. I've no feelings for her any more. The fact that she's dead, well, it's sad. She was a good teacher. But we were no longer on speaking terms.'

'Why did you split up?'

'That's my business.'

'It's mine now.'

'I think I'll call my solicitor.'

'That just makes you look guilty of something.'

'I've studied law. I know my rights. I also know I'm the first person you'll try to hang this on.'

'Strange choice of words there, Steve.'

'What do you mean?'

He was one cagey fucker, McKeown thought. 'You know what happened to Cara.'

'Is that a question or a statement?'

'Statement.'

'I have no idea what happened to her.'

'Then you won't mind telling me where you were this morning.'

O'Carroll let out a long sigh. 'I was at home, then I came into work.'

'What time?'

'Around ten. Usual time.'

'I'm sure we can verify when you arrived. Can anyone vouch for your whereabouts before then?'

'Nope. Are we done here?'

'No, we are not.' McKeown scratched the side of his jaw, trying to get a handle on his opponent. One thing was sure. O'Carroll would make a great poker player. 'When was the last time you saw Ms Dunne?'

'Are you deaf? We split up. I don't know when I last saw her. Now, I'm calling my solicitor. Unless you're here to arrest me, I'd like you to leave.'

'We need your fingerprints and a sample of DNA. Elimination purposes.'

'After I contact my solicitor.' O'Carroll stood up and moved behind the bar, where he started to slam bottles into the cooler.

Nodding at his colleague, who'd remained standing at the door, McKeown rose, shrugged on his jacket and pulled the door open to a blast of freezing air. His boss would certainly be interested in this O'Carroll character.

'I'll be back,' he said, feeling like Arnold Schwarzenegger. Now, if only he could get rid of the smell of vinegar from his fingers …

CHAPTER ELEVEN

Once Lottie had updated Kirby, they found Boyd and entered the building, heading towards the locker room where a member of staff stated she'd seen Fiona heading after her shift.

SOCOs were already in place. They'd found a small area on the floor with a trace of blood. Fiona's head wound, Lottie thought. After a cursory look around, she told Kirby to check the lockers and showers, while she and Boyd took the stairs to the roof. They were constructed of stone. By the time they reached the top step, she felt her head spinning.

'No sign of a struggle along the way,' Boyd said. 'That's if she was brought up here against her will.'

Examining the door in front of her, Lottie twisted the old brass knob. The door opened outward without objection. The wind slapped her in the face as she stepped outside. It took her a moment to catch her breath. She had donned overshoes and gloves, and Boyd, still suited up, carried a brown paper evidence bag. Just in case they found anything suspicious. Two SOCOs were already taking photographs.

'No footprints,' Boyd observed.

'It's been snowing steadily,' she said.

Walking carefully across metal pallets placed by the SOCOs, they reached the area from where it was likely Fiona had taken her last steps.

Boyd crouched down and swept away flakes of damp snow. 'What time was the body discovered?'

'The witness says it was after three when he parked his car,' she said.

'That's over an hour ago. And as you say, it's been snowing constantly.'

She glanced at the SOCOs. 'Any footprints?'

Both shook their heads. One said, 'If there were, they've been obliterated by the snow.'

She caught Boyd glancing at his watch as she moved to the edge of the parapet. Inching sideways until she was lined up with the scene below, she looked over the area then drew her eyes back to the ground around her. Hopefully SOCOs would find something.

'Are all the staff and visitors accounted for?' she asked Boyd.

'They're being interviewed in the canteen.' He was edging back towards the door.

'And the patients?' God, but he was being a pain in the arse.

'Most are confined to bed. Uniforms are checking each person against the register. I think it's all a waste of time. It's obvious she jumped.'

'I don't think she did. She was getting married tomorrow.'

'I rest my case,' Boyd said.

Lottie cringed at the sarcasm lacing his voice. She was so cold she was unable to come up with a smart reply. Instead she said, 'Fiona is the second person found dead clothed in a wedding dress in the space of a few hours. It's suspicious, Boyd.'

Across the vista, towards the horizon, she thought she saw a light moving through the trees. 'What about the outdoor staff?'

'What do you mean?'

She kept her eyes fixed, ignoring the blizzard tearing through her jacket. 'Gardeners? Site maintenance? I thought I saw someone. Among the trees. What's over there?'

'I'll have to check.'

'If my memory serves me correctly, there are life-sized statues depicting the stations of the cross, and further on there are allotments or vegetable gardens. A river runs through the land at the edge of the forest.' She recalled, somewhere from the dregs of a memory, her mother bringing her out here when she was a child, to pray and light candles in the chapel for her missing brother.

'What are you thinking, Lottie?'

She could feel the warmth of Boyd's breath on the side of her face as he spoke. 'I'm thinking there's someone out there looking up at us. Come on.' She turned on her heel.

Boyd remained where he was. 'Are you not staying here to look around for possible evidence?'

'SOCOs have it in hand, and anyway, the snow will preserve it – if there is anything here. Find me someone who knows the layout of the land around here.'

'After that, I have to leave. I'm sorry, but it's important to me … to my mother.'

'Go, then.' She wanted to say more, to talk to him, to find out what was going on, but now was not the time. Later. Tomorrow. Yes, definitely tomorrow.

With one last glance towards the area where she'd seen the light, Lottie rushed through the door and down the stairs, all the while feeling like a shadow had been cast over her.

While Boyd organised uniformed officers before he headed off, Lottie fetched a large torch from the boot of the car. She inched along a narrow footpath that cut a snow-covered lawn in half. Her brain was telling her she was wasting her time, but her gut was telling her Fiona Heffernan had not committed suicide. The blood on the locker room floor, and the wedding dress. They'd found two dead women dressed in wedding gowns, and that added up to highly suspicious circumstances. Cara and Fiona had both been murdered; she just had to prove it.

She reached the end of the path where it split into a V. Moving to the left, she crossed a stone bridge. The water below flowed furiously, moving too quickly to freeze over. On the other side, the path veered right. She thought she saw a light flicker through the trees. Ducking down, she forged on, with branches snagging her hair and her boots sinking in the deep snow. The torch cast a beam ahead of her and she was sure there were no footprints other than the trail she'd left behind. After a few moments, she found the source of the light.

Among the stations of the cross statues, a crucified Jesus hanging on a large wooden cross loomed before her, lit by a spotlight on the plinth. She stepped forward. This must be the light she'd seen. Then again, the spotlight was static, and she'd been sure the light had been moving. The wind?

As she turned to head back, the trees rustled and snow pelted down. She pulled her hood tight, heading along a path she had yet to walk, and as she made a right towards the abbey, her eyes followed the direction of the river. The land was flat where the snow laden-trees broke ranks. Beyond them lay a house and a farmyard. At the perimeter hedge, a man stood with a lamp in his hand. Lottie waved her torch in greeting, though he was fifty paces away from her. He didn't acknowledge her; just stepped backwards, turned and walked away. Slow, determined steps. Then he was gone.

She felt as if an icicle had slipped down inside her clothes. Making her way quickly, she hoped McGlynn would have news for her, because she sure as hell wasn't wasting any more time out in this no-man's-land if she wasn't dealing with a murder.

*

Christy Clarke wiped a trickle of water from his eye as he walked carefully back to his house. The yard was like an ice rink and his wellington boots were not doing him any favours. It wasn't tears of emotion, he told himself. Just the cold.

In the kitchen, he tried the tap again. The pipes clanked. A gush of brown water spluttered onto the mugs in the sink and splashed up on his green waxed jacket. He waited. Looked out of the window. The water drained to a dribble and stopped. He took the wrench out of his pocket and went back outside.

The water pump was in a barn beside the pig shed. He'd already spent the best part of the day trying to fix it, and he'd been sure it was working when he'd finished. But the dirty dribble of water told him otherwise. Now, with his hands in fingerless gloves, he set to work again, hoping that this time he'd get it right.

A car skidded into the yard. He heard its door open and shut.

'What are you doing in there?' Beth said.

He didn't turn around. She reminded him too much of her mother when her voice slit through his soul with that tone.

'What does it look like?' He tightened the wrench around a bolt.

'Have you not got the water fixed yet? God, Dad, I wanted to have a bloody shower.'

'Spray on some of that fancy deodorant for now. I'm doing my best.'

'Right!' Indignation laced her voice. 'A coffee might warm me up. I'll put the kettle on.'

'There's no fucking water,' Christy said. He looked over his shoulder, but his daughter had already stomped into the house.

The wrench slipped and nipped the top of his index finger. He stuck it in his mouth to stem the flow of blood and wondered how he was ever going to make things right again. Without warning, a sob belched from his throat and the anxiety that had been gathering like a fluff ball in his chest erupted in a fit of shakes. He leaned against the cold concrete wall of the pump house and succumbed to the racking sobs that tore from his lungs.

'Dad!' Beth shouted from the back door. 'I can't make coffee. There's no water!'

Christy sniffed away the last of his tears and bent over the pump without answering his daughter. He could do no more here. The problem must be inside.

'Out of the way, lass.' He opened the cupboard door under the sink.

'It took me ages to get through the village. I couldn't even stop to buy bottled water. Is there something going on at the abbey?' Beth was rooting in the bread bin.

'Must be getting ready for the wedding tomorrow.'

'Fiona and Ryan's wedding? No way. They're just having a small affair. I was only invited to the meal, that's how small it is. I doubt that much activity is warranted. I'll head over to have a look.' She stood with her empty mug in one hand and a slice of bread in the other as her father fiddled with the tap under the sink.

'God damn it to hell,' he said as water flowed freely into the sink. 'It was the inside pipe that was frozen all along, not the pump.'

Beth put her mug on the counter. 'I'll have a cuppa when I get back.'

'Where are you going?'

'I told you. To the abbey, for a snoop.'

He saw the wince curl her face inwards and her teeth grit before he realised he had gripped her arm so tightly his fingers had turned white.

'Stay and drink your tea with me. I've been on my own all day.'

'Let go of my arm, Dad.' A flush of red had spread across her deathly pale skin.

He dropped his hand and took a step backwards. 'Sorry, darling. Don't know my own strength half the time.' He filled the kettle, making a fuss of taking her mug and his own over to the table.

Eventually she relented, hanging up her coat and sitting down.

'What's wrong? Is it the VAT returns? I'll put them on a spreadsheet for you.'

He kept his back to her. Stared out at the snow falling diagonally like spikes across the yard and wished his only child wouldn't be so curious. It was bound to lead her into trouble. And Christy Clarke knew all about trouble.

CHAPTER TWELVE

When he had finished the dance routine, Trevor pointed his finger. 'You, you and you, up here. Quickly.'

As he waited for the two youngest girls and one of the teenagers to join him on the stage, he cast his eyes upwards. The front row of the balcony was empty. He shrugged away the nervy feeling of having been watched. It was probably Giles, the theatre manager, who was apt to prowl around in the darkness, keeping a wily eye on proceedings or on the young girls. But Trevor wasn't at all certain that was who he'd seen. The show was sold out, so Giles had no need to worry about opening night. It could bomb and he'd still make a profit. If it hadn't been the manager up there, who had it been?

'It's nearly time to finish. What do you want us to do now?'

He was awakened from his daydream by the voice of one of his charges. Jasmina, Tasmania? Her name escaped him. He stared at the perfect eyelashes, the purple shadow sparkling on the lids and the flawless make-up. A dash of jealousy streaked through his veins and his fingers involuntarily slid along his chin, bumping over acne that had forgotten he was no longer a teenager.

Another voice boomed out. 'Trevor, come down here!'

'I'm busy, Giles. I haven't time to be—'

'Now! This is important. Outside.'

Trevor watched Giles turn on his heel quicker than a ballerina and march out the door.

'Go on,' Shelly said. 'I'll run through the routine with the girls once more. The session is almost finished anyway.'

'Thank you.' Trevor jumped off the stage, picked up his towel and wound it around his neck to soak up the sweat pooled at the base of his throat.

The theatre bar was eerily quiet. The smell of stale beer clutched the peeling paint to the walls. He made his way to the smoking area. The heavy fire door resisted his push before it swung open with such force that he found himself propelled outside, where a high stool blocked his fall.

'Bloody hell.' He brushed down his knees and came face to face with his employer.

'Sit,' Giles said, pointing to the stool.

The Perspex roof dipped with the weight of snow, and when a bout of shivers shook his body, Trevor realised he should have put on his cardigan before venturing out in the sub-zero temperatures. 'I haven't time for games. What do you want?'

'I said sit.' A dark shadow crossed Giles's eyes, so Trevor did as he was bid.

Once he was seated, he knotted his feet around the rung on the stool and waited in the cold. Giles balled his hands into fists and bit down on his lip. His belt had an extra notch bored into it, over which his stomach flopped. Trevor couldn't stop himself staring as the manager's belly visibly inflated, the strain manifested on his face. The dark eyes widened and the flabby pink lips opened.

'What have you been up to?'

Trevor's body tensed and he scrunched up his face in confusion. 'I don't know what you're talking about. I've been rehearsing night and day.'

Moving around the stool, Giles wheezed, remaining otherwise silent.

Feeling a little braver, Trevor said, 'You'd better tell me what you think I've been doing wrong, because the suspense is killing me.'

The slap caught him on the back of the neck. He almost fell off the stool. Instead, he jumped up, his feet dancing to a silent tune. 'What the hell was that for? You can't go around hitting people. I'll report you for bullying!'

The hand that caught his arm was firm. The breath assaulting him was minty with the hint of an illicit cigarette. Giles would have you believe he didn't smoke, but Trevor knew otherwise. Trevor knew a lot of things about his boss that very few others knew.

'You won't report me for anything!' Giles gave him a push. 'Sit down and listen to me, like a good little man.'

Ready to argue, Trevor tensed his muscles, but he decided to let curiosity get the better of him. He sat. 'What do you want to talk to me about?'

'A little birdie told me something ... What's the word I'm looking for?' Giles seemed to be consulting an invisible dictionary in his mind. 'Let's say I heard something salacious about you. If you don't want anyone else to know, you will keep your mouth shut about you know what.'

'I have no idea what you're talking about.'

'That's good. You can't tell tales out of school then,' Giles laughed.

'I really have no idea what you mean.' Trevor held his breath as Giles continued to walk around him.

'You can do what you like outside of dance school, but in here, you need to keep your dirty little paws off Shelly.'

'Shelly?' A strangled laugh escaped from Trevor's lips. 'I think you've got it all wrong there.'

'Perhaps, but I know things. I watch you all the time. Even when you don't know I'm around. Remember that.'

'Okay. Can I leave now?' Trevor wondered again if it had been Giles watching him from the balcony. Probably, though the fecker was never around when he was supposed to be. You never knew when he was likely to creep up on you. Slimy bastard. His skin crawled.

After another slow circle around the stool, Giles came to a sudden stop. Trevor held his breath. A sigh of cold air snaked down his back. He spied a magpie pecking at the snow on the wall at the edge of the smoking hut, its black wings stark in contrast to its white chest and the snow. That wasn't good. Not good at all.

'I want you to do something for me,' Giles said.

*

Ryan Slevin dropped his camera bag on the hall table.

'Is that you, Ryan?' His sister's voice screeched from the kitchen above the din of his three young nephews fighting over something or other. He smelled garlic. A lot of garlic. He blamed all those cookery shows. While her boys were in school, Zoe spent most of the day in front of the television soaking up exotic recipes. He knew *MasterChef Australia* was her favourite. Hence fish for dinner every second day, interspersed with crackling pork belly. And, of course, spices and garlic. Always garlic.

He hung his dripping-wet coat on the crowded hook, untied his boots and shoved them underneath, on the floor.

'What did you cook today?' He kissed his sister's forehead, noticing that it was slick with sweat. The kitchen looked as if thirty *MasterChef* contestants had spent the day there, trying to concoct a dish that had yet to be invented.

'Something new,' she said. 'Fish basted with fresh garlic sauce. I made it myself. The sauce, not the fish.'

'Sounds great,' Ryan lied. 'Where are the boys?'

Zoe nodded to the table. He lifted up the edge of the cloth and spied his nephews sitting cross-legged on the floor.

'What are you three up to then?'

'Hiding,' five-year-old Tommy said.

'Playing,' added four-year-old Josh.

'Seek,' said two-year-old Zack.

'Well, I found you. Scoot into the sitting room. I bet *Fireman Sam* is on.'

The three of them crawled out between Ryan's legs and at last the kitchen fell into silence.

'I collected your suit from the cleaner's,' Zoe said. 'It's hanging on the front of your wardrobe.' She sniffed back a tear. Tendrils of once-blonde hair fell across her eyes and she brushed them away with her elbow. Both hands were covered in flour.

'Why are you sad?' he said.

'Oh, you know.' She turned back to the stove. 'Tomorrow is your happy day. How exciting for you and Fiona. But at the same time, I can't stop thinking of our parents' disastrous marriage, and you know my own is not …' She sniffed again. 'We spoke about it before, but now I honestly think Giles is having an affair. Ever since Zack was born, he's never home. Not for a minute do I believe he's needed at the theatre twenty-four-seven.' She wiped the flour from her hands onto her apron and hunched her shoulders.

Ryan felt his heart break a little for his younger sister, but he couldn't quell the rise of anger.

'Zoe, I intend to make my marriage work. Me and Fiona are older than you were when you got married. And wiser, I hope.'

'I know, but you have to be one hundred per cent sure of her.'

'Where is this coming from? You never said anything like this before.'

'It's just ... Fiona is very possessive and strong-minded. You're not. You're a big softie, especially where she's concerned. You've never even met her family.'

'She has a sister in Australia. There's no mystery there, so stop trying to find one.'

'She never speaks about her parents or her life before she came to Ballydoon. You have to admit it, Ryan, Fiona's a bit odd.'

'Jesus, Zoe, just because she's not an extrovert and—'

'I know, but there's just something ... I can't put my finger on it.'

'Well, I'm marrying her tomorrow, so you can stop thinking up excuses not to like her. Okay?'

Zoe turned. He caught a whisper of a smile at the edge of her mouth. 'Okay.'

'I'll have a shower. When is *that* likely to be ready?'

'*That?* I'll have you know, Ryan Slevin, *that* is my highlight dish of the week. Fish straight from the sea.'

'Caught it yourself, did you?'

'Smartarse,' she laughed. 'I ironed your good shirt too. For tomorrow.'

'You're the best sister ever.' He gave her a hug but hadn't the heart to tell her he had bought a new shirt especially for the occasion.

As he pulled away from his sister, Ryan heard the ding-dong of the doorbell. 'Are you expecting anyone?'

'It might be Fiona.'

'The night before our wedding? I don't think so. I know we want it all low-key, with no fuss, but no matter what you think of her, Fiona is a traditionalist at heart.'

He went to answer the door.

*

Waiting for the door to open, Lottie glanced around the small estate on the edge of Ballydoon village. Boyd had rushed off to Galway. She hoped he would be safe on the bad roads; she'd told him to text her when he arrived.

The address she had for Ryan Slevin was a terraced house belonging to the Bannon family. She'd been informed that Zoe Bannon was Ryan's sister.

Kirby ambled up the path, his burly face puce from the couple of steps' exertion. 'I hate being the bringer of bad news,' he said.

'Part of the job,' Lottie reminded him.

A roar of kids' shouting preceded the door being opened, followed by the pungent aroma of garlic.

She flashed her ID card at the man standing before her. 'Hello, are you Ryan Slevin?'

'I am. Have I done something I'm not aware of?' His face lit up with an amused smile and she couldn't help noticing a smudge of flour on the cheekbone under his eye. She had to resist the urge to wet her finger and wipe it away. He had the air of a teenager, despite his height, build and beard, though she suspected he was in his thirties.

'Can we come in, please?'

'It must be serious,' he said, but Lottie heard devilment in his tone. Around his legs, three ginger heads appeared.

'Who's that?' the tallest boy said.

'Shush, Tommy. Come this way, please.'

A woman appeared, untying a dirty apron. She shuffled the children out of the way. 'What's going on?'

'I'm Detective Inspector Lottie Parker and this is my colleague Detective Larry Kirby.'

Lottie wended her way around the children and their mother and followed Ryan into a sitting room that looked like a play area.

Toys were scattered everywhere, and a noisy cartoon blasted from the television. With the children evicted to their mother's care, Ryan bundled up the toys and deposited them in a heap by the side of the television, which he switched off.

He sat into a tired armchair. Lottie perched on the edge of the couch, and Kirby fell into the tattered cushions beside her.

'So, what do you want from me?' Ryan said.

'I'm afraid we have some bad news, Mr Slevin,' Lottie said.

'The name's Ryan. What bad news?' He shifted uneasily, straightening himself upright.

'You're engaged to Fiona Heffernan, is that right?'

'Fiona? Yes, I am. Has something happened to her?'

'I'm afraid so.'

'A car accident? Oh God.' He buried his head in his hands. Lottie could no longer see his face. 'Fiona hates driving in bad weather. Is she okay?' He stood suddenly. 'Can I see her? Is she in Ragmullin hospital?'

'Please sit down, Ryan.' She detested this part of her job. 'The news is very bad. We found Ms Heffernan this afternoon. I'm sorry to say that she's dead.'

Ryan sat, his eyes questioning. 'What? How? Oh my God!'

'It wasn't a car accident.' She noted the changing expressions on his face. Questioning. Incredulity. Horror. He appeared genuinely shocked.

'What? What happened? I can't believe this. We're getting married tomorrow. This is her second chance. To make a good life for herself, with me. Oh God, no ...'

Scanning the cramped sitting room, Lottie wondered if this was where Ryan had intended to live with Fiona, but it was too early for questions of an intrusive nature. She just needed to find out where he'd been this afternoon.

'Are you okay to continue? Do you want your sister—'

'No. Don't say anything to Zoe, please. I'll tell her when you're gone.'

'You said this was Fiona's second chance. Was she married before? Divorced?'

'No, nothing like that. She had a long-term involvement with a bloody prick of a fellow; she was still with him when we met. She was so damaged after that so-called relationship ... but we were good together.' He paused. Raised his eyes to Lottie. 'Tell me, please, what happened to her?'

'Her body was found around three this afternoon.' Lottie thought how best to frame her words. 'It looks like she, em ... fell from the rooftop of Ballydoon Abbey.'

'Oh my God. This is just awful.' Ryan ran his hand through his hair then along his bearded chin before resting his elbows on his knees. 'I hope she didn't suffer.'

What an odd statement, Lottie thought. She was trying desperately hard to get a handle on Ryan Slevin. 'We'll have a better picture as to what happened after the post-mortem.'

Ryan's stare caught her unawares. It was penetrating, and any trace of laughter had disappeared from his eyes. 'You mentioned the rooftop. What was she doing up there?'

'We're still establishing the facts.'

'But ...' It was as if realisation had suddenly dawned on him, and a burst of anger replaced his disbelief. 'You think she jumped? No. No way would Fiona do that. We're getting married *tomorrow* and she loves her little girl. What about Lily? Is she okay? Who's looking after her?'

Lottie swung around and scrunched her forehead in a question to Kirby. He shook his head, eyebrows raised. This was the first they'd heard of a child.

'Fiona has a daughter?'

'Yes. Lily,' he repeated.

'Do you know where she is?' Lottie said urgently.

Ryan jumped up, clenching a hand into a fist and thumping it into the other. 'You mean to tell me no one has gone to pick her up from her after-school club? She'll be terrified.' He pulled his phone from his pocket and furiously scrolled through his messages and calls. 'No one rang me. They may have been trying to contact Fiona.'

'We took her handbag and phone from her locker. They're signed into evidence,' Kirby said.

'And you didn't notice anything on her phone or in her bag about her daughter?' Lottie said.

'No, don't think so.' Kirby looked down at his notebook.

'What age is Lily?' Lottie turned to Ryan, anxiety constricting her lungs.

'She's eight. She goes to the after-school club when Fiona's at work. Oh God, you didn't know she had a child?'

'We're on it straight away. What's the name of the club?'

'Little People. It's in Ragmullin.'

'Kirby, make some calls.'

As he went out to the hall with his phone, Lottie turned back to Ryan. 'Who was Fiona in a relationship with before she met you?'

'Colin Kavanagh, and I wouldn't call it a relationship. That word means there has to be love involved, and I don't think the emotion figured in that man's vocabulary, let alone his heart.'

'Where does he live?'

'In a big old house, a converted barn, outside the village. Down by the lake.' He gave her the address.

Lottie wondered if the fact that Fiona died in her wedding dress was a statement. Had Boyd been right? Was it Fiona's way of telling Ryan she no longer wanted to marry him? That killing herself was better than the prospect of life with him? No, it didn't make sense. She had thought it suspicious all along, and now, the news that Fiona was the mother of a little girl compounded her theory of murder. Especially after also finding Cara Dunne dead in a wedding dress. She hoped Lily was okay. Probably still at the after-school club. Eyeing the door, she heard Kirby talking on the phone.

Returning her attention to Ryan, she said, 'I'm sorry to have to ask you these questions at this difficult time. Can you account for your whereabouts this afternoon?'

'What do you mean?'

Why did people answer questions with more questions? 'Just routine.'

'But you said Fiona jumped …'

'No, I said it looks like she fell. She was found on the ground. We have to look at all the evidence.'

'She could have been pushed, is that what you mean?' Without waiting for her to reply, he held up his hand. 'I know, I know. Wait for the post-mortem. I'm in the newspaper business. I understand the language.'

'This afternoon, where were you?'

He slumped back on the chair. 'At work. In the *Tribune* office. I'm a photographer for the paper.'

'You were there all afternoon?'

'Yes. No. I can't remember. I know I was working. I came straight home. I had to eat my dinner then write a short speech for tomorrow. Only there's no tomorrow any more, is there?'

As his body crumpled into a heap and sobs tore from his throat, Lottie let him have his moment of grief. Kirby returned, shaking his head.

'The child is not at Little People,' he said. 'The manager tells me Lily had a class at three o'clock at the dance school in Ragmullin

Theatre. Her mother had arranged for a member of staff to bring the child there, and she herself was to pick Lily up afterwards.'

'So where is she?' Ryan moaned.

'I phoned the dance school,' Kirby continued. 'Colin Kavanagh is listed as the contact if Fiona is not there to collect Lily.'

Ryan shot out of the chair and faced up to Kirby. 'Kavanagh is Lily's father. Thank God she's safe.'

'Sit down, Mr Slevin,' Kirby said. He turned to Lottie. 'No one at the theatre remembers phoning him to pick Lily up.'

'We're leaving now,' she said. 'We need to call to Mr Kavanagh.'

Ryan's body seemed to deflate. 'Let me know when you find her. I have to know she's all right. The boys love her.'

'And you? Do you love her?' Lottie pressed.

'Of course I do. As if she were my own daughter, for Christ's sake.'

As she followed Kirby to the front door, Lottie turned around in the cramped hallway. 'Where were you going to live after the wedding?'

'I have a cottage. Far side of the village. I've renovated it. It was like our own little dream home, and now those dreams are … shattered.'

'We'll need to have a look there.'

He dug around in his pocket and extracted a bunch of keys. He twisted one off the ring. 'Here. Take it. It's a spare.'

The kitchen door opened. Zoe stood there with a million questions in her eyes. 'What's going on, Ryan?'

'I'll leave you to it,' Lottie said, and pulled the door shut behind her. She sat into the car beside Kirby.

He said, 'So who is this Colin Kavanagh when he's at home?'

'You'll never believe it …'

CHAPTER THIRTEEN

The narrow road around by Doon Lake was treacherous in the bad weather conditions. Lottie clutched the door handle, ready to escape if they skidded. But Kirby kept the car straight.

'Can't believe a high flying Dublin solicitor is living here, in the back of beyond,' he said.

'Well, he is, and his reputation is not very pleasant.'

The gates, with an intercom, were designed to keep outsiders out. Lottie identified herself, and Kirby drove the car up the winding avenue. She couldn't see much of the house in the darkness until the outdoor lights came on, casting eerie shadows up and down the massive barn-like structure.

The door opened before she had one foot on the bottom of the three steps. A tall man stood there.

'Where is my daughter? Have you found her?' Lottie sensed a sudden movement of fear in her abdomen. The child wasn't here. 'Not yet, Mr Kavanagh. Can we come in?'

The tall, white-haired man opened the door wider and guided Lottie and Kirby into the vast expanse of hallway. He closed the door and stood with his back to it without inviting them further into his home.

'I've had calls from your people about Lily,' he said. 'What's Fiona done with her?'

'Mr Kavanagh, is there somewhere we can sit?' Lottie said. As she studied him, the dread settled into the pit of her stomach. If the little girl wasn't at Kavanagh's house, where was she?

'You can talk to me here. I don't like gardaí in my home.' His eyebrows knitted into a ribbed frown. She noticed that he wasn't as old as his white hair indicated. Face long and sharp. Eyes green; irises that appeared as if they were feathered with sprigs of seaweed. Mid fifties, probably; a good twenty years or so older than Fiona, she figured.

'I regret to have to inform you that your ex-partner, Fiona Heffernan, was found dead this afternoon.'

'She's dead? You're joking me.' His eyes travelled from Lottie to Kirby. 'You're not? She *is* dead?'

'I'm afraid so.'

'You'd better come on in.'

He walked ahead of them into a dark room that Lottie could only describe as a library. It seemed out of place in the modern construction. Three walls were lined, floor to ceiling, with books, some leather-bound, probably first editions. Two brown leather sofas and a chaise longue were the only furniture besides the bookshelves. The fireplace was banked with logs, and flames raged up the chimney. Lottie moved towards the heat and stood with her back to the fire, allowing the warmth to de-ice her body.

When Kavanagh was seated, he indicated for Lottie to sit too.

'If it's okay with you, I'll stand. Fiona was found dead in the grounds of Ballydoon Abbey this afternoon. It appears she might have fallen from the roof, but we are—'

'Fallen? What was she doing up there? And Lily? The call I got was about my daughter.'

'Did you collect the child from her dance school this afternoon?'

'What? No, I did not. No one called me. Jesus Christ! Where is Lily? Did Fiona pick her up? Maybe before her … accident.'

'I'm not sure.' Lotte tried to digest the enormity of the fact that the little girl was most likely missing. The dread she'd felt when her own daughters had been abducted just six weeks ago reared its head and threatened to consume her. She had to remain professional, though. No point in showing her distress to Kavanagh. 'I've yet to draw up the sequence of events. This is an ongoing investigation.'

'You mean to tell me you don't know where my daughter is?'

Kavanagh's arrogance appeared to be negating his concern. Lottie felt her nerves grating with aggravation. If Boyd was here, he might call Kavanagh a prick under his breath, and right now she couldn't think of a better word for him.

'If Lily isn't with you, who do you think she might be with?' Dear God, she thought, let him know someone who might have collected the child.

'I know who. That bastard Ryan Slevin!' Kavanagh bolted out of the chair, in the same manner that Ryan had not ten minutes ago.

'I've just come from Ryan's. Lily is not there.' But she hadn't checked Ryan's sister's house. She'd logically assumed the girl was with her father. Fuck!

Kavanagh said, 'What about that cottage where he intends to live? Have you checked that?'

'I've sent a squad car there. The thing is, you are the only other contact for the after-school club and the dance school. Where were you all afternoon?'

'In my office.'

'Can anyone corroborate that?'

'I work alone. My secretary is on extended maternity leave. I've downsized my office so I have just a receptionist in three days a week.' Pausing to catch his breath, he continued, 'You should be asking that Slevin yob where *he* was.'

'Let me do my job, Mr Kavanagh. We don't know what's happened to Lily yet, but can you think of any reason why Fiona might want to kill herself?'

Kavanagh sat down and crossed his legs, cradling an ankle on one knee. Lottie noticed a definite tremble in his hands.

'Fiona's a complicated individual.' His face flushed as he spoke. 'You'd have to know her to realise where I'm coming from. She loves … loved Lily unconditionally. Loved her job too. I don't think she ever really loved me. Maybe that's why she continuously turned down my offers of marriage and refused to have Lily carry my name. I have no idea what she ever saw in Ryan Slevin.'

'When did you split up?'

'About two years ago. My daughter was six at the time. Fiona had changed the instant the baby arrived. She shut me out a lot. I can understand a little of it. I'm twenty years older than her. But I could never get my head around how she hooked up with Slevin.'

'When she left where did she go?' Lottie was sure Zoe Bannon's house hadn't enough room for Fiona. She must have had her own place.

'I rented a house in Ragmullin for them. Top-notch, top dollar. I wanted Lily to be comfortable. I love my daughter.'

Lottie took down the address and made a call for it to be searched. 'Do you have much contact with Lily?'

'Every second weekend. She has her own room here.'

'Can I see it?'

His face reddened. 'I did not kidnap my own daughter, Inspector.'

'I never said that.'

'You implied it.'

Lottie was growing weary of him. 'If you or Mr Slevin did not pick up Lily, who do you think did?'

He nudged his chin with a finger. 'I have no idea. But in the morning, I'll be sending correspondence to that dance school. It is outrageous that they could let an eight-year-old leave their care without properly checking credentials.'

'When was the last time you spoke to Fiona?'

'Sunday night. She came to pick Lily up after she'd been here for the weekend.'

'Was anyone else with her?'

'She was alone. That bastard knows better than to show up on my doorstep.'

'One final question. Do you know of any reason why someone would want to harm Fiona?'

'What? She was a nurse, for God's sake. Everyone loved her.' He stood and walked to the door. 'Find my daughter and bring her home.'

'We will.'

'Fiona was a good mother. I would stake my house on it that she did not throw herself off any roof. She either fell or she was pushed.'

'Okay. Can I see Lily's room now?'

Kavanagh directed her up the winding stairs to a loft-like mezzanine. Lily's bedroom was overflowing with cuddly toys, a doll's house and every toy Lottie cared to imagine. The double bed had a *Frozen* duvet. A net canopy adorned with butterflies hung over it.

She opened drawers and the wardrobe and gasped at the array of clothing. 'Are these all Lily's?'

'I like to ensure my daughter is well cared for.' Kavanagh stood inside the door, his head touching the bare timber ceiling. 'She's okay, isn't she? Please tell me nothing has happened to my little girl.' He picked up a photograph from the dresser and handed it to her with tears in his hard eyes.

Lottie had no idea where his daughter was, but her heart was fluttering a warning not to be taken in by appearances. She gazed at the smiling face of the young girl in the picture. Long blonde hair framed her elfin face. Freckles dotted her nose, and her smile was infectious. Two slides clipped her hair away from her blue eyes. The little girl had a familiar look about her. Daft, Lottie thought. She'd never set eyes on either Lily or Fiona before today.

'Can I borrow this?'

'Of course.'

In the en suite bathroom, she picked up a small toothbrush. 'I'll take this for a DNA sample.'

She felt Kavanagh's eyes boring through her as she sealed the toothbrush in a clear evidence bag.

'Let me know as soon as you find her.'

'I will, I promise,' she replied, thinking how out of place amongst the child's toys he looked.

At the front door, she said, 'Thank you, Mr Kavanagh. We will be in touch.'

'You'd better be, because I can guarantee you I will be snapping at your heels every step of the way.'

As Lottie followed Kirby out to the car, she had no doubt in her mind about the sincerity of Kavanagh's last words. All the rest, now that was a different matter entirely.

*

Beth lay on her bed and propped the box on her knee. She took out the brochures and skimmed through them. Sun, sea and sand. That was what he'd promised her. She felt a pool of warmth inch its way from her abdomen up to her chest. She'd been in love even though she knew he could never love her back. And she had made a promise to him. A promise not to tell anyone of their plans. But then it was too late.

Settling the papers back into the box, she fixed the lid and slid it under her bed. She plugged in her phone to charge and tapped the screen alive, then flicked through her apps and brought up the news. Nothing exciting apart from the weather. Doom and gloom. She logged into Facebook. Her notifications lit up like a Christmas tree. What the hell?

Throwing her legs over the edge of the bed, she sat up and clutched the phone tightly in her hand, scrolling through the posts. A body had been found in the grounds of Ballydoon Abbey. Someone had taken photos and videos, but they were all fuzzy. She scanned the comments, her journalistic antenna on high alert. Suicide, some were saying; a woman had jumped from the roof. Still more commented that she had been found in a wedding dress. Someone else said that that was earlier in the day. At Hill Point. Shit, that was the tip-off she'd got, and then her dunce of an editor had stuck his oar in, preventing her from investigating it.

This one, though, she had to see for herself. Why shouldn't she get these scoops? If she hadn't such an old-fashioned editor, things would be different. She thought of the national papers. The web-based news outlets. Her blog. Yes, she could break a great story that way. Make a name for herself. Then she thought of the story she was secretly working on. That made her mind up for her.

She would have to sneak out past her father. The weight of so many illicit escapes was becoming too much of a burden to bear. She'd been told it wouldn't be for much longer. That was what she'd been promised. It was what had kept her going, living in the arsehole of nowhere. Then everything had changed.

She left the light on, pocketed her phone and slipped out of the house.

CHAPTER FOURTEEN

When she returned to the station, Lottie issued a nationwide alert for eight-year-old Lily Heffernan. The principal at St Celia's primary school supplied a list of teachers, parents and children, and Lottie organised a team to contact everyone.

She checked with the after-school club, but no one had seen the child since she'd been dropped off for her dance class. Kirby headed to the theatre to check out the situation there and get a list of staff and students, while Sam McKeown did the same at the club. Already, roadblocks had gone up around the town, but she knew it was too late. They'd lost the crucial two-hour window that experts claimed was critical in any child abduction case. Or maybe the little girl had just run away and was waiting for her mother somewhere? Lottie crossed her fingers instinctively.

As she awaited the return of her detectives, she ate a Mars bar and gulped a lukewarm coffee that she'd fetched from the canteen. She was convinced she was dealing with two murders and a missing child. Her brain constricted in pain with all that was going on, and as she looked at Lily's photograph, her heart lurched in her chest thinking of where she might be. That made her think of her own family. She'd have to go home soon. And Boyd. He had, as yet, no knowledge of Lily Heffernan's disappearance.

She took out her phone and called him. It went to voicemail. She hung up without leaving a message. He had enough on his plate with his mother. If it actually was his mother he was meeting. Shit, why had she thought that? She shook her head to rid herself of suspicions.

Three hours had passed since Lily's dance class ended, so that was the timeline they had to use. Three hours since the little girl had disappeared.

She couldn't sit doing nothing. She dumped the half-drunk coffee in the bin and moved to the door, deciding to walk to the theatre to clear her head.

The snow on the pavements was beginning to freeze. The Christmas lights were lit and Main Street looked brighter than she'd ever seen it. Every second string of bulbs was blue, and it gave a winter wonderland feel to the town. As she turned down Gaol Street, she was struck by the line of stalls along the road. All shuttered. The road closed to traffic. The lights at the after-school club were still on, and the theatre, at the end of the street, had a large Christmas tree swaying outside on the path.

Entering the theatre through the sliding glass doors, Lottie welcomed the blast of heat. She spied Kirby standing beside a life-sized crib. Two men were seated on chairs. Being interrogated, it looked like.

'Hello,' she said. 'I'm Detective Inspector Lottie Parker.'

She smelled the dank odour of dampness. It was an old building, built on the site of Ragmullin's gaol over a hundred years ago. She shivered at the thought of the reported ghosts walking the vacuum between the roof and ceiling and strolling through the underground chambers, their chains clanking, trailing a fetid stench in their wake.

Kirby turned to her. 'I've completed a search of the building with the help of uniforms. No sign of the child. This is Giles Bannon, theatre and dance school manager.' He pointed to the older of the two men.

'Bannon?' Lottie felt the wheels whirring in her brain. 'Any relation to Zoe Bannon?'

'She's my wife.'

'Oh, right,' Lottie said, thinking she should have been informed of this.

'What has Zoe got to do with anything?' Bannon looked up indignantly.

Lottie paused, trying to align her thoughts. 'You know we're investigating the disappearance of eight-year-old Lily Heffernan, your future step-niece?'

'I do.'

'Lily's mother Fiona was due to marry Zoe's brother Ryan tomorrow, you know.'

'Of course I bloody know. All that hullabaloo about it being a small ceremony while inviting twenty or thirty people they don't even know to a shindig at the Railway Hotel. Ryan has my head fried.' He paused, then added, 'This gentleman has informed me that Fiona is dead. There won't be any wedding now, will there?'

Instantly Lottie had an urge to smack his smug face. She felt Kirby tug on her sleeve. Somehow she managed to keep her temper concealed.

'I was about to commence the interview,' Kirby said.

'We should do this at the station,' she told him, thinking it might soften Giles Bannon's edges a little. She nodded towards the other man. 'Who are you?'

He lifted his head, his eyes dancing about wildly. He was either high, excited or terrified.

'Trevor Toner,' he said. 'I'm a dance tutor.'

'Were you tutoring Lily today?'

He nodded.

'Speak up,' Kirby said.

'Yes, I was. Me and Shelly. We were rehearsing for the show. It's on next w-week and the kids are b-brutal.'

'Brutal?' Lottie wasn't sure if his stammer was permanent or if he was scared witless.

'I mean they're b-bad. Unrehearsed.'

'And when the class ended, who collected Lily Heffernan?'

'I don't know.' He rubbed his hands together so feverishly that Lottie was sure she could see flecks of skin flittering in the half-light. 'They always rush to the d-door. Sometimes they don't even bother to change out of their dance shoes.'

Giles Bannon stood. No matter how she tried, Lottie couldn't marry his image with Zoe's slight frame. He was overweight and smelled of sweat. Was that what she'd sensed when she'd walked into the building? Perhaps there were no ghosts after all.

'Do the students have to be signed in and out?' she said.

'Yes. Usually,' Bannon said. 'But at this time of year, with a show coming up, it's usually a bit ad hoc.' He walked to the glass door and appeared to gaze out at the crooked Christmas tree.

'Ad hoc? What do you mean?' Lottie moved to his shoulder. She didn't like talking to anyone's back.

'It's always a rush. The kids, they've been in school all day, then dance class, so they like to dash home.' He turned, keeping his back to Lottie. This annoyed her even further.

'Are you telling me you have no record of anyone signing Lily out?'

'That's what I'm saying.'

Trevor Toner stood up, glanced at Bannon then back to Lottie. 'I usually help Shelly check the kids in and out. But I was a little late getting out front today.'

'Shelly who?'

'Shelly Forde.'

'Where is she now?'

'Gone home,' Bannon interjected. 'As has everyone else. And I need to leave too.'

'Can I see the register?' She would keep him as long as she could.

Bannon turned and walked across the foyer, his steel-tipped shoes clicking on the smudged tiles. At the reception desk, he lifted a ring binder and brought it back to Lottie.

She skimmed the unintelligible signatures. 'I'll take it with me.'

'Take what you like. The kid isn't here.' Bannon had resumed his vigil at the door.

Lottie directed her attention to Trevor Toner. 'What was Lily's mood like today?'

He shrugged. 'I didn't take much notice of her. All of them were under-rehearsed, so she didn't stand out or anything.'

'Do you know her well?'

The man's already pale face turned ashen. 'What? No. Not like that. Oh God, you don't think I did anything to her, do you? I'd never hurt a child.'

A grunt from Giles Bannon alerted Lottie. She felt the hairs on her arms perking to attention. 'Have you something to add, Mr Bannon?'

He swirled round, his face puce. 'I'd like you to leave now.'

'That's not going to happen now or any time soon.' She turned to Kirby. 'Accompany them to the station to record their state-ments. I have a forensic team on the way. This entire building is out of bounds.'

'For how long?' Bannon said.

'Until I say so.' She sighed loudly.

McKeown picked that moment to arrive, his height and bulk dwarfing Bannon, who took a backward step.

'Interview them separately,' she said. 'Locate Shelly Forde. I want all three in interview rooms when I get back.'

While Trevor Toner seemed to shrink into himself, Giles Bannon appeared to relish the challenge. And then he spoke the words Lottie despised.

'I want my solicitor.'

Uniforms had the building sealed off and a team were searching the auditorium row by row, for the second time. Lottie doubted the little girl was hiding or being hidden anywhere in the theatre. It was more likely she had wandered off or been taken away. She'd ordered the CCTV footage to be secured from the theatre reception area and, as there was none on the outside of the building, officers were checking nearby businesses. The chances of finding anything on CCTV were slim, mainly because Gaol Street would have been packed that afternoon with the markets, the street cordoned off to traffic. She would have to rely on witness statements, and she knew how unreliable they were.

As she signed herself out at the crime-scene tape, Lottie was certain SOCOs wouldn't arrive until morning. They were stretched as it was, with the two potential crime scenes resulting from the deaths of Cara Dunne and Fiona Heffernan.

Walking back to the station, the street coloured sepia under the yellow street lights and blue in places from the twinkling strings overhead, she was consumed with a deep sorrow. Where was Lily Heffernan?

She passed the courthouse, all cordoned off with renovations stalled since the deaths of the workers in a freak crane accident. It had cast a damp blanket over the town, and it was only with the festive spirit in the air that normality had started to return. But now, with two murders and a missing child, the abnormal was once again thrown back into the mix.

Shaking her head, she continued her journey. Her next job was to brief Acting Superintendent David McMahon. That was one prospect she did not relish. After that, she was going home to her own family. She needed to hug them and be hugged.

Kirby and McKeown both looked like they could do with a week in bed. Lottie supposed she portrayed the same grim image. Before she did anything else, though, she had to hear what Bannon and Toner had had to say for themselves.

'We had to let them go,' Kirby said. 'They'll be back in the morning to give their official statements.'

'Why on earth did you let them go?'

'A solicitor arrived,' McKeown said. 'Bannon was all smiles. Like two pigs in shite they were.'

'Stop. You'll give me a headache.' She already had one.

'In all fairness,' McKeown said, 'he was within his rights to call a solicitor.'

'Rights?' Lottie fumed. 'An eight-year-old girl is missing, and her mother is lying on a slab in the mortuary.'

'Sorry, boss, but the way I see—'

'Has anyone informed the superintendent?' She was in no mood for pontificating. She wanted facts.

'He's attending some Christmas dinner thing in Dublin Castle,' Kirby said as he sat down, a gasp of air escaping from his chair. 'He's not answering his phone.'

'All teachers, students and parents have been contacted, with no result,' McKeown said. 'We've Lily's photograph circulated and alerts out, and the night team have been briefed.'

'Not much more we can do for now,' Lottie said. 'Go home and be back at six a.m. The duty sergeant can contact us if there are any developments.'

'If that's what you want,' McKeown said.

'Have we any update on Cara Dunne? Anyone talk to her friends or work colleagues?'

'I had a word with her ex-fiancé, Steve O'Carroll. He's the assistant manager at the Railway Hotel.'

Kirby said, 'Bannon mentioned that was the hotel where Fiona Heffernan's wedding reception was due to take place.'

'What did O'Carroll have to say for himself?' Lottie asked.

'Not much,' McKeown said. 'I checked him out. He spent four years studying to become a solicitor. Failed his finals spectacularly and never got to practise. Now he's living in Ragmullin. He refused to answer any questions. I got the feeling he hadn't much regret over the break-up with Cara.'

'Okay, thanks. Once the post-mortem confirms Cara Dunne was murdered, I want him in here.'

'Sure, boss,' McKeown said. 'For what it's worth, I think he was acting very strange.'

'Acting strange does not say he's guilty of anything.'

'Still, he didn't seem too put out by her death.'

'We'll follow up with him tomorrow. You two are off duty now.' As McKeown fetched his coat and left, she turned to Kirby. 'The belt used to hang Cara Dunne. Any word from forensics?'

'I was working on it,' he said, 'before Fiona and Lily happened.'

'First thing in the morning, I want a report on my desk.'

'Sure,' Kirby muttered.

She switched off the light in her office, closed the door and left Kirby to whatever he was at. Her legs felt like lead as she made her way down the stairs. A hot shower would be welcome. And then she was putting her feet up for the night. She tried calling Boyd again. He still wasn't picking up. What was going on with him?

CHAPTER FIFTEEN

As he walked along the narrow footpath on the wide street, the only street in Ballydoon, he was acutely aware of the evil crawling along in his wake. He walked slower than usual. The weight had settled, the burden of the darkness lodged on his shoulders like a shroud on a dead person. When he crossed the bridge, he heard the river flowing. Snow banked up at the edges, and reeds bowed their heads in a solemn salute. He turned into the grounds of the abbey and raised his face to the black sky. No moon. It was blotted out by the pulsing clouds of the night.

He could see a light haze ahead. Two garda cars. A white van. And the tent. Had they not taken away her body? Surely by now she should be lying naked in a morgue, slit open from chest to pubic bone. Her entrails extracted, weighed and noted. Sealed in plastic bags awaiting return to the empty cavity. And her hair. Oh, her hair …

He ducked under a tree and made his way along one of the many pathways he knew so well. Hands now tightly scrunched into fists, deep in his pockets. If anyone approached him, they were getting a punch. And fuck the consequences.

Along here there was less snow. The path, sheltered by trees, led back over the river and around the statues. He stood at the fence. Behind him, the garda activity might as well have been in another country. They were oblivious to where the real action lay. The real clues. The real reason.

He watched the farmhouse. He couldn't see much of the yard in the dark; only the light from the windows. He knew what was in there. Knew who was in there.

He chuckled to himself, a wide smile creasing his face in two, before continuing on the path. His hands were more relaxed now. He had no fear of being found. Not where he was going. No one would find him. Ever. Never. No.

CHAPTER SIXTEEN

The day had been excruciatingly long. Lottie was sure she could feel each one of its minutes dragging at the muscles of her legs. She needed to sit. To lie down. To rest. But her second job was just about to begin. Her family. Not that it was a job, but all the same, there was no time for leisure. She wished, just for a second, for someone to sit with her so that she could unload her worries and fears. And she wondered how she would get through the night with the weight of little Lily Heffernan's disappearance pressing down on her like a cement block.

She heard muted voices as she hung her jacket on the banister. She cocked her ear to listen up the stairs. Nothing. The sound was coming from the sitting room. Opening the door, she stuck her head around it.

'Leo?' She felt a shiver slip between her shoulder blades.

After McMahon, Leo Belfield was the last person she wanted to have to talk to tonight. Her half-brother from a complicated family tree. A captain in the NYPD. Once he had discovered his true family, he had travelled over to Ireland regularly. He'd been injured during the course of her last case, and Rose, Lottie's mother, had taken on the task of nursing him better. What was he doing here at this late hour?

'Hello, Lottie.' He stood up from the couch, where he'd been sitting with her daughters. There was no sign of baby Louis, or indeed Sean. The former most likely in bed and the latter probably in his room, gaming on his PlayStation. The idea that her son might be doing his homework was remote. 'Can I have a word in the kitchen?'

'*My* kitchen,' Lottie said under her breath as she led the way. Though it wasn't really her kitchen, she thought. She was only renting the house.

She was happy to see the room had been tidied up. The laundry had been put away and a saucepan was sitting on the hob. Even the floor looked as though a sweeping brush had scraped over it. Rose had been in.

Leo pulled out a chair and sat. Lottie remained standing. She'd rather be looking down at him. She heard footsteps hammering down the stairs. Louis crying. A door opening.

'Sean!' Katie yelled. 'You're an eejit. You've woken Louis. I'll swing for you.'

'Whatever,' came Sean's reply.

Lottie rushed to the hall. 'What's going on out here?'

'That dope woke Louis,' Katie said, and disappeared up the stairs.

Sean was searching through the pile of coats on the banister.

'Where are you going?' Lottie tightened her grip on the kitchen door.

'Out.'

'Where?'

'Anywhere but here.' He dragged a jacket from the pile and opened the front door.

'It's late, Sean.'

He turned on the step. 'I don't care. I need air. This house is suffocating me.'

'Don't be long.' Lottie felt powerless to stop him heading out into the night.

'Everything all right?' Leo said.

Returning to the kitchen, she shrugged at him and lifted the lid of the saucepan. Chicken stew. She switched on the hob. 'What do you want, Leo?'

He pulled out a chair. 'Will you sit for this chat?'

'Sounds serious.' She sat.

Leo's hands were clasped together on the table. His eyes replicas of her own. Emerald green. 'I know you've been involved with solicitors over the Kitty Belfield probate.'

'And?' Lottie believed Kitty Belfield to be their grandmother.

'You know I have a claim on the Farranstown estate?'

'Yes, I do.'

'After that episode with my twin sister, Bernie, I thought I wanted no part of our heritage.'

'To be honest, Leo, you don't need it. Alexis left you well off, didn't she?'

She hadn't meant to sound bitchy, but she knew that was the way her words had come out. Alexis had passed herself off as Leo's mother, having left Ireland with him as a baby. She was the half-sister of their mother, Carrie King. Long story.

'True,' he said. 'She left me with real estate in New York. I've yet to wind up her company.'

'Why do you need to have an interest in Farranstown, then?' Lottie couldn't keep her voice from bristling.

'Will you listen to me? Legally I have a claim on the estate.'

'Right!'

'There's no need to get your Irish temper riled up. I've discussed all this with Rose. She's in agreement.'

Lottie pushed the chair with the back of her legs and stood, shaking her head. 'I might have known my mother had her paw stuck somewhere in the middle of this pie.'

'I'm trying to help you here, if you'd only listen.'

'I've had a long bitch of a day. Get to the point.'

'Lottie, I want to buy you out.'

'You what?' She could feel her jaw slacken. She had not been expecting this.

'I want to buy you out. I'll take over dealing with the legal stuff. The probate and all that.'

'But why?' She sat down again.

'I'd like to help you. You don't need a noose like Farranstown House around your neck. When the legalities are dealt with, I want to sell it. It's good development land, stretching right down to the lake.'

Perhaps now was not the time to tell him he'd have a hard time getting planning permission for a development on the shores of Lough Cullion, the source of Ragmullin's water supply.

He continued, gesticulating, his excitement visibly building. 'I'll get it valued. Pay you your share. You won't have to worry about it after that.'

'It could take years before it's sorted out.'

'I don't mind. I can pay you from Alexis's estate. I have to go back to New York. I want to return to work. I've had enough of Ireland for the moment, to be truthful.'

'I don't blame you.' Lottie felt the beginning of a smile warm her face. Maybe having a half-brother wasn't so bad.

'There is one condition, though.' His green eyes darkened to a deep viridian.

Her body deflated and she straightened her back in readiness. He was being an arsehole. Building her up just to let her down.

'What is it?'

'I want you to sign legal documents. And once everything is valued, I'll pay you half.'

'Feck off.' She rolled up her sleeves before standing and heading for the stove.

'I'm serious, Lottie. That estate could be worth five, maybe ten million euros.'

She found a wooden spoon and stirred the stew. Kept her back to him. Millions? Jesus. She'd never thought of Farranstown in terms of money, just as a nuisance she could do without.

'What do you say?' he persisted.

'I don't know. This is sudden.' Still she stirred, with the chicken breaking up into straggly bits in the sauce.

'Think about it. You'll get half up front. You'll have nothing else to do with Farranstown. The proceeds will help you find a house of your own.'

'I quite like this house,' she said.

'But it's not yours, is it? You're indebted to Tom Rickard.'

'That's my business, Leo.' But he was right. Rickard was baby Louis' grandad, and he had been kind enough to give her the house almost rent-free. She knew it was his way of keeping tabs on Louis. Tiredness itched behind her eyes; they felt like sand after the tide had ebbed.

'What if the probate doesn't go through?' she said. 'Someone else might have a claim on the place.'

'I'll worry about that. If I get the forms drawn up, will you sign?'

It seemed such an inconsequential task. Just her signature. Nothing to fear. But Lottie couldn't help feeling that maybe, just maybe, it might be the biggest mistake of her life so far.

CHAPTER SEVENTEEN

It was late when Boyd returned to his flat. His journey west had taken him two and a half hours; the traffic into Galway had been atrocious. But he'd driven home in an hour and a half.

He slipped off his jacket, then his shoes, and from the refrigerator he took out a can of lager. He felt like something stronger, but Kirby had demolished the bottle of whiskey last night.

As he sipped the beer in the silence of his own space, he thought about the evening he'd just had and hoped Lottie wouldn't be inquisitive about his need for another absence in a few days. He would just have to don a poker face and lie.

Taking a few deep breaths, he lay back on the couch. He closed his eyes and wondered just what he was going to do. A ring on the doorbell and he sat up straight. It was late. Lottie? God, no. Not at this hour.

He opened the door.

'Sean? What are you doing here? Do you know what time it is?'

'Can I watch some telly with you?' The teenager stood on the step, a forlorn picture with a sheet of sleet pelting down behind him.

'Come in.'

Sean flung his jacket on the back of a chair. Boyd picked it up and hung it in the hall. When he returned to the living space, the television was on and Sean was huddled in the corner of the couch.

'Where have you been? Your jacket's soaked.'

'It's Chloe's, so I don't care. I've just been walking around town.'

'Want to talk about it, bud?' Boyd picked up his beer but didn't sit.

'I just want some peace.' Sean looked up at him, his blue eyes swimming like the ocean. 'You don't mind, do you?'

'Once your mother's okay with it.'

'She doesn't care.'

Oh no, Boyd thought. He had become a confidant for Sean over the last few years and he reckoned the boy saw him as a substitute father figure. But he could really have done with just his own company tonight. He had too many things to think about. And listening to the woes of a teenage boy railing against his mother was definitely not on his agenda.

'I have to text her. To let her know you're here.'

'Whatever.'

'One episode of something and then you're off home.' Boyd took the remote control from Sean's hand and paused the screen.

'You're worse than her, you know,' Sean muttered.

Boyd waited for the tirade, but silence crawled into the air between them. He gave in. Sat down and unmuted the sound. Then he sent a quick text to Lottie to let her know her son was with him.

'Can I have a Heineken?' Sean chanced.

'No you cannot. Do you want your mother to skin me alive after she's finished with you?' Boyd laughed.

Sean laughed too.

*

The rattling of the windows made the hair stand on the backs of his hands. Father Michael Curran rose from his chair and walked to undo the heavy gold tie-back on the curtains. As Ballydoon parish priest, he had lived in the ancient parochial house for the last five years, and through each one of those winters the old sash windows had rattled and creaked constantly. It had never bothered him before tonight. Never mind the windows, he thought, *he* was rattled. With the subdued lighting in the room, he could see little outside. Black and wild. Leaning closer to the pane, he tried to see beyond his own haggard reflection. Suddenly a branch crashed against the glass. Jumping backwards, his legs collided with the chair, and as he fell onto the seat, he yelped in pain.

He had to go to bed. The night was closing in and it was fifteen minutes past his bedtime. Routine had got him through his life thus far. He didn't want to admit that it was something of an obsession now.

Closing the autobiography he had been reading, he stood, undid the other tie-back and went to drag the curtains across the window.

From the depths of his throat, a strangled screech escaped. His blood froze. He stepped backwards once again, his progress halted by the legs of the chair.

A face, plastered flat against the wet glass.

The priest recoiled, hands shaking, legs jellied. His feet slithered from his slippers and he turned on his ankle. No physical pain, just a twisting deep in his stomach. He looked out again. The face had disappeared. Shadows jumped around like skeletons dancing wildly. Branches slapped against the window, sounding like bones cracking in double-jointed fingers.

A knock. Sharp and insistent.

He swung around. His heart was beating so loudly in his chest it reverberated in his ears. He had no idea if the persistent knocking was from the window or the door. He blinked rapidly in confusion and looked at the window again. No face. Had he imagined it?

Steps.

Footsteps.

In the flagstoned hallway outside the living room. *Tap tap tap*. More ominous than the knocking on the window. The priest wondered if he had left the door unlocked. No, he would not have done that. Creature of habit. He always locked the doors.

Another *tap tap*.

Still Father Curran was sure the sound was from his imagination, despite his vow never to venture to the dark side.

And then he heard the strangled cry of the swans.

*

She was warm, and at the same time she felt cold. The covers were hairy and she wanted her own fleece blanket.

It was dark, but Lily didn't mind that. She liked the dark. Her mum told her the fairies only came out in the dark. They were her friends, the fairies.

But she didn't know why she wasn't at home in her own bed. That wasn't right. Her mummy always put her to bed. Except for the nights she stayed with her daddy. His hair kind of scared her. Once, he'd even tried to cut *her* hair, but she'd screamed his house down so he put the scissors away. But he was her daddy and she loved him.

Her *Paw Patrol* Zuma toy. That was what she wanted. Or her Peppa Pig doll. Even her Winnie-the-Pooh. She knew she was too old for teddies, all her friends said so, but she couldn't sleep without them. Maybe if she cried and screamed someone would fetch her mummy, and her mummy would bring in her teddy. Had she done something wrong? Was that the reason?

She'd got into the car. Sat in the back while the seat belt was strapped across her chest. There was no booster seat for her, but she'd said nothing, kept her mouth shut. She hadn't even cried. Not one little bit. So if she'd done all that, why was she here on her own?

Maybe she'd just have to try to sleep with the hairy blanket and pretend it was her teddy. And in the morning, her mummy would wake her up and tell her it was all a bad dream.

*

The child lay sleeping. Breathing in and out. So calm and unaware of the torturous world she inhabited. The blanket was bunched up under her elbow like a comforter. He wanted to reach out a hand and smooth her beautiful long hair away from her angelic face. But that might wake her. And a sleeping child was easier to manage than a screaming brat.

His breath carried in the air in sync with hers.

He kept his hand deep in his pocket. Safe in there.

In. Out. On her breathing went.

For how long? he wondered.

How long would she have in this world created by adults, inhuman to children?

He bunched his fingers into a fist, tight in his pocket.

It was not his call to make. Who should live and who should die.

It came from an authority higher up the food chain than him.

And still he watched.

Her breaths.

In.

Out.

*

The other boys called him names. They sneaked up on him, pulled at his short, tight hair, laughed and ran. No one ever hung around long enough to hear what he might have to say.

He had to keep his hair cut. No way was any teacher ever going to do that to him again. No way in hell.

He kicked a can across the playground and listened as it clattered into a gully. Picking up a stick, he hit the can and it rose out of its place of refuge to land on the concrete.

'Boy! That's vandalism. If you don't stop, you will turn into a criminal.'

He turned to see the man hurrying his way, his coat fluttering and flapping around him, like a dirty sheet on a washing line. Like the sheets he had to sleep in at home. Discoloured and smelly.

He'd never thought he'd miss his old school, but once he was six, he had to transfer to the all boys' school. It wasn't fair. He'd liked playing with the girls. They usually folded up in tears at his approach even before he pinched them. He supposed it wasn't really playing, what he was doing.

His arm was gripped so tightly he dropped the stick. His chin was grabbed by putty fingers and his face turned upwards with a sharp twist. The man's breath was stale and pungent. The boy gagged, though he tried to show no emotion. Once you cried or whimpered, they knew they had cracked you and surviving the torment became harder. And if his home was notified of his wrongdoings, his backside became a welter of blisters and burns; his arms a pulse of yellow and purple bruises. All because he was too weak. But not today. Hairy face could hump off.

The boy did something he hadn't done before.

He laughed hysterically.

As he waited for the phone call home to be made, he was glad he'd had his hair cut. At least he wouldn't have to suffer that indignity.

CHAPTER EIGHTEEN

Thursday

Lottie awoke with pain pulsing behind her eyes. Her dreams had been filled with horrific images that she knew would haunt her until the cases were closed.

In the shower, she found little relief. If Cara and Fiona had been murdered, it was highly likely they'd died at the hand of the same perpetrator. Therefore it was even more likely that Lily Heffernan was in the clutches of a murderer. She shivered at that thought and tried to wash it away with warm water.

Memories of the bones of her brother Eddie found in an unmarked grave, exploded in her head. No, don't go there, she warned herself. Lily had to be safe. That was the thought she needed to cling on to as she dried herself, ignoring the little pieces of fluff from the towel sticking to the hairs on her arms.

Did someone kill Cara Dunne, then head out to Ballydoon to kill Fiona Heffernan before travelling back to Ragmullin to abduct the little girl? How was that even possible? It *was* possible, she conceded. There was little blood involved in the killings; no knives or guns had been used. The killer would have been clean and free to mingle, to drive, to abduct.

With her head still spinning, Lottie pulled on a pair of black jeans and a white long-sleeved T-shirt and headed into work without having anything to eat.

She arrived at the station before any of her team but Acting Super-intendent McMahon's car was already in the yard. Inhaling the aroma of fresh coffee, she rushed along the corridor. She needed to review yesterday's activities before she attended the post-mortems. First, though, she had to find out the status of the investigation into Lily's disappearance.

The foul humour she'd woken up in got worse instead of better. Usually work acted as a balm to the trouble she left at home. But Sean was becoming unmanageable. She'd sat up until he waltzed in the door after three a.m. Okay, Boyd had let her know he was with him, but still, her son was being awkward just for the sake of it. She shook her head and tried to forget home life and concentrate on work.

Despite the two deaths yesterday, her main concern was the missing child, Lily Heffernan. She checked the bulletins, but there had been no reported sightings of the little girl. She needed to interview Trevor Toner and Giles Bannon from the dance school and get updates on the reports from parents, kids and teachers. There was so much to do. It was looking like an abduction. If the child's mother had committed suicide, had she made arrangements for her daughter? Someone to care for her; someone to collect her? Wouldn't she have left instructions with Ryan Slevin or Colin Kavanagh? Not if she had reason to distrust them, Lottie thought. Not if one of them had murdered her. Not if someone else had murdered her.

She crossed her legs and leaned back in the chair as a feeling of dread lodged squarely in the centre of her chest. She feared for the child. When she looked up, McMahon was standing in the doorway. He had the habit of appearing out of nowhere like an unscented gas. His appearance usually heralded trouble.

'Good morning, sir.'

'Tell me about this missing child.' He straightened the collar of his shirt and opened his suit jacket. A double-breasted waistcoat shielded his torso.

'Lily Heffernan has been missing since four o'clock yesterday afternoon, last seen at her dance rehearsals in Ragmullin Theatre. We have everything in place to try to locate her.'

McMahon sat and stretched his arms across the desk. For a moment she thought he was about to grab her hands, but instead he slammed both fists loudly on the wooden surface. His voice betrayed more than a hint of anger as he spoke, its timbre low yet menacing.

'I don't want to listen to your shite, Inspector. I don't want to be finding out about missing kids on the fucking radio on my way into fucking work. I don't need *Morning Ireland* informing me of things I should know about first-hand. Do you understand what I'm saying?' He raised his hands and flicked his black fringe out of his eyes.

Rather than slink into her chair, Lottie straightened her shoulders, ready to do battle.

He was still talking, his tone now an octave higher. 'I expect my second in command to keep me fully abreast of matters of interest; matters that make the national goddam news at seven o'clock in the morning while I'm sipping my skinny bastard latte in a paper cup. Do you hear me? I do not expect that the first time I hear about it is on the airwaves filling my car.'

Jesus, he was repeating himself so much, it was making her headache worse. 'I tried to contact you last night, sir. But unfortunately you were up in Dublin at your fancy dinner, and—'

'Don't!' He held up a finger. 'Don't spout shite at me. I can't stand your insubordination. You're one inch away from being out that door. Do you hear me?'

'Yes, sir.' If she added up all the inches, she'd reach a mile, she thought.

'Update me, then.' He folded his arms and sniffed away his derision.

'Well, it's like this ...' She fought the urge to mirror his posture. 'We are investigating two deaths. One was a teacher called Cara Dunne. She was found hanging in her bathroom, wearing a wedding dress. No suicide note has been recovered. I'm sure she was murdered. We're currently gathering information and I'm attending her post-mortem shortly. Then yesterday afternoon, the body of Fiona Heffernan was discovered in the grounds of Ballydoon Abbey.'

'Ballydoon?'

'It's a village, less than fifteen kilometres from Ragmullin, and—'

'I know where fucking Ballydoon is. Go on.'

'The abbey is a nursing home. Fiona was a nurse there.'

'Get to the point.'

'Her death is being treated as unexplained until the post-mortem is completed. She might have jumped from the roof or – and I think this is more likely – she may have been pushed. We haven't found a suicide note and she had a gash on her head. We found blood on the locker room floor. The fact that she was wearing a wedding dress, just like Cara Dunne, makes her death look highly suspicious.'

'Right. The little girl. Tell me about her.'

She could see he was struggling to keep his temper down. She hoped when it exploded, she wasn't in its trajectory.

'No one at the scene mentioned anything to us about Fiona's daughter. The only thing of interest I heard there was that Fiona was due to get married the next day. Today, actually. Detective

Kirby and I visited her fiancé, Ryan Slevin, who informed us of the existence of Lily. She is eight years old, and as I said, she was last seen at a local dance school.'

'And you neglected to inform me of this development?'

'Sir, we tried. You were not answering your phone.'

'Someone could have left a message for me.'

Lottie shrugged. She had no idea if anyone had left a message or not.

'Carry on,' he said, puffing out his cheeks, which were now so red, she felt he might expire.

'I met with Fiona's ex-partner, Colin Kavanagh. He is the child's father. He claimed to be no wiser than Ryan Slevin as to the child's whereabouts. At that stage, I issued the alert. There seems to be some animosity between Slevin and Kavanagh.'

'Wait a minute. Did you say Colin Kavanagh? The solicitor?'

'Yes, sir.'

'Ah, for fuck's sake. He will be all over us like baby oil.'

'You know him, sir?'

McMahon nodded, biting the inside of his cheek. It was a few moments before he spoke again. 'Kavanagh used to work in the Dublin criminal court when I was in the Drugs and Organised Crime Bureau. A shrewd bollocks to meet across the table.'

'Why do you say that?'

'He's a defence lawyer for some of the most notorious crime gangs in the city.' He scrunched his eyes and flicked his fringe, his flush retreating a little. 'I thought he'd retired.'

'Well, he retired to Ragmullin, or just outside of it, to be correct. He operates a small office with a few clients, as far as I can gather. Sounds dodgy to me.'

'You don't work for twenty-five years with the scum of the earth without some of that scum sticking to you,' McMahon said. 'I'd lay my car on it that the disappearance of his daughter has something to do with his past dealings.'

'Perhaps his past also has something to do with the death of Fiona Heffernan.'

'You don't think it is suicide, then?'

'It's currently unexplained. I'm meeting with the state pathologist as soon as I can get away. I'll keep you informed of any developments.'

McMahon stood. 'Tell me again about the death from earlier in the day.'

'Cara Dunne. Early thirties. Schoolteacher. Found hanging in her bathroom by a neighbour. Ms Dunne had a recent engagement breakup from the assistant manager of the Railway Hotel, Steve O'Carroll.'

McMahon moved to the door. He spoke over his shoulder. 'I'm taking an active role in the missing kid investigation. I want to know about everything you uncover. Let Sam McKeown act as go-between. He seems to be the only one around here capable of doing a proper job. And keep me informed after the post-mortems or I'll have someone else sitting in your chair before you can say *I give a shit.*'

'But sir—'

'No buts. And I'm doing all the press conferences. Don't forget I'm the boss around here.'

'Right, sir.' *Arsehole*, she said under her breath as he left.

She felt the day she had been planning so perfectly in her head was now shot to pieces. A defence lawyer for crime gangs? Colin Kavanagh had suddenly become more than a grieving ex-partner. He was now firmly a person of interest. If Fiona had been murdered, Kavanagh was definitely in the cross hairs as a suspect. But what was his link to Cara Dunne? And where was his little girl?

CHAPTER NINETEEN

Ryan Slevin was awakened by one of his nephews slamming the bathroom door and Zoe yelling from the kitchen telling him to be quiet.

Today should have been his wedding day. He had the day off work and now he had nothing to do. His Fiona was gone. And so, it seemed, was Lily. Lifting his laptop from the floor, he checked on the work he'd done in a stupor last night. Then nudged open the file called *MY WEDDING DAY.*

His love for Fiona would never be confirmed in public. No piece of paper to proclaim their unity to the world. Nothing. It was all gone. And in that moment, as strange as it seemed, Ryan felt a surge of relief. He was going to move into the cottage on his own. Be his own boss for once in his life.

As he pulled on his clothes, he thought of how empty his life would be without Fiona. Yeah, he'd loved her, loved being with her, but the sex was only so-so, and Lily could be a little minx at times. He looked at his reflection in the wardrobe mirror, then opened the narrow door to find a clean shirt. There, hanging on a hanger, was his white one, ironed crisp by Zoe. He tried to still the trembles convulsing his chest. Fiona was gone. There would be no wedding today. No wedding ever. Not to Fiona, in any case.

Closing the wardrobe door, he sat back on the bed and glanced at the laptop again. He was about to shut it down when he noticed he had an email. Not from anyone he recognised, but it had not been directed to the spam folder. He placed the laptop on his knee and clicked the email icon. As he read, his teeth began to chatter, and it had nothing to do with the cold in the room.

Closing the laptop, he wondered how the hell he was going to handle this shitstorm.

*

Chills palpitated through the morning air and the snow lay deep on the ground, but the weather app on her phone promised rain by afternoon. At least then she should be able to drive to and from work unhindered.

At the sink, Beth listened to the noisy pigs. With the morning light rising behind the sheds in the yard, she thought about last evening, when she'd stood at the garda cordon watching the activity from a distance. The only information she could garner was that a woman had been found dead, clothed in a wedding dress. No one could confirm if it was murder or a suicide. She'd eventually given up. As she'd walked back down the avenue to head home, a car had pulled up alongside. And the nurse, Alan Hughes, had given her chapter and verse.

Poor Fiona. Poor Ryan. The upside of it all was that she had an article for next week's edition of the *Tribune*. If her editor allowed it. She sighed. By then, it would be old news.

Dropping two slices of bread into the toaster, she was aware that she hadn't heard any movement from her father. He was usually in the living room struggling with returns or mouthing off about his solicitor or accountant. Always drama where Christy Clarke was concerned. She smiled at the little robin with his red breast perched on the snowy window ledge. Her mother used to say a robin was a sign someone was going to die.

She sat at the table and scrolled though the news on her phone. Shit! How had she missed this last night? A child was missing from Ragmullin. She thought of Lily, Ryan's future stepdaughter. Surely not her. Holy friggin' cow.

'Dad! Dad! Did you hear the news this morning?' She jumped up, ran to the living room, waving her phone in the air.

The room was empty. Papers scattered all around the floor. The net curtains blew gently in the breeze from the gap along the bottom of the sash window.

'Dad?'

She clattered up the wooden staircase. Maybe he was still asleep. She paused on the top step. Clamped the hand holding the phone to her chest. The robin!

'Dear God in heaven, if you're really up there, don't let my daddy be dead. Please.'

At his door, she knocked gently. No answer. She twisted the old black knob and pushed the door inwards.

Her dad wasn't in his bedroom. She searched every room in the house. He was nowhere to be found. She checked for his jacket, and noticed the one he usually wore still hanging on the back of the door. But his wellingtons were missing from the boot room. Dragging her own jacket over her shoulders, she ran out to the yard. Over to the pig pen.

'Dad! Where are you?'

No reply; only the screech of the animals.

Looking around in desperation, she remembered her phone. She pulled it out of her jeans pocket and, with freezing fingers, tapped in her father's number. It rang out. She called the number again. Holding the device away from her ear, she listened intently. No sound of it in the yard. She ran back into the house. Dialled again. No vibration or ringtone. Nothing.

With nervous energy propelling her, she flitted from room to room. He definitely wasn't in the house. Could he have headed into the village? To his garage? He'd closed it down about a year ago. She scrolled for the number just in case. Rang it. Nothing.

What to do now? Phone the gardaí? Was that an overreaction? She was being totally irrational. His car was gone; maybe he had driven to the shop for the morning newspaper.

She tried to recall last night's events after she'd returned from the abbey. The look on his face when she'd related the gossip she'd heard. That in all likelihood Fiona Heffernan had committed suicide. The bride-to-be of her colleague Ryan Slevin. What had her father said? *Good enough for the bastard.* Why had he said that? He'd left her sitting in the kitchen with her mouth hanging open and slammed the door on his way to the living room.

Now she sat in the exact same spot with her lips firmly jammed together. She had no idea what to do besides keep ringing and texting him, check out his usual haunts and then head into work.

CHAPTER TWENTY

The mortuary, traditionally known as the Dead House, was attached to Tullamore Hospital and was as cold and uninviting as always. Once she was suitably robed up, Lottie entered the cutting room. Jane Dore, the state pathologist, nodded over her mouth mask at the assistant pathologist, and Tim Jones began the process of bagging organs that had been removed for weighing and analysis.

'Sorry I'm late,' Lottie said.

'It's okay. I started a little early on Cara Dunne. I've yet to get to the second body ...' Jane scrutinised the pages on her clipboard. 'Fiona Heffernan.'

Standing beside the five-foot-nothing pathologist, Lottie felt like a giant. 'What conclusions have you reached about Cara's death?'

'She has the nicest pair of hands I've seen on a corpse,' Tim Jones said.

'What?' Lottie stared at him.

'Not that it makes any difference now she's dead.'

She looked at Jane, whose eyes had darkened into a scowl.

The pathologist led the way to the door. 'Come into my office.'

Lottie followed her. The office was a cubicle off the main cutting room, everything pristine and sparkling bright. Stainless-steel desk and filing cabinet. She waited while Jane tapped on her computer and pages began to spew from a printer.

'Cara Dunne was quite a woman,' Jane said.

Lottie leaned against the cabinet and watched as Jane shuffled the pages into a neat bundle.

'What do you mean? Did she kill herself?'

'No, she did not. In her last seconds of life, she fought bravely and furiously. Her hands, nails and neck bear the results of a defiant struggle.'

Lottie blew out a small breath of relief. Her instinct had been correct. 'Do we have DNA? Fingerprints?'

Jane shook her head. 'I've checked, and I'd say the assailant wore gloves and was well protected. But I've swabbed her nails. Hopefully we will get something.'

'But you said—'

'Will you let me tell you?'

'Go ahead.' Lottie folded her arms and waited. She was itching to get a murder investigation up and running.

'In simple terms, her death was caused by asphyxiation. The ligature caused her neck to compress and slowly smother her to death.'

'She was strangled?'

'The victim was strung up and hanged until she died. She was murdered. I've noted the technical data in my report.'

'You mentioned that she struggled. How did someone get the belt around her neck and put her up on a stool?'

'I don't usually speculate, as you know. However, I imagine she was surprised.' Jane raised one eyebrow.

'Perhaps the assailant already had the belt tied in a noose,' Lottie said. 'The bathroom she was found in was small and compact. Easy enough for someone larger and stronger to subdue her in there.'

'Possibly,' the pathologist said.

'It doesn't make sense, though. She had to have known him.'

'That's your—'

'My job. I know.' Lottie didn't want to listen to the pathologist's mantra. She just wanted something to go on. 'And the only forensic evidence you have is what may be beneath Cara's nails?'

Jane physically bristled. 'I've picked up hairs and fibres. They may or may not be from the assailant. The results will take some time. And before you ask, she was not sexually assaulted.'

'Okay.' Lottie was thinking: why target this teacher who had just returned from morning Mass? Living on her own. Not bothering anyone. Or was she? She'd have to work through Cara's circle of friends and her possessions in the hope of finding something that would point her in the right direction. For now, her number one target was the ex fiancé, Steve O'Carroll.

Jane said, 'I'd start by finding out if she owned the belt. It looks like a man's belt. If it's not hers, he brought it with him. Premeditated. He knew what he was doing. I've sent it for further forensic analysis. I noticed something scratched into the leather. It could be initials. Possibly BD or more likely BB. I asked forensics to find out what it is.'

'Thanks Jane. That's good.' Lottie scratched her head. 'There's no sign of a struggle in her apartment. No damage to the lock. She let him in. She knew him.' She looked up at the pathologist. 'I'm assuming it's a man. What do you think?'

'Definitely someone with a lot of upper-body strength. Has to be taller than her. She's five foot four.'

'Thanks, Jane.' As she turned to leave, Lottie said, 'And what about Fiona?'

'Tim has her prepped and waiting. If you want to hold on ...'

'I'd better get back to the station to set up the jobs book and organise a full incident team to investigate Cara's murder. Have you had a chance to glance at Fiona's body yet?'

'Don't be fishing, Lottie. I'll let you know when I've finished.'

'Not even a cursory look?'

Jane sighed, tapped the mouse and read something on the computer screen. 'The gash on her forehead. That's what makes this appear suspicious. In my opinion, it happened before she hit the ground. There was some blood on the dress. Not drops, so it must have transferred as the dress was pulled over her head. When we cut the dress from her body, I noticed bruising on the brachial, the underside of her humerus.'

'Her upper arm?'

Jane nodded agreement. 'The bruises might be totally unrelated, but I'll know once I do the post-mortem how soon before death they occurred. I'll email my preliminary report once I have it completed.'

'So her death is suspicious?'

Jane gave her assent with a quick rise of her tightly plucked eyebrows and a diminutive nod.

As Lottie made her way back down the cold, sterile corridor, she heard her name being called. She turned round. The assistant pathologist was standing at the cutting room door.

'Tim?' she said. 'Did you want me?'

'I wanted to apologise for my behaviour yesterday at Cara Dunne's apartment. My comments were totally out of order.'

'Apology accepted.' Lottie made to leave. He remained standing at the door. Jane came out of her office and looked from one to the other. Tim retreated.

Making her way to her car, Lottie couldn't help feeling Tim Jones had wanted to say something else before Jane's appearance had stopped him. Her detective's brain mulled it over on her way back to Ragmullin, but by the time she arrived at the station, all she wanted to do was get working on the murder of Cara Dunne. And that of Fiona Heffernan, because she knew from Jane's demeanour and words that the death would also be classed as murder. And, of course, she had to find Lily.

A microphone was shoved under Lottie's nose as she picked her way carefully along the icy footpath outside the station.

'Detective Inspector Parker. A minute, please? Cynthia Rhodes, national television.'

As if she did not know the curly-haired bespectacled reporter, sporting her trademark black leather biker jacket.

'Ms Rhodes,' she said, attempting to sidestep around Cynthia. The microphone followed her.

Cynthia said, 'Can you tell us what you're doing to find Lily Heffernan?'

Lottie stopped. 'As you can imagine, this missing child is a top priority for us at the moment. We're doing all we can to ensure the safe return of Lily to her family.'

'Do you think that whoever killed Lily's mother, Fiona Heffernan, has taken the little girl?'

Where had that come from? Lottie herself hadn't even received confirmation that Fiona had been murdered. 'I'm not going to speculate as to what may or may not have happened.' Shit, she would have to say something professional, otherwise the urge to slap Cynthia might overwhelm her. 'I would ask the public to be vigilant and keep a lookout for Lily, and to call our crimewatch number with any information they might have.'

'I'm sure you can understand the trauma Lily's father, Colin Kavanagh, is going through, seeing as your own daughters were recently abducted. Can you tell us what you personally are doing to find her?'

Lottie's skin prickled. 'Acting Superintendent David McMahon will hold a press conference later. Perhaps you can direct your questions to him.' She tried to turn, but her sleeve was tugged, pulling her back in front of the camera.

'Why aren't *you* speaking to the media? Have you been demoted?'

Demoted? Ha. That was a joke. 'You must realise we are dealing with the suspicious deaths of two young women. I am senior investigating officer on all the cases. Thank you for now.'

'Two murders, then?'

Shit and double shit. 'Suspicious deaths, I said. You need to clean the wax from your ears.'

You've done it now, Parker. Lottie sighed, disentangled her sleeve from Cynthia's hand and, ignoring a host of shouted questions, escaped inside. All she had to do now was avoid her boss for the rest of the day. McMahon would not be pleased.

CHAPTER TWENTY-ONE

After morning Mass had ended, Father Curran headed to the cabin behind his house. He hadn't slept a wink, listening to the rattles and cries of the wind. It was all a figment of his imagination. Seeing that face at the window, lurking in the dark, had brought nightmares rushing back. That was why he couldn't sleep. Had he really seen it?

He stripped off his jumper, white collar, shirt and trousers. From a gym bag he extracted shorts and vest. When he was ready, he stepped onto the treadmill. Working up a sweat was one way of exorcising his demons. Not that he believed his demons were of the supernatural variety. No, his were flesh and blood that had stalked him all his life.

Once beads of perspiration began to bubble on his forehead and drip down his nose, he upped the tempo. Run, run, run. Faster, faster, faster.

A shadow crept through the crack in the door like a spider web, growing larger as it approached. Father Curran pressed a button on the machine, slowing his run to a walk. Sensing someone behind him, he twisted his head around so quickly he fell to the ground. On hands and knees, he scanned the area behind him. Nothing. No one. He returned his gaze to the door. It was still barely open. It hadn't moved. Or had it?

Raising himself to his knees, he stayed still until his breathing returned to normal. As he stood and moved back to the treadmill, the door opened wide.

'What are you doing here?' he said.

'Sorry for disturbing you, Michael.'

'Please don't be so familiar with me, Father Burke. I've told you before to address me as Father Curran. Respect the collar.'

His morning was totally ruined. He switched off the machine and got his towel from his bag, feeling every one of his seventy years dragging at the muscles of his legs. He hastily dried his face, conscious that he was in shorts and vest. Father Joe Burke was younger than him – early forties, he thought – and he disliked the fact that he'd seen him out of his clerical garb. 'What do you want?'

'Em, I wanted to let you know … The bishop asked me to inform you, eh …'

'For heaven's sake, man, spit it out.' He didn't like Father Burke. He was not a true priest. Rumour had it that he'd cavorted with women in a parish in Wexford or some such place before he came to Ragmullin. Then he'd taken a sabbatical. If the church grapevine was correct, he was also the bastard son of an unmarried mother. Father Curran couldn't help the grunt of derision that escaped his lips.

'It's Cara Dunne. She's dead.'

Father Curran eyed the younger priest, watching for signs of a lie. 'Cara? Really? Why were you sent to tell me?'

'I've no idea. Maybe because you used to be on the board of management of the school where she teaches.' Father Burke sat on a wooden bench.

'I've nothing to do with the school any more, and I didn't ask you to sit down.' Father Curran flicked the towel against the bench and the younger man jumped up. He could have sworn he said *bastard* under his breath. Well, he knew who the bastard was in this room.

'Sorry. I'll go. Just doing what the bishop asked,' Father Burke said.

Father Curran followed him to the door. 'Off you go. I don't like to be disturbed.'

'Do you want to know how she died?'

'I suppose you're going to tell me.'

'Reports say it was suicide.'

When the door had banged shut, Father Curran let the air escape his body without realising he'd been holding his breath.

When he switched the treadmill back on, his feet felt lighter and his run quicker.

CHAPTER TWENTY-TWO

In the incident room, Lottie threw her damp jacket on a lukewarm radiator. Brushing off her encounter with Cynthia, she consigned it to the depths of her subconscious, where she dared not venture any time soon.

Standing in front of the gathered detectives and uniformed officers, she listened to their voices murmuring in conversation. The sound gradually faded. They all looked up expectantly.

'First off,' she kneaded her hands, encouraging the blood to circulate, 'I've met with the state pathologist. She has completed Cara Dunne's post-mortem, and based on her findings, we are dealing with murder.' She pointed to the photo of the young woman pinned to the whiteboard, then picked up a marker and wrote the word *murder* and yesterday's date beneath it. As the investigation gathered legs, the board would fill up with suspects, timelines, maps and evidence. Hopefully.

'We need to build up a picture of Cara. Everything we can find.'

'I've already interviewed her fiancé,' Sam McKeown said. 'I also spoke to some of the teachers at Cara's school. She taught in Ragmullin. Convent of Mercy. I'll get through the rest of the list this morning.'

Lottie tapped a pen against her forehead. 'The fiancé?'

'Smarmy dude by the name of Steve O'Carroll. He's the assistant manager at the Railway Hotel.'

'Did he account for his whereabouts yesterday morning?'

'Said he'd been at home before he reached work at ten. He invoked the dreaded S word.'

'Asked for his solicitor.' Lottie felt the heat rush through her cheeks. If only she could get it to her fingers.

'I also asked him why the engagement ended.'

'And?'

McKeown rubbed a hand over his shaved head. Was he hoping the action would lead to a light-bulb moment? Lottie wondered.

'Bit cagey, as you'd expect. But he expressed little emotion when I informed him of Cara's death. Said they split up three months ago, but wouldn't say why.'

'I want him in here, solicitor or no solicitor. Take fingerprints and a DNA sample. Got it?'

'Yes, boss.' McKeown tapped his iPad.

'Cara didn't teach at the school Lily Heffernan attended, did she?' Lottie checked her notes.

'No. Lily went to St Celia's primary. Oh, and one of Cara's colleagues said that she'd been on sick leave for the last three months.'

'Why?'

'Stress.'

'When did you say her engagement broke down?'

'Three months ago.'

'So it wasn't work-related stress that kept her out of school. Get a photo of O'Carroll on that board so we can all see him.'

McKeown scrolled through the hotel website and tapped an image. The printer at the back of the room whirred. He picked up the page and pinned it to the board. Lottie stared at the smooth jaw and swept-back hair.

'What age is he?'

'Thirty-seven.'

'Weird-looking guy,' Kirby said.

'Not half as weird as you looked this morning,' McKeown muttered.

'Less of the wisecracks.' Lottie studied O'Carroll's photo and found his dark eyes a little unsettling. 'As I said, bring him in for an official interview. And I want to know if he had any connection to Lily or Fiona Heffernan.'

'Right, boss.' Kirby answered for them all, knocking a stack of pages from the table to the floor. 'Sorry. Just looking for something to write on.'

'Okay.' Lottie felt a wave of despair for her detective. He seemed to be diving further into the depths of ineptitude. She brought the focus back to Cara. 'If O'Carroll can account for the relevant time, perhaps Cara's murder is the work of an ex-pupil with a grudge or something. But that's like a needle in the proverbial haystack. Talk to everyone who knew her. I need to go through her things. That suitcase, for one.'

'When SOCOs are finished with it, I'll bring it in,' Boyd said.

She glanced at his tired eyes. He looked shattered. His shirt collar was askew and his tie knotted untidily. Not like Boyd at all. She wondered if Sean had said something he shouldn't have last night. She was still mad at her son. He'd had no right to be there. He should have told her where he was going. She'd have to have serious words with him. Later.

'Okay, thanks, Boyd.' Trying to gather her thoughts into a coherent thread, she continued.

'According to the state pathologist, Cara Dunne was asphyxiated by the belt around her neck after she was strung up. It appears to be a man's black leather belt. Find out if it belongs to this Steve O'Carroll, though Jane said there are letters scratched into it. She thinks it could be BB or BD. See if it means anything to anyone.

Jane also says that the victim put up a good fight. Hair and fibres have been sent to the lab. No sexual assault. Cara was five foot four. Her assailant must have been taller and stronger. There was no sign of a break-in or disturbance at the apartment and there's no working CCTV in or around the building. The neighbour, Eve Clarke, says she heard loud voices some minutes before she gained entry to check on Cara.'

'Her murderer has to be someone she knew.' Kirby again.

Lottie leaned her head to one side. 'Not necessarily. She was a teacher. Probably trusting, and generous with her time. Perhaps she was the kind of person who allowed a stranger into her apartment.'

'Was she a prostitute, then?' McKeown said. A trickle of titters permeated the room.

'That's not even remotely funny.' Lottie stood erect, commanding attention. 'We know relatively nothing about this woman. Who are her family, her friends? You'd better come back to me with information. Plenty of it, and by the end of the day.'

'Yes, boss,' McKeown said.

'And the neighbour. Eve Clarke. She needs to be formally interviewed.'

'Is the teacher's death linked to the nurse at the abbey?' Boyd said. 'They were both wearing wedding dresses.'

'The state pathologist hadn't commenced the post-mortem on Fiona Heffernan before I left. She's of the opinion the death is suspicious, because of the gash on her head, and suggests it occurred prior to death. Plus Fiona had significant bruising on her upper arms. We won't know anything further until I get the preliminary report. We haven't found a suicide note and her little girl is missing. Two victims in wedding dresses could point to the same killer, and if you find another connection between them, I want to be the first to know.'

'Right, boss.' A collective murmur threaded through the room.

'Maybe it was a suicide pact,' McKeown said.

Lottie ignored his comment.

'Fiona Heffernan was thirty-four years old and due to marry her fiancé Ryan Slevin today at three o'clock in Ballydoon church. Lily, her eight-year-old daughter, is her only immediate relative residing in Ireland, apart from an ex-partner, Colin Kavanagh. She had a married sister in Australia.' Lottie thought about the hurried phone call yesterday evening. Fiona's sister had told her that she'd decided not to travel for the wedding; she had young children and it was too expensive. 'I believe Fiona was murdered and that person could have Lily.'

Kirby filled the silence. 'There's a nationwide alert for the little girl. Plenty of calls coming in, though nothing positive yet. Interviews are ongoing with everyone at St Celia's primary. Uniforms are following up with all the parents we spoke with yesterday. So far, no clues to what happened to Lily.'

'Okay. Did you find anything in the locker room at the abbey?'

'Just a towel on the ground and her clothes inside the locker. SOCOs have her handbag and phone. I'll see when we can get them.'

'Sooner rather than later. McKeown, you keep Acting Superintendent McMahon up to date on Lily's case, and we need to interview the staff from the dance school where she was last seen.' She glanced at her notes. 'Trevor Toner, Giles Bannon and Shelly Forde. Lily's disappearance is more than likely linked to what happened to her mother. That little girl has to be found. Alive.' She paused to catch her breath, then added, 'Any more questions?'

'What about the media?' Boyd said.

'The press office and our super will handle it.' She was sure McMahon would relish the pieces to camera. She was glad to stay clear of it.

'In summary, we have two dead women. I want their friends and colleagues interviewed. I want their movements traced in the hours and minutes leading up to their deaths. Then go back, day by day. Find witnesses. Someone who saw anything or anyone suspicious or unusual. I need to know what those women had for breakfast, dinner and tea, and with whom. And find out what's on their phones and laptops. See if the victims have a common link. Got it?'

Murmurs of assent chimed with chairs scraping across the floor. Uniformed gardaí and detectives made ready to escape.

'We'll have a further meeting later this afternoon. I want Steve O'Carroll, door-to-door reports, CCTV and anything else you can bring me.' She gave up trying to keep a semblance of order as the incident room emptied. Her team was small, but it was good. They were not new to this. They knew what they had to do.

*

Eve Clarke was already staring at the line of milk cartons on the shelf before she realised she had left her apartment. She paused with her hand outstretched and looked down at her attire. Beneath her coat she saw the legs of her pyjamas, her feet clad in only her UGG slippers. She'd walked for ten minutes on the snowy and slushy footpaths. What had she been thinking? Or not thinking, more like.

Grabbing the nearest carton, she made her way between the aisles up to the cash desk. She didn't even look around to see if anyone recognised her. She couldn't take the embarrassment. Keeping her head low, she handed over the milk. Put her hand in her pocket for cash and it came out empty. She tried the other one. Also empty. Damn.

'I'm sorry, I came out in such a rush I left my purse at home.'

Without listening to the cashier, she fled from the shop. Sleet was falling in sharp sheets on top of her bare head. This had never happened to her before. Must be the stress of finding Cara yesterday, she thought, trying to console herself. But she didn't feel consoled. A nervous tingle began at the base of her skull and worked its way over her scalp and down to her forehead. By the time she reached Hill Point, she had a full-blown headache and was soaked to the skin.

'That didn't take you long.'

Eve looked up to see a garda standing by the crime-scene tape at the steps to her block. Had she spoken to him as she left earlier? She couldn't recall.

'Left without my purse.' She made to edge by him.

'Lucky I remembered you.'

'Why's that?'

'No entry without ID. We've been informed that we're now dealing with a murder.'

'What?'

'It's a crime scene up there. Your neighbour. It looks like she didn't commit suicide. Murdered. A teacher, too. Who would have thought?'

Who indeed? Eve gathered her coat round her body and rushed into the building. This was turning into the worst-case scenario. How was she going to keep things normal with so many guards and detectives and guys in white suits around?

She had to clear her head. Properly clear it. She had too much to lose.

CHAPTER TWENTY-THREE

Kirby informed Lottie that Trevor Toner had arrived for his formal interview. Without a solicitor. She perked up her eyebrows at that nugget of information.

'Interview Room One?'

'Yeah,' Kirby said. 'I'll sit in with you.'

Toner appeared to be even more nervous than he'd been last night, but he had showered and dressed in clean clothes. His crown of hair was combed, the sides shaved tightly. Lottie thought he looked like the type of thirty-something-year-old whose mother still sewed his name on a strip of white linen on the inside of his jumper. He was wearing a pair of jeans at least a size too big for him, a checked cotton shirt buttoned up to his throat and an FAI training hoodie.

'Play soccer, do you?' she said, trying to put him at ease.

'What? Oh, this? No. I got it in the Oxfam shop in town. A fiver.'

'Cool,' Kirby said. 'We're recording this – okay with you?'

Trevor nodded. Lottie noticed he was wringing his hands into each other as Kirby made the introductions for the recording.

'How long have you been a dance tutor?' she said.

'Five years.'

'I see you're thirty-six. What did you do before dancing?'

'I've always been a dancer. I mean, it's five years since I opened the dance school.'

'Lily Heffernan. How long has she been a student of yours?'

He ran a finger along his chin, and Lottie noticed the shake in his hand. 'I'm not sure. Maybe ten months or so. She's in the show that's starting next week.'

'Tell me about yesterday.'

'Not much to tell. We were rehearsing on the main theatre stage. They were so bad.' He shook his head. 'It was soul-destroying, after all my hard work. Shelly took them for a while.'

'Did they annoy you so much that perhaps you took it out on Lily?'

His eyes rounded like marbles. His mouth formed a perfect O. 'No. What do you mean? Oh God. I never laid a finger on her. You have to believe me.'

'Someone did, because she's missing. Did you see anything unusual yesterday? About Lily or anyone else?'

'No. Wait a minute. I thought … I noticed … Oh, it's nothing.'

'Noticed what?' Lottie leaned forward, resting her hands on the table.

'When I was on the stage, demonstrating the routine, I thought I saw someone watching from the balcony. But it might just have been the lights blinding me.'

'Did you investigate?'

'No. I forgot about it until now.'

Lottie eyeballed him. 'You sure about that?'

He dropped his head. 'Yeah.'

She decided to change direction. 'Giles Bannon. What's he like to work for?'

'Giles?' The eyes darted from Lottie to Kirby and back again.

'Yes. Giles. The theatre manager.'

'He's … I suppose he's okay, like.'

'You don't seem sure.' She leaned back and folded her arms.

'He's fine.' A tap of a finger on the table.

'Hard taskmaster?'

'Talk to him yourself,' Trevor said, a hint of bravado tingeing his voice.

'I intend to.'

'Have you spoken with Shelly?' he asked.

'She's on my list too. Why?'

'She might know more than I do.'

'About Giles as a boss, or about Lily Heffernan?'

He scratched the shaved side of his head, over his right ear. 'You're confusing me on purpose.'

'You're confusing yourself,' Lottie snapped.

'She – Shelly – was there when the kids were leaving.'

'Where were you?'

'I can't remember anything about Lily.'

'You didn't see who picked her up?'

'No.'

'No one signed her out.' She had checked the register. 'Is that unusual?'

'It's usually a mad rush. Not everyone signs the book.'

'Bad practice,' Lottie said. 'Tell me about Shelly Forde.'

'What about her?' He fidgeted on the aluminium chair.

'What's she like? Dependable? Good worker?'

'Shelly's a brilliant dancer. She's never late for class and helps me out loads. Don't annoy her.'

'Why not?'

'She's … a nice girl … a good dancer. I like her.'

'Is she your girlfriend?'

'Are you joking me?' His mood lightened for the first time since Lottie had entered the room. 'Shelly is like a sister to me. The sister I never had.'

'Are you from around here, Trevor?'

'Yeah … originally.'

'You live in a bedsit on Main Street.'

'What about it? I'm not a kid.'

'Fall out with your parents?'

'I just need my own space.' He dropped his eyes and picked at his fingernails.

'Have you got a girlfriend or boyfriend?'

He raised his head and squared his shoulders. 'That's a very personal question and I don't think it's any of your business.'

'Trevor. An eight-year-old child has gone missing. She was last seen at your dance class, so let me be the judge of what is or is not my business.' She watched as he digested her words. He remained silent. She'd get there another way. 'Lily's mother was found dead yesterday.'

'What? Oh God, this is a disaster.'

'What is?'

'I mean … Fiona was nice. You know.'

'I don't know. Tell me.'

'I only met her a couple of times. She was friendly, but she seemed sad. This is so awful.'

'Sad? How?'

'I can't explain it. I can't believe all this is happening to me.'

'Nothing is happening to you, Trevor. Not yet, anyway.'

'You know what I mean. I don't understand what's going on. Can I go now?'

'You can go, but if you think of anything that might help find the little girl, contact me straight away. Don't leave town. We need a DNA sample and your fingerprints.'

'I think I need my solicitor for that.'

Lottie groaned.

When Trevor had left, she turned to Kirby. 'What do you make of him?'

'Not a lot.'

What are you not telling me, Trevor? Lottie wondered. Because she was sure he had held something back. They always did. She believed 'economical with the truth' was a statement attributable to witnesses and suspects alike. But she had nothing evidential to hold him on. She flicked through the file. According to Shelly Forde, whom Kirby had talked to last night, Trevor had not left the theatre after rehearsals. But what about Giles Bannon?

*

He stood outside the Oxfam shop and stared in through the window. It was dark inside. He could not see what treasures might be hanging on a rail for him to find. His hands were frozen. He shoved them into his hoodie pockets and walked down Gaol Street.

He tried to ignore the stallholders as they opened the shutters on the wooden huts, casting an idle eye as he walked. Shiny baubles, hand-painted. Holy statues carved out of bog oak. He could see how a little girl could be mesmerised by all the colours and glitter.

Still trembling from his interview at the garda station, he crossed the road at Cafferty's. At the stall outside the pub he stopped and stared. Dolls. Tiny things. Some looked like voodoo dolls. He cringed. Thankfully they were hanging at the back from hooks on a crooked shelf. Out front there were proper dolls with pink ribbons and frilly dresses on their stuffed bodies. He wondered if perhaps this stall had held some special wonder for Lily. If she had been waiting around on the street for her mother, would she have been drawn here like he had been drawn?

He raised his head from the display just as a man came from the back of the stall, his arms loaded with more dolls. Trevor turned away quickly and rushed across the street to the theatre.

*

Before Lottie could formally interview Shelly Forde, Acting Superintendent McMahon said he'd take the interview with Sam McKeown.

'I'm sure you have plenty to do with the two dead women cases,' he said.

'But sir—'

'But nothing. Come on, Sam.' McMahon's voice echoed in her footsteps as she returned to the office.

Boyd arrived with the old brown suitcase from Cara Dunne's flat, and Lottie followed him to the evidence room, trying to keep her rage in check. As he placed it on an empty table, she looked at it eagerly, hoping it might give her a clue as to what had happened to the teacher.

'It's been examined by SOCOs?'

'Yeah, and dusted for prints,' Boyd said. 'It's a wild goose chase, if you ask me.'

'No one is asking you, Boyd,' she said.

'Wow, you're bristly this morning.'

'Didn't sleep well. Lily's face haunted me all night.' She felt her heart skip a beat as she thought of the little girl, alone somewhere, asking for her mother. She looked back at Boyd and caught him staring at her. 'What?'

'Thought I might be haunting your dreams.'

'That would be a nightmare.' She poked him gently on the arm, let her hand slip down and squeezed his. 'I've got this. Fetch yourself a cuppa. You look like you could do with something to warm you up.'

'I could answer that … but you know what I'd say.' He smiled and left her to the old brown suitcase.

She pulled on gloves and flicked the first catch. It clicked open. Then the second. She raised the lid. A swarm of dust motes rose in the light streaming through the grubby window. She peered into the case.

White linen garments. Neatly folded. Lace, that to her untrained eye appeared hand-crafted, circled the collar of the first item. She lifted it onto the table. It looked like an old-fashioned nightgown, buttoned to the stand-up collar. She didn't unfold it. Not just yet. She wanted to see what else was in the case.

She took out another item of clothing. Beneath it rested a third. All similar. Was it a trousseau of some sort? Heirlooms from Cara's grandmother, perhaps. At the bottom of the case she found items of underwear. Knickers and knitted stockings. Two ancient-looking cotton bras. Playtex Cross Your Heart, with four rusted hooks on the back of each. They looked like something her mother would have worn, back in the day. Where had they come from? Why had Cara got them? Questions that might or might not have relevance to the murder investigation.

Letting out a gasp of air, Lottie realised she'd been holding her breath in anticipation of what she might find. Disappointment coloured her vision. She should have known she'd find nothing to help her.

She ran her fingers along the lining of the case, hoping to discover a hidden compartment, but there was nothing.

Boyd returned with two mugs of coffee. He handed her one. 'Find anything interesting?'

'Ancient clothing, that's all.'

He put down his mug, donned a pair of gloves and picked up one of the bras. 'She must have been a couple of cups larger at one stage.'

'Show me that again.' She inched the label away from the cotton and held it to her eyes. 'Forty DD.'

'And that means what exactly?'

'Boyd, you know full well what it means.'

He grinned, then pulled out a chair and sat down. 'I was right?'

'There's no way Cara Dunne was ever a forty DD.'

'Does that bring us any closer to finding out who murdered her?'

She shook her head slowly. 'Nothing makes any sense.'

'Put them back. Lock the case and forget about them. Let's do some real detective work.'

'Have you discovered something I should know about?' Lottie folded the clothes neatly back into the case.

'Jane Dore was on the phone. She wants you back in Tullamore.'

'I've been there already this morning.' Lottie felt heat prickle her skin in frustration. 'Did she say what it was about?'

'No. But she sounded like it was urgent.'

'I'll ring her first. I'm not driving again in this weather unless it's absolutely essential.'

'She did mention Fiona Heffernan and murder in the same sentence, though.'

'Get your coat, Boyd. You can drive.'

CHAPTER TWENTY-FOUR

'Sorry for dragging you back, but I thought you might like to see this for yourself.'

Jane spoke as she walked around the body. Fiona Heffernan was lying on the stainless-steel table, her chest open, skin and muscle peeled back, ribcage sawed away. Tim Jones had his back to them, weighing an organ in the background.

'I'm anxious to hear what you've found.' Lottie fixed her mouth mask, then joined the pathologist at the table. The smell of death clung to the back of her throat. She gagged and swallowed, then composed herself and looked into the cavity.

'Nothing of interest there,' Jane said. 'Normal healthy thirty-four-year-old. Has given birth. No evidence of any disease in her organs. Bloods will be sent for screening.' She raised Fiona's arm and Lottie noticed the bruises Jane had mentioned earlier that morning.

'What does the bruising suggest?' she asked.

'It suggests that someone with hands much bigger than hers gripped both her arms tightly.'

'Is there a connection to Cara Dunne's death?' Lottie felt the stirring of anticipation in the pit of her stomach.

'The gash on her forehead happened before the wedding dress was put on. Have you examined the roof?'

'Yes. Nothing was found there. But blood was found in the locker room. We're awaiting the forensic report.' Lottie noticed that Jane hadn't answered her question about the deaths being connected. But that wasn't unusual for the pathologist. She dealt with facts. They had the wedding dress link, but she wanted hard evidence.

Jane said, 'Wherever she was before she reached the roof may be the initial crime scene.'

She'd have to check the locker room herself, Lottie thought. 'Thanks, Jane.'

'That's not what I brought you out in this awful weather for, though.'

A tingle began between her shoulder blades as she watched the pathologist move to the top of the table to stand behind the victim's head.

'Join me,' Jane said.

'What am I looking at?' Lottie peered at Fiona Heffernan's long dark hair.

Spreading it out in a fan, Jane said, 'Do you notice anything?'

Lottie shrugged. 'I'm not sure what I'm supposed to see.'

Parting the hair further, Jane pointed to a section close to the right-hand side of the skull. 'See there?'

'Yes!' Lottie peered closer. 'There's a clump of hair missing. Did someone pull it out?'

'No.' Jane moved her fingers closer to the scalp.

Lottie could see what the pathologist meant. 'Someone cut out a piece of her hair?'

'Exactly.'

'Oh my God!' Lottie exhaled. 'Perhaps she did it herself?'

'The lack of growth tells me this was done just before death.'

'She cut a chunk of her own hair and then threw herself off the roof?'

'Did you find a *chunk* of hair, as you call it?' Jane said.

Lottie eyed Boyd over her mask. He was lounging at the door, having failed to venture any further. She wondered why. He wasn't usually squeamish. 'Can you find out?'

He said, 'I'll check with SOCOs, but I don't think any hair was found.'

'The body was clothed in a wedding dress and underwear. Bra and knickers,' Jane said. She moved to a bench and picked up a small plastic evidence bag. 'I found this lodged in the victim's bra.'

'That looks like hair,' Lottie said, taking the bag. 'Human?'

'It is,' Jane said.

'Fiona's?' Lottie asked, but she knew it did not belong to the woman on the cutting table.

'It's blonde.'

'Whose?' Lottie suspected that Jane knew, because her eyes were twinkling with excitement.

'I can't be sure without a DNA match, and there are no roots with which to carry out analysis ...'

'But?'

'But to my eye, it looks very like Cara Dunne's hair.'

'Sweet Jesus. What the hell?' Lottie stared over at Boyd, who looked as dumbfounded as she felt.

'Come with me,' Jane said. She walked briskly towards an adjoining room and pointed Lottie in the direction of a second body. Cara, with her chest neatly stitched up. Standing at the woman's head, Jane parted the hair and held up the evidence bag.

'Let me get this straight.' Lottie felt her head buzzing with this new information. 'Someone cut a piece of Cara Dunne's hair, and that same piece of hair was found on Fiona Heffernan's body.'

'Seems so.'

'And there's a piece of Fiona's hair missing that you have yet to find?'

'Correct.'

Lottie's brain whirred in confusion. 'We'd better do a fingertip search of the abbey. If we don't find Fiona's hair there, then it could be that someone else is a target, or … there's already a third body somewhere.'

'And if you have a third body, you have—' Boyd began.

'A serial killer.' Lottie turned to look at him.

'That's not all,' Jane said.

'Shit.'

At an evidence drawer, the pathologist extracted yet another tiny bag.

'More hair?' Lottie felt her jaw slacken. 'Where did that come from?' She examined the hair through the transparent plastic. 'It's not blonde like Cara's, or jet black like Fiona's. It's kind of a dirty brown. This doesn't make any sense.'

Jane filed the sample back in the drawer. 'Follow me.'

Lottie walked in the pathologist's footsteps to her office, Boyd trailing in their wake.

Jane clicked on the computer. 'We had a suicide victim. Found two weeks ago. Robert Brady, aged thirty-six.'

'Out at Lough Doon,' Lottie recalled.

'Yes. He was found suspended from a tree in the forest. He'd been there maybe a week. The attending doctor deemed it suicide immediately and the body was cut down and brought here for a post-mortem. As no foul play was suspected, I was not involved.'

'What has this got to do with my victims?'

'The post-mortem was carried out by my assistant.'

'Tim Jones?'

'Right.'

'I'm at a loss to know where this is headed, Jane.'

'Tim agreed on suicide. Plain and simple. He brought me the file to ensure he'd done all that was required. I read it and agreed. Nothing suspicious. The only odd thing was the handful of brownish hair found in the pocket of the trousers.'

'Did it belong to the dead man?'

'I don't know. It wasn't suspicious at the time, and he's well buried now. But when I discovered that locks of hair had been cut from Cara and Fiona, I remembered that detail.'

Lottie leaned back in her chair, stared at the cracked ceiling. After a few seconds, she lowered her eyes to look into Jane's. 'Was any of the victim's hair cut off?'

'It wasn't noted in the post mortem report.'

'Can I see the report?'

'I'll email it to you.'

'Thanks.' She stood up and moved to the door. 'What do you think we're dealing with here, Jane?'

'I actually have no idea.'

CHAPTER TWENTY-FIVE

The young woman standing at reception grabbed Lottie as she was keying in the code to enter the bowels of the station.

'Hey, let go.' Lottie twisted her arm, bracing herself for an attack.

'You're Detective Lottie Parker.' The young woman dropped her hand.

'Detective Inspector, if you must know.'

'Can I have a word? Just for a minute.'

Lottie glanced at the desk sergeant, who shrugged his shoulders. 'I'm awfully busy. Make your complaint at the desk.'

'It's not a complaint. I tried ringing earlier.'

Lottie squinted at the young woman. She was dressed in a green parka jacket, the furry hood resting on narrow shoulders. She'd seen her somewhere. Recently? She wasn't sure.

'Are you a reporter?'

'Yes, Beth Clarke. I work at the *Tribune*. That's not why I'm here, though. Please. Just a minute of your time.'

Lottie acceded to the request with a shrug. She told Boyd to go on ahead as she opened a door to her right. A small interview room, more like a cupboard, used mainly for form-filling.

When they were seated, the room clouded with whatever scent Beth Clarke was wearing. Lottie welcomed the fact that it distilled the odour of death clinging to her skin from the mortuary.

'What can I do for you?' She studied the emotions flickering across the young woman's face. This was a mistake. Why was she a sucker for distressed individuals? 'Beth, I'd appreciate it if you told me why you're here. As I said, I'm extremely busy.'

'It's my d-dad. I c-can't find him.'

Oh, here we go again, Lottie thought. She was about to direct the young woman out to the front desk, but something stopped her. A yearning in her eyes. They were so inky, they were almost black. What was really troubling Beth Clarke?

'Your dad? What's his name?'

'Christy. Christy Clarke. He was at home last night when I went to bed … at least I think he was. But he wasn't there this morning.'

'And where do you live?'

'Ballydoon village. Dad owns the pig farm on Doon Road. Do you know it?'

'Is it close to the abbey?'

'Our farm backs onto it. There's been a lot of trouble over run-off – effluent – seeping into the river, but Dad is adamant it's not coming from our place.'

Lottie's inquisitive brain wanted to ask about the trouble, but she had to get to the crux of the matter. Beth seemed a little more relaxed now.

'What age is your dad?'

'He's … I'm not sure. Fifty-five or something. Old, anyway …'

Lottie grimaced. 'Is your mother at home?'

Beth's pale cheeks flared bright red. She dropped her head. 'My mother left us, years ago. I think she ran off with another man.'

'I'm sorry.'

'No need to be sorry. I try not to think of her, if I'm honest. Apparently she's back now. Living in Ragmullin. I don't want to talk about her, though.'

'No problem.' Lottie folded her arms. 'Have you looked around for your dad?'

'He's not in the house or on the farm. There's no sign of his car, either. I asked in the village and I even went to the garage my dad used to run. It's closed down now but he's not there anyway.'

'Look, Beth. I don't want to sound heartless, but your dad is a mature adult and has probably just gone off to clear his head for a few hours. He might be here in town, or he could have gone to Dublin for the day. Why don't you go home and wait for him? Keep ringing his phone. I'm sure he'll contact you eventually.'

Beth stood up so quickly the table shuddered in the confined space. 'You don't understand. He's been under so much pressure lately. The taxman's been hounding him. He can't balance the books. The pigs are neglected. He's neglecting himself. He's hardly left the house in weeks except to go to the shop in the village. This is totally out of character and—'

'I'm sorry,' Lottie held up her hand, 'but he has to be missing for at least forty-eight hours before we can class him as a missing person. Go home and wait.' She knew it sounded harsh, but she had murders to deal with, and a missing child. Standing, she said, 'I hope you understand.'

'I don't understand.' Spittle landed on Lottie's chest from the angry young woman. 'You have alerts out for the little girl. Why can't you do it for my dad?'

'It's different for children. You're a reporter. You know the way things work. If you're that concerned, why don't you put his photo on your Facebook page and get your friends to share it. I'm sure someone will spot him.'

'Thanks for nothing.'

The door slammed.

Lottie remained standing in the small room for a moment, the sound reverberating in her ears. She knew she should be heading up to the incident room to digest Jane Dore's information, but instead she ran to the front door of the station. Beth was nowhere to be seen. Before she knew what she was doing, she was standing at the counter in the offices of the *Tribune*.

'Can I speak with Beth Clarke, please.' She showed her ID.

The young woman looked behind her to the open-plan office, where files and newspapers were strewn in bundles over the floor. 'Anyone seen Beth?'

'I'm here.' Beth Clarke came out of a door marked *Toilet*. 'What are you following me for?'

'I want to ask you about Ryan Slevin.' Lottie noticed the older man in the corner raise his head.

'Ryan's not in,' Beth said. 'His fiancée died yesterday, as I'm sure you know.'

'Can you confirm that he was at work yesterday?'

The older man stood. 'I'm the senior editor here. Nick Downes. Yes, Ryan was in yesterday, though he left early.'

'How early? Why?'

Downes shrugged. 'Something to do with his wedding. Can you remember what time it was, Beth?'

'Afternoon sometime.' She shrugged. 'I don't know. You should ask him yourself.'

'Is he here today?'

'What do you think?' Beth said, and moved away from the desk.

'Tell me, Beth, in your opinion, was Ryan in love with Fiona?'

'That's a funny question. He was getting married, wasn't he?'

'People get married for all sorts of reasons, not necessarily love.'

'Gosh, you are one cynical woman.'

Lottie bristled. 'I'm trying to get a picture of the man who was about to marry a young woman who has died suddenly.'

'Looks to me like you want to fit him up.' Beth sat at a desk piled high with newspapers and rested her feet on a bundle on the floor.

'Beth,' Lottie said. She wished she didn't have to talk over the counter, but no one seemed eager to let her into the general office. 'I'm sorry you can't find your dad. I know you're mad at me, and I understand, but I can't do anything at the moment.'

'I'll look for him myself.'

'He could be back at home now, for all you know.'

'He'd ring me if he was. I left enough messages. Years ago, my mother left me in the dead of night. Dad saw what that did to me. I don't believe for one second he would do the same.' Beth's eyes flared before she turned back to her desk and switched on her computer.

'Are you any relation to Eve Clarke?' Lottie asked.

'Never heard of her.'

There was nothing further to be gained here. Lottie turned on her heel and made her way out onto the street. The thought she carried with her back to the station was that Beth Clarke was hiding something. She was either covering for Ryan Slevin or holding a candle for him. Either way, Lottie would find out.

At the station, Boyd directed Lottie to the interview room.

'Steve O'Carroll, Cara's ex-fiancé, is waiting for us.'

'With his solicitor?'

'Not yet.'

Boyd made the introductions for the recording and Lottie studied the man seated on the other side of the table. O'Carroll had his hair tied back. His suit was black and his shirt white, worn like a uniform – pressed and pristine. He was thirty-seven, according to the copy of his passport in front of her.

'Thanks for agreeing to this chat, Mr O'Carroll,' she said.

'You needn't think I'm going to be taken in by your chumminess. I know how this works.'

'Are you happy to begin without your solicitor?' She saw his eyebrow arch and knew he was consumed with curiosity. He wanted to know what she knew. She would have to be careful not to fall into his trap.

'For now.'

'Right so. You've worked at the Railway Hotel for how many years?'

'It's all here.' He handed over his employment record, which he'd brought with him.

'Thank you. You've been there eight years. Good place to work?'

'It's okay.'

'You began as a barman and are now assistant manager. No manager vacancies come up?'

He squirmed on the chair, but his lips turned up in a smile. 'Not yet.'

'Ever thought of trying a different hotel? Some of the big ones up in Dublin or over in London?'

'No.'

'Why not?'

'Is this relevant?'

'I'm just curious.' She was trying to get a handle on his personality, and so far, he was giving nothing away: his hands on his lap beneath the table, his face grim as a headstone.

'Don't waste your time on me, Inspector. I had nothing to do with Cara's death.'

'How long had you known Cara Dunne?'

'Maybe three years.'

'You were engaged to her.' A statement.

'I was.'

'For how long?'

'A year.'

'And you broke up three months ago, is that correct?'

'In a manner of speaking, yes.'

'What happened?'

'We were no longer compatible.'

'How did you reach that conclusion?'

'Is this relevant?' he asked for a second time.

'Answer me and I'll know.'

After a sigh, he trained his eyes on a spot above her head and said, 'She changed. Became possessive and a right nag. Bossing me around about the wedding and stuff. We argued. End of story.'

'So you broke it off?'

'Yes.'

'How did Cara take that?'

'Not very well.'

'In what respect?'

'As far as I know, she'd been off work since. Took up religion big-time.'

'And how do you know all this? Was she in contact with you?'

'She never left me alone. Every single day. Calls. Texts.'

'Did she harass you at work?'

He ran a hand over his mouth and nose and sniffed, then replaced his hand under the table. 'No. She never called to the hotel. She'd booked it for our reception. I asked her to slow down. But no. Full steam ahead she went, like a runaway train.'

'It all became too much for you?'

'Yeah.'

'Why did you propose to her in the first place?'

A slight smirk itched at the corner of his lips. 'I got walked into it, didn't I? A few drinks one night, and she says how nice it'd be to have a ring on her finger. I agreed, thinking I was in love. Wrong. She focused on this mad wedding, saving like mad; wouldn't even go out for a drink with me. If I'm honest, she became a boring wagon.'

Lottie cringed at his choice of words, but let it slide. 'Surely you knew her well enough before then?'

'Obviously not.'

'Cara was a thorn in your side. You did something about it and—'

'Hold on there a minute.' He smacked the table. 'I never said that. Don't be jumping to the wrong conclusions.'

It was the first real emotion Lottie had seen from him. Consternation, or fear?

She picked up a copy of his clocking record from the hotel. 'You clocked in at ten o'clock yesterday morning. Where were you before then?'

'At home.'

'What time did you get up?'

'Jesus, I don't know. The usual. Eight o'clock.'

'And what did you do from eight a.m. until ten?'

'Had a wank, jumped in the shower. Then I got dressed. Cooked my breakfast and ate it. Washed the dishes and left for work.'

'Did you drive or walk to work?' She knew he lived on the outskirts of town. An easy ten-minute walk, but taking account of the bad weather, more like fifteen.

'I drove. I've my own parking space in the yard.'

'Is there CCTV in the yard?'

'No. It's private. Staff only.'

'Cameras at your house?'

'What is this? Why would I need them at home?' His face clouded. 'If I'd thought I'd be needing an alibi, I'd have made sure I had someone stay over for the night.'

'I'll need all the hotel CCTV.'

'Why?'

'To prove you were there when you say you were there.'

'Get a warrant.'

He was smug. Too smug. Had all the answers, and he was getting under her skin. 'Do you own a black leather belt?'

'I own maybe five or six. Why?'

'I'll need to see them. Do any of them have the inscription BB or BD?'

'Not to my knowledge.'

'Will you consent to us taking a sample of your DNA? For elimination purposes.'

'I will not.'

'Why not?'

'I've been in and out of Cara's apartment for the last few years. I'm sure my DNA is all over the place, and you'll try to frame me for her death if you find just one hair or fingerprint belonging to me. I've done nothing wrong. Now I'm waiting for my solicitor.' He folded his arms and clamped his mouth shut.

End of, Lottie thought.

CHAPTER TWENTY-SIX

Lottie was back in Cara Dunne's apartment, searching for a lock of hair.

If the suicide from three weeks ago was suspicious, and her theory of a serial killer was correct, then the lock of hair from that victim had to be here.

'This is ludicrous,' Boyd said.

'Won't do you any harm to have a look. You take the living room.'

SOCOs were working away in the bathroom. She went to the bedroom. Suited up and gloved, she traced her hand along every surface, inside each drawer and through all the clothes. Nothing. She knelt by the edge of the bed and checked each blanket, each sheet as she turned them down. Still nothing.

'It's a wild goose chase,' Boyd shouted from the other room.

She ignored him. Went on checking. Carefully she took Cara's nightdress from under the pillow and ran her fingers through the folds.

'Boyd!'

'What?'

'Got something.'

He rushed into the room. 'It's not much, is it?'

'Boyd, it's a lock of hair. Cara had blonde hair, and—'

'Fiona Heffernan had long black hair. What colour is that? Ginger?'

'Could be light brown with a tinge of red. Hard to know.' But she thought Boyd was right: it was ginger.

'Who the hell does it belong to?'

'It could be from the suicide victim Jane mentioned. Or it could be someone else entirely.' She put the lock of hair into an evidence bag.

'Lottie?'

She looked up. Boyd's face was paler and thinner than normal. His eyes were watery. Had he been drinking again last night? She wanted to reach out to hold his hand, to tell him not to worry.

'What?' she said.

'Could it belong to the little girl?'

'Oh shit.' A cold finger of dread slithered down her throat. She felt sick. 'No. It couldn't be. Cara was murdered before Lily went missing.'

'Thank God.'

'And Lily has fair hair.' Lottie stood up from the bed. 'Did you find anything?'

'A lot of dust.'

'This makes no sense.'

'She wasn't much of a housekeeper.'

'Don't, Boyd. Now is not the time for jokes.'

'I wasn't joking. I'd end up asthmatic if I lived here.'

She cast a final glance around the bedroom and moved back into the living area. She hoped SOCOs found something they could use from the samples they were gathering in the bathroom. 'Let's get this logged in at the station.' She fingered the evidence bag with its piece of treasure. 'Jesus, Boyd, we need to find the little girl.'

She shrugged her arms out of the white suit and grabbed her jacket. She was in the corridor before Boyd had his zipper undone.

The next-door neighbour was peering through her slightly open door.

'Eve?' Lottie nodded a greeting. 'Can I have a word, please?'

'Sorry. I'm not feeling very well. Another time?'

'Now would be a good time for me.'

'I was about to lie down.'

'Just a quick word.'

The woman went to shut the door, but Lottie held her hand in the way, hoping it wouldn't slam on her fingers. It didn't. She checked over her shoulder, but there was no sign of Boyd. She followed Eve Clarke inside.

The living room, which had appeared so slick and bright yesterday, seemed to have taken on a darker hue. Clothes were strewn on the backs of chairs, and the venetian blinds had snagged halfway. Lottie could see into the kitchenette, where dishes were spread around haphazardly, as if someone had taken them out of the cupboards while looking for something and had forgotten to put them back where they belonged.

'I'm sorry for disturbing you,' she said, lifting a magazine from a chair and sitting down.

Eve gave a long, exasperated yawn and leaned against the window ledge, folding her arms. She was still in pyjamas. Her feet were bare and dirty.

'What do you want to know? I'm exhausted with all the noise from next door. When will they be gone?'

'As soon as they finish. Will you sit down?'

'I'm grand here.'

'Eve, I need to confirm your whereabouts yesterday morning.'

'I was here alone. I told you that.'

'Can anyone else verify it?'

Eve unfolded her arms and leaned towards her. 'No.'

Lottie heard the woman's teeth grinding and saw her eyes flitting about the room as if she was expecting someone to jump out of a cupboard. What was going on? She was sure she smelled alcohol, and Eve had the look around her watery eyes of someone who took more than she could handle.

'Are you sure?'

'I was here. Alone. For shit's sake, what's this all about?'

She reminded Lottie of her daughter Chloe when she acted like a petulant child. Lottie stood and faced her.

'I'll tell you what it's about. Your next-door neighbour was brutally murdered yesterday morning. You entered the apartment and found the body. You have yet to consent to your DNA and fingerprints being taken. If you do not consent, I will arrest you for obstruction of justice, and I'll get a court order to tear your home apart. That's what it's all about.'

'Okay, okay.' Eve flapped her hands in the air. 'No need to get your knickers in a twist ...' She stopped gesticulating. 'You sure she was murdered?'

'Yes.' Lottie folded her arms and leaned against the wall.

Eve gulped loudly. 'I've nothing to hide. I like my privacy. I don't like cops sniffing around, you know ...' Her voice trailed off, and she looked away and twiddled with the cord for the blind. It slapped down suddenly onto the windowsill and she leaped back as if bitten. 'Damn useless yokes.'

'Has something frightened you, Eve?'

'A woman was murdered next door and you ask if something frightened me? I'm scared. It's not safe around here. I thought she'd taken her own life. I never thought for one second it could be ... something else.'

'It was made to look like suicide.'

'That's cruel.'

'Sit down, Eve. We need to talk properly.' Lottie was fast losing patience. She tried to keep her voice even when what she really wanted to do was shout at the woman.

As if sensing her restrained anger, Eve sat at the table.

Lottie joined her. 'Listen to me. We can do this here, or at the station. Which is it to be?'

'I've nothing to hide.' Still not answering the question.

Lottie sighed. 'Can you run through yesterday morning from the start?'

'I got up around eight thirty. Went to the shop for fags. Came back. Looked at telly. Then I heard the voices.'

'Did you see or hear Cara before that?'

'No. But I know she goes to Mass every morning and usually visits an old friend out in the nursing home at least once a week.'

'Who is the friend? Which nursing home?'

'Sister Augusta, I think she's called. She's in Ballydoon Abbey.'

'Really?' Lottie sensed her eyebrows arching. 'Why didn't you mention this to me yesterday?'

'You never asked, did you?'

'Okay. Do you have a partner? Anyone to vouch for you?'

'I have no one. I left my husband years ago. Christy put everything and everyone before me and I'd had enough of it.'

'Christy?' Before Lottie could ask anything further, a knock at the door interrupted her. She looked over at Eve, who slowly got to her feet.

Boyd stood there. Face flushed, hands fluttering as he beckoned Lottie out.

'What's the fuss?' she said as he gripped her elbow and wheeled her down the corridor, away from a startled Eve.

'Come on, we have to leave.'

He kept walking. She pulled away from him. 'Hold your horses. I was in the middle of an interview.'

'You can continue it at the station later. This is important.'

'Boyd, unless you tell me, I'm not budging an inch.'

'We have another one.'

'Another what? For Christ's sake ...' She followed him. 'Tell me, Boyd.'

'Another murder made to look like suicide,' he said over his shoulder as he took the stairs downwards, two steps at a time.

CHAPTER TWENTY-SEVEN

Lottie felt like blowing red raging flames through her nostrils at Boyd when they arrived back at the station.

'I'm sorry,' he said. 'I just thought it was important to look at it straight away. McKeown was adamant we had to read it immediately.'

Lottie flopped behind her desk and picked up the post-mortem report that Jane Dore had sent through.

'Robert Brady. Thirty-six years old,' she read aloud while Boyd sat on the chair in front of her.

'Go on.'

'I don't need an audience. Why don't you get something to eat? You look like death warmed up.'

'Jesus, Lottie, you're not my mother.'

'How is your mother?'

'Fine.' He grunted and shoved the chair back. 'I sent the lock of hair to the lab for analysis.'

'What hair?'

'The hair you found at Cara Dunne's apartment.'

'Let me know when there's a report back.' But she knew forensic analysis could take weeks. She also knew it was useless for DNA, but perhaps it could be matched to the cutting found on Robert Brady's body. She needed to know one way or the other, and unless she got Jane to call in a favour, it'd be weeks before she'd have a result. She continued to read aloud, even though Boyd had returned to the main office.

'Five foot eleven. Weighs seventy kilos.' That sounded light to her. 'Hey, Boyd, what weight are you?'

'Around eighty kilos. Why?'

'Just wondering. You're six something in height; this guy was five eleven.' She read the remainder in silence. 'Jesus, Boyd,' she exclaimed.

'What now?' He got up from his desk and sauntered back into her office.

'This Robert Brady. He had shoulder-length ginger hair.'

'Same as we found at Cara's.'

'We need that comparative analysis completed immediately. Tell Jane to request expediency.'

'You're asking her to call in favours?'

'Yes, I am.'

As Boyd made phone calls, she read the remainder of the report. There were no more major revelations. The assistant pathologist, Tim Jones, had classed it death by suicide due to compression of the carotid arteries. He mentioned bruising on the neck and fingers, but decomposition had ruled out further tests. McKeown had been right to call her back from Eve Clarke's. This was too much of a coincidence. Once the hair analysis was complete, she was certain she'd be looking at perhaps the first of three murders.

She told Boyd.

'Your boss won't be happy,' he said.

'He's your boss too.'

'I know, but another murder will skew his performance reports.'

'We'd better get cracking before he finds out then, hadn't we?'

Boyd scuffed the floor with his shoe. 'You're forgetting about the wedding dresses angle.'

'Robert Brady was hardly going to wear a wedding dress ...' She flicked through the report again. 'He was wearing black trousers and a white shirt.'

'Part of a wedding suit?'

'I don't know what to think.'

But something gnawed away in her brain. Brady might not have been the first victim. Where had the hair come from that was found on his body? And the fact that Fiona was missing a lock of hair convinced her that they would soon find another body. Not if she caught the killer first. She stood up and stretched.

The big question was, how did little Lily fit into it all? Lottie dug her nails into the palms of her hands, then checked for updates on the child. Lily was all over the news and social media, but no one knew where she was. McMahon was on top of it, so what else could she do? She decided to follow up on something Cara's next-door neighbour Eve Clarke had said.

CHAPTER TWENTY-EIGHT

The location looked different in daylight. Crime-scene tape whispered a lonely tune as it fluttered in the wind, and the uniformed garda resembled a frozen statue.

Lottie showed her ID and entered the main door of the abbey. Boyd stopped outside to have a puff on his e-cigarette. She wondered how long that fad was going to last.

The abbey reminded her of an old convent school building. Long tiled hallways, high ceilings, and narrow arched stained-glass windows dulling daylight and throwing a criss-cross of rainbows on the floor.

Needing to ensure they'd missed nothing, she headed to the locker room, glancing back to see if Boyd was on his way. Not a sign of him. She was sure the e-cig was for show, and that he'd lit an actual cigarette once she'd disappeared inside.

SOCOs had taken samples of the blood from the floor, and Fiona's locker was still cordoned off with tape and bore the remains of black fingerprint dust. She hoped the killer had left his or her mark. Something to give her a clue to their identity. She raised the tape and dipped under it.

The locker door was open. Fiona's uniform had been taken away for analysis. As had her clothes. Lottie recalled there had been a shirt, a sweater and a pair of jeans, folded on a shelf. On the floor of the locker was a pair of robust boots, perfect for walking in the snow.

But Fiona would never get to walk anywhere again. A hooded fur jacket with a Primark label was scrunched up on top of the boots. The pockets held coins, till receipts and tissues. She wondered why Kirby or SOCOs hadn't bagged the receipts. She did so now, tut-tutting at the sloppiness of others. A quick glance showed the receipts were from Tesco, with itemised grocery products, dated the day before Fiona's death. It reminded Lottie that she had yet to check out Fiona's home, even though she knew McKeown and Kirby were there right now.

Running her gloved fingers into all the crevices of the locker, she came up empty. She got down on her hands and knees and noticed a piece of paper on the ground under the locker. Sliding her hand in, she drew it out. A photograph of Lily.

'Fuck you, Kirby.' She swore aloud.

She'd trusted him to do his job efficiently while she and Boyd had examined the roof yesterday afternoon, and he'd missed this. His performance since Gilly had died was bordering on negligent. If she'd known about the photograph when they'd found Fiona's body, they'd have been alerted to Lily earlier and perhaps have prevented the child disappearing.

She studied the photo. It was more personal than the one they'd used on the nationwide alert. The little girl really did have an infectious smile. Her eyes danced in the light, her hair flowing in the wind. A moment captured by her mother to savour in times when she was not with her daughter. The irony made Lottie shiver.

As she slid the photo into an evidence bag, she thought again about the wedding dress. What had made Fiona bring it to work? Had she been trying it on? Then a thought struck her. Was it even hers? Hurriedly she texted Kirby to check Fiona's house for a wedding dress.

Walking up the stone steps, she reached the roof. SOCOs had been through the whole area, but she wanted to see if there was even a hint of Fiona's hair anywhere. Why was the hair so important to the killer? Why the dresses? Shaking her head, she stood at the edge of the roof and looked out over the snow-covered gardens. She found her eyes drawn to the wooded area where she had walked in the dark of the previous evening. Her skin prickled as she recalled the sensation of someone watching her after she'd stumbled across the life-sized statues. From up here, with the snow blanketed everywhere, she could not see them. They seemed to have melded into the winter landscape along with the killer. With a final glance at the tented area below, she returned inside.

With still no sign of Boyd, she hurried along the main corridor, where she found a nurse in an office. She asked to see Sister Augusta. After following the winding corridors, trying to remember the directions, she found the nun.

The room was bright and airy. Blue and yellow wallpaper. Sunflowers. The hospital bed had rubber sheeting visible around the mattress. The cabinet was bare. No flowers, no water or biscuits or grapes.

'Who's there?' croaked a voice. 'Get me water.'

Lottie introduced herself and said, 'Will I fetch a nurse?'

'They're useless. Pour me a glass, like a good little lassie.'

'Let me see if there's anything in here.'

As Lottie opened the cabinet to check, a bony, long-fingered hand clasped hers.

'What are you snooping in my drawers for?'

'You asked me …' She disentangled her hand and stepped back.

The old nun's face was as white as the sheets on which she lay. Her long silver hair was combed neatly, with a parting down the middle; her face was a crevice of peaks and troughs; her mouth devoid of teeth and her lips ashen. Lottie had checked before arriving and knew Sister Augusta was the same age as her mother, Rose, but the similarity ended there. Cancer was eating the nun from the inside out, and from what Lottie remembered of Adam's illness, she didn't think she had much time left on earth.

'Do you mind if I have a chat with you?' She pulled up a low-backed chair and sat beside the bed.

'Get me a drink first.'

'Sure.'

She found a nurse and returned with a jug. She poured and held the glass to the nun's lips.

'I'm not an invalid,' Sister Augusta snapped, 'but thank you.'

When the nun was settled, Lottie said, 'I'd like to talk about Cara Dunne.'

'She never came.'

'When?'

'Yesterday. She comes every week. I might look dead to you, but I'm not there yet. I know about everything going on here, no matter how much it might look to you that I'm on the way out.'

'I didn't think that at all.'

'Your expression says you did. Someone belonging to you died of cancer.'

Lottie took a deep breath. She didn't want to talk about Adam. It was still raw. Too raw. Even five years later. But she found herself replying, 'My husband.'

'God rest his soul. It's an awful disease. I pray every hour of the day for God to take me. To take away this pain. I think he wants me to serve out my purgatory on earth, so that I can fly straight to heaven.' The nun cackled a half-laugh.

'I'm afraid I have some bad news,' Lottie began.

'Cara's dead, isn't she?'

'I'm sorry.'

'When she didn't arrive yesterday, I knew something had happened. And then poor Nurse Heffernan jumped off the roof.'

'Who told you that?'

'That other nice nurse. What's he called?' A spindly finger tapped the side of her head, and before Lottie could supply the name, Sister Augusta said, 'Nurse Hughes. He told me to call him Alan, but I'm old school, you know.'

A racking cough split the air, and Lottie looked around for a box of tissues to hand to the nun. The room was barer than a cell.

'How did she die?' Sister Augusta said when her coughing had subsided.

'I'm sorry to say that at first it looked like she killed herself.'

'But not now? Is that what you're telling me?'

Lottie gave the nun a half-smile. Sister Augusta's brain was still quick, even if her body was failing her.

'She was murdered.'

'I see.' A series of slow nods followed.

'Can you tell me anything about Cara to help me understand why someone would want to harm her?'

Deep rattles accompanied the nun's breaths. Lottie waited.

'I'm sure there are lots of people who'll be happy she's gone. Made life hell for some.'

'In what way?'

'Ruled the classroom, she did.' Sister Augusta cackled as if this was funny.

'Oh.'

'When she was a child, I mean. I don't know anything about what she was like as a teacher, but I'd say she hadn't changed much.'

'Did you teach her?'

'No, but I heard.'

'She was a tough kid, then?'

'She could stand her ground.'

'Do you know of anyone who might have held a grudge and killed her?'

'I don't know. But she was hard. That was the old way. Not now. Cara said that's why there are so many delinquents around.'

Lottie scratched the side of her head in confusion. 'Were you friends?'

'No.'

'But she visited you every week, didn't she?'

'This might sound like the ramblings of an irrational old nun, but I think she wanted to watch me die.'

Lottie stared at the saliva gathering in a white streak at the edge of Sister Augusta's lips. 'That sounds a little unchristian.'

'You'd have to have known her. She was damaged.'

'How?'

'I can't recall.'

Lottie was beginning to think Sister Augusta was losing her mind as well as her life.

'Did you know she'd been engaged?'

'Everyone knew. She flashed that diamond around like she was God's gift. It was like she had accomplished some great feat. If she'd climbed Croagh Patrick, that would have been an accomplishment. She was a silly girl. Didn't even do that well for herself in the love stakes.'

'You knew Steve O'Carroll?'

'Never met him. The way Cara talked about him, I thought he was the greatest doormat ever invented.'

That didn't correspond with Lottie's only experience of O'Carroll. 'What was Cara like after they broke up?'

'Dark and dangerous. Her eyes, they were like black bullets. If someone could spit fire, she could.'

'I heard she turned to religion.'

'She turned to the devil himself.'

Confusion reigned inside Lottie's skull, causing her to scratch her head again. 'Did anyone make threats against her?'

Sister Augusta closed her eyes, her head sinking further into the pillows. 'I don't know for sure. A few weeks ago, she arrived in a fluster. I don't think she had anyone else to talk to. She offloaded it all on me.'

'What did she say?'

'Something about meeting someone. Watch out for the past, she said. It catches up with you.'

'You think it might have had something to do with her teaching?'

'It was more personal than that.'

'Her ex-fiancé?'

Sister Augusta began to cough uncontrollably. Lottie held the glass to her lips and allowed the nun to sip until her breathing returned to something akin to normal.

'Talk to Father Curran. He might help you.'

'Father Curran?'

'He lives in the village. He was to celebrate the sacrament of marriage for poor Nurse Heffernan today.'

'Okay. Did he know Cara as well?'

The nun seemed to have a faraway gaze in her eyes. She was staring somewhere over Lottie's shoulder. Lottie glanced behind her, but there was no one there.

'The little girl,' Sister Augusta said. 'Nurse Heffernan's daughter. Where is she?'

As another bout of coughing engulfed the nun, Lottie felt she was on a Ferris wheel, she'd been going round in so many circles. 'Lily is missing.'

The nun resumed her uneven breathing but said nothing. Just a slight nod of her head told Lottie she'd heard her.

'Are you okay?' Standing up, she looked for a bell to call a nurse.

Sister Augusta spoke then. Her voice clear but weak.

'It's all about the child.' She closed her eyes. 'All about the child.'

'Tell me. Please,' Lottie said, frantically.

But the woman had slipped into a deep sleep.

*

Boyd walked in a semicircle outside the main door. He lit up his second cigarette of the day, having abandoned his e-cig, and watched as the SOCOs finalised their work. A band of uniforms were carrying out a fingertip search of the area with long-handled tongs. Boyd thought they were wasting their time. They were dealing with someone meticulous and careful. Someone who planned.

In his trouser pocket, his phone vibrated. He glanced at the screen and frowned as he answered.

'How's it going, Sean?' he said. 'Did your mother flay you alive last night?'

'No, but she's unbearable. Can I ask you something?'

'Go ahead, bud.'

'Can I live with you? Only for a while. A day or two. That's all.'

Boyd took a deep breath. He had asked Lottie to marry him, and he knew her kids would be part of the package. But he wasn't their father, and anyway, he wasn't about to step on her toes over her son.

'Sean, you need to talk to your mother. Tell her how you're feeling. She understands.'

'No she doesn't. You do.'

A thought struck Boyd. 'Sean, are you supposed to be in school?'

'You know what? You're even worse than her. Always on about school and homework. I have to live too, you know. Thanks for nothing.'

'Sean … Sean?'

Boyd looked at the phone. The lad had hung up. The cigarette had gone out. He lit it again. He should go inside and help Lottie. Tell her about Sean. But his head was spinning. From everything he had to think about, or the nicotine? He looked at the damp cigarette clutched between his long fingers. Took another drag and quenched it before returning it to the packet to finish off later.

CHAPTER TWENTY-NINE

Father Michael Curran lived in the parochial house beside the church, at the entrance to the village. It was an old two-storey building sporting a mahogany door.

While waiting for someone to answer the doorbell, Lottie peered around the side of the house. The garden was well kept, with a large shed in one corner.

When the door opened, the priest ushered them inside. Father Curran was a fit-looking seventy-year-old. His white collar looked wider and higher than the one worn by her friend Father Joe Burke, and he was dressed in a flowing floor-length black cassock. She wouldn't be surprised if he conversed in Latin.

Once they were inside, sitting down, he said, 'How can I help you?'

'I want to talk about Cara Dunne and Fiona Heffernan.'

He gave her a half-smile, and she felt her insides curdle as if she'd just tasted sour milk.

'Would you like some green tea? And I've wholegrain bread. Healthy food helps you live longer.'

She wondered if he was into protein shakes and that sort of crap. Sean had been on about them recently. 'No thanks, we're fine.'

'Had you a question for me?'

She studied the priest. He was sitting erect in a wingback leather chair. The room was spotless, but the furniture smelled and looked old.

'I believe you were supposed to conduct a marriage ceremony today, between Ryan Slevin and Fiona Heffernan.'

'So sad. It's the talk of the village, you know. Fiona was a lovely person.'

'Did you know her well?'

'Not really. Met her properly for the first time when she came with Ryan to make arrangements for the wedding. A small affair, she said. She didn't believe in making a huge fuss, from what I could gather. Saving her money, she said. Clever young woman financially.'

Lottie caught his unspoken words. 'But not clever in other ways?'

'You are quick, Inspector.' He smiled fully and she could see his perfect dentistry. 'I admired Fiona for working hard and raising her daughter. You are aware that she and Colin were never married?'

'Yes.'

'The fact remains that the child was born out of wedlock. That's a mortal sin. A sin for which she was loath to beg forgiveness, despite my insistence she should repent.'

Blowing out a breath of warm air, Lottie counted to three and squared her shoulders. 'If you are so against her mortal sin, as you call it, why did you agree to perform the marriage ceremony for Fiona and Ryan?'

He sniffed back a snort. 'That lad could have made something of himself. But what does he do? He takes photographs for the newspaper. Upsetting people. He's just like that young one, Beth Clarke. Come to think of it, she was here this morning, banging on the door looking for her father.'

'Do you know where Christy Clarke is?'

'I don't, and I can't understand how he would let his daughter be involved in gutter journalism.'

This statement puzzled Lottie. She had never considered the *Tribune* to be anything other than a mouthpiece for local news. What had they published to incense Father Curran?

Before she could explore it further, Boyd said, 'How well do you know Ryan Slevin?'

'He lives in the village. His sister Zoe is a nice lady. Married to Giles Bannon. Three beautiful boys. Lovely children.' That grin again.

Lottie couldn't stop the somersaults in her stomach. There was something particularly off-putting about the old priest.

'And Fiona Heffernan,' she said. 'You say you didn't really know her?'

'I often saw her at the abbey when I visited the sick. She was a nurse there.'

'I know that.'

'She used to live with Mr Kavanagh. Don't know why he opted to live in sin with her. Then she upped and left him.' Father Curran arched his eyebrows and his lips slid sideways. 'He lives down by Lough Doon. You know the legend of the Children of Lir?'

Lottie did, and she didn't want to hear it from him. She believed the priest was trying to direct her away from talking about Fiona. She was up to a bit of redirection herself.

'Tell me what you know about Cara Dunne.'

The face remained solid as a block of lard. 'I was sorry to hear of her death. Suicide. Shocking. I had no idea she could commit such a final sin.'

'She was murdered, actually.'

The priest's stony expression morphed from indignation to bewilderment. He cocked his head to one side, then the other, as if he was trying to make sense of what he'd heard. 'But I was told—'

'You were told wrong,' Lottie said. 'How well did you know her?'

Father Curran's posture slumped and his eyes clouded over. He held onto the wooden arms of the chair. 'I was on the board of management of her school for a while. She was a good teacher. Stern, but good. Unusual in one so young. After her engagement broke down, she sought me out for guidance.'

'How did you guide her?' Boyd said.

'I guided her back into the arms of Jesus.'

Boyd grunted and Lottie threw him a dagger look, but she felt the same. Listening to religious mumbo-jumbo wasn't going to solve Cara's murder. She said, 'I need to know anything you can tell me about Cara.'

The priest seemed to be in a world of his own as he said, 'Last night, I heard the voices calling and crying. It must have been her soul on its way to purgatory.'

'God grant me patience,' Lottie muttered. She felt Boyd's eyes boring into her. She kept her focus on the priest. 'What voices?'

'The windows were rattling and I heard cries echoing throughout the house, though I was the only person here.'

Lottie got that. Wind and old houses had conjured up many a slumbering ghost in recent times. 'How long had you known Cara?'

He turned his head slowly. Blinked. As if he was coming out of a fugue state. As if he was wondering why she and Boyd were there. 'She joined the Convent of Mercy school straight from college. I was the chaplain there, as well as being on the board.'

'And you became friends?'

'She used to fill me in.'

'Fill you in?'

'When the boys reached the age of seven, they transferred to the all boys' school while the girls stayed at the convent school. It was beneficial to be forewarned of any troublemakers.'

'Were you the chaplain at the boys' school too?'

'I examined them on their religious knowledge in preparation for Confirmation.'

'Doesn't really make sense to me,' Boyd interjected. 'Whether they were troublemakers or not – surely that was the concern of the teachers, not a priest who visited the school maybe once a month.'

'Once a month?' Father Curran mocked. 'I went there every day. I took the teaching of the catechism very seriously. I had to ensure the staff did too. I set weekly tests.'

'And if someone failed a test, what did you do?' Lottie couldn't help the flush to her cheeks.

'They studied even harder. I've been teaching for over forty years.'

'You were teaching at the time of corporal punishment, then.'

'Yes. The belt was a good master.'

'And when the belt could no longer be used, what did you do then?'

'My methods were all above board, Inspector.'

Lottie decided to bring the rambling priest back on track. 'When was the last time you saw Cara?'

'She visited her friend at the abbey every week.'

'Sister Augusta?'

'Yes.'

'How did Sister Augusta become friends with Cara?' Boyd said.

'You should ask her, if you can get a word out of her.'

'I talked to Father Joe Burke,' Lottie said. 'He was filling in for you yesterday at the abbey nursing home. Why was that?'

'I had things to do. Being parish priest is a responsible role, one that I take very seriously.'

'I don't know a lot about it, to be fair,' she said.

'I thought not. If you took more notice of the teachings of the Church rather than drowning your soul in society's depravity, you'd be better off, don't you think?'

She wanted to shout back at him, but Boyd touched her arm, restraining her. She took a deep breath. 'You know nothing about me. I hope it stays that way.'

He laughed then, and that outraged her further.

'Lily Heffernan,' she said.

'What about her?'

'When did you last see the little girl?'

'What has she got to do with me?'

'You tell me.'

The priest rubbed his chin. 'I saw on the news that she's missing.'

'Did her mother bring her to any of the meetings about the wedding?'

'She did. And I told her the child was a stain on God's love.'

'What?' He was getting under Lottie's skin so intensely, she wanted to scratch the hell out of it.

'As I said, a child born out of wedlock is a sin. I told her that before I could perform the wedding, she and the child would have to renounce Satan and—'

'You what?' Lottie leaped to her feet. She'd thought those types of sentiments had died away. How wrong she'd been.

'She did renounce Satan. I was happy to officiate.'

Lottie kept shaking her head. She couldn't waste time listening to him.

'When was the last time you laid eyes on Lily?' Boyd said.

'I don't know if I can answer that with any accuracy.'

'Why not?'

'She was often in the village. She sometimes played with the Bannon boys. So I don't rightly know when I last saw her.'

'Yesterday, maybe?' Lottie said.

The priest leaned his chin on one finger dramatically. 'I can't say for certain.'

'You're refusing to answer me?'

'I'm saying I can't say for sure when I last saw her.'

Lottie made for the door.

Boyd said, 'A young man took his own life a few weeks ago in Doon forest, by the lake. Did you know Robert Brady?'

With her hand on the door, she watched as the drama drained out of Father Curran's face.

'That name is unfamiliar to me.'

He clamped his lips shut and showed them out without another word. He didn't need to say a thing. His face told her he had uttered a lie.

CHAPTER THIRTY

After leaving the village, Boyd drove them to Fiona's rented house in Ragmullin. It was situated in an upmarket area, on the Dublin side of the town. Constructed in the last ten years, its garden was still unfinished, with cement blocks and sand piled into one corner beneath a dusting of snow. A deflated yellow football lay inside the wall. Builders were working on new houses to the rear.

Lottie pulled on a forensic suit and went inside. McKeown was busy searching through a cabinet in the living room and Kirby was mooching around in the kitchen.

'Find anything?' she said.

'It's very bare,' Kirby replied. 'Anyone could have lived here and you wouldn't know a thing about them. No photos or posters. Not even in Lily's room. No personal effects or jewellery either.'

'Fiona was getting married and moving out,' Lottie said. 'Maybe she already had her stuff in the cottage.'

McKeown looked up from his task, perspiration glistening on his pate. 'We've been through the cottage already. There's nothing there that could belong to Fiona or her daughter. We only came across male clothes and stuff.'

'Any sign of her wedding dress?'

'It's upstairs. Hanging on the front of an almost empty wardrobe,' Kirby said.

'Then the dress she was found in had to have been brought by the killer into the abbey. How did no one notice it?' Lottie folded one arm around her waist and rested the other on top.

'It could have been hidden in a patient's room, or another staff member's locker.'

'Have you checked out the staff?'

'Yes. All accounted for from the start of Fiona's shift to the fall from the roof,' McKeown said.

'It's not a very secure building. Anyone could have walked in,' Kirby pointed out.

'With a wedding dress hanging over their arm?' McKeown scowled. 'I don't think so.'

'I was just saying,' Kirby said.

Now wasn't the time to reprimand him over the photo under Fiona's locker, though Lottie itched to have it out with him. No, finding the little girl safe was more important. She picked up a bundle of newspapers from a chair. Five copies of the local paper, the *Tribune*.

'Interesting,' she said, flicking through them.

'What is?'

'There are quite a few here.'

'Maybe she forgot to put out her recycling bin.'

'You're missing my point, Kirby.'

'Which is?'

Lottie put down the papers. 'I don't know.'

As she went up the stairs, she was still bothered by the news-papers. In what she supposed was Fiona's bedroom, she saw the off-white wedding dress hanging on the wardrobe. Full-length, long-sleeved, with a high neck and pearl buttons down the back. A very different style to the one in which the body had been found. Wedding dress retailers needed to be checked out, to trace its purchase.

She opened the wardrobe door. Finding very little inside, she scanned her eyes over the room. Impersonal. That was the word that sprang to mind. Also, bare.

In Lily's room, she used the same word again. Plain pink duvet cover and pillowcases. Matching curtains. Her clothes were neatly hung up and her shoes arranged in a row beneath the window. There did not seem to be enough clothes for a child of her age, even though there were plenty at Colin Kavanagh's house. McKeown had said there was only male clothing at the cottage. Where was all their stuff?

Two books on the bedside cabinet; no toys. Lottie felt her heart lurch as she thought of her grandson's toys. She immediately felt sorry for a child she'd never met. She hoped desperately that no harm had come to the little girl.

Back downstairs, she told Kirby to bag the newspapers. 'Are you nearly finished?'

'There's nothing here, boss,' he said.

'I know, and that's what's bothering me.'

It was well into the afternoon by the time Lottie and the team gathered in the incident room. She recapped the last thirty-odd hours.

'Regarding Cara Dunne, have we anything back from forensics on fingerprints or DNA?'

'It's too soon,' Boyd said.

'Keep on at them.' She stifled a yawn. Food! She needed to eat, and soon. 'Toxicology reports are pending on both Cara and Fiona's bodies too.'

'We found nothing at Fiona's house except the wedding dress.' Kirby said.

'Yes, apart from the wedding dresses, the only other connection between our victims is that Fiona was a nurse at Ballydoon Abbey and Cara Dunne regularly visited a sick nun there. We need to clarify whether the two women ever met or talked. Then we have the missing locks of hair from each body and the locks of hair recovered on or in the possessions of both women.'

'Explain, please,' Kirby said.

Lottie pointed to the photographs. 'This lock of blonde hair was found in the underwear of Fiona Heffernan. In her bra, to be exact. It has been sent for analysis, but to the naked eye it looks like Cara's. The state pathologist has confirmed that a section of Cara's hair had been clipped from the base of her skull. She also found that a lock of Fiona's long black hair had been cut from her head. That has yet to be found.'

'Perhaps it will be on the next victim,' McKeown said.

Lottie stared at him to see if he was making a joke, but his face was serious.

'It's likely Robert Brady was the first victim,' Boyd said, eyeing McKeown.

'I'm coming to Brady,' Lottie said, and turned to the room. 'Boyd and I searched Cara's flat earlier. There we found, in the folds of her nightdress, a lock of ginger hair. It's possible it came from Robert Brady.'

'I worked that case,' McKeown said. 'Everything pointed to suicide.'

'I need a fresh pair of eyes on it. Kirby, find out all you can about Brady. If he was the first to die at the hands of this killer, there has to be a link to Cara and indeed Fiona.'

'We can't even find a link between the two women, apart from the fact that they both had a slip of hair cut off and were dressed in wedding gowns,' Kirby grumbled.

Lottie folded her arms and leaned against the wall. 'There has to be something, however inconsequential it may appear to be.'

McKeown stood and walked to the board. He stood beside Lottie, the minute stubble on his head sparkling under the artificial light. He loosened his tie and pointed to a photograph of the abbey.

'Fiona worked there. Cara visited a patient there. Who did you say she was?'

'Sister Augusta. I interviewed her earlier.' Lottie straightened her back. 'See if you can link Brady to the abbey too.'

'Right, boss.' McKeown returned to his seat, stretching his long legs out in a gap between two tables.

'The state pathologist has confirmed that a lock of hair was found in Robert Brady's pocket,' Lottie said. 'In light of the current cases, it's likely he did not commit suicide.' She eyed McKeown pointedly. He didn't blink.

'If we follow that line of thought,' he said, his voice deadpan, 'there could even be a victim before Robert Brady.'

'It's possible, but we have no idea who that hair belonged to,' Lottie said.

'Right,' McKeown lowered his head. 'I might have missed something on the Brady case, so I've started to rework it. Before you assigned it to Kirby, I may add. I found an article in the *Tribune*. The issue published the week after Brady's body was found has a photograph of the scene. The photograph is credited to Ryan Slevin.'

Boyd bolted up straight. 'There you have your link.'

'What link?' Kirby said, as if waking up from a slumber.

'Ryan Slevin took the photograph of the Brady scene,' Boyd said, 'and then his fiancée is murdered and her child goes missing.'

'That's what I'm thinking,' McKeown said.

Boyd shot a glance at McKeown and Lottie wondered if there was animosity between her detectives. She hadn't time for infighting. Turning her attention to the board, she said, 'Do we have a photograph of Brady?'

'I'll get one,' McKeown said.

'Any update on the search for Lily Heffernan?'

'The super is gung-ho on press releases and television appeals. No sighting of the kid as yet, and we found no clues at the house. All the teachers, parents and pupils at her school have been interviewed, as has everyone connected with the after-school club and the dance school. Nothing so far.'

Lottie thought for a moment. 'Giles Bannon is the manager of the dance school. He's married to Zoe, Ryan Slevin's sister. Ryan was to marry Fiona today.'

'Everyone is related to everyone else in small towns and villages,' Kirby said.

'I know, but I want Bannon interviewed.'

'I interviewed him this morning,' McKeown said, 'after Shelly Forde.'

'And?'

'Bannon was in his office sending emails at the end of the dance class. If we need to dig further, we'll have to secure a court order to seize his computer and phone.'

'But where was he when Fiona met her death? Where was he when Cara was strung up?' Lottie turned to the board, lacking in photographs of suspects. 'He's a person of interest in Fiona's death now. Boyd, call him in. I want to personally interview him. Say it's a follow-up on Lily.'

'Right,' Boyd said.

'And Shelly Forde. Did she have anything enlightening to say?'

'Nothing to add. Just the same stuff about the rush of kids at pick-up time. And the register only being signed by some parents. She didn't see anything unusual and she has no recollection of Lily leaving the theatre.'

Lottie said, 'Trevor Toner mentioned he thought he saw someone hanging around the theatre during the class. Anyone else mention that?'

'No,' McKeown said.

'When I spoke to Sister Augusta earlier, she said, "It's all about the child." I think it's worth bearing that in mind.'

'Something to do with Father Curran?' Boyd said.

'Who is Father Curran?' Kirby said.

'He's Ballydoon's parish priest. He was to officiate at the marriage of Fiona and Ryan. He comes across as old-school Catholic. But when I asked if he knew Robert Brady, he clammed up. See what you can find out about him.'

Kirby scribbled a note.

'I also want a background check on Colin Kavanagh,' Lottie added as she sorted her files and papers into a bundle. 'And make sure we get a DNA sample from Steve O'Carroll.'

'Right, boss,' Kirby said. 'What about the wedding dress?'

Lottie gathered the files to her chest and thought for a moment.

'McKeown, find out where Cara bought her wedding dress. See if the one she was wearing was hers or something the killer brought with him. And find out where Fiona bought her dress, then trace the dress she was discovered in. Maybe it will lead us to her killer.'

Or it could be like a star in the sky, she thought. Something you know is there but is totally unreachable.

CHAPTER THIRTY-ONE

Beth parked her car outside the garage her father had owned for twenty-something years. He'd only closed it down last year, citing loss of earnings, with no one interested in buying second-hand cars any longer. The boom had returned for some people, but not all, she thought sadly.

As she stepped onto the pavement, she was surprised to see a man walk from behind the building and head for a silver BMW.

She coughed loudly into her hands and rubbed them together. 'Cold day,' she said redundantly.

The man stopped walking.

Her breath caught in her throat. She had no idea why he was snooping around the garage.

'It's very cold indeed.' He zapped the lock open and made to sit into the car.

She noticed it had a current registration. Doing the figures in her head, she reckoned it was worth about fifty grand. Probably more if he had all the bells and whistles in it, which he most likely had.

'Were you looking for Christy Clarke?' She moved closer to the glistening monstrosity of German engineering.

'I was. But he's not there. Do you happen to know where I might find him?'

She was about to say she was Christy's daughter, but a knot twisted in her gut and stopped her. He must know who she was, but she wasn't giving him any advantage. Her journalistic senses were on the highest alert.

'Can I give him a message from you?' She was trying to draw him out.

He waved her away. 'It's okay. I'll track him down myself.'

As she watched him drive away, she wondered why Colin Kavanagh was looking for her father.

After finding Christy's car parked at the rear of the garage, Beth made her way inside and called out, 'Dad? Are you in here?'

Her voice echoed back at her. She flicked a switch and the light tube flickered a couple of times before the showroom was bathed in brightness.

'Dad?'

No answer.

She made her way around the cars, wondering why they hadn't been offloaded when the garage had closed, or why the bank hadn't repossessed them. The door to the office was shut. She put her hand on the handle but didn't depress it. Some internal warning system was clanging bells in her head, telling her to turn away. To run. To get the hell out.

She laid her ear against the door and listened. Silence.

'Dad? Are you in there? I've been worried sick about you.'

She had no idea why she was talking to a wooden door. Stalling. She was the only living being in here. Now what had made her think that? But she knew. She knew before she opened the door that something horrific was on the other side.

Taking a deep breath, she swallowed her fear and entered the office.

The scream left her before she knew she had even opened her lips. A surge of vomit shot from her stomach to her mouth and she clamped a hand firmly there, keeping it from spewing outwards. Swallowing the acidic liquid, she found she was rooted to the spot. The urge to run to her father's side was overwhelming, but she couldn't move.

She sank to her knees and pulled her phone out of her pocket. Then she dialled 999.

*

The garage door was guarded by a uniformed officer, while another garda hunkered down beside the young woman who was seated in the squad car. Lottie jumped from the car before Boyd had time to pull the handbrake. She raced over to the squad car.

'Beth,' she said, addressing the tearful girl. 'I think you should see a doctor. You've had an awful shock.'

When the two red eyes cut through her, Lottie turned and walked to the garage.

The uniformed garda signed her in.

'No one enters unless I say so,' she told him. 'Got it?'

'Got it.'

The garage was old-fashioned. No modern double-height glass walls with coffee machines and reception desks here. It was obvious even to someone who knew little or nothing about cars, as she did, that Clarke's Garage had been unable to compete with the glossy showrooms in Ragmullin. She noticed, however, three Mercedes lined up along one wall and two BMWs at the other end. Not old bangers then. Odd.

'What type of car business did Clarke run?' she asked Boyd.

'High-end, if this lot is anything to go by.'

'You'd imagine when he closed down that he'd have sold the cars.'

'Perhaps the bank took the garage and left everything here.' Boyd glanced around, his eyes gleaming as he inclined his head to look in the window of the nearest Mercedes. 'Or maybe he was just a useless businessman.'

'Maybe,' Lottie said. 'Where's the body?'

Boyd led the way to a door to their left. A man with a medical bag in his hand was on his way out.

'I confirmed the death,' he said and kept walking.

'Who is he?' Lottie said to the uniformed garda standing at the office door.

'Local GP. We called him when the body was discovered.'

'And Beth found the deceased?'

'Yes, the young lady called 999. I was first on the scene. She was in a bad way.'

'She was inside the office?'

'On her knees at the door. Poor thing.'

'Thanks,' Lottie said, and entered the office.

The man lying across the chair was definitely dead. That much she could see from the lack of a face. Blood spatter on the wall behind him.

'Gunshot?' she said.

'There's a shotgun by his hand,' Boyd said. 'McGlynn is on his way.'

'We'd better not venture in any further. McGlynn will have my guts for garters.'

'You're right there. But there've been plenty of people traipsing through here in the last few minutes; he'd have no reason to have a spat with you in particular.'

Lottie scanned everything that was visible to the naked eye. 'I'd be inclined to call it a suicide, but after the two murders yesterday, we can't be sure, can we?'

She thought of how she had dismissed Beth earlier in the morning when the girl had arrived at the station concerned about her dad. Guilt wormed its way through her blood. Feck, she thought, she should have been more considerate. But events were happening with such velocity that she was struggling to keep up. She itched to get over to the body, to check if he had a lock of hair missing or one on his person, but she didn't want to compromise the scene. 'Is it really Christy Clarke?' she said.

'Without a face, it could be anyone,' Boyd offered, and went back out to have a word with the garda at the door.

'Boyd!' It was unlike him to be so insensitive. Something was eating away at him, and she wanted him to share it with her. Could it be related to Sean showing up on his doorstep? But now was not the time for sorting out personal matters.

A bustle of activity at the door caused her to turn around. Two paramedics with a stretcher trolley had arrived. Too late for them. Too late for the victim.

'We need a positive ID, and to find out if he owned the gun,' she said. Boyd was staring at the victim's decimated face. He had gone deathly pale and staggered slightly. 'Are you okay?'

'I need a toilet,' he said.

'You should find one in the pub across the road …'

Before she could finish her sentence, Boyd had bustled his way out between the startled paramedics. She watched as he ran across the road, bursting through the pub's double doors. She was torn between following him to make sure he was all right and staying with the victim. She needed to wait for McGlynn, but she also wanted to check on Boyd.

She stayed where she was.

*

After the garda had taken down all she had to say, which wasn't a whole lot, Beth told him she was feeling better and wanted to go to

Zoe Bannon's house. Once he'd run it by the inspector, he arranged for a colleague to take her there in the squad car.

She needed to talk to Ryan or Zoe. A friendly face might help her, because she couldn't go home. Not yet. Not to an empty house with her father's unfinished work littered across every surface.

She rang the doorbell as the squad car pulled away. Zoe opened the door, holding her youngest son in her arms, with her two other boys wrestling in the hallway behind her.

'Oh God, what's happened to you, Beth?'

'Can I come in?'

'Of course, you can. Head to the kitchen. You look awful. Have you the flu? There's an awful dose doing the rounds. I suppose you heard about poor Fiona. I can't get my head around it at all. Poor Ryan … well, I don't know what to say to him. Oh, sorry, here's me prattling on. Sit down. Did you hear all the sirens? Something must be going on in the village. Did you notice anything? That bridge is an accident waiting to happen. Do you think there was a crash?'

As Zoe flung school bags and jumpers to the floor, Beth burst into tears.

'Oh pet, what's wrong?'

'It's Dad. He's … he's dead. Oh my God, Zoe, I don't know what to do.'

Zoe crossed herself and Beth winced through her tears. Ryan's sister was like a mother to everyone, and that made her think of her own mother. For a moment she wished Eve was here. She quickly dismissed the thought.

'I'll put the kettle on,' Zoe said.

'I don't want a thing. It'll make me sick. After what I've seen … It was terrible.'

'Do you want to talk about it?'

'I'm not sure I can.' Beth pulled at a corner of the tablecloth and wound it around her hand. Twisting and twisting, so hard she almost dragged it from the table to her lap.

'What happened, Beth? Tell me.'

'Is Ryan here?'

'He's probably up at the cottage. He's in a state. And what with Lily missing too ...'

'No word yet?'

'Not a dicky bird, poor little mite.'

Beth gulped down a sob that was threatening to engulf her. She had to talk, otherwise she felt she was going to curl up and die.

'Dad killed himself.'

'Oh dear Mother Mary in heaven. That's terrible. You didn't ... you know ... find him, did you?'

Beth nodded. 'He'd shot himself. In the face. In the garage. Why did he do that?'

'Oh hun. That's just awful.' Zoe flopped onto a chair. 'I can't even begin to imagine how you must feel.'

'Don't try. It's awful.'

'Do you think you should ... you know ... tell your mother? She's in Ragmullin, you know.'

Beth felt the colour flare up her cheeks. 'I'm aware of where she is, and for all I know, she could have driven him to it.'

'You don't mean that.'

'I do. Every word of it. She abandoned us. Went off and made a new life for herself, so Dad said. God only knows what she's been up to.' Beth couldn't control the burst of trembling convulsing her body. Her knees rattled so much they bumped off the underside of the table.

Zoe stood. 'I'll make that tea.'

Taking her hand, Beth pulled Zoe down to her eye level. 'Listen to me. I think a lot of things might be unearthed if the guards start looking into Dad's death.' As Zoe drew away from her, Beth added, 'We can't let anyone find out about you-know-what.'

'Don't be silly. Why would the guards be looking into it just because Christy killed himself?'

'I know from my job what that detective inspector is like.'

'Oh Beth, this is such a mess.'

Beth stood and grabbed Zoe's elbows, forcing the woman to look into her eyes. But as she was about to speak, the chime of the doorbell broke them apart.

CHAPTER THIRTY-TWO

With Boyd by her side once again, Lottie rang Giles and Zoe Bannon's doorbell for the second time in as many days. She'd agreed to allow Beth to stay here until she was formally interviewed. Ideally the interview should take place at the station, but Lottie needed to hear first-hand how she'd stumbled across her father's body, so she decided to strike early.

Once inside, tea was insisted upon, and when she had it made, Zoe went to join her children in the sitting room, leaving Lottie, Boyd and Beth in the cluttered kitchen. The smell of garlic was still as strong as the evening before.

'Are you positive it's your dad, Beth?' Lottie said, ignoring the teapot and cups in the middle of the table.

The young woman seemed to nudge one shoulder upwards in an 'I don't know' or a 'could be' gesture.

'Please talk to me.' Lottie noticed that Beth's eyes were dry but red-rimmed. 'Would it help if I asked Zoe to join us?'

Beth shook her head. 'It's okay. I can talk. Just … It was a shock, you know. Finding him like that … my dad … and it *was* him, I'm sure.' She swallowed a loud sob. It sounded more like a hiccup.

'It's okay to cry.' Lottie wished Boyd would engage the girl in conversation. He was a lot better at comforting bereaved family members than she was. But he was studying his hands. She felt like giving him a nudge but didn't.

'I don't want to cry,' Beth said. 'I want to scream and shout. It's not fair, you know. Not fair at all.'

After allowing her a moment to compose herself, Lottie said, 'When you called to the station this morning, I thought you were being a bit premature in declaring your father missing. I'm sorry I couldn't do anything at the time. Can I ask, though, why were you so worried?'

Again Beth shrugged one shoulder. This time she spoke. 'He's been under so much pressure lately. Hasn't been himself at all. First he was grumpy and angry all the time, then he became so distant. And the last few days he's been acting like he's been terrified of something.'

'Terrified?'

'Sorry, I shouldn't have said that. I don't know what I'm saying.'

'What was your father terrified of? Was it anything that would make him take his own life?'

Beth wrapped the tablecloth round and round her fingers. 'Do we have to do this now?'

Lottie was certain the young woman knew more than she was telling. 'Why did you go to the garage?'

'I'd tried everywhere else, I suppose. I couldn't stay at work and do nothing.'

'Any idea where your dad might have been all day?'

Opening her eyes wide, Beth said, 'He wasn't in the garage when I checked this morning, so I don't know where he was. If I'd been a little earlier, maybe I could have saved him.'

'It will be up to the pathologist to rule on time of death,' Lottie said.

'And his cause of death?' Beth prompted. 'Will the pathologist confirm he killed himself?'

'Why do you say that?'

'I don't want to believe he did *that*. I heard the way everyone was talking about poor Fiona. It was sickening. Do you realise how hard it'll be for me to continue living here?'

'Don't be thinking like that.'

Beth folded her arms on the table and buried her face in them. 'You don't understand.'

Lottie put out a hand and smoothed her hair. 'Actually, I do. Very much so.' She felt her voice break a little. Her own father had taken his life with a pistol in his mouth when she'd been just four years old. She'd known very little about it at the time, but she'd lived through the devastating effects in the aftermath.

Beth raised her head, sniffling. 'Sorry. I can't believe he would hurt me that way. I never thought, not in a million years, that he could do something like that. Never!' Her voice rose in an unnatural shriek. Lottie touched her hand. She had to make the girl focus.

'Take a few deep breaths. Look at me. Does your dad own a shotgun?'

'Yes.'

'Where does he normally go during the day?'

'I don't know. I leave for work around eight every morning. Usually he's already fed the pigs by then. Oh God, I'll have to feed them now. I hate the mucky bastards. The smell of them.'

'Don't think of them for now. You're telling me about your dad's routine.'

After another sniff, Beth said, 'Sometimes he goes to the shop. For milk and the newspaper, and bread if we're out of it. I don't know why he was at the garage this afternoon. It's been closed for over a year.'

'But the cars I saw in there look new,' Boyd said. Lottie welcomed his interjection.

Beth continued. 'I work in Ragmullin every weekday. Some weekends too. I'm on call twenty-four-seven. Ridiculous for a local paper, but I do podcasts and I write a blog as well. Sometimes my stuff gets picked up by the online news sites.' She paused and shook her head. 'I honestly don't know what my dad does all day.'

'Are you sure his car wasn't at the garage when you checked this morning?' Lottie asked.

Beth closed her eyes, as if envisaging her earlier actions. 'It wasn't there, that's why I didn't go in then. I left work early and went home, and when he still wasn't around, I headed back to the garage to check again. That's when I found his car parked out the back.'

'Did you see or speak to anyone?'

'Only Colin Kavanagh. He was there walking around, looking for dad.'

Lottie raised an eyebrow at Boyd. 'Lily's father?'

'Yeah. He and Dad are … were acquaintances. He advised Dad on stuff to do with the business, as far as I know.' Beth scrunched up her nose like a child who didn't want to eat her broccoli.

Lottie's heart broke for the young woman. Beth wasn't much older than Katie. She felt a twinge of guilt gnaw her heart. She hadn't checked in at home all day. Shit. Then she wondered about Kavanagh's connection to Christy Clarke. Kavanagh had lived with Fiona Heffernan for years and was the father of her child. She didn't believe in coincidence, but she knew it was possible, especially in a small village. And Lily was still missing.

'Did you ever hear any rumours about why Fiona left Colin?'

Beth's eyes opened wide. Was that a streak of fear that had flitted across them before a veil of tears sheathed them again? 'I … I think Fiona said he was too old for her.'

'And Lily? Colin can't have been happy to see another man raise his daughter, can he?'

'I don't know what you mean. Ryan loves Lily as if she were his own. And Mr Kavanagh had rights to her, so there couldn't be any problem, could there?'

'I don't know,' Lottie said. 'If you think of anything, will you let me know?'

'Can I go home now? I'm wrecked.'

'Why don't you stay with Zoe tonight?'

The blue eyes turned almost ebony as Beth replied, her voice wavering like she could cry again any second. 'I'm only friends with Zoe because of Ryan. I work with him. I wouldn't feel … comfortable here. I want to go home.'

'Have you any other family?'

'Just Dad. My mother is estranged from us.'

'Who is your mother, Beth?' Lottie knew what the girl was going to say even though she'd already denied knowing the woman.

Beth stood and moved to the sink. She filled a glass with water. Turning back, Lottie noticed the shake in her hand as water spilled over the side.

'My mother's name is Eve Clarke. And I hate every bone in her body.'

CHAPTER THIRTY-THREE

They left Beth in the care of Zoe Bannon. She only agreed after Boyd worked his charm and convinced her it was best not to be alone.

'This is a right mess,' Boyd said as they headed for Colin Kavanagh's house.

'Why do you say that?' Lottie asked.

'For starters, yesterday morning Eve Clarke discovered the body of Cara Dunne. That initially looked like a suicide but is now a fully fledged murder investigation.'

'Go on, Sherlock.'

'And this afternoon Eve's ex-husband Christy is found with his brains blown out. Also looks like a suicide.'

'You don't think Christy Clarke killed himself?'

'I don't know what to think.'

'You're right on one thing,' Lottie said, staring at the snow pelting against the window. 'It *is* a right mess.'

They lapsed into silence as the car sped along the narrow, slushy road. She could detect that Boyd was uptight. She felt like burying her head in his shoulder and seeking the comfort of his body close to hers. He'd been so distant lately, she feared their wedding might never take place.

'We can sort it, though,' he said. 'Don't worry.'

'I'm not worrying about the case.'

'What's the scowl for then?'

'I'm concerned about you.' She could have sworn his hands tightened on the steering wheel as she spoke. 'What's up with you, Boyd?'

He turned his head slightly without taking his eyes off the road. 'I'm fine, Lottie. Absolutely fine.'

'We are getting married, Boyd. I promise you.'

'You don't even want anyone to know.'

'I need to get my head around how it will affect our working relationship, and then we can tell my family and make the arrangements. Are you excited for us?'

He concentrated on the dark road ahead. 'I am.'

She didn't believe him. He was up to something. But right now, she felt she had enough on her plate with two murders and a suspected suicide. Not to mention a little girl who was still missing. She radioed the station for an update. It turned out there was little to report. Lily Heffernan was still missing. No sightings. But Kavanagh had been ringing the station constantly, and was filling the news channels with pleas for his daughter's safe return.

Lottie rang home. Just to check her family were all okay. And that was when Katie told her about her plan.

'No fucking way,' Lottie said when she'd hung up.

'What are the Parker kiddies up to now?' Boyd winked, winding her up more.

'Katie wants to fly over to Tom Rickard in New York. For Christmas, for fuck's sake.'

'It might be good for her to get away.'

'I thought you were on my side!' Lottie fumed. 'She wants to bring baby Louis with her and get this ... Chloe wants to go too.'

'Well, they've been through a horrendous experience recently. Let them off.'

Lottie tried to twist around in the seat, restrained by the belt across her chest. Trying hard not to hyperventilate, she said, 'Boyd, would you ever shut up. What do you know about kids, anyway?'

'Nothing, Lottie. Not a thing.'

She breathed long and hard as Boyd kept his eyes on the road. The headlights made the snowflakes sparkle and flutter before they disappeared, and she felt herself sinking into the seat. She had a missing child to find, and now her kids were running rogue. Life seemed to be unravelling around her. Nothing new there, she thought.

Boyd idled the engine at the gates to Colin Kavanagh's house while Lottie went to the intercom. No reply. She walked back to the car, looking around in the dark.

'There's no one home,' Boyd said, getting out and searching his pockets.

'Don't light a cigarette,' Lottie said. She went to the car boot and extracted two torches.

'Why not?'

'Because I really want one. But I don't want one. Follow?'

He zipped up his jacket and nodded. 'What do we do now?'

'I wouldn't mind a snoop around.' She handed him a torch.

'The gate's locked,' he pointed out.

'Never stopped me before.'

She began walking along the perimeter hedge. From experience, she knew it was virtually impossible to secure a property out in the countryside unless you constructed a ten-foot-high wall all the way round. And Colin Kavanagh hadn't done that.

'Wait up, Lottie. What do you think you're doing?' Boyd caught up with her.

'Looking for a gap.' She shone the torch up and down as she walked, ducking beneath overhanging branches, and realised just how dark it was without the haze of street lights, even in the distance.

'You're mad.'

'I know. You must be too. You're following me.'

'I'm afraid you'll fall down a rabbit hole like Alice in Wonderland and be lost for ever.'

'You wish.' She smiled to herself as Boyd kept pace behind her. 'Anyway, Alice got back out.'

'Knew you'd have a smart reply.'

'Wait up. Hold my torch. Shine it there.' She paused at a break highlighted in the hedge.

'This is ludicrous. Kavanagh is a solicitor, for God's sake.'

'All the more reason.'

As Boyd held the two torches, she considered the tiny gap. Pulling aside bramble branches, she made an opening large enough to squeeze through. She held back the briars with the sleeve of her jacket over her hand for protection and watched Boyd grunt and grumble as he joined her on the other side.

'This is totally illegal,' he said, straightening up.

Bits of dead leaves stuck to his hair and Lottie plucked them out. She slid her arm around his waist and leaned into him.

'Not now, Lottie.' He pulled away from her as if she'd scalded him with boiling water.

'I can't figure you out,' she said, feeling a chill of rejection knot her chest.

'That makes two of us. Come on.'

Making their way stealthily, they came to the edge of what she supposed was a vast lawn. The torches guided them as they crept forward.

'I don't see his car,' Lottie said, still irritated by Boyd's rebuke.

'Could be in the garage.'

'Keep that beam low. You don't want to alert dogs.'

'Dogs?' Boyd said. 'You never mentioned he had dogs.'

'I don't know if he has or not. Just be careful.'

'Remind me again why we're doing this?'

Pausing, she said, 'Kavanagh's been on to the station constantly demanding we find Lily, and yet he was seen by Beth at her father's garage shortly before Christy's body was found. I just want to see if he's home or not.'

'He didn't open the gate for us. That tells me he's not home.'

'Maybe he is.'

'Or maybe he's out searching for Lily.'

'Or he's pretending to be mourning the death of a friend while trying to figure out how to deflect the blame away from himself.'

'You think Kavanagh killed Christy Clarke?'

'I'll hold my thoughts until the post-mortem is completed and SOCOs have done their jobs.'

'So we're breaking and entering on one of your whims?'

'Something like that.'

They reached the house. It loomed up in the dark, as forbidding as it had been yesterday when she'd been here with Kirby.

'Do you think I should ring the doorbell?'

'Lottie, there isn't one light on in the house. He's not here. Come on, it's time we went home.'

'Give me a minute.' Shining the torch along a pebbled pathway, she followed the beam around the side. She put one foot on the paving at the rear of the house and suddenly motion sensors triggered lights attached to the back wall.

'Shit!' She jumped backwards into Boyd, who leaped away from her.

'Holy God, you scared the gizzard out of me,' he gasped. 'Now you've done it.'

'I have, haven't I?' She stepped further forward and listened. 'At least there's no alarm going off.'

'Bit useless out in the middle of nowhere.' Boyd pocketed his redundant torch. 'Do you even have an idea of what you're looking for?'

'Not really.'

Peering in through the windows, she saw no sign of life. She tried the latch on the back door. Locked. She moved further along. Still nothing. As she went to make her way down the expansive lawn surrounded by hedges, every light inside the house suddenly came on.

Colin Kavanagh stood at his back door.

Lottie walked up to Kavanagh, straightening her shoulders, Boyd at her side.

'Can we have a word?" she said.

'I'm calling your superintendent,' Kavanagh said, rage filled spittle shooting from his mouth.

'Acting superintendent,' Lottie said.

'I'm calling the Garda Commissioner. The Minister for Justice, or whoever I can lay my hands on, will learn of your trespassing. You will be arrested for this.'

'I'm sorry.' But she wasn't. 'When you didn't answer the intercom, we thought something dreadful might have happened to you, so we decided to conduct a search of the area to see if access could be gained another way. Did you know there's a gap in your defences?'

'Do you think I came down in the last shower of rain?'

'No, sir,' Boyd interjected. Lottie caught his glare and turned her head. 'We're sorry for having disturbed you. We'll be on our way now.'

She squared up to Kavanagh. 'Why didn't you let us in?'

'I've just arrived home.'

'Oh, where have you been?'

'None of your goddam business. Now leave, or my first call will be to your superintendent.'

'Acting superintendent,' Lottie reminded him again.

'I'm adding arrogance and ignorance to my opinion of you.' Kavanagh's face flared under the back-door light. The whole area was lit up like a Christmas tree, and Lottie thought he looked like Santa Claus. He just needed the beard.

'Can you account for your whereabouts this afternoon?'

'Huh! Not to you I won't.'

'When did you last see Christy Clarke?'

'He was here this morning, if you must know.'

'Why was he here?'

'He called for a chat.'

'Oh. And what was the chat about?'

'Inspector Parker, that is nothing to do with you. It would answer you better to find my daughter.'

'Why were you at Clarke's Garage today?'

'No comment.' He stepped closer, and Lottie could smell a sweet, tangy odour coming from his body. 'Tell me, what exactly are you doing to find my daughter?'

'We have a dedicated team working to locate her. Which reminds me, I will need a detailed itinerary of where you were all day yesterday and what you were doing.'

He straightened his back, towering over her. 'What are you accusing me of?'

Lottie was not easily intimidated. 'I'm asking pertinent questions that I'm sure you as a solicitor would agree with. What do you keep in that cabin?' She pointed to a shed-like structure under the trees at the end of the lawn.

'If you were doing your job, you'd know that your people have already searched my property. Leave. Now.'

'I'm certain you already know, but Christy Clarke was found dead this afternoon. I'd appreciate it if you could come to the station tomorrow morning for a formal interview. No need to bring a solicitor. I'm sure you can advise yourself.'

With that, she grabbed Boyd by the sleeve and steered him around the side of the house and onto the gravel avenue.

'His car is there now,' Boyd said. 'He was telling the truth about being out.'

Lottie kept moving at a gallop. 'Let's see what we can get out of him tomorrow.'

'You won't get a chance. He'll have McMahon whipping your arse.'

'I'd really like to know where he was before he arrived home just now,' she said, clipping in her seat belt as the gates slowly slid closed and Colin Kavanagh's house was plunged into darkness.

CHAPTER THIRTY-FOUR

The incident room was abuzz when they returned to the station.

'Why all the phone activity?' Lottie said.

'Kavanagh's just offered a twenty-thousand-euro reward for information about Lily,' Kirby said.

'Shit. All the cranks and crazies will be out now.'

She shook off her coat and moved to the head of the room, each footstep imprinting her anger on the floor. She had no idea how to obstruct her daughters' plans to go away for Christmas. If she kept working, she might be calm enough to have a half-decent conversation with the girls when she got home.

Appraising the incident boards, she noted the victims' photographs and wondered if Christy Clarke's picture was about to join them. It was piercing her chest like a thorn bush, the feeling that Clarke's death had not been by his own hand. Or if it had been, had someone coerced, blackmailed or threatened him into killing himself? On the second board, the photo of Lily Heffernan.

She faced the room.

'Listen up, guys. Come on,' she cajoled. 'It's late and I've a home to get to, and I'm sure you all have too. First of all, I want to update you on the recent death of Christy Clarke in Ballydoon village.' She filled them in as best she could, then, having determined that there was still no sighting of Lily, she continued, 'Where are we in relation to the investigation into the death of Cara Dunne?'

The door had been left open to allow air to circulate, and she noticed McMahon lounging against the door, his arms folded tightly across his waistcoated chest. His eyes were boring through her. Shite!

Kirby said, 'We have a history of Cara's work life to date. A very simple work history if you want my opinion. When she finished college, she joined the Convent of Mercy primary school, where she taught for ten years. Her colleagues say she was a hard but fair teacher. Even the kids' parents liked her.'

'You need to find out about her life before she went to college.'

'Yes, boss.'

'Anything in relation to Steve O'Carroll?'

'He was an okay guy, according to Cara's teacher friends. Their words, not mine. One said that Cara was so in love she tended to neglect her friends, and she was completely devastated when he broke it off.'

'O'Carroll said she harassed him. Any reports on that?'

Kirby shook his head. 'No. The other things we already know. She found religion. Went to Mass daily. Visited the abbey nursing home weekly.'

'Anything else?' Lottie bunched her hands into fists. This was getting them nowhere. 'Any mention of Father Curran?'

'Give me a minute.' Kirby licked his finger and flicked through the papers on his knee.

'Why don't you use an iPad?' McKeown grinned. 'You can take notes in your phone and sync it—'

'Here it is,' Kirby said, holding up a crumpled page. 'Father Michael Curran. He gave her a reference for the job at the school.'

'He must have known her or her family,' Lottie said.

'Will I interview him about it?'

'Leave it to me.' Lottie kept her focus on her team and avoided catching McMahon's eye. Thinking about her chat with the priest, she decided to go for it. She looked at Kirby. 'Anything to link the priest to Robert Brady?'

'Not so far.' His cheeks reddened and Lottie guessed he hadn't done much investigating. He said, 'I've just started, really.'

She glanced up from under her lashes to the back of the room. McMahon was still there. She didn't want to mention Colin Kavanagh because she sensed he was the reason her boss was lingering.

'Anything further to report on Fiona Heffernan's death?' she said, bungling on into the abyss.

McKeown said, 'I'm finding it difficult to trace the wedding dresses.'

'So much for your fancy iPad.' Bitch was her middle name today. 'Didn't I ask for a second-by-second account of each victim's movements?' Vacant stares greeted her. She was losing control of her team. 'Tomorrow, guys, I want reports on my desk.'

'Right, boss.'

'We have someone killing brides-to-be or ex-brides-to-be, and once the media get a handle on this, we'll have headlines striking fear into the heart of Ragmullin.' She glanced at the photo on the second board. 'Fiona's daughter, Lily. What's been done to find her?'

'I have uniforms scouring all the CCTV we've recovered from the area,' McKeown said. 'I've put out a request for dash-cam footage for the relevant time on Wednesday, and Colin Kavanagh has organised a TV appeal, so—'

'Inspector Parker. My office.'

Lottie caught sight of McMahon's back as he exited with a swivel on the heel of his polished shoe. The onslaught was going to hit her at some stage; she might as well face it now.

'Right. Be back here at seven a.m.' She gathered her things and picked up her bag from the floor.

'Do you want me with you?' Boyd asked as she swept by him. 'For moral support?'

'Thanks, but I think one of us getting into trouble is enough for now.'

Throwing her bag on the floor, Lottie leaned against the wall. McMahon's office only had one chair. His own. She supposed it made him feel powerful making people uneasy. Well, feck him. She clutched the files to her chest and waited. He marched around his desk and sat, a squeal of air escaping from the leather beneath him. He ran his hand along the rim of his coal black fringe as if wiping perspiration from his brow, then looked up at her.

'Colin Kavanagh,' he said. His voice was quiet. Too quiet.

'Sir. What about him?'

'What did you do to him?'

'Not a damn thing.'

'You must have done something, because he's been on the phone to me.'

'Shit.'

'Exactly. Shit.'

'I'm sorry, sir.'

'Explain.'

'Well it's like this. I went to talk to him about the death of Christy Clarke, who was found in Ballydoon with his brains painted on the wall behind where his head used to be—'

'Quit the melodramatics.'

She suddenly wished she had somewhere to sit. The files in her arms weighed a ton. 'A witness saw Kavanagh sniffing around Clarke's Garage. I wanted to interview him. About that, and about Fiona and Lily.'

'And you decided to *sniff* around Kavanagh's property while he wasn't there, is that it?'

'Yes, sir. I mean, no, sir. I had no idea if he was there or not.'

He smiled, his teeth gleaming in the artificial light. 'Good work.'

Had she misheard him? 'Good work?'

'I'm being sarcastic, Inspector. His daughter is missing and you go rattling his cage. Have you no sense?' He held up a hand. 'No, don't answer that.'

She let out a strangled sigh. 'Anything else, sir?'

McMahon's sardonic smile disappeared. 'Kavanagh has offered a reward, and that tells the public we are incompetent. I've already had the commissioner on to me.'

'Lily is our priority, but I'm also investigating two – possibly three – murders.' Her stomach rumbled, filling the air in the room. She had to get out of here.

'That's beside the point. If you're not up to the job, I can give it to someone else.'

She took a long breath and moved over to his desk. 'No, I can do it. I was just explaining all we're dealing with. And Kavanagh's reward has the phones hopping, taking more resources.'

'Keep Kavanagh happy.' He mussed his hair with long fingers and bit down on the side of his lip. 'Can you do that?'

'I will try, sir.'

'And find his daughter.'

'Yes, sir.' She turned to leave, then chanced, 'About Cynthia Rhodes. Has her report aired yet?'

'What report?'

'Oh, nothing. She must have binned the interview.' Relief flowed through Lottie's veins.

'She did not bin it. It was an absolute mess, if you want to know.'

She groaned. 'Sorry.'

'I have enough to think about without Cynthia fucking Rhodes. You really know how to press my buttons.'

'Right.'

She rushed out of his office before he had a chance to explain which buttons she was hypothetically pressing.

*

When Beth entered the house, the silence hit her immediately. It was more than the absence of sound. It was as if everything had been muted, and what was left behind was an empty hole. She threw her keys on the table and dragged off her coat, suddenly aware that this was what would greet her from here on in.

She stood in the middle of the kitchen and glanced around. Even when her father had been out in the yard, there was always hustle and bustle. Footsteps. Kettle. Phone. Coughs and shouts. Now? Just a big empty nothingness.

Without moving a muscle, she listened intently. The pigs were squealing. The snow had started up again. It blew hard against the window pane. But despite the squeals and the near blizzard outside, the air was somehow calm.

She turned from the window and surveyed her surroundings. There was some noise after all. The refrigerator hummed and the freezer buzzed. She moved to switch on the radio, but halted, her hand in mid-air. It was usually her dad who listened to the radio, while she followed the news on her phone.

Slumping onto a chair, she bit her lip and buried a sob in her throat. She'd have to be strong. He'd expect that of her. But why had he done that to himself? To her? Had he found out what she had hidden from him?

She leapt up off the chair and rushed to the living room. It was in disarray as usual. A single tear rolled down her cheek towards her nose. At the desk, she picked up a page scrawled with figures. Her poor father and his VAT return. Why hadn't she helped him?

'I'm sorry, Daddy,' she said to the mess of a room, which now felt bare and vacant despite the clutter. 'I've not been a good daughter.'

She switched off the light. Closing the door, she made her way up the stairs to have a shower. Hoping against hope she could wash away some of her sorrow.

CHAPTER THIRTY-FIVE

After sorting out jobs for the skeleton night crew, Lottie went home to sort out her own lot.

Her mother met her at the door. 'I dropped off a casserole. I know what you're like when you're stuck in the middle of a case.'

'Thanks. Can I ask you a question?'

'Sure.'

'Did you convince Leo to buy me out of Farranstown House?'

'You're too nosy for your own good, young lady. I'll say one thing, though. Don't look a gift horse in the mouth. Get some rest. You look like the wreck of the *Hesperus*.'

Shaking her head, thinking how her mother always got a dig in, Lottie watched Rose walk slowly to her car. She was getting more stooped. The once straight and strong Rose Fitzpatrick was ageing quickly. But Lottie had little sympathy, because at that moment she felt older than her mother.

She dropped her coat on top of the multitude on the banister. The smell coming from the kitchen reached her nose. She was ravenous. First, though, she checked her children. All appeared to be in good form, greeting her with silent nods. Picture with no sound, as Adam used to say. They were waiting to see what *her* form was like. Not good, she silently transmitted.

Katie followed her into the kitchen. Switching on the stove to reheat the casserole, Lottie heard her drag a chair out from the table. The chair legs screeched on the tiled floor.

'Where's my cute little man?'

'Louis is in bed.' Katie sat down. 'Mam, can we talk for a minute?'

'Sure.'

Obviously her elder daughter hadn't got the memo. Lottie joined her, bracing herself for a row.

Katie joined her hands on the table. 'Like I told you on the phone, Mam, I want to bring Louis over to visit his Grandad Tom for Christmas. I think it would be good for Chloe to come too. Tom says New York is fab at this time of year.'

Lottie turned up her nose. 'I presume Tom Rickard's paying for it?'

She didn't like Tom funding Katie's trips, but Louis was his grandson and she couldn't deny him access. She felt a squirming niggle like a hungry worm under her skin. Was he buying her family out from under her? Was Leo doing that also?

'I knew the first thing out of your mouth would be about bloody money,' Katie snapped.

Lottie held her hands up and attempted a wry smile. 'I always do that, don't I?'

'You do.'

'That aside, I'm not sure it's a good thing to be away for Christmas. Granny will miss you. And what about Sean?' *She* would miss them.

'We asked Sean,' Katie said quickly. 'He says he doesn't want to travel.'

'Are you certain you asked him?'

Katie dipped her head. Lottie wasn't sure what that meant.

'He'll be like a grizzly bear over the holidays with just me for company.'

'You're thinking of yourself again.'

'I'm thinking of your brother. His moods are black enough without this on top of him.'

'Okay.' Katie counted on her fingers. 'One, leave the money aside. Two, leave Sean out of it. Three, we want to go. I think it'd be great for Louis.'

'It's cold in New York.'

'It's cold here too.'

'I'll miss you all being here.' There, she'd said it.

Katie reached out and took her hand. 'No you won't. You're in the middle of a case. And you know what you're like with a murder investigation.'

'What do you mean?'

'You forget all about us. You lose yourself in the job. You're never here anyway. You don't listen to us.' Katie snapped her hand back. 'And you … you float off into another world.'

'No I do not.' Lottie clasped her own hands into each other.

'You do. When you have big cases, you get stressed. All the bloody time. You won't even notice if we're here or not. Mam, I'm not asking your permission. Me and Chloe are adults, and anyway … Tom has the tickets booked.'

Lottie felt her jaw drop. 'You did this to me before. Broke my heart, Katie.'

'Oh, get real, Mam. Even Boyd can't break your heart. Why don't you hurry up and marry him? What are you waiting for? We don't mind, if that's what's holding you up. Sean loves him. I know you do too.'

Lottie felt her cheeks flush. Her own daughter knew more about her than she did herself. Guilt framed a shadow around her, and in that moment, she thought she might never break through it. 'I've failed as a mother,' she whispered.

'Mam! Stop feeling sorry for yourself.' Katie stood. 'I smell something burning. Did you leave the stove on?'

'Oh shit.' Lottie jumped up to switch it off.

'By the way, Uncle Leo was here earlier.'

Swinging around, she stared at her daughter. 'Uncle?'

'Well, that's what he is, isn't it?'

The word stuck in Lottie's craw, conjuring up images she'd seen in the course of her work. Horrors perpetrated by so-called uncles on defenceless children. She sensed her thoughts were irrational, but in reality, she knew very little about her half-brother.

'Don't call him that,' she said. 'Please, Katie. And watch yourself around him.'

'What the f—'

'Katie! Just be careful. He's not allowed in this house again unless I'm home. Got it?'

'Granny was with him. Feck's sake, Mam, you're such a pain in the hole.'

'I've had enough of this. I need to eat.'

'There you go again. Just when I wanted to have a proper conversation with you. It's always about you. You. You. You.'

'Katie!'

The girl was half out the door. Over her shoulder she said, 'And for your information, *Uncle* Leo is booked on the same flight as us.'

The door slammed shut. Lottie slumped against the stove. She snapped her hand away from the heat and watched the tips of her fingers redden. She should run water from the cold tap over them, but she just stared, waiting for the blisters to rise. She deserved it, after all.

As tears stung behind her eyes, she wondered how she was going to right all the wrongs she'd visited on her family over the years. Somehow, she felt it might be too late.

*

The night crew were busy updating files and PULSE, the garda national database. Kirby sat at his desk with a McDonald's meal. He tipped the chips onto a sheet of photocopier paper on his desk and tried to tear open a sachet of ketchup with his teeth. It ripped, and ketchup spurted onto his face and hair.

'Holy Jesus,' he said to the empty room.

Tipping the chips to one side, he scrunched the page and wiped his face with it. He wanted to throw the whole lot in the bin, but he was starving. He devoured the chicken nuggets, stuffed the chips into his mouth and swallowed the coffee, which was now cold.

Burping loudly, he bundled the wrappers into the box and dumped it in the bin. On his desk, he spread out a copy of Beth Clarke's article that had appeared in the *Tribune* the week after Robert Brady had been found dead. If Brady's death had not been a suicide, he sensed maybe there might be a clue here.

As he read, he couldn't help admiring the young journalist's technique in handling the sensitive subject.

Robert Brady had been thirty-four years old, an unmarried and unemployed builder's labourer. He'd lived in Ragmullin all his life. Neighbours told Beth Clarke that they fondly called him Bob the Builder, but that the change in him had been massive after his employer had gone bust a year ago and the workers had been let go. Brady had struggled to get another job. With only odd jobs coming his way, he'd struggled to pay his mortgage. Lost his house to the banks. Struggled to live.

Kirby put his name into PULSE. One misdemeanour turned up. Drunk and disorderly. Brady had kept his nose virtually out of trouble. Good lad, Kirby thought, feeling an affinity with the dead man.

He returned to the article and noticed the name of the person who had reported the body hanging in the woods. Colin Kavanagh. He read on. Two men who'd been looking for fir trees for Christmas found the body, but with no phone coverage in the forest, they'd run to Kavanagh's house to raise the alarm. Kavanagh, the thorn in the boss's side. That might give her a bone to chew on.

Pushing back his chair, Kirby switched off the computer and dragged on his coat. Time to go home. He paused in the middle of the office. Maybe he'd stop off in Cafferty's to stave off the boredom before another lonely night.

He made his way out of the station and into the snow. Yes, he thought, a couple of hot Irish whiskeys would do the job.

CHAPTER THIRTY-SIX

Beth showered and changed into clean black jeans, T-shirt and a knitted sweater. She felt hollow, like someone had stuck their hand in her chest and pulled out her heart. She walked slowly down the stairs and grabbed her jacket from the banister.

She flicked off the hall light. Passing the living room, she noticed the light in there was on. A shadow moved. She screamed, clutching her hand to her chest.

'What the hell are you doing here?'

Colin Kavanagh raised his head. He was seated on Christy's chair. The paperwork that twenty minutes ago had been scattered all around was now in neat piles on the desk.

'Ah, Beth. Hello.'

'I asked you a question. Why are you here, going through my dad's papers?' She stepped into the room, glancing around to see if anyone else had entered her home. 'How did you get in?'

'The back door was unlocked. You should be more careful now that you're living alone.'

'My dad's blood is not yet cold in his veins and you barge in here, preaching to me. You are the pits.'

'That's no way to speak to your elders. Did Christy not teach you any manners?' He pointed to a chair in front of the desk. 'Why don't you sit down?'

'Why don't you get out?' Beth felt her flesh flare with rage. 'You're trespassing.'

She watched as Kavanagh tidied the last sheaf of pages before leaning back into her father's chair. He joined his hands behind his head. 'Trespassing? Now, Beth my darling, that's where you're mistaken.'

Had she misheard him? Blinded with rage, she was certain of one thing. She wanted Kavanagh out of the house.

'I'm asking you one last time to get out. Otherwise I'm phoning the guards.'

'Phone away. You'll only make a fool of yourself.'

'What are you talking about?' She was unwilling to concede defeat, but the trauma of the last few hours raced through her body like an unfettered pony and she sank onto the chair. Kavanagh's white hair shone like a halo in the gleam of light from the lamp. Shadows flashed up and down his long face. Beth felt a shiver travel the length of her spine, and her entire body shuddered.

'I'll tell you what I'm talking about.' He unlocked his hands and his body seemed to curl like a snake as he reached forward and picked up a sheet of paper. 'Read this. It's a legal document. It states that I am the owner of your late father's house and business. All of it. Lock, stock and steaming pig shit.'

Beth's hands froze on her lap like two cubes of unbreakable ice. It could not be true. 'What are you saying?'

'Your father signed everything over to me. Did he not tell you?'

'When? Why? I don't understand.'

'When your mother left him, Christy felt it was the best course of action to prevent her from getting her dirty, cheating paws on anything remotely connected to him.'

'I don't believe that for a minute. My mother never came looking for anything. She had no right to, anyway. She was the one who left.'

'I suppose you never wondered why she ran off with another man?'

'That didn't concern me at the time, and it doesn't concern me now. I can't believe Dad would come up with such a crooked plan all on his own. What did you promise him?' Beth failed to suppress a sense of rage. She knew the likes of Colin Kavanagh. Sleazebag was usually uttered in the same sentence as his name. Now she was convinced he had cheated her father out of his livelihood; stolen her inheritance.

'I offered him a way out,' Kavanagh said smugly. He leaned back, this time keeping his spine erect. More threatening, Beth thought.

She couldn't stand it any longer. She jumped up 'Fuck you. You might have seen him as a lightweight, an inconsequential excuse for a human being, but he was my dad! He was the only person in the world who loved me. Let me tell you, I won't let you get away with this.' She paused, her breath dying on her lips, exhaustion rattling her knees. 'I'm coming after you.'

His guffaw filled the room. She steeled herself against physically cringing. She had to appear strong, though she felt like her insides were breaking into a million pieces.

'You are so funny,' he said. 'You should be on the stage. Maybe Giles Bannon might have a role for you in one of his piss-poor shows.'

How could he mock her like this? How could he have fleeced her father? In that instant, Beth loathed Colin Kavanagh with more hate than she thought a human heart could possess. Fiona had been right to leave him.

She let fly. 'Your daughter is missing. You should be more concerned with her than with me. God knows what sick fuck is having his way with her right now.' She instantly felt horrible saying those words, but she received the reaction she craved.

Kavanagh thumped the desk. 'What do you know about Lily? Have you done something to her?' Suddenly the hardness floated away from his eyes. They watered, and his hands trembled. 'I have to find her. She's my daughter and I love her, just like your father loved you, even if it looks like he didn't. You have to understand that. Tell me if you know where she is.'

Beth couldn't help the smile she felt spreading across her face like a warm breeze. Kavanagh's face told her she had him rattled, if only for a moment.

He stood up. She dropped her smile as he stepped around the table and towered over her.

'Don't threaten me, Beth Clarke. Not about my daughter. Ever. Just don't.'

*

Ryan Slevin was surprised that the garda forensic team had left his cottage in a surprisingly good state.

It had been his and Zoe's parents' home. When Zoe married Giles, she'd moved into his house in the village. She'd been good enough to let him stay with her for the last six months while he worked every evening and weekend transforming the cottage. For Fiona and Lily.

He stood at the kitchen window and peered out at the darkness. He couldn't stay here any longer. Much as he loved the cottage, getting away from Ballydoon and Ragmullin was now his main aim. December wasn't a good month to sell property, but he hoped the cottage would be snapped up quickly.

He turned from the night. Opening a cupboard, he took out his spare camera and checked to see if the gardaí had confiscated the SD card. It was still there. They'd probably been looking for evidence that a crime had occurred in the cottage. But there wouldn't be any, because Fiona had died at the abbey. That much was perfectly clear.

The caw of crows travelled down the chimney. He didn't like birds. It was okay photographing them from a distance, but the thought of them flying down the wide chimney and landing in his living space made the hairs on his arms shoot up.

He'd have to put a cowl on the chimney if he was going to have to live here for any length of time. Pocketing the SD card, he slid the camera back onto the shelf and closed the cupboard door. He stood stock still when he heard a loud knock on the door.

'Ryan? Are you in there? Let me in. Please.'

'Beth?' He lifted the latch.

She burst inside, her face a mess of tears, and threw herself into his arms. 'Oh Ryan. Help me.'

'Is there someone after you?' He looked out over her head, staring deep into the night. It was dark save for the light spilling forth from the depth of his cottage.

'Zoe told me you'd be here. I had a shower and then ... He was there. He's a horrible man.'

'Who are you talking about?' He disentangled himself from her grasp and led her into the kitchen, sitting her down.

She seemed to gather her wits quite quickly and blinked back her tears. 'First Fiona, and now my dad. Why, Ryan? Why?'

'I have no idea what you're talking about. Start at the beginning.'

'I left work early. I had to look for my dad. I thought he was missing, you see.' She paused, catching her breath. He didn't see, but he nodded for her to continue. 'I couldn't find him anywhere. I'd even called to the garda station. But that detective said I had to wait forty-eight hours or something. I searched the village. No one remembered seeing him. And then ... then I saw his car at the rear of the garage ...' She began to cry again.

'What garage?'

'Dad's old garage. I had the spare key and I went in. Oh Ryan. He … he'd killed himself.'

'Your dad?'

She nodded, sobbing hysterically. 'Why would he do such a thing?'

He shook his head. How would he know? Christy Clarke had never had much time for him. 'Maybe he was in debt or something.'

'That's what I thought. And then, just now, he was in my house.'

'Who?' Ryan scratched his head. 'Your dad?'

'No, no. Colin Kavanagh.'

Feeling his skin prickle, he hooked a gentle finger under Beth's chin and lifted her head so he could look into her eyes. 'That prick Kavanagh was in your house? What did he want?'

'H-he was s-sitting at my dad's table, his desk, going through his paperwork,' she sobbed.

'The cheek of the pig.'

'He said Dad had signed everything over to him. The farm. The house. Everything. Leaving me with nothing. What am I going to do?'

'Back up there.' Ryan tried to think logically. 'Was Kavanagh your father's solicitor?'

She shrugged. 'He must have been, I suppose. I never got involved in all that stuff.'

'Christ, Beth, this is serious shit.'

'I know.'

He'd offer her a drink, but he had no alcohol in the cottage. Tea, maybe? But Beth looked like she was too far gone for tea.

'Do you want to head into the village for a drink? You could probably do with one. I know I could.'

'Maybe.' She leaned into him and he hugged her. 'Oh Ryan, I don't know what to do.'

'I do.'

CHAPTER THIRTY-SEVEN

The village pub was pulsing with a crowd in for a football club table quiz. Lottie smelled silage and fried food, though she hoped the two odours did not emanate from the same source. The atmosphere was loud and warm. The decor cool yet old-fashioned. The barman struggled with the crush of bodies and shouts for more beer, shots and shorts.

After her mini meltdown with Katie, she'd abandoned the casserole, called Boyd and convinced him to drive out through the snow to Brennan's Pub in Ballydoon, just to see if they could pick up any gossip on the recent death of Fiona Heffernan. That was what she told him anyway, though Katie's words still crunched in her ears. She wondered how Boyd was going to fit into her madcap family. Easily, probably.

He was on his second pint and she felt that if she drank another sparkling water she'd pop. She really wanted a glass of wine. A big glass, not a piddling small one. Full to the brim, so she'd have to lean down and put her lips to the rim. First a sip, then a glorious gulp. The image was so vivid in her mind that she tasted the crushed grapes in her mouth. She pictured a place where she could float to after a bottle or two. Oblivion. A dot in infinity where all her troubles disintegrated into nothing. After the argument with Katie and the burn on her fingers, she'd known there was only one person who could keep her from downing the bottle of cooking wine she kept at the back of the cupboard.

'What are you thinking about?' Boyd said, and sipped his drink.

'You don't want to know,' she muttered, the smell of alcohol consuming her.

'That dirty, eh?' he grinned.

She hit him on the arm, her mood lightening. A tiny bit. She hadn't hit that hard, had she? But Boyd had somehow dropped the pint. Smithereens of glass flew everywhere on the floor. Beer seeped into the old, scarred floorboards and people tried to get out of the way, dancing little jigs.

'I'm sorry,' Boyd said, leaping to his feet. 'So sorry.'

'It's okay,' Lottie said. 'Sit down. Don't be a lug. Here's the barman.'

Boyd sat, and she stared at him as a lad appeared, mop and brush in hand. The floor was cleaned quickly and the glass swept up. In the few minutes it took, Boyd sat like a statue on the low three-legged stool, his knees almost at his chin as he crouched forward. She noticed how sunken his cheeks were. Her heart dipped, landing somewhere in the pit of her stomach.

'Boyd?' Her voice was drowned out by the din. It was the quiz interval. Leaning into him, and a lot louder, she said, 'What's wrong?'

Instead of crouching closer to speak, he seemed to pull away. 'I broke a glass. I'll get another drink when that crowd clears away from the bar.'

'I'm not talking about your stupid drink. What's up with you?' She was almost sorry she'd posed the question. She wasn't at all sure she wanted to know the answer, because somewhere within her soul, she sensed Boyd wasn't going to tell her good news. They were engaged, though he'd yet to produce a ring. Was it another woman? No, not just when she had committed her heart to him. She felt her breath die in her throat.

'Me? *Moi*?' He smiled with mock incredulity. 'I'm as right as rain. Or snow. Or whatever the weather is deciding to do outside at the moment.'

'You sure?'

Inclining his head, he landed a quick kiss on her cheek. 'I'm grand. Honestly. I'll get that pint.'

He stood and moved to squeeze in at the bar.

She wasn't sure she believed a word he'd said. She should have protested. Probed and prodded like the detective she was to find the truth, but a moment after Boyd stood up, the door opened and Ryan Slevin walked in followed by Beth Clarke.

Transfixed, Lottie watched as they searched for a seat. Unable to find one, Beth lounged against a spare bit of wall and Ryan headed to the bar. Someone got up, put on their coat and left the pub. Beth sat on the vacant chair, directly in Lottie's line of vision.

When Boyd returned, looking a little flushed, she said, 'Did you notice Ryan Slevin at the bar?'

'No. Is he here?'

'Yes. With Beth Clarke.'

'That's not a crime.'

'I know, but—'

'They work together,' he continued. 'Don't they?'

'Yeah.'

'And they've both lost loved ones in the last day or two, so what's the big deal?'

'I never said it was a big deal.' She folded her arms. 'Jesus, Boyd, you're impossible sometimes.'

'Me? It's you who's making a song and dance about two grieving people out for a drink together.'

'Shh. I might be able to hear what they're saying.'

'Are you mad?' Boyd said. 'It's noisier in here than a school playground at break time. Enjoy your drink and chill.'

'I would if I had a drink.'

'Oh shit. I forgot to get you another.'

'I mean a drink with alcohol in it. Preferably one hundred per cent proof.' She really did want one now. Because suddenly everything seemed a little too much for her, and she wanted to experience an hour she would not remember later. An hour. Even half an hour. She'd settle for that. Yes. Definitely.

'Don't go there,' Boyd said, his voice soft but serious. 'Not now. Not ever. You're doing so well.'

'Yes, Rose.'

'You're scaring me, Lottie.' He sounded totally unconvinced by the half-smile she flashed him.

'It was just a thought. You know, one of those irrational things that pop into my head now and again.'

'I know too well.' Boyd laughed and went to buy her another bottle of water.

His laugh made her feel a little better. Maybe he wasn't hiding a woman from her somewhere over in the west. He returned with the drink and she kept her eyes on the couple just inside the door. She sipped the water, imagining it was a glass of dry white wine.

'They seem very close,' she said.

'Who?'

'Ryan and Beth.'

'Stop staring.'

'She just placed her hand on his knee, and he's put his hand over hers. He didn't try to swat it away.'

'I wouldn't swat yours away if you wanted to put it on my knee.'

'Shut up, Boyd. I'm trying to listen.'

'You're a madwoman.'

'You've said that many times before.'

'I thought you never listened to me,' he said.

'I do. Sometimes.' She kept staring at Ryan and Beth. 'I wonder if we could move closer to them.'

'Lottie, I'm finishing this pint and you're driving me home and then you're going to sort out Katie and Chloe. Forget about work. For now.'

'But this could be important.'

The pub door opened and, bending his head of white hair so that it wouldn't graze against the lintel, Colin Kavanagh entered.

In a flash, Ryan was on his feet. Before anyone could react, he was thumping and punching the solicitor and a streak of invective flew from his mouth. Lottie drew her eyes to Beth. The girl was immobile. In the next instant, Boyd was on his feet, trying to separate the two men.

Wending her way through the crowd, wondering how Boyd had managed it so quickly, Lottie joined them. Kavanagh was being held back by Boyd, while Ryan Slevin was still mouthing out at him. Lottie grabbed his arm. It didn't stop him shouting.

'You're a thieving bastard, Kavanagh. A good-for-nothing fraudster. No wonder Fiona couldn't stand you. You're a bloody fuckwit. You—'

'Now, Ryan, sit down.' Lottie put a hand on his other arm. He shrugged it off.

'Bloody guards. Never around when you need them, and then they go poking their noses in when you don't want them.' Spittle landed on Lottie's cheek. She wiped it away calmly and eventually forced Ryan to sit on a stool.

'I want him arrested. He assaulted me. I'm making a formal complaint,' Kavanagh spouted.

'Shut up,' Boyd said.

'You've been drinking,' Kavanagh said.

'I'm off duty, and it's none of your business.'

'Everything in this village is my business because I own more than half of it.'

The crowd swelled around them and men began shouting angrily. Lottie filtered out the words and concentrated on how to defuse the situation.

'I think you should go home, Mr Kavanagh.'

The tall man glanced around. Seeming to sense the hostility in the bar, he turned on his heel, dipped his head again and left.

'Phew,' Lottie gasped. 'That was close.'

'What do you mean?' Boyd said.

'I thought he might have a swing at you.'

'Chance would be a fine thing.'

She turned her attention to Ryan. 'Any more of that carry-on and you'll spend the night in a cell.'

'Kavanagh's the one who should be in a cell.'

'Why do you say that?'

'He's robbed poor Beth blind.'

Beth moved beside Ryan. 'I can talk for myself and fight my own corner. There's no need to be an arsehole, Ryan.'

'Oh really?' He looked like he was about to cry. 'This place is too jammed. I'm going home.'

'I want a word,' Lottie said.

He ignored her. 'You coming, Beth?'

Beth picked up her jacket from the floor. 'I suppose so.'

Lottie grabbed her elbow. 'Is everything okay?'

'How would it be okay? My dad blasted his head off with a shotgun and that bastard stole every penny from him. No, I'm not okay.'

'What do you mean?'

'Ask Colin Kavanagh.' Beth wrestled her arm from Lottie's grip and pushed past Ryan. Before Lottie could ask another question, Ryan had left too.

As the crowd dispersed back to their quiz and drinks, she said, 'I think I've had enough of this place.'

'Let's go,' Boyd said.

Outside, the snow had started to fall again. There was no sign of Ryan or Beth. Lottie made her way down the street to the car. Boyd caught up with her.

'You seem unusually on edge tonight,' he said.

'Well, you were very quick to jump into the middle of that row back there. I'd say you're more on edge than me.'

There was something in the way Boyd hung his head that melted her anger. She leaned into him and put her finger under his chin. The longing to be held in his arms superseded the other emotions vying for her attention; she was so lonely it hurt physically. She was the expert on knowing what lonely meant and she thought Boyd got it too. He turned from her, though, shrugging off her embrace.

'What is it?' she said.

'Now isn't a good time.' He was shaking his head as if there was something caught in his hair and he was trying to cast it away.

'What do you mean?'

He paced the length of the car then back again. 'I'm not in the right headspace.'

'Oh, I see.' But she didn't see at all. 'Would your headspace be in Galway? Some young one there keeping a bed warm for you, is there?'

'Will you listen to yourself?'

'And would you ever piss off?' She unlocked the car and sat in.

As Boyd moved around to the passenger side, she locked all the doors.

'Lottie? You're being childish. Let me in.'

She gunned the engine, pulled out of the parking space and skidded along the road. Taking a sharp left, she looked in the rear-view mirror to see Boyd fading to a dot, standing with his hands on his hips, shaking his head in dismay.

Yeah, she might have been childish, but it felt good. His floozy in Galway was welcome to him. If he'd given Lottie an engagement ring, she'd have flung it out the window.

CHAPTER THIRTY-EIGHT

Her three little boys were asleep at last. Zoe folded up Tommy and Josh's washed and dried uniforms; Zack's clothes were still in the washing machine. She welcomed the few snatched moments of peace. Moments like these were rare in her life. There were always adults or children around. Her legs felt heavy, as if the blood in her veins was lead resting around her ankles. She picked up the three blue rain jackets and went to hang them on the hall stand.

Catching sight of her reflection in the mirror, she gasped aloud. She hardly recognised herself. When had that happened? The frozen image stared back at her. Her hair was threaded with streaks of grey. Natural grey, not the new fad of hip grey that women paid a fortune for in a salon. Her eyes, so like Ryan's, were narrow streaks of tiredness and her forehead was creased with deep furrows. She hung up the boys' jackets and walked back down the hall.

In the kitchen, she opened a packet of biscuits and had chomped her way through four or five when the front door opened. Giles was home. So much for her peace.

'I'm in here,' she said, hurriedly sweeping crumbs from the table into her hand. 'There's fish stew in the pot.'

'Fish again?' He flopped onto a chair and unfolded a newspaper on the table.

'There was so much left over from yesterday, I didn't want to waste it. I know you don't like waste.' She ladled a few scoops onto a plate and switched off the stove. 'Did you hear the news?'

'I'm trying to read it, if you'd shut up.'

Zoe placed the plate at his right hand. He picked up a fork and shoved a bite into his mouth with one hand still on the newspaper.

'Ouch. That's mad hot,' he said.

'Blow on it,' she said, 'like the kids do.'

The rustle of the paper as he bunched it into a ball grated like nails on a chalkboard.

'Fuck you,' he said, throwing the paper onto the floor.

'I just swept up.' She stood her ground, though she just wanted to go upstairs, fall into bed and sleep.

'Sweep it again.'

She didn't move.

'What are you looking at?' He paused with the fork halfway to his mouth, sauce dripping onto the table. His lips were wet and flabby. While she'd been losing weight, it seemed Giles had ballooned. Must be all the butter and cream from her new recipes.

'You, Giles. I'm looking at you. You might think you can talk to Trevor and Shelly at the dance school like that, but for Christ's sake, I can't take much more of it.'

He shoved the plate away, kicked the newspaper under the table and pulled her towards him. She fell to her knees with the grip he had on her.

'You're hurting me,' she whispered.

'Good. You know how important my work is, don't you?'

'Of course I do.'

'I expect you to keep this house straight while I'm out. I don't like coming home to a pigsty.'

'I do my best.' God, why did he make her feel so worthless?

'No you don't. I actually have no clue what you do all day.'

'I've little Zack to mind, and I bring the boys to school and pick them up. Giles, please, there's something I have to talk to you about.'

'Sweep up that mess first.'

'Listen to me. I want to return to my job.' Giles had insisted on her extended maternity leave, and even though she had hated working for Colin Kavanagh in his solicitor's office, it allowed her a sense of freedom.

'What are you talking about? You can't even do a day's work at home.'

'I'm going mad here. We need the money and I really want to go back.'

'No,' he snarled.

She shot upright and, as if possessed by some alien spirit, drew her hand backwards to smack him. He caught her wrist and twisted it.

'I get enough shite at the theatre; I expect a little bit of respect, not to mention a clean house, when I get home.'

'Christy Clarke is dead,' she spat at him.

She waited for the reaction. Got one. The purple that had infused his face drained away. His eyes bulged. She could see the yellow in the corners of the whites, with veins snaking towards the pupils.

'I don't believe you.'

'He's just gone and blown his fucking head off. You know what that means?' For some reason, she was actually enjoying his discomfort, though she knew what Christy's death spelled for them.

'What?'

'We are fucked, Giles,' she spat.

'Jesus, Mary and Joseph.' He put out a hand to grasp hers, but she sprang backwards as if he had a disease. 'What are we going to do?'

'I thought, seeing as you are such an *important* person according to yourself, you might be able to come up with a plan.'

'Fuck you, Zoe.' He burst from the chair. She cowered behind her hands, but he had gone. She could see into the hall, where he grabbed his coat and was out the door, slamming it behind him.

A cry from upstairs.

'And fuck you too, Giles,' she shouted after him. 'You've only gone and wakened the boys.'

*

Steve O'Carroll sat staring at the reservations program on the computer screen. His boss would have a fit when he returned next week from Gran Canaria sporting a tan bought on the back of good sales. Well, he was going to be very disappointed. With the Slevin-Heffernan wedding cancelled, small though it was, there'd be no Christmas bonus this year. The deposit was secure, but nothing else had been paid for. The flowers, the decorations, the waiting staff and chefs. And the food going to waste; the freezers were stocked to the brim. Steve hated when that happened, but then hadn't he cancelled his own wedding? That made him think of Cara. He heard an uneasy click-click in his ears and swung around in the chair. The sound was a pair of heels walking across the floor of the empty bar.

'Anyone serving in this dive?'

He looked out through the half-open office door. No sign of his barman behind the counter. He appraised Eve Clarke's looks from his vantage point. She was one of those women who thought she was God's gift to man, when in fact she was middle-aged, caked in make-up and wearing false eyelashes. Trying too hard to shed her years, he surmised.

'Service!' she yelled, like she was in some city saloon.

She could wait.

He turned his attention back to the screen and worried his fingers through his ponytail, wondering what he was going to do.

*

Eve hadn't really wanted to go out for a drink, but the thought of Cara Dunne having been murdered next door gave her the shivers. She had slapped on her face, then dragged on a pair of white jeans and a blue blouse, forgetting she was no longer living in Spain and it was zero degrees outside.

Sitting on the high stool, she tapped a coin on the counter. When Steve O'Carroll eventually came out to serve her, she said, 'Where's your new barman?'

'No idea. What can I get you, love?'

'I'm not your love. Gin and tonic. Hendrick's if you have it.'

She watched admiringly as he bent down to get a glass. When he stood, she saw his shoulder muscles flexing beneath the tight-fit white shirt.

'Not many around tonight,' she said. Small talk. He deserved no more.

'No.'

'And no wedding crowd to tend to after that Heffernan girl was killed. Must be bad for business.'

He placed the gin and a small bottle of tonic water in front of her. 'Anything else?'

'I'm sorry about Cara,' she said, counting out coins from her purse.

'Yes, bad luck.'

'You think so?'

'What are you implying?' His eyes narrowed as he dragged the coins into his hand.

'Just thinking, you were together for a long time.'

'Not that long.' He appeared nervous, twitching his stupid pony-tail. Who did he think he was, going around like that in Ragmullin?

'Still, you must be devastated.'

'I'm not.'

'That's a bit harsh. She was a good woman. I was grateful when she told me about the vacant apartment next door to her.'

'Another two euros.'

'What?'

'You're short two euros.' He jangled the money in his hand before closing it in a fist.

'Sorry.' She searched her purse, not wanting to break a note, and found some coins wrapped up in a receipt. 'Here you go.'

He placed the money in the till and made to return to the office.

She said, 'It's a murder, you know.'

'What is?'

'Cara's death. The guards are all over the place. You can't move without bumping into one of them.'

'Really?' He came back to the bar.

She had his attention now. 'Oh yeah. Very grisly. I found the body. Awful.'

'*You* found the body?'

'I did. I'm still not the better of it.'

'Did they ask about me?'

'Who?'

'The guards.'

'Yeah. A woman detective. All legs. Too thin, if you want my opinion. Probably doesn't have time to eat. Can't remember her name now.'

'Must be that Parker one. She's a detective inspector.'

'If you say so.' Eve had little recollection of the conversation, never mind the name.

'What did she talk to you about?' More nervous twisting of the ponytail, and Eve noticed a ribbon of perspiration bubbling on his upper lip. It wasn't that warm in here, she thought.

'You'd like to know, wouldn't you?'

'I would.'

'And I'd like another one of these. On the house.'

'Hendrick's again?' Now he seemed eager to please.

She smiled, showing off her dental work. 'Sure thing.'

As she drained the gin through the black straw he'd placed in the glass, she thought she might get more than a free drink out of Steve O'Carroll tonight.

*

Trevor Toner watched the night close in on itself as he stood outside the door to his flat smoking a spliff. It had been a funny sort of day. Not funny ha-ha, just weird. If he didn't buck up and get his act together, his show might be pulled. It was shite anyhow. He had to admit his interest had disappeared out the theatre door with little Lily Heffernan. But he needed to make the show work. If it was a success, more and more parents would sign their little darlings into his classes, hoping he could transform two left feet into ten twinkle toes. He promised he would make them stars with one hand, while pocketing their cash with the other.

He looked up at the dark windows above his head and pulled up the collar of his jacket. He'd have a pint first.

He walked up Main Street until he reached the Railway Hotel. He wondered who might be working tonight. Not Steve, surely. Not after Cara's death yesterday. Then again, knowing Steve, anything was possible. He pushed open the door to the lounge bar and peered inside.

Not too many here tonight. A couple down at the end and one man on his own at the table under the window. A woman was deep in conversation with Steve at the counter. No sign of the new barman. As he took a step onto the black-tiled floor, the woman turned her head sideways.

Edging backwards, Trevor was through the doorway and out on the street before he caught his breath. As he fled, he felt like someone had walked over his grave.

*

Lily was so tired, even though it seemed like she'd slept for hours. She had no idea where she was, and she felt too weak to move her legs. She'd not heard a sound all day.

She wondered where her mummy was. Sometimes she was late picking her up, but Lily always waited for her. Never ran off home on her own or got into strange cars. Not until yesterday. But it wasn't a strange car. It wasn't a stranger. And that was what upset her the most. None of it was fair. Tears stung like needles at the back of her eyes. But she was a big girl now, and big girls weren't supposed to cry.

A fluttering sound made her hold her breath. What was that? Her heart beat against her ribcage and her stomach growled. She was hungry and couldn't remember the last time she'd eaten anything. Not proper food like her mummy cooked. A pang of something she couldn't describe hit her, and she had a terrible feeling she might not see her mummy ever again. No!

Trying to sit up, she found she could only move one arm. Her head was sore, her hair felt sticky and her mouth was dry. She had never felt so scared in all her life. Not even when Johnny Burns had pulled her hair in junior infants and spat in her orange juice and … She couldn't remember what else Johnny had done to her that first day at school, but she knew her mummy had had to buy her a new cuddly toy to get her to go in the next day. Was it Peppa or Winnie-the-Pooh? She tried hard to remember which toy she'd got because she thought it was important to remember little things like that. But she couldn't remember and that made her even sadder.

Listening, Lily heard the sound again. At least it wasn't a mouse, she thought. Her mummy hated mice and had screamed once and jumped up on a chair when one ran out of the cupboard she'd just opened. Lily thought that was so funny. Not now. She didn't want to have to jump up on a chair. Because she could not move.

The fluttering got stronger and closer, like footsteps.

Lily screamed as something soft touched her forehead.

*

In the yard, the man stood as still as the rising breeze allowed. The squeal of pigs was ear-splitting. He raised his face to the heavens, welcoming the fresh crispness of snowflakes, something to clear his palate. His body trembled as rain surrounded him in a damp misty fog.

Her car wasn't around. There were no lights on in the house. If it wasn't for the animals, the night would be silent.

Talking careful steps on the slimy cobbles, he moved to the window beside the back door. Peered into the darkness. Nothing. Maybe he'd go inside and wait for her to return. As he walked towards the door, the darkness was lit up by the shimmer of lights from the front of the house. He listened. The thrust of an engine, gears changing down, the shriek of brakes.

She was home.

He felt a stirring in his groin.

She had the most beautiful hair.

Long and shiny.

Beth Clarke was just who he needed.

CHAPTER THIRTY-NINE

Lottie idled the car outside her mother's house. The lights were on. Rose was still up. Or perhaps it was Leo. She had to talk with him. To see why he was colluding with her daughters behind her back. She had to do something to forget about Boyd. Switching off the engine, she got out of the car and found the key to the door.

Inside, the sound of laughter echoed. Damn you, Leo Belfield, she thought. How can you get on with my mother while I have to wade through a battlefield to have a normal conversation with her? She shook the thoughts out of her head and pushed open the door.

'Hello,' she said.

Leo stood up and pulled out a chair for her. Ignoring it, Lottie sat on another.

'What brings you out on this miserable night?' Rose said, her arms folded as she sat on an easy chair by the stove.

For some inexplicable reason, Lottie felt an anxious twist in her chest. She recognised it as jealousy. She was jealous of the friendship that had blossomed between Rose and Leo. Leo, who was not Rose's blood relative but who was Lottie's half-brother. All her father's doing.

'Just passing,' she lied. 'When are you flying home, Leo?'

'In a few days.'

'Really?'

'Yeah.'

She noticed how he'd developed an Irish accent in the weeks he'd been in Rose's company. She wondered what other habits he'd picked up from her mother.

'It's wonderful that Leo's agreed to accompany the girls.' Rose beamed a smile so bright Lottie thought she might pass out from the dazzling false teeth.

She felt the blood drain from her skin. It was all Rose's doing. The girls going to New York for Christmas. It had to be. But she wasn't going to give her the satisfaction of admitting she knew this.

'Are you going straight back to work?' she said to Leo.

'I'm taking another month or two off. My lieutenant is okay with it.'

'Good for you.' Lottie could taste the sarcasm dripping from her words. 'Any holidays planned?'

'I'm going to spend some time showing Katie and Chloe a good old New York time.'

'Like fuck you are!' Lottie shot out of the chair.

'Charlotte Fitzpatrick Parker! Language.' Rose put out a hand. 'Sit down.'

'No, I won't.' She leaned towards Leo. 'What are you playing at, eh? Trying to wheedle your way into my life through my girls, is that it?'

'I've no idea what you're talking about,' Leo said.

'Of course you do. First you try to buy me off with Farranstown House, and then you go behind my back contriving for my family to be decimated at Christmas. What game are you playing?'

'I honestly don't know what you're talking about. Rose said it would be a good idea.'

Lottie turned to her mother. 'You're never happy unless you're controlling my life. Well listen here, the pair of you. *I* am Katie and Chloe's mother, and I say if they can travel and who they can travel with. Not you.'

'Sit down and calm down.' Rose stood, pointing to the chair.

Lottie brushed by her. 'I've had a bitch of a day, and so far, a bitch of a week, and I can do without conspirators conniving behind my back.'

Without a backward glance, she ran from the house, wondering why on earth everyone and her mother was against her. Rain fell on her head like a dark, damp shadow. With her hand on the car door handle, she shivered uncontrollably. Were things about to get worse? Surely not. But then again, she was Lottie Parker and her protective shield against evil had worn away to a fine filament.

Driving home, blinded by tears of frustration, she craved a friendly arm around her shoulder, a tender kiss on her cheek and maybe a few comforting words whispered in her ear. Boyd? No, she'd burned that bridge tonight.

She let herself into her house, in darkness and silence. Everyone was asleep. She went to the cupboard in the kitchen. Grabbed the bottle of wine. All night she'd been thinking of opening it. Downing it. Wallowing in the acrid tang of it. She knew what it tasted like. She lifted the bottle to her nose. Inhaled the sharp scent she knew was there without opening it. She wavered. Her hands trembled.

Could she live with herself if she drank it?

Could she unravel all that she'd built up, in one night of weakness? Could she hell.

*

Cynthia Rhodes was like a dog with the proverbial bone. She held the bottle of red in one hand and knocked with the other. As she waited for the door to be opened, she tapped her boot on the ground.

'Hello, handsome,' she said, wriggling in past him. 'Fancy a nightcap?' She took a corkscrew out of her pocket. 'I came prepared.'

'Jesus, Cynthia, do you know the time?'

'I learned it in primary school, so yes, I do.'

She smirked, put the bottle on the small coffee table and handed him the opener. Taking off her leather jacket, she kept her eyes on his and followed his gaze as they travelled over her sheer white blouse. She smiled as his mouth opened. Wearing the red bra beneath it had been a class move, even if it was a cliché and two years old from Primark.

'Are you going to open that or offer it up?' she said.

'Eh, em …'

'Let me do it,' she said, and took the corkscrew from his hand. 'What about some nice music? To put us in the mood.'

'I thought you only came here for information,' he said, and sat on the couch.

'Oh yes, I want that too.'

'I think you need to stop persecuting Lottie. It doesn't look good for the force.'

'You mean she's not making the force look good, darling.'

'Honestly, you should just attend the press conferences and give up doorstepping her.'

She didn't like his tone. They were losing the mood she'd worked to create. Inching closer to him, she handed over a glass.

'Let's not talk about Lottie Parker.'

'Let's not,' he said.

She sipped her drink and thought about how she was going to get the information she wanted.

But she knew.

It was a long night that did not bring her some reward.

*

With the bottle in hand, Lottie checked her phone as she walked from the kitchen to the sitting room. Missed call. She squinted at it. Maybe she needed spectacles. No way could she afford them. She recalled the conversation with Leo, the prick, about Farranstown House, and wondered about the length of time it would take the money to hit her account once she signed the papers. If she signed.

The phone vibrated again. She answered.

'Lottie, I'm sorry it's so late, but I wanted to check in with you. You know. To see how you're coping.'

'Father Joe.' She flicked on a lamp. 'Why do you think I can't cope?'

'I didn't say that.' There was a smile in his voice. 'I just thought you looked a bit harried yesterday. I care for you … for your well-being and all that.'

'And all that.' She laughed and sat on the couch. Placed the bottle in the centre of the coffee table and stared at it.

'So how are you?'

'I'm fine.' I'm not, she thought, but she didn't want to tell him that. He was too nice. Too caring. A good friend. She couldn't confide in him right now. The unopened bottle mocked her.

'How is Boyd?'

'Why are you asking about him?' She wished she'd brought in the corkscrew. Wished the bottle had a screw top.

'You're full of questions with no answers.' His voice was carefree. No admonishment.

'Answer one for me,' she said, delaying the urge to drink. She pulled her legs up on the sofa and nestled her ankles beneath her.

'I'll try.'

'What can you tell me about Father Curran?'

'Not much,' he said without preamble. 'He's been around a lot longer than I have.'

'I gathered that.'

'He's a good man, Lottie.'

'I never said he wasn't.'

'You implied you don't like him just by asking about him.' He paused, and she waited in the silence for him to continue. 'He's good to the sick. He visits the abbey.'

'Anyone in particular that he visits?'

'Now that you mention it, whenever I've stepped in, there is one patient who always asks after him.'

'Sister Augusta?'

'Yes. She's of his vintage, so perhaps they knew each other before she was hospitalised.'

'Was he always based in this diocese? Do you know where Sister Augusta hails from?'

'Lottie, what are you getting at?'

'I don't know, to be honest.'

'I can nose around.'

'Thanks. Father Joe—'

'Joe.'

'Joe, do you think Father Curran could have had anything to do with either Cara Dunne or Fiona Heffernan's deaths?'

'Wow, that's a big leap. I informed him of Cara's death. The bishop asked me to do it. Father Curran used to be on the board of management of Cara's school.'

'How long ago?'

'I think he retired about a year ago.'

'Can you find out more?' Lottie said.

'I'll snoop around.'

'Thanks. Did you know either Cara or Fiona?'

There was a long pause. 'I meet many people.'

'Fiona was a nurse at the abbey. Surely you saw her there?'

'What difference would it make to your investigation?'

Why was he being evasive? Or was it just her exhausted brain seeing things that were not there? 'I thought you could give me an insight into the type of person she was. I need to find out why someone killed her.'

'I'll rack my brains and get back to you. She was a good nurse and a nice person. That's what I know from the few times I ... met her. Anyway, you're sure you're okay?'

'Boyd asked me to marry him,' she blurted out.

'Wow. Can't say I didn't see that coming.'

'I eventually said yes, but now ...'

'You're not sure?'

'I think he might be seeing someone else. I don't know what to do.'

'Why don't you talk to him about it?'

'It's not that easy. What would you do?'

'I've never been in that position.'

She listened to the long pause, his breathing soft and gentle.

'Do you ever have doubts, Joe?'

'I went through a crisis of faith once and had to take a sabbatical. It helped.'

'The time you found out about your mother?'

'Before that. About eight or nine years ago. I was going through a difficult time. I left the priesthood for a year.'

'What did you do?' she said. 'Sow your wild oats?'

'I had a good time. Met some nice women, if you want to know. But I missed the Church. I returned refreshed.'

'That's good.'

'You never make anything easy for yourself. Talk to Boyd. No point in beating yourself up when you don't have the whole picture.'

'Thanks, Joe.'

'I wasn't being cynical.'

'I wasn't either. Honestly, thank you. It's good to talk.'

'You'd better get some sleep. I'll see what I can find out.'

'About Boyd?'

'No, about Father Curran,' he laughed.

'Oh, right. Thanks. Goodnight, Joe.'

She sat with the phone in her hand and thought about the conversation she'd just had. But her mind was like a reel of unconnected wires. She couldn't find the end of one to help unravel the lot. Just like my life, she thought, her eyelids weighing heavy.

CHAPTER FORTY

He walked around in a tight circle. Cold air followed in his wake. The windows rattled as rain pelted against them. The snowstorm had turned and the rain didn't seem to be letting up any time soon.

Reaching across the bench, he pulled the stand towards him. His table. His worktop. He chuckled to himself as he took a mouthful of coffee. It had cooled sufficiently so as not to burn his sensitive mouth. Setting the mug down, he thought that perhaps he should buy a fancy coffee machine. One of those ones that used little pods. The coffee always smelled nicer out of them. But he knew he could never afford a proper one. A jar of instant and a kettle would have to do.

He stretched his legs and flexed his ankles one way then the other. He needed the blood to flow more freely before he began. He'd once had a Fitbit. It was good to keep him abreast of his health and activity. All the kids had them. An accessory, as much as their phones. But he'd got rid of it. He didn't trust anything that could monitor your movements, with or without your consent.

Settling on the wooden chair at his bench, he pinned the wire into the stand with the latest specimen before him. Carefully he opened the plastic bag and extracted the prize.

Ah, it was as beautiful as the others.

He took up the wire figurine and began his work.

It never left me. That first day at school and what that teacher did to me. And the next day, and the next. It went on and on.

The second day was far worse than the first. I remember it was raining and none of the kids could go outside for the lunch break. I was able to swallow the banana, the only thing in my lunch box. I'd have loved some orange squash to wash it down, but I had none and no one offered me a sip of theirs. A loud snip caused me to glance towards the head of the room. She stood there, beckoning me with the scissors. I looked around, hoping she was silently calling someone else. She caught my eye.

'Yes, you. Up here. Now!'

The sound of munching and soft chatter died away with my footsteps as I approached her desk.

This time she pulled me to her side and made me face the room.

'No one comes into my classroom with lice in their hair. Nits multiply by the millions. I don't want to go home scratching my head for the weekend.' She held up the scissors, the steel glinting under the light bulb. I felt the coldness against the back of my neck; felt the tug of hair on my scalp. And I heard the snip as she hacked at my hair. Uneven chunks fell to the floor and I tried in vain to hold my cries in my throat. The other kids laughed. One loud burst of noise. I dug my hands in my trouser pockets to keep them from flying to my ears.

I knew that one day someone would pay for it. People think little children don't remember things that far back in their lives, but I can say that it is those incidents that have defined me. Her actions have moulded me into what I am today.

Oh, I kept the feelings dormant for a long time, but it was the humiliation at the hands of another that awakened the latent need in my being. The need to seek redemption. People will flounder around like goldfish in a bowl looking for the answer. And when they find it, the revelation will come too late. That's when they will realise they are swimming in a bowl that's too small for them. They will know that I can watch them through the smeared glass. I will have the rod out and waiting. Not to catch them. Oh no, that would be too simple. I have better plans for them. For all of them.

They will never again humiliate another human being.

They will never break another vow.

Fucking goldfish.

CHAPTER FORTY-ONE

Friday

The night felt like it had been one long day, as Lottie waited for the sun to come up. It defied her by refusing to appear. Rain had fallen incessantly during the night, and everywhere was wet but still bitterly cold.

Sitting on the damp kerbstone, she pulled her knees up to her chin like a child. Probably get flu, she thought, but she'd worry about that when or if it happened. At least she had overcome the episode with the wine. Had shoved the bottle into the furthest corner of the cupboard. Her sleep had been restless but she'd remained sober. Thanks to Father Joe.

Her husband, Adam, smiled at her from the engraved photograph on the headstone. The plot looked bare; even the birds had deserted the branches overhead. She'd come to wallow in the silence. To escape the confines of her house. Her family. To hide in the shade of the trees. But she'd forgotten, with the cemetery expansion, that most of the trees had been cut down. Without their shelter, an east wind cut across the field, blitzing the back of her head.

She pulled her jacket tighter around her and closed her eyes, feeling strangely comforted in this place of the dead. It was as if she had stepped out of her own reality and inhabited a few moments of existence in another universe. One where she could still talk to Adam and sit in the silence of her own thoughts. She hoped she was doing the right thing. Moving on. The drizzle became a downpour and her mind drifted out of the past because she knew she had too much to do in the present.

She stood, pressed a finger to her lips and then to the photo. She meandered towards the gate, up past the plot of little angels, glanced at new graves marked with wooden crosses, mounds of freshly dug clay turning to mud under the precipitation. The recently deceased, leaving their grieving families behind. Oh God, Lily, she thought as her heart thudded. She had to bring the little girl home, and not in a white box.

And after abandoning him in Ballydoon last night, she had to face Boyd.

'What are you doing in there, Kirby?' Lottie ran her hand through her hair and her fingers snagged in the damp, matted mess. She thought she might actually look worse than Kirby did. She banged twice on the car window before it whirred down.

'Oh, good morning, boss,' he said. 'Sorry, I must have nodded off.'

'At this hour of the morning? Is there something you're not telling me?' She spied dried ketchup in his hair, and the odour coming from the car was of unwashed flesh.

'Not really. I'll be inside soon. Just need to do a few things first.'

'What on earth could you be doing out here, for God's sake?' She noticed that the back of his car was piled high. Pillows, a duvet and what looked like a suit jacket. He couldn't be living in his car, could he?

'Just give me a few minutes.' He tried to straighten his tie, and she noticed he was still wearing yesterday's shirt.

'As long as you're okay.'

'I'm fine.' The window whirred up and closed tightly.

Lottie walked away. She had enough problems without getting involved in Kirby's domestic woes. As she keyed in the code to gain access to the office, she already knew she would get involved. Kirby had been through so much in the last six months. Losing Gilly was tough; she knew grief could eat you up and spit you out just as quick. He needed someone to watch out for him; a kind word was sometimes all it took. Despite that, she had a feeling Kirby had spiralled well past the kind-word stage.

Boyd was sitting at his desk, head down, reading a report. Should she ignore him and sidestep into her own office? Or meet the beast head on?

He did not lift his head. So, he was pissed off.

'Did you get home okay?' she couldn't resist asking.

'No thanks to you.' His head remained bowed. 'I had to call a taxi and it cost me a fortune.'

'If it's any consolation, I'm sorry for leaving you there.'

'You should be.'

'Right.' She took off her jacket and went to hang it up in her office. 'I take it my apology is not accepted.'

'Take it any way you like.'

She returned to his desk, leaned on it with both hands. 'I got mad at you. That's all. You've been acting indifferent recently. Skiving off to Galway. You won't tell me why. Have you a girlfriend there and are afraid to dump me, is that it? What else am I to think?'

When he looked up at her, she stepped back. His usually bright hazel eyes were dull, circled with dark rings; his face was dragged down by his grey hue. Had he too slept in his car? Or was he missing his new girlfriend? Stop, Lottie, she told herself.

'You left me out in that godforsaken place, Lottie, so I really don't care what you think.' He turned his attention back to whatever he'd been reading.

She wanted to bitch back. To say something smart or even hurtful, but her tongue stuck to the roof of her mouth, like it did when something scared the life out of her. And in this moment, Boyd was scaring her. She pivoted and marched into her office, slamming the door behind her and slumping onto her chair. Boyd and Kirby were acting so far outside normality, it was truly frightening. Something was going on. Something she was excluded from. And Lottie did not like being on the outside looking in.

Her desk phone rang.

'I hope you're having a better morning than I'm having, Jane.' Lottie tapped her computer awake.

The pathologist had her official voice on full volume. 'I've carried out some preliminary analysis on the hair specimens found on the bodies.'

'What did you find?' Lottie sat up straighter now.

'I've no DNA matches or anything like that. It's dead hair. But I can tell you this. The size of the specimens we have does not match the amount taken from the bodies.'

'Explain, please.' Lottie furrowed her brow.

'It's obvious that more hair was cut from Cara Dunne's scalp than that which you found on Fiona Heffernan's person.'

Lottie digested this information. 'Does that mean what I think it means?'

'If you haven't found the hair anywhere else, it could mean the killer is keeping trophies.'

'Bastard. I mean, thanks, Jane. Anything else?'

'That's it for now.'

Lottie hung up and considered this new turn of events. It was all so bizarre.

Before she could go check what the rest of the team were up to, Kirby opened the door and edged into her office like a sheepish schoolboy.

'Sorry about earlier, boss.' His face folded into a hangdog expression.

'Are you living in your car?' Lottie had had enough of pussyfooting around.

He took a deep breath before blowing out his cheeks. No words were forthcoming.

'Sit down,' she said. He did. 'Tell me what's going on.'

'It's like this, boss … You see, after Gilly died, things went a bit haywire for a while. Truth be known, things were skewed before then. I missed a few payments. Then the landlord decided he was selling the apartment. I hadn't a leg to stand on, so to speak, because I'd not paid the rent. On Monday, I ended up out on the street. Or in my car, to be exact.'

'You could have told us. We're your friends. I'm sure someone would put you up until you find somewhere. Or a hotel. Did you think of that?'

'I didn't want to go begging to any of you. Anyway, I'm broke.'

'How can you be broke? You earn a decent wage here, and all that overtime … You do claim your overtime, don't you? Even though I know the super despises it. Messes up his budgets.'

Kirby shrugged. 'I couldn't get my head together. You know. Drinking, and placing a few bob on the horses. I don't have much left at the end of the day.'

'Starting now, Kirby, you're getting your shit together. No detective of mine is going to be found sleeping in his car.' When she saw the look of hurt on his face, she knew what it had sounded like. A superior officer worried about the image of the force. 'Please don't take that the wrong way. I mean it as a friend.'

'Thanks, boss.'

'If none of the others can help you, I might have a spare room next week. My girls are talking about going to New York for Christmas, and—'

'Oh God, no, I can't accept a room from you, even in the short term. I'll have a word with Boyd. He's got a good couch.'

'Good luck with him,' Lottie growled. 'He's been like a bear with a sore head all week. What's up with him?'

Kirby shook his head. 'He is very moody. But he hasn't confided in me. Something might be up with his mother or sister. He's over in Galway a lot more than he used to be. Do you want me to ask him about it?'

'No.' But she did want to know what was going on in Boyd's life.

'I may look like an eejit, but I'm not one,' Kirby said. 'I won't go asking him straight out. Maybe over a pint, or a coffee. I'll find a way.'

'Thanks. And the offer of a room stands. For now, find somewhere other than your car to live.'

'Yes. And thank you.' Kirby bowed his head like he'd just had his confession heard in a claustrophobic box and was anxious to escape to fresh air to do his penance.

She hated to say it, but she had to. 'Kirby, you missed the photograph of Lily in the locker room.'

'I know. I'm sorry. I'll work twice as hard on the case. I promise.'

'You do that. You can go.' She didn't know which of her emotions was dominant at the moment. Anger at Boyd or pity for Kirby. She fought to untangle everything going on in her head.

When she looked up, Kirby had returned with a sheet of paper.

'Sorry, boss.'

'Go ahead.'

He sat down and passed the page over. 'Last night, before I left, I had a read of the *Tribune* article by Beth Clarke about Robert Brady's suicide.'

'What about it?'

'You can have a read yourself. I highlighted a few things that might interest you.'

'Summarise it.'

'Well, Robert Brady was known locally as Bob the Builder. He used to work for a building firm before it went bust, and then did odd jobs on his own. I got to thinking … Cara Dunne.'

'You found a link to Cara? What is it?'

'The belt used to strangle her. Remember it had the initials carved into the leather?'

'Yes.'

'I think that might be BB for Robert Brady. Bob Brady. Or Bob the Builder.'

'I see where you're going with this. Get the belt checked against Brady's DNA and fingerprints, if they're on file. We need to search his home and belongings.'

'That's the problem.'

'Why is it a problem?'

'Brady was a bit like me in a roundabout way. He'd lost his home to the bank. He was living rough for a few months before he died.'

'Have we any way to trace *where* he was living?'

'I'll see what I can do.'

'Where are his possessions?'

'I'll try to find out.'

'Do that, and locate someone who knew him. Friends, family – anyone who might have cared for him or his stuff.'

'Sure thing.' Kirby stood.

'Ring the mortuary. Find out what happened to Brady's body. And if he has anything to do with this mess, let's hope he hasn't been cremated.'

'Will do.'

'And Kirby?'

'Yes, boss?'

'Good work.'

Once she was alone, Lottie read through Beth Clarke's article. The writing was tender and caring. Not one word of coldness or judgement. She was struck by a moment of clarity. Beth Clarke had known Robert Brady.

CHAPTER FORTY-TWO

Lottie led the early-morning team meeting in a daze. She wanted to get on the road and talk with Beth about Brady. First, though, she needed to make sure the team knew what they had to do.

McKeown was first in with his news. Which turned out to be no news really.

'You asked me to follow up on Cara Dunne and Fiona Heffernan's online presences. Both had deactivated their social media accounts. Cara in the last three months and Fiona a year ago. Their mobile phone providers gave me listings of their calls and texts.'

'Well?'

'The call histories are a bit scant. The last call Fiona made was to Ryan on the morning she was murdered. There is also one call around lunchtime. Unregistered number, but we're trying to trace it. Other than that, nothing unusual. Cara's phone has numerous calls to Steve O'Carroll. None of which appear to have been answered. No texts. It's possible she or someone else wiped the phone clean.'

'Anything online? Emails?'

'Just a submission of a sick note for Cara to her principal. Nothing on Fiona's.'

'They were quiet women then, in the world of social media.'

'I've read over all the statements from neighbours and any friends I could locate. Both women's movements in the days leading up to their deaths were normal. Nothing out of the ordinary sticks in anyone's minds.'

'When did Steve O'Carroll last have contact with Cara?'

'He says it was weeks ago. Haven't found anyone to dispute that.'

'And Fiona? Was there anything unusual in her relationship with Ryan or Colin Kavanagh that anyone noticed?

'There's a nurse at the abbey. The man who found her body.'

'Alan Hughes,' Lottie said.

'Yeah, that guy,' McKeown said. 'He says Fiona was very distracted for the last few weeks. He put it down to wedding nerves at first, but after he found her body, he thought about it again. He tried to pinpoint when her mood changed from excitement about the wedding to what he called "manic behaviour".'

'Did he pinpoint it?'

'He says it was about three weeks ago. She became flustered at work. Didn't want to tend Sister Augusta. And whenever the priest was doing his rounds, Fiona was nowhere to be found.'

'Three weeks ago,' Lottie said. 'That's when Robert Brady died.'

'He was found just over two weeks ago,' Kirby said.

'The pathologist said he was dead for a week before his body was discovered.' She looked at Brady's photograph on the board. 'Because Kirby thinks it was his belt that was found around Cara Dunne's neck, and because a lock of hair was found on his person, Brady's death is definitely suspicious.'

'Jesus, boss, we have enough to be getting on with,' Sam McKeown whined.

Lottie ignored him and thought of the priest's changing demeanour when she'd mentioned Brady's name. 'I believe Father Michael Curran could be a link in these murders.'

'How?' McKeown wasn't giving up easily.

'He gave Cara Dunne a reference for her job ten years ago. He met with Fiona about her wedding and also saw her regularly at the abbey. That is, until she started to avoid him.'

'Maybe she was avoiding him because of his attitude to her being an unmarried mother?' Boyd offered into the mix.

'She'd been an unmarried mother eight years at that stage, so I doubt anything the priest said about it could have upset her too much.' Lottie looked to McKeown. 'What's the status of the investigation into Lily's disappearance?'

'CCTV hasn't turned up anything unusual. The lads are now looking at the dash-cam footage that was handed in after a further appeal.'

'Wasn't Gaol Street cordoned off to traffic?' Lottie said.

'Yeah, but cars were still able to cut through the car park at the side of the theatre and travel down the hill out of town.'

'Right, keep an eye on that.'

'Will do. Oh, and Colin Kavanagh has been on radio and television bad-mouthing us while appealing for the return of his daughter. He's offered a reward.'

'I heard,' Lottie said.

'We have no evidence that Lily was abducted,' Kirby said. 'Now the loonies are out in force, blocking the phone lines.'

Lottie said, 'I think it's better to have Kavanagh on the airwaves than knocking on my door.' But she was worried. Lily had been missing too long. 'Could she have wandered towards the canal or the river?'

'The canal is frozen over,' McKeown said, 'but we've had it and the river checked. No joy.'

'Keep me informed of any developments,' Lottie said. 'Lily's disappearance must be linked to her mother's death, so we have to make headway on Fiona's murder.'

'Yes, boss,' McKeown said.

'Anyone got anything else to add?'

Head shakes and murmurs greeted her. 'Right. I want Colin Kavanagh interviewed in connection with Christy Clarke. And I want the belt identified conclusively. First, though, I'm going to chat with Beth Clarke.'

With Boyd still in a strop, Lottie headed out to Ballydoon on her own.

As she drove, slush washed along the roadside and the rain beat a tattoo on her windscreen. Branches that had been laden with snow were now bare and black, and the landscape was decidedly greyer as she sped along the narrow road into the village.

Brennan's Pub had its doors and windows shuttered. The corner shop was open; clear plastic covered bales of briquettes and gas cylinders. Crime-scene tape still hung around Clarke's Garage with a lone drowned-looking uniformed officer standing guard.

She still had to receive word from the pathologist on whether there was anything suspicious about Christy Clarke's death. Making a mental note to follow up once she was back at the office, she turned left before the entrance to the abbey and drove to the farm.

Beth's blue Volkswagen Golf was parked haphazardly in the yard. Lottie pulled up behind it. Rain and mud flowed under her boots when she got out of her car, and the air was foul-smelling. That stalled her for a moment until she spotted the large sheds and heard the animals squealing. She was immediately transported back to a year ago, when she'd stood in a similar yard where a man had met his death through the blades of a slurry agitator. Shrugging off the shiver that ran through her, she approached the back door, the obvious door to try when in the countryside.

After a second burst of knocks, it still went unanswered. Looking all around, she noted a well-worn pathway. She walked along it until she reached the hedge. Beyond, through the spills of rain, she had a direct line of sight towards the roof of the abbey. And in between, the wooded area with the eerie-looking white statues. Was this where someone had been standing a couple of evenings ago, while Fiona Heffernan lay dead on the ground beside the abbey? It seemed likely. Had it been Christy Clarke she'd seen, or his daughter? Perhaps even someone else?

As the rain stung her face, she tightened the hood of her jacket, shielding herself against the sharp rain, and turned away.

'Oh my God!' she exclaimed. 'You shouldn't creep up on people like that.'

The kitchen was neat and tidy. Lottie felt like having a mug of tea or coffee to warm her up, but Beth didn't offer anything. They sat at the large wooden table across from each other.

'I'm sorry for scaring you, but you were trespassing on my father's property. Although I suppose that's not strictly true now.'

Beth's eyes were red-rimmed and her hair, equally red, was wild and loose. Lottie could see the young woman was wound up so tightly that at any second she could unravel and spring in all directions. Her job was to ensure she learned the truth from Beth. Experience had taught her that truth was usually revealed in twists and turns, and more often than not, it was smothered in lies.

'Explain what you mean,' she said, smiling kindly.

'It's difficult for me to talk about it. My last image of my father, which I'll have for the rest of my life, is a grotesque mask of blood and flesh. That's not right, is it?'

'I'm sorry you had to find him. No daughter should have to see that,' Lottie said. 'I know exactly how you feel.'

'Do you?' Beth fiddled with a crumb on the table. 'You must see some sights in your job. I'm sure nothing shocks you.'

'Everything shocks me. Inhumanity comes in many forms, not necessarily personified by visible violence, but the things I see don't harden me to the trauma families have to go through after a death.' She paused, surprised to see Beth listening intently. 'What did you mean a moment ago?'

'It's Colin Kavanagh. It's all his fault. That's the reason why Ryan went for him in the pub last night.'

'What did he do?'

'I'm not sure. I haven't had time to go through Dad's paperwork, but he was here yesterday when I got home from Zoe's house. Sitting out there at Dad's desk.' She pointed to the door that led to the rest of the house. 'He had the cheek to say he owned all of our assets, including this house.' A cry broke from Beth's throat and tears threatened at the corners of her eyes.

'Really? Do you think that's true?'

'It could be. He was Dad's solicitor, as far as I know, and Dad was acting very strangely lately. I told you all this yesterday. It kind of makes sense now. I think he may have signed everything over to Colin Kavanagh. What I can't get my head around is why. I don't believe it was because of my mother, like Mr Kavanagh said.'

'Your mother? Eve Clarke?'

Beth nodded.

'What did Mr Kavanagh say about her?'

Beth abandoned the crumb and pinched the bridge of her nose with her finger and thumb, as if she was trying to remember the exact words. 'He said Dad didn't want my mother getting her hands on his money. But Dad never voiced that concern to me. Never. That's why I don't believe it.'

'Leave Mr Kavanagh to me, Beth. I'll talk to him, and when I find out the truth, I'll tell you. No need for Ryan or anyone to be throwing punches. Okay?'

'Okay.' Beth dropped her hand from her face and fiddled with the crumb again until it disintegrated between her fingers. She glanced up, her eyes full of grief and fear.

Lottie felt a twinge in her heart. 'Is something else worrying you?'

'Isn't it enough to have my father kill himself and that Fiona's dead? No explanation for either death. I'm a journalist, but I'm also the daughter of one of those victims and a friend to the other. I want answers.'

'I've just told you, I will let you know.'

'Right. In about six months, when there's an inquest.' Beth's lip curled with derision.

'I'm warning you, Beth, don't go snooping. Too many people have died already, and a little girl has disappeared.'

'Poor Lily. Inspector, do you think the deaths are connected?'

Lottie didn't answer. She thought about the wedding dresses and the locks of hair. Other than that, there was nothing concrete to link the victims to each other. So why had they been targeted by a killer? She still had no confirmation as to whether any hair had been shorn from Christy Clarke. She shivered at the thought that the evidence might have been obliterated by the gunshot. She needed the post-mortem results. And she was haunted by the fact that eight-year-old Lily was still missing.

They sat without saying a word, rain beating against the window, the pigs squealing and crows cawing loudly outside. Was this the time to bring up Robert Brady?

Beth said, 'You know about Robert Brady, I suppose.'

Serendipity, Lottie thought. 'Yes. He was found hanging in the forest by the lake. Near here, wasn't it?'

'Not far from where Colin Kavanagh lives,' Beth added, her lip curled. 'You know Robert did some work on that barn Kavanagh bought?'

'Did he?'

'Yeah. And he worked on Ryan's cottage. Then the poor sod ended up living in his van. That's so unfair.'

'Did you know Robert?' Lottie asked, thinking she must get the team to follow up on his living arrangements. She studied the young woman's face intently. 'Please, Beth, I need to know if I should be looking into his death.'

'You haven't enough to be looking into?' The curled lip returned.

'I'm trying to establish facts. Following the evidence, tracking clues, investigating victims' lives. That's police work.'

'A bit like journalists.' A half-smile, lined with sadness, broke on Beth's face. The effect lifted her whole demeanour and her eyes lost their emptiness momentarily.

'If there is anything you think might be suspicious about Robert's death, then I need to know.'

Beth stood. 'Would you like a cup of tea?'

She did, but not now. 'The tea can wait.'

The young woman sighed, sat down and found another crumb to play with. Lottie counted the seconds in the silence.

With her elbows on the table, one shoulder raised as if cradling her head, Beth concentrated on the crumb as she spoke.

'I liked Robert. He was one of those inoffensive people. A bit simple, my dad called him. But he wasn't. Not really. He was clever with his hands. Always making things. He was a great builder. He was even known as Bob the Builder. You know, after the cartoon character? He never went anywhere without his builder's belt. Always showing off his work tools. Lads made fun of him, and girls laughed at him. I just felt sorry for him.'

'Did you befriend him?'

Beth blushed. 'I did, in a way. Though he must have been more Ryan's or Zoe's age than mine.' She started to cry.

'What's the matter, Beth?' Lottie reached out and took the girl's hand in her own. 'You can tell me.'

'I'm not sure I can.'

'If you want me to keep it between us, I will do my best. Until such time I think it might have a bearing on the other deaths. Okay?'

Beth sniffed away her tears and rubbed her nose on the end of her sleeve, childlike. 'The company Robert worked for folded, and he only had odd jobs here and there. The bank took his house. His self-worth disintegrated. Can you imagine what that can do to a person? To wake up every morning and only have a van to live in; to have nothing to look forward to. And you know what? I might have no father. No home, if Kavanagh is telling the truth.' She smiled ruefully. 'But at least I have my job.'

'And you have your mother.'

'Don't mention that woman. She abandoned me. She's dead to me, corny as that sounds.'

'Tell me about Robert,' Lottie coaxed.

Beth shook her head, but after a few seconds, she relented. 'I met him when he was doing some work at Ryan's cottage. He was polite, but quiet in himself. It struck me as odd that Ryan didn't appear to like him. Made him redo all the skirting boards, saying they were shoddy. That kind of thing.'

'If Ryan didn't like him, why did he engage him to work for him?'

'It was Fiona. She recommended him.'

'Fiona knew Robert too?'

'She must have done. Maybe it was because of the great job he did converting Kavanagh's barn. Have you seen it? The house? It's amazing.'

Lottie grimaced at the memory of the breaking-and-entering escapade. 'Yeah, I've seen it. You told me previously you thought Fiona left Colin Kavanagh because he was too old for her. Is there any other reason?' She knew she was changing direction in her line of questioning, but it was something she needed to know.

'Maybe money wasn't everything to her. If he's so obnoxious in public, who knows what he's like behind closed doors.'

'Do you think Robert might have known Cara Dunne?' Lottie said. Beth opened her mouth to speak, then shut it again. 'Come on, Beth, help me out here.'

'I don't know if he knew her or not.'

'Did he ever go by the initials BB?'

She shrugged. 'As I said, some people called him Bob the Builder.'

'Anything else you want to tell me about him?'

'If he hadn't been homeless, I think his death would have been investigated more thoroughly. Vulnerable people are easily forgotten – by the authorities and people in general. Easy targets to whitewash out of your consciousness. I'm not convinced Robert was ...' Beth paused. 'I don't think he'd gone far enough ... to kill himself.'

There was something else. Something she was holding back. Lottie tried again. 'What are you not telling me, Beth?'

'I've said enough.' She stood up suddenly.

'When did you last speak to Robert?'

'Ages ago. When will Dad's body be released for burial?'

'I'll check when I get back to the office and let you know.' Lottie stared at her. 'How well did you actually know Robert?'

'Not well enough, obviously.'

'Any idea where his van is?'

'Try the caravan park at Lough Doon. The day he died, he had to get out there somehow, hadn't he? Can you leave now?'

'One final thing. Will you go through your father's paperwork to see if you can help me confirm what Kavanagh said is true?'

'Okay.' Beth held the door open and the rain splashed inside. 'Can I ask you something?'

'Sure.' Lottie zipped up her jacket.

'What do you think has happened to Lily?'

'I'm trying to find out.'

'I'll see if I can discover anything that might help.'

'Beth?'

'What?'

'You be careful.' Lottie stepped out into the deluge.

CHAPTER FORTY-THREE

Beth stood at the window and watched the detective making a call in her car. Who was she contacting, and why? Had Beth said something she shouldn't have? She replayed the conversation in her head. No, there was nothing that had given anything away. If the detective found out things in her own way, Beth had nothing to fear. Then she remembered the warning to be careful. Could she be in danger?

She shivered, though the kitchen was warm. Icicles of foreboding trickled down her spine and flew around to her abdomen. She felt like someone had dunked her into a barrel of freezing cold water. With trembling hands, she slid a bobbin from her wrist and whipped back her hair at the nape of her neck.

As she turned away from the window, she missed the shadow passing by.

In the living room, she sat at her father's desk and began the task of trying to understand what he had been up to with Colin Kavanagh. A surge of energy propelled her. This was real investigative work, something she had always wanted to do, though not in these circumstances.

She fleetingly wondered how Lottie Parker remained sane with all she had to deal with. Beth knew that if it was her, she would slowly go mad.

*

Lottie sat in the car, pondering her next move.

There were so many half-truths, and an almost total lack of evidence, but there was enough to convince her that maybe some or all of the deaths were linked. She just had to find what connected the victims. She felt a rush of adrenaline. The connection would be found in Ballydoon. Each one of the dead – Robert Brady, Cara Dunne, Fiona Heffernan and Christy Clarke – was linked to the village in one form or another. Sister Augusta had said *It's all about the child.* So how did the disappearance of little Lily Heffernan fit in with the deaths?

Lottie had a feeling she was looking at this the wrong way around, but no matter what she tried, she couldn't make anything fit. A jigsaw with more than one piece of blue sky missing. One thing she knew for sure: Beth Clarke was afraid of something or someone. And Lily was still missing.

She wished Boyd was with her.

Taking out her phone, she rang him and was relieved when he agreed to come out to Ballydoon. She told him where she'd be, then drove away from the Clarkes' as the rain dissipated. What had Beth omitted? She felt it was something crucial to the murders. As she drove, she phoned Jane Dore's office. Still no progress on Christy Clarke's post-mortem. It would be afternoon before Jane got to him. Then she rang Kirby. And he told her something new.

As she drove down the narrow road, she felt everything was like a pot on a stove. They kept throwing things into the mix and soon, very soon, it was all going to boil over. She hoped that when that happened, there would be at least one definitive answer to take hold of and run with.

*

Beth walked away from her father's desk. She needed a cup of coffee before she started. Something to spur her on. She'd slept with her eyes open last night. The back door had rattled as if someone had been trying to get in. But she had it double-bolted. At times like this, she wished her father had relented and let her get a dog. But no, he'd said it was too much of a worry, with livestock in neighbouring fields.

She listened to the hungry pigs outside. Much as the idea appalled her, she knew she'd have to feed them. Then she'd have to sort out someone to take them or sell them for her. Or was that now Kavanagh's responsibility? She had no idea.

Her phone rang in her jeans pocket. She checked it. Zoe. She didn't want to talk, so she let it go to voice message. Later, when she was feeling up to it, she'd see what Zoe wanted. A message popped up on the screen. A text. Zoe again.

Beth reluctantly opened the message.

One word. *HELP*.

*

He wasn't too worried that he'd been unable to get into the house last night. There'd be another time. He'd continue to keep his eye on her, without her knowing, like he'd done with the others.

From his vantage point he'd admired the long-legged detective as she'd got into her car. She had beautiful hair, but she needed to care for it better. He'd watched as she drove away, and wondered just how much of a problem she was going to be.

He fingered his prize in his pocket. The silky feel of the hair was like gold dust in his hands. He had more like it, but the urge to feel Beth's hair in his hands was becoming too intense. As he was debating with himself whether now was a good time to strike, the door opened, and she rushed out and jumped into her car.

Another opportunity missed. But there would be others. Of that he was completely sure. And if there were none, he was well able to manufacture them.

He smiled as the smoke trailed from the exhaust pipe as she turned the car in the yard and drove away. Oh beautiful young Beth, you are just the tonic I need.

He drew back into the undergrowth, at one with nature, where he knew no one would ever find him.

CHAPTER FORTY-FOUR

At the entrance to the lakeshore, Lottie stood by her car, glad the rain had stopped. She cocked her head to one side, listening to birds singing loudly in the trees. She didn't like birds. They were fine up high, away from her; other than that, they gave her the shivers.

On the water, she saw swans swimming and thought it unusual for December; surely it was too cold for them. After a while, the birdsong and the trumpet of the swans was obliterated by the noise of a car engine. She waited while Boyd joined her.

'I've never been to this lake before,' he said, buttoning his coat and turning up his collar against the cold air.

'My county is a soft bed of springs and lakes,' she said. 'Doon is the mythical one.'

'Bit odd having a gate out here in the middle of nowhere,' he said, looking around.

'There are fishermen's caravans further down. It's probably to keep burglars away.'

'Right!' Boyd laughed dubiously. 'Nothing stopping them walking around the gate and through the bushes.'

Lottie smiled. 'The caravans were checked out, weren't they?'

'They were. No sign of Lily.'

'I want the site searched again, and this time they're to look for Robert Brady's van.'

When he'd phoned it in, Lottie said, 'Boyd, can I ask what you had to go to Galway for?'

'I told you. My mother had an appointment at the clinic. I had to bring her. No need to be so suspicious.'

'But your mother can drive, can't she?'

'Did you call me all the way out here to interrogate me?'

Lottie shrugged. He was too evasive. Maybe she'd give his mother a ring. When she had time. For now, they both needed to concentrate on work. 'I want to see where Robert Brady was found.'

Boyd sighed. 'It's been over two weeks since his body was discovered. The entire area was probably flattened by ambulances and the like, not to speak of the snow.'

As they walked, she said, 'Do you know the legend of this lake?'

'I'm sure you're going to tell me.'

'The Children of Lir,' she said, 'Google it, as Sean says.'

'I'm not sure it will help us solve any murders.'

They reached the wooded area that Boyd had pointed out from a drawing saved on his phone.

'Where did you get that?' she said.

'It was on Robert Brady's report. Kirby's been going over it. Thin file, as you'd guess.'

'Open and shut,' she said, and wondered about McKeown's original thoroughness. Had he fucked up?

'Through here.' Boyd held up a branch to let her duck through the gap.

'I had a look at the photographs in the *Tribune*,' she said. 'Beth and Ryan got close enough to the scene.'

'Do you think maybe that has anything to do with why their loved ones have died?'

'Because a reporter and a photographer were at the scene of a suicide?' Lottie raised his eyebrows sceptically. 'Doubtful, I'd say.'

'Maybe we should check with Ryan to see if he has any other photos from that day.'

'Worth a shot,' Lottie conceded.

'That's if we're to disbelieve the evidence telling us Brady took his own life.'

'Evidence?' Lottie said. 'Open-and-shut cases rarely get that far. And I'm not sure the assistant pathologist, Tim Jones, did a good job.'

'He conferred with Jane, didn't he?'

'Yes, but I'm reserving judgement for the moment.' Lowering her head beneath the brambles and thorny branches, she added, 'Why would Robert come way out here? It doesn't make sense.'

'Colin Kavanagh's house is half a mile across the field at the edge of the woods.'

'And Kavanagh called in the location of the body, after the men who found it knocked on his door.' Lottie paused. 'Kavanagh's name appears every which way I turn.'

'Every which way but loose.'

'What?'

'A Clint Eastwood film. You know, the one with the ape.'

'Jesus, Boyd,' she nudged his elbow, 'we've gone from cursed swans to an ape.'

He laughed. 'Just about sums up these muddled cases.'

'And for your information, it was an orang-utan, not an ape.'

'More confusion,' he said, and gripped her arm as she almost tripped on a root.

She felt a warm surge at his closeness. 'I rest my case.'

They arrived at a small clearing, the ground soft and well trodden, possibly from the snow. The tinkle of water pierced the air as it dripped from ferns and branches.

She said, 'Is this the right place?'

He straightened his back and stood beside her. 'How did they find him? It's so far in.'

'Two local men were scrounging through the woods looking for trees to flog for Christmas. They found more than they bargained for. Kavanagh's house was the closest, so they raised the alarm with him.'

'Convenient,' Boyd said.

'Gosh, those bloody birds are loud, aren't they?' She pulled up her hood just in case one of the damn creatures decided to swoop down and nest in her hair.

'Did Beth mention whether Brady had any underlying health issues?'

'No, but she was definitely holding something back. Insinuated that we hadn't investigated thoroughly because he was homeless.' Lottie absorbed the scents of the forest and the dim shadows of her surroundings, praying that the dark clouds would smother the rain until they got back to the car.

A large tree trunk loomed up in front of her, its branches knotted around it. She leaned her head backwards, looking up.

'How did Brady get up there?'

'Climbed?'

'What did the report say?'

'I can ring Kirby. He has the file on his desk.'

'You won't get coverage here. Check it when we get back.'

As she walked around the tree, Lottie sensed she was missing something. She stared up through the bare branches. Clouds scudded across the sky, partially hidden by the canopy above her head, and for a few moments light glinted through the gaps. She looked down at her feet, and falling to her knees, she began to scrabble around the base with her bare hands.

'What are you at?' Boyd said.

'I thought I saw something just now.' She dug through fallen twigs and mushy leaves. And then she saw what had caught her eye. 'Got any gloves?'

Boyd handed her a pair from his pocket. 'What is it?'

Slipping them on, she carefully lifted the prize from its resting place.

As she held it aloft, light glinted off the piece of jewellery in her hand.

'It's a clue.'

CHAPTER FORTY-FIVE

The cross, attached to a silver chain, was about two inches in length and had a stamp on the back, marking it as silver. Lottie placed it in an evidence bag and put it in the boot of the car. Once they checked the scene photographs, she was sure they'd confirm the piece of jewellery had not been there when the body had been found.

She followed in her car, with Boyd driving on ahead. As they made to pull into the driveway outside the church, another car sped out, almost clipping hers. She caught sight of a head of white hair. That man was turning up everywhere, and just like a slug, he left a trail behind him wherever he'd been. She wondered what business Kavanagh had with Father Curran, and his reason for leaving in such a hurry.

Boyd had already pressed the doorbell when she joined him on the step.

'Was that—' he said.

'Colin Kavanagh, yes.'

Receiving no reply at the door, they walked around the side of the house and came to a shed. Pushing the door inwards, they stalled.

Father Curran was seated on a spinning bicycle, eyes closed, mouth open, and pedalling like his life depended on it. He was bare-chested, wearing tracksuit bottoms and worn-looking runners on his feet. There was also a treadmill, and weights on the floor.

'Father Curran?' Lottie said.

His legs stopped moving before his mouth. Eventually his grunts ceased. 'Holy Mother, what are you doing in here?'

'I'm a mother all right, but I'd question the holy bit,' Lottie said, trying to be light-hearted. 'Can we have a word?'

'No, you ...' His words caught in his mouth as he struggled to regain equilibrium. 'I need a minute.'

He alighted from the bicycle, picked up a towel from a bench behind him and ran it over the back of his neck before wiping perspiration from his face.

He looked his age now, she thought. An old man trying to keep in shape. A walk might be better for him, rather than all this equipment.

Straightening his back, he stared at her, pupils so dark she could hardly see the cool blue of the irises.

'Wait here while I go to the house to get dressed,' he said.

'We'll come with you.' She stood her ground.

As though admitting defeat was an alien concept, he moved into her space, quickly followed by his body odour. She smelled incense. That's mad, she thought.

'What do you want from me?' he said.

'Why was Colin Kavanagh here just now?'

'Colin?' The priest appeared mystified. 'I'm afraid that's my business.'

'It's my business when people have been murdered and a little girl is missing.'

'So sad.'

'What is?'

'The little girl being abducted.'

'Do you know that for a fact?'

His flushed face paled significantly. 'You're twisting what I say. It's common knowledge around here that she was taken.'

'Is that what Kavanagh told you?'

'What he told me is confidential. It was a conversation between friends.'

'So Colin Kavanagh is a friend of yours.'

'An acquaintance.' The priest moved to the bench, sat down and dragged a black sweater over his head. When he looked up, Lottie almost recoiled from his icy stare.

'How long have you known him?' she said.

'Since he moved here from Dublin.'

'Was Lily with Fiona when she called to discuss her marriage ceremony?'

He bowed his head momentarily. 'I cannot recall.'

'Can you recall anything about Robert Brady?'

Watching the priest closely, Lottie noticed an immediate change in his appearance. His face dropped some of its years, and a small twinkle of light caught his eyes. And then, in the next instant, it disappeared. What had she just witnessed?

'Robert was an unfortunate individual,' Father Curran said softly.

'How well did you know him?' Boyd asked.

'My only interaction with him was while he was in the village doing odd jobs. He was a devastated man.' He looked over at Lottie, as if challenging her to disagree. 'He came to me looking for advice.'

'I'd say that was good.' She couldn't help herself.

'What advice did he request?' Boyd said.

'He needed direction in his life.'

'And you were well equipped to deliver that, were you?' Lottie snapped. 'Did you send him to Mass like you did Cara?'

Father Curran directed a stony glare at her.

'When was this meeting?' Boyd again.

'Must be about six months ago, if memory serves me. He was in a bad way. No work, no money. Inconsolable.'

'And did he take your advice?'

'Evidently not. He committed a mortal sin by taking his own life. I pray for his soul, every day.'

'Enough of this bullshit,' Lottie said, pacing the claustrophobic cabin. 'What advice did you give him? Repent of your sins and follow the way of the Lord, maybe?'

'Something like that.' The priest's chin jutted out. He was not allowing her to intimidate him.

She ceased moving and glared. 'You believe Robert Brady committed a mortal sin, yet you claimed his body and had him buried in the cemetery. That doesn't make sense to me.' Kirby's phone call earlier had informed her that undertakers acting on Father Curran's behalf had taken Brady's body to be buried.

'He is not buried in the cemetery.' The priest twisted the towel into a knot.

'What?'

'I said all the prayers I could for his soul, then I had him buried outside the walls of the cemetery. In unconsecrated ground. As it should be.'

'Oh for Christ's sake.' Lottie paced a tiny circle. Was this man for real?

'Do not take the Lord's name in vain.'

She stepped into his space, eyeing him coldly. 'That poor man had no one in this world, and now he has no one in the next.'

'It is written in the doctrine I studied.'

'Don't you know it's all changed now?'

'I believe what I believe.'

She took a few breaths to align her thoughts. 'Where were you the day Robert died?'

'When was that again? My memory is not what it used to be.'

As she tried to recall the exact date as determined by the pathologist, the galvanised-metal roof above her head rattled with loud pecking. Birds. Goddam birds.

'His body was found two weeks ago,' Boyd said. 'It's estimated he'd been dead for maybe a week before that.'

'I would have said morning Mass, worked out here in my gym, and then conducted my daily rounds for the sick at the abbey.'

'Have you been to the site where Robert was killed?'

'The site?'

'The forest at Lough Doon.'

The priest stared at the roof, where the birds were now pecking with greater intensity. 'I need to get this place insulated.'

'Answer the question, please.' Lottie gritted her teeth.

'Do I need my solicitor?'

'If that's the way you want to play it, I can take you into the station to have you questioned. Six hours initially, and then a further six when my superintendent approves it. And he will.'

'That would be Acting Superintendent McMahon, wouldn't it? Colin told me about him.'

'What?' Lottie said.

'Apparently your superintendent and Mr Kavanagh go back a long way,' Father Curran said smugly.

'Are you refusing to answer the question?' Lottie said. 'Did you visit the site where Robert Brady's body was found?'

'Yes, I went there a week ago. To pray at the place where Robert lost his battle with his faith.'

'Did you leave anything behind?'

'I assume you mean a silver cross and chain at the foot of the tree?'

'I do.'

'It was already there. So, Inspector, you need to look for someone else.'

She was not going to believe him that easily.

'Are you prepared to let us take your fingerprints and a sample of your DNA?'

'Not unless you have a warrant. Do you?'

She opened her mouth to object, but closed it again. 'I'll get it. Don't think about leaving town.'

'It's a village, not a town, and I've nowhere else to go. Good day, Inspector.' He turned back to his spinning bike.

Lottie felt Boyd taking her by the elbow and steering her out into the damp air. She gulped a welcome breath. It felt fresh after the cloying atmosphere of the shed. She'd need to take a shower.

CHAPTER FORTY-SIX

Sitting with Zoe in the cluttered living room, Beth felt the urge to tidy up some of the toys. To pile them all into a basket or box; to run a cloth over the dresser; to spray Febreze on the couch. But she sat tightly on the arm of a chair and watched as Zoe ran her fingers up and down the edge of the old-fashioned net curtain that insulated her in her own world.

'You need to go outside. Get some air, Zoe.'

'I need to escape from Giles. He's getting worse. Domineering and demanding. I'm afraid of him.'

'Can you afford to leave him?'

'No.'

'What are you going to do?' Beth said.

'I need your help.'

'I've nothing, Zoe. Now that Dad is dead.'

'What do you mean?'

'Colin Kavanagh tells me he owns it all. I went through Dad's papers last night. I still have to find evidence to prove what Kavanagh says, but he has no reason to make it up.'

'I'm so sorry about your dad, Beth, honestly I am. But it leaves us in a right mess.'

Beth held Zoe's stare. She had no idea what her friend meant. 'How could Dad's death leave you in a mess? I don't understand.'

Moving away from the window, Zoe stood in front of the mantelpiece. 'I never told you this, but Christy came to Giles maybe three months ago. He wanted an investor. Someone to put money into the farm. You know, after the garage went belly-up.'

'Tell me Giles didn't give him money ...'

'He gave him fifteen thousand euros. All our savings. He said Christy told him he'd double it in a few months and return it with interest. Now your dad is dead. How can we get that money back?'

Beth shoved her hands between her crossed knees, hiding the uncontrollable shaking that had engulfed them. 'How could you give him money without telling me?'

'He put a good business proposal to Giles. At least I think it was a good one. Giles can be convincing where money is concerned. Now we're broke.'

Beth stood up, her mind racing. 'I'm sorry about all that, Zoe, but I can't help. You'll have to talk to Kavanagh.'

She heard a door open and shut.

'Zoe, where are you? I need a cup of tea.' The voice travelled from the kitchen.

'I'll be there in a moment.'

'Can't he make his own cup of tea?' Beth said at the sound of water pouring from a tap into a kettle.

'What about the cars in the garage?' Zoe said. 'All those Mercedes and BMWs. Can't you sell those and get us our money back?'

Beth couldn't help the laugh that broke from her throat. 'Zoe Bannon, you know I can't do that. You know why too. So don't go there. Right?'

'But—' Zoe began. The rest of her words were drowned out by the insistent ringing of the doorbell.

*

Before heading back into Ragmullin, Lottie decided to call to Ryan Slevin to ask him about the photos he'd taken in the forest when Robert Brady's body was found.

'That priest is a lying bastard,' she said, standing outside Zoe Bannon's door, her finger pressed to the doorbell.

'Don't you need permission to bury a body somewhere other than in a cemetery?' Boyd said.

'Yes. We can follow that up at the station. Maybe then we can get his DNA and fingerprints, and perhaps some answers.'

'Do you think Father Curran left the chain and cross under the tree?'

'He says he didn't,' Lottie said, 'but I don't believe a word out of his mouth.'

The door opened and the space filled with the bulk of Giles Bannon.

'Mr Bannon, we'd like a word with Ryan.'

'He's not here. Try the cottage.'

'Can we come in, please?' She kept her foot ready to wedge in the space if he made to slam the door on her.

'I've already told you he's not here. So piss off.'

'No need for that,' Boyd cut in.

'Look, my wife is distraught about Fiona and Lily. She can't even make me a cup of tea. Has Lily been found yet?'

A twinge of guilt squeezed Lottie's chest. 'We're doing everything we can to find her, before it's too late.'

The craggy face dropped some of its animosity. 'You'd better come in.' Bannon walked down the hall.

In the kitchen, he switched off the kettle and pulled on his Crombie. The heat from the stove was overpowering, and Lottie wondered how long he was going to stand there in his overcoat. She felt like divesting herself of her own. Without being invited, she pulled out a chair and sat, indicating for Boyd to do likewise. After a thirty-second stand-off, Bannon sat down too.

'I've work to be getting back to.'

'What could be so important that you can't give me five minutes?' Lottie said.

'The annual dance show is supposed to be opening next week. There are sets to organise, musicians to pay, costumes to sort. You wouldn't believe the stress.'

'You're going ahead without Lily?' Lottie said.

'I know it sounds harsh, but the show must go on, and she was only in one dance. How much longer are you going to have the theatre cordoned off?'

'For as long as it takes.'

'Right. Hopefully you'll find her soon.'

Lottie hoped so too, but she was finding it hard to get the measure of Giles Bannon.

'Did you know Robert Brady?' She watched his face intently.

'I've heard of him. Odd-job man, wasn't he? Hanged himself.'

'That's being reinvestigated.'

'Really?' Bannon pushed his chair backwards and stood.

'Yeah, really,' Lottie said.

'He worked on Ryan's cottage, didn't he?' Boyd said. 'Surely you can tell us something about him?'

'Talk to Ryan. I've nothing to tell you. I have to leave now. Let me know if you find Lily. Poor pet.'

Lottie opened her eyes wide and Boyd shrugged his shoulders. Giles Bannon already had the front door open to usher them out.

'What did Robert do to you?' Lottie was intrigued now.

'He did nothing to me. I think he was a friend of Fiona's. Talk to Ryan, if you must.'

There was nothing to do but leave.

Outside, Lottie said, 'That was interesting. Bannon is the type of man who tells you more about himself by saying very little.'

'True. Seems like he didn't know Brady but still didn't like him. Will we track down Ryan to see if he can shed light on it?'

'There's no point in adding to greenhouse gases with both of us driving, is there?' Lottie said. 'Leave your car there and come with me.'

As she pulled away from the house, she kept one eye on the rear-view mirror, watching for Bannon to emerge. Instead, she was rewarded with a swish of the living room curtain. From behind it, Zoe stared at her, her face a mask of what Lottie thought looked like terror.

CHAPTER FORTY-SEVEN

With all that had happened, Lottie realised she hadn't yet been to Ryan's cottage. Members of her team and SOCOs had searched it for Lily. They'd uncovered nothing that could lead to a reason why Fiona had been murdered or why Lily had disappeared.

'The hair, Boyd, that's what bothers me.'

'You could do with a trim all right.'

She laughed, despite the enormity of the cases they were working. 'You know what I mean.'

'It's a bit odd, I have to admit, because it doesn't lead us anywhere.'

'It proves that at least two if not three people were murdered by the same person. Taking a lock of hair for a trophy? For what?'

'I don't know,' he said. 'Any word on Christy Clarke's postmortem?'

'Not yet. The man was under tremendous pressure, according to his daughter. Maybe Colin Kavanagh was one source of that pressure. But if it's suicide … Oh, I don't know what I'm talking about.'

'Do you even know where you're going?'

She squinted through the windscreen. A mist was falling, and it felt like she was driving through dense fog. 'I think it's the next left.'

Grass threaded the middle of the road and bare bramble branches criss-crossed out over the edges. At last, through the mist, she saw the outline of a small whitewashed cottage, surrounded by trees. A black car was parked at the front door. She pulled up behind it.

Boyd knocked loudly. No answer. 'If that's Ryan's car, where is he?'

'Let's have a look round the back.' As she walked, she peered through the windows, but the two front ones had blinds pulled down. Paving stones marked the way. A square patio by the back door, with two wheelie bins and nothing else. She lifted the lids. 'Empty.'

'No sign of Slevin,' Boyd said, glancing around. 'There's a walkway up that way, through the trees.' He pointed.

Lottie followed the line of his finger. It was trodden down grass rather than a path. Like what they'd walked through to find Robert Brady's body. She noticed footprints. 'Shit.'

'What?'

'Come on.'

'Where are you going now?'

'To look for Ryan before he ends up with a haircut he didn't ask for.'

'You're mad, woman.'

She took off, slipping and sliding, listening to Boyd panting behind her.

'Wait, Lottie. I can't keep up.'

'Stay at the cottage, then.'

'I can't let you go off on your own.'

She stopped and stared at him. 'What's the matter?'

He gulped down breaths in quick succession. 'I keep slipping. My shoes aren't right for this.'

'Go back and try to get into the house. See if there's evidence of an altercation or something.'

'Something?'

'Yeah.'

'Why do you think Ryan might have come this way?'

'Fresh footprints. Look. There. They could belong to him or they could be someone else's.'

'I see what you mean. I'll check the house and call for backup.'

'I'll go a little further. Don't worry, I'll be fine.' She grinned. 'Nice of you to worry, though.'

He turned without answering her and walked back towards the cottage.

Feck you, Boyd.

She continued to hurry up the path. It inclined further with each step. The mist seemed to be worsening. She could see little more than two steps in front of her. Should she call out? What if the killer was hiding somewhere? What if she called and stopped him just in time? What if Ryan was the killer? Too many questions, she warned herself.

'Ryan! Ryan! Where are you?'

Branches crashed against her face as she quickened her pace; her feet lost traction in the marshy terrain and she slipped. Getting back up, she thought, this is madness. She had no evidence that anything had happened to Ryan. For all she knew, he could be in bed, conked out. Or knocked out. Or dead. She found her phone. One bar of coverage. She called Boyd. 'Any sign?'

'I found a key under one of the bins. He's not inside. Come back …'

The signal died. She'd left the radio in the car. Rookie mistake.

She shouted through the trees, 'Ryan? Answer me.'

She'd been moving through the undergrowth for maybe five minutes when she heard it.

A soft keening, like someone crying.

What the hell?

Swiping branches and bushes out of her way and disentangling her hair and clothing from briars, she ran as fast as she could through and over the natural obstacle course. All the time heading upwards. It was denser than the forest where Robert had been found, and she had no idea where she was. Shit.

Her breath was coming in quick bursts as she tried to gauge which direction to take, knowing in her heart it was useless. There were no longer any footprints to guide her. The ferns and grass were up to her knees. No evidence of it having been trampled on recently. She looked around frantically. She was totally lost. Leaning against a rotted tree trunk, she tried the phone again. Dead as a dodo.

Suddenly she heard a branch snap.

'Who's there?'

Another snap, and the crunch of footsteps.

'Ryan? Is that you?'

Moving away from the tree, straining to hear, she focused on the direction of the sound. It was behind her.

Before she could turn around, she felt the roughness of a hand over her mouth and another around her neck. Kicking wildly, she tried to get free, tried to injure whoever had grabbed her. Whoever it was, they were stronger than her. Too strong.

Black dots appeared in her vision as air was cut off from her throat. She couldn't breathe. She was still struggling, but it was useless. The dots became rounder and bigger. Her vision dimmed and she saw her children and grandson, fading into the distance. And then she thought she saw Adam with a hand out, beckoning, right before blackness overwhelmed her and her body slumped down, down until it was lying on nature's floor.

CHAPTER FORTY-EIGHT

In Ryan's cottage, Boyd went through all the cupboards and drawers, knowing everywhere had already been searched and nothing found. His chest hurt from having run after Lottie, and he thought his blood pressure had gone through the roof. He was on the wrong side of fit, for sure.

As he searched, he concluded that the cottage was basically empty of anything edible, legible or comfortable. No food. No letters or newspapers or books. Empty cupboards. Bare armchairs. Even the beds had no linen on them. It was as if someone had stripped the dwelling naked in anticipation of decorators. Ryan had told them it was to have been his home with Fiona and little Lily, but that did not ring true. Boyd felt as if it had never been intended to be a home. It was too ... What was the word he was searching for? Sterile. Yes. That was it.

He opened the bedside cabinet doors, the wardrobe, foraged through the sparse refrigerator, the bathroom cabinet. All virtually empty. Not even an out-of-date carton of milk or a toothbrush. Every wall was freshly painted, and he could see how someone had taken care with the kitchen refurbishment. Had that been Robert Brady's work? There wasn't even junk mail in the house. Lottie would call it weird. Lottie! He tried her number again. Nothing. He'd called for backup; they should be here soon.

He glanced at the time on his phone again. How long was it since she'd taken off on her hike? Ten, maybe fifteen minutes. He heard the rumble of car engines and opened the front door to see Kirby and McKeown alighting from a car, with two uniforms squashed into a squad car parked behind them, strobe lights flashing.

'What's going on?' McKeown said.

'Inspector Parker took off into the forest,' Boyd explained.

'Why did you let her go alone?'

'She sent me back. Ryan Slevin was supposed to be here, but there's no sign of him.'

'I think we should look for the boss,' Kirby said, taking out a cigar and lighting it. 'This isn't a crime scene, is it?'

'I don't know what the hell it is,' Boyd said, feeling a tightness in his chest. Anxiety for Lottie? 'Can you get Google Maps on your phone?'

'I haven't even got one bar of coverage, let alone Wi-Fi.'

'We need to see where that forest path leads.'

'I've a map in the car.' Kirby went back to fetch it.

'Is Slevin now a suspect for his fiancée's murder?' McKeown asked.

'All I know is that we don't know where he is at the moment.' Boyd eyed McKeown. 'Are you sure you did a thorough investigation into the Robert Brady death?'

McKeown took a step forward. 'Are you accusing me of not doing my job properly?'

Boyd could see steam rising from the other man's ears. 'I only asked a question, no need to get your hackles up.'

'It sounded accusatory.'

'Maybe you took it that way because you're guilty of something.'

'Oh for fuck's sake, Boyd, spit it out before it eats you up.'

'Robert Brady's suicide might be more of a suspicious death, possibly another murder.'

'Because of the snippet of hair found in his pocket?'

'Because of the belt.'

'DNA results aren't back yet. Nothing's been confirmed.'

Boyd felt his pocket, searching for cigarettes, and came up with his e-Cig. Blasted thing. He took a puff anyway. 'I have a strong suspicion the belt used to hang Cara belonged to Robert Brady.'

McKeown said nothing, shifting from foot to foot.

Boyd fiddled the e-cigarette between his fingers, trying to figure out why McKeown was acting so defensively. 'If we can establish that the belt is Brady's, it proves that whoever killed Cara Dunne had access to the dead man, or at the very least, his belongings. It suggests, therefore, that Mr Brady may not have committed suicide.'

'The pathologist ruled it suicide. End of.'

He sounded like a teenager, Boyd thought.

Kirby walked back through the mist. 'I have the map now, but it's not much use.' He unfolded it. 'Which way did she head?'

Directing them around the side of the house, Boyd pointed to the pathway through the trees. 'Is that on the map?'

'No. But a section of the forest stretches for about a kilometre that way. It follows a steep slope upwards before it dips down again.'

'What's on the other side?' Boyd said.

'According to this, it's the village.' Kirby pointed proudly at the damp paper in his hand.

'Maybe she's gone there,' McKeown said, his voice sounding calmer. 'Have you tried Slevin's phone?'

'There's no coverage here, as you know.' Boyd reiterated Kirby's comment.

Kirby pumped his chest out, full of importance, and eyed their shoes. 'You stay here, Boyd, in case she comes back. We'll head into the forest.'

'I'll go with you.' Boyd needed to be doing something; McKeown was grating on his nerves like steel wool on ceramic. 'McKeown, leave the uniforms here and drive into the village. Kirby and I will meet you on the other side of the forest.'

'How am I supposed to know where that is?'

'Take a photo of the map with your phone. From what I can see, it's somewhere close to the abbey. And if you can't find it, open your mouth and ask someone. The old-fashioned way.' Boyd turned to Kirby. 'Come on, let's go.'

Without waiting for McKeown's reply, and cursing his soft shoes, Boyd took the lead.

With Kirby wheezing behind him, he easily reached the place where he'd left Lottie. The mist had turned to fog, making it difficult to see ahead. Broken branches showed him her trail. 'This way.'

'Very dark in here, isn't it?' Kirby moaned. 'What's your take on all these murders?'

'Hard to know, but I don't like how Colin Kavanagh appears at every corner.'

'Where is he?'

Pausing for a second, Boyd said, 'I don't mean he's actually here.'

They carried on, ducking and diving through the undergrowth and overhanging branches.

'Shh!' Boyd said, stopping suddenly. Kirby clattered into his back.

'What? I'm after stepping in shite of some sort. Jesus, Boyd, the fucking smell.'

'Shh.' With his finger still to his lips, and his head to one side, Boyd listened intently.

Alert now, Kirby whispered, 'It sounds like a bird or something.'

Running now, abandoning any semblance of protocol, Boyd shouted, 'It's a woman, Kirby. It could be Lottie!'

*

Beth arrived home and sat at her dad's desk. Opening the scanner app on her phone, she started to scan documents. She knew her head was not in the right space to take it all in or to be aware if she stumbled across anything relevant, so she snapped everything, hoping something might yield a clue as to why he'd shot himself. She felt the truth was a story far beyond her journalistic talents.

She heard a loud hammering. Someone was at the door.

The detective again, probably. Why couldn't she leave her alone? Maybe Beth could find a bone to throw her. Abandoning her scanning, she went to open the door.

Wet and muddied, Ryan almost fell in on top of her.

'Ryan! You look like something the cat dragged in. What happened?'

'Let me sit down for a minute.'

'Come in.' She led him to a chair. 'Ryan, losing Fiona that way was awful, just terrible, but you need to mind yourself. I'm serious.' She put out a hand to touch his cheek, an act of tenderness, comfort for a friend, but he swiped it away.

'You shouldn't be thinking about me,' he growled. 'You've lost your dad too.'

'We're united by our grief, then. Gosh, that sounds too poetic for this horror show.'

'You're so good with words, Beth,' he said, a half-smile tickling the corner of his mouth. 'Put the kettle on.'

There was something in his tone that sent a shiver through her. Busying herself with the tap and kettle, she said, 'Have you heard anything from the guards?'

The chair scraped across the floor. Suddenly he was at her shoulder. 'What do you know?'

He was too close to her. Way too close. She swung around and scooted around his sweaty body to wipe invisible crumbs from the table with her hand. This is becoming a nervous habit, she thought. 'I had a detective here earlier.'

'What did you tell them?' He followed her around the table.

She kept a step ahead of him. 'Shouldn't you ask what they were asking about?'

'Well then, what were they asking?'

Pausing because she'd run out of table to trek around, she said, 'She wanted to know about Robert.'

'Is that all? Nothing about your dad or Fiona?'

'My dad and Fiona? I don't understand.'

With dirt clinging to his clothes, Ryan puffed and panted, strained wheezes rising from deep in his chest. 'About their deaths, I mean.' He paused. 'Shit, Beth, why were they asking about Robert?'

She shrugged, unable to figure out what to say to placate him.

'What did you tell them?' he repeated.

The kettle hissed, then whistled, breaking the tension that had sprung up like a wall around them. Ryan slumped onto a chair, pulling at his face with dirty fingers. Beth fetched mugs from the cupboard and milk from the refrigerator.

An unsettling feeling lurked in the pit of her stomach like a sour liquid as she noticed the way Ryan kept his eyes on her while she moved around the kitchen. She filled the teapot and put it on the table.

'Ryan, you're scaring me. What's going on?'

'You really don't want to know.' He lifted the pot and poured the tea.

Beth stared, without moving a muscle. Ryan was not being Ryan; he was not the man she knew. She was sure something much worse than Fiona's death was the cause of the yellow in his widened eyes and the pallor of his skin.

She just couldn't decide if his look was one of fear or menace.

CHAPTER FORTY-NINE

Boyd dropped to his knees at the tree trunk.

'Lottie! Are you okay?'

Stupid question. With trembling hands, he lifted her head. She slumped forward and he caught her in his arms. She was sitting on the wet forest floor. Face purple. He put a finger on the side of one eyelid, opened her eye up then let the lid fall back. Felt her throat for a pulse. Shallow breaths.

'Thank God,' he said. Cradling her in his arms, he willed her to wake up. To open her eyes of her own accord. 'Come on, Lottie, please …'

She started to cough. Eyes flashed open. 'Boyd?'

'Thank goodness.'

'Give her some air.' Kirby put a hand on his shoulder.

'I'm okay,' she whispered, her voice raspy.

'What the hell happened?' Boyd said, anger replacing his fear. 'How could you be so stupid? Who did it?'

'Boyd,' Kirby said, and pushed him out of the way. 'Slow down. Give her space.'

Boyd fell backwards.

Lottie gasped for fresh air. 'He tried to stop me,' she said. 'Bloody bastard.'

'Who? Who tried to stop you?' Boyd said, scratching muck from his trousers.

'Didn't see … Came up behind me. I heard a sound, like someone crying.' Her eyes flashed with something. At first he thought it was fear, but as she went to stand, he knew it was rage.

'Fucker tried to stop me.'

'What did he try to stop you from?'

'Don't know. I was heading that way.'

She lifted her arm slowly and pointed through a gap in the trees to her right. He followed the direction with his eyes, squinting through the dense leaves, but couldn't see anything. Leaving Lottie with Kirby trying to get a signal on his phone, he moved through the thicket. He was fully aware he could be destroying evidence of her attacker, but he had to see what was beyond.

As he climbed, the copse thinned out and a dim winter glint appeared. He reached the top, gasping at the beauty of the landscape before him, but he still couldn't fathom out what might have caused someone to attack Lottie.

Hearing footsteps behind him, he turned around ready to attack. It was only Kirby, with Lottie in tow.

'You should have stayed where you were to wait for help,' Boyd said.

'What's the focal point down there?' she said, ignoring him.

'The abbey,' he said, looking to the right of the village.

'No. I mean in our direct line of sight. Look there.' She pointed. 'What do you see?'

Tracking the line of her finger, he said, 'Clarke's Garage?'

'Exactly.'

'I don't understand.' He started downwards, but felt her hand on his sleeve, holding him back.

'Wait.' She hunkered down and studied the ground around them. 'Over there.' She started to move. 'Come on.'

He caught up with her. Could she not listen to advice? 'Lottie, you need to see a doctor.'

'I'm going to personally strangle him.'

'The doctor?' He tried a joke. 'You look like shit.'

'Pot and kettle. See, there.' She pointed to the trees. 'Cola cans and wrappers. Someone was definitely here.'

'It's like a lookout or a den.' He wondered how she was still able to focus. His own head was thrumming.

'We need SOCOs up here,' she said.

'Probably just kids or teenagers.' But he didn't think so. He tried to visualise the line of sight from the vantage point where he stood. Straight down into the village. 'You really think someone was staking out Christy Clarke's garage?'

'I do. Let's head there. We need to find Ryan Slevin. Kirby, you stay and guard this area until we can get a team up here.'

'On my own?' Kirby sounded doubtful.

'I think you're safe enough,' she said. 'I reckon whoever it was is long gone.'

'You sure you're okay, Lottie?' Boyd said. 'You need to see a doctor. I don't think—'

'Boyd,' she said over her shoulder. 'Shut up.'

He had to smile at her gumption. As they made their way downwards, he stayed right behind her, ready to catch her if she collapsed.

*

Lottie could hardly keep her frustration under wraps. Running a hand along her throat, she relived the touch of fingers, squeezing, tighter. Then nothing.

They walked through a gap in the hedge and onto the road. A line of six council houses stood before them, appearing out of sync with the countryside. As they reached the garage, she felt a wave of nausea engulf her and leaned into Boyd.

'I still think you need to see a doc—'

'If you mention the word doctor once more, I'll throttle you, Boyd.'

'I don't think you have the energy to walk, let alone choke me.'

The garage looked more bereft now than it had done yesterday. All the garda and forensic activity had been completed and it was back to its lonely existence. The dirty windows. The space within lined with expensive cars.

'I wonder, has there been any luck checking the registrations?' she said.

'Meant to tell you earlier: McKeown found out they were all reported stolen from Dublin within the last year.'

'Really? Why didn't they remove the plates?'

'I presume whoever *they* are thought no one in their right minds was going to look for stolen Mercedes and BMWs in the arsehole of nowhere.'

She tried the handles of the car doors and found them all locked. 'Where are the keys?'

'In the office, perhaps,' Boyd said and made to enter the blood-spattered space.

'I hope the post-mortem is completed soon. I need to know what happened to Christy Clarke and how, or if, his death fits in with the others.' She stopped at the sight of the bloody walls and felt sick at the thought that entered her head. 'And little Lily. I hope to God the child is unharmed.'

She felt a breeze on the back of her neck and whirled round to see McKeown marching through the main door, rubbing his hands together.

'Jesus, but it's bloody cold out.'

'You took your time getting here,' Boyd said.

'When more uniforms arrived at the cottage, I followed your trail up the hill. Kirby's still there. I got two bars on my phone and called in SOCOs. Gave them direction to the lookout or whatever it is. For what it's worth, I think it's a waste of our time and theirs. No one gets ambushed over a couple of crisp packets and a Diet Coke.'

Feeling the flush of anger colour her cheeks, Lottie said, 'Someone attacked me, and I think it presented them with enough time to remove something from that den. SOCOs might be able to determine what that was, and then maybe we can identify *who* it was and why they were so anxious to keep it hidden.'

'Right,' McKeown said.

Lottie thought he didn't look very sure. 'Have you a problem, Detective?'

'No, boss. Not at all.'

'When we get back to the office, find the original stolen car reports. Track where they were taken from and liaise with the local stations to see what they've come up with. Do your utmost to trace how and when those cars arrived in Ballydoon. Got it?'

'Got it.'

'And I want forensic analysis on the cars too. I want to know who drove them here and who handled them. Now drive me and Boyd back to his car. It's at Bannon's house. And arrange for mine to be driven back from the cottage. Can you do that without making a fuss?'

She instantly regretted talking to McKeown so sharply. Being the newest member of her team, he had yet to grasp her fluctuating moods. Plus, like all of them, he was also working Lily's case. She put a hand to her head to stop it thumping. They were going around in circles and she felt she was in a maze with no one to guide her.

CHAPTER FIFTY

When Giles Bannon arrived at the theatre, he nodded at the garda who was manning the door and headed inside. Waste of taxpayers' money, he thought. In his office, he brushed down his coat and checked his shoes were clean. He found deodorant in a drawer and sprayed it liberally under his arms through his shirt. Satisfied, he went to check on rehearsals.

The hall was empty except for Trevor on the stage. Bannon kept his eyes firmly fixed on him as he completed a rehearsal of his solo dance routine, his body lithe and full of energy. He wondered idly how Trevor hadn't made the big time, with his skill and flair. There was no denying he had a talent for dance, far above any Giles had seen, even better than the professional groups who performed here. No, there was something keeping Trevor rooted to the town. Giles had an idea what that might be; he just needed more proof.

'Well done.' He clapped slowly as the dancer blinked against the spotlight.

'What are you doing there?' Trevor picked up a towel from the side of the stage and made his way down the steps into the auditorium.

'Watching you.'

'You shouldn't lurk in the shadows like that. Anyone might think you were a pervert.'

Giles laughed loudly. 'Oh shut up. There's only one pervert in this room and it's not me.'

'What are you talking about?' Trevor made to walk past, but Giles grabbed his arm and pulled him close. 'Get your hands off me.'

'Where's Lily?' Giles said. 'What did you do with her, you sick fuck?'

Trevor's face paled instantly. 'I never touched her.'

Giles smiled. 'Come on, you can tell me. I won't tell the guards.'

'There's nothing to tell. Let me go.'

'Colin Kavanagh has put up a reward. I could do with the money, so tell me.'

'If I knew anything about Lily, which I don't, you'd be the last person I'd tell.' Trevor wrenched his arm free and strode though the double doors.

Before they could slam shut in his face, Giles caught one and stood watching as Trevor picked up his gear bag and headed for the exit.

'I'll find out,' he shouted after him. 'And when I do, you're going to be one sorry arsehole.'

*

The air was bitterly cold, but the scent of cinnamon and pine followed Trevor like a smoke trail. Walking past the market stalls, his shoulders slumped with an invisible weight. His legs moved automatically, but it was as if the soles of his feet were sticking to the ground.

Oblivious to the chatter of the happy Christmas shoppers, he bundled his way through the crowd. Up the street, turn right. Keep on walking. Keep your head down. Don't drop your bag. He'd be there soon. Hopefully. And then he could wash away the stench of Giles Bannon's words. But the further he walked, the louder the venom-laced invective roared, beating a racket against his eardrums.

Louder and louder.

Pervert. Pervert.

Maybe he was. Maybe that was what his thoughts were constantly saddled with.

He reached his door. Scrabbled around in his bag for his key.

He had to get inside. Now! Once in there, in his own private habitat, he'd be safe.

Inside, he walked around his small room, scratching his arms vigorously. The place was a mess. All that furniture, and the suitcases stacked up in the corner. Clutter taunting him. He had to get rid of everything soon, before it crowded him out. But first, he thought, he had to exercise.

He completed his stretches and arched his back, raised and dropped the kettle bells until he could no longer do so. Still he felt as if every muscle in his body was taut, like strings ready to be plucked. He brought up Spotify on his phone and tapped his favourites. Bannon was a bollocks. He'd sent the email, hadn't he? What else did he want from him?

As the music played, he stood by the small rectangular window and lifted the curtain. He was looking directly at a brick wall. He craved the day when he'd have enough money saved to either rent or buy a proper place. He'd been told it would be soon. That was before.

He turned away from the window and opened the cupboard. He found a box of Weetabix and put a couple into a bowl. He didn't bother fetching milk. He moved to the chair and sat with the bowl on his knee, chewing the dry cereal as if it were a biscuit. His knees jigged. Not even the music calmed him.

He heard a door open, then close somewhere in the building. He felt a hand rest on his shoulder and fingers gently massage his neck muscles. Closing his eyes, he released his pain in one long shriek.

But there was no hand.

Only his memory of what once had been.

He ran both his own hands up along his throat, around his ears and into the hair on top of his head. He tugged, trying to pull out the loneliness, knowing he couldn't. His heart was broken, his life in shreds, and he had no one; no one in the world to talk to.

At last, he composed himself and sat cross-legged on the floor, the palms of his hands facing upwards on his knees, his eyes staring at the cracked ceiling.

In his own silence.

Alone.

*

Resting her head on her desk, her hands on her knees, Lottie allowed the coolness of the timber to feed through her skin. This was becoming a habit, she thought as her eyelids drooped, but before she could fall asleep, she rustled herself back to life. There was no time for rest. Lily was out there somewhere. She had to find the poor little girl. She also had a murderer to stop before he killed again.

Her email icon pinged. An update from Jane Dore, the state pathologist. The encrypted file contained the preliminary report on Christy Clarke.

She entered her password and scanned downwards for the confirmation she needed.

No gunshot residue on the victim's hands.

Christy Clarke had been murdered.

How did he fit in with the deaths of Cara and Fiona, though? She shook her head, willing energy into her flagging body. She read some more. Tried to find anything relating to Clarke's hair in the myriad of words merging on the screen before her eyes. Nothing.

She rang the morgue.

'Hi, Jane.'

'You just caught me. I'm on my way out.'

'It's about Christy Clarke. Did you check his hair?'

'I sent you my report.'

'I know, but I'm seeing double at this stage. Can you tell me? Now, please?'

She heard the sound of keys being placed on a desk, followed by clicking on a keyboard.

Jane said, 'It's not conclusive, because his skull was shattered. In addition, he had thinning hair to start with. Therefore I cannot confirm one way or the other if some of it was cut off, or if he was killed by the same person who murdered the two women.'

'But you do think the same person killed Fiona and Cara?'

'Lottie, I don't know. All I can say is that both women had a section of their hair removed, and a cutting of Cara Dunne's hair was found on Fiona Heffernan's person.'

'And it's possible that the hair found among Cara Dunne's possessions was Robert Brady's. Plus you have the lock of hair found on his body. That hasn't been accounted for yet.'

'I haven't found any of Fiona's hair on Christy Clarke.'

'Maybe the killer is keeping it for another victim.'

Jane said, 'It's also possible that the cutting of the hair and the planting of it was not carried out by the killer. Have you considered that? There is no evidence that it was done at time of death.'

When Lottie finished the call, she considered what Jane had said. Weighing it all up, she was as certain as she could be that she was dealing with one killer. But the wedding dresses? What did they mean? She was confident they were not a coincidence.

She shot out of her chair and opened the door.

'McKeown, have you any update on the wedding dresses?'

'I hadn't a chance to run it by you.' He tapped his iPad screen. 'The dress Cara Dunne was wearing she purchased locally, six months ago. The dress Fiona Heffernan was wearing has yet to be traced.'

'Where did Fiona buy her own wedding dress?'

'Same shop as Cara Dunne. True Brides, here in Ragmullin.'

'And the staff there, have they been checked out?'

'All accounted for at the times of the murders.'

'They're sure the dress Fiona was wearing wasn't purchased in their store?' She crossed her fingers, hoping for a miracle.

'They're sure.'

'Shit.' She thought for a moment. 'It was a new dress, wasn't it?'

'Looked to be.'

'And the shop staff, were they able to tell you anything about it? Any hint as to where it might have originated?'

McKeown swiped his finger along his iPad. 'It's possible it was bought online.' He turned the tablet towards her.

She squinted at the image. Unable to hide the disappointment in her voice, she said, 'It's not the same.'

'No, it's not, but it's the nearest replica the staff know about. They think it could have been customised or custom made.'

'Damn. So we're looking for a seamstress or tailor, and also a hairdresser or barber.' She felt her body physically deflate. 'Get a photograph of the dress Fiona was found in. Circulate it through the media. Someone has to recognise it.'

'If it was purchased online, it could have come from China or God knows where.'

'Just do it.'

He nodded and busied himself doing as she'd instructed.

'I want the team in the incident room in an hour, with comprehensive updates on everything, including little Lily.' She fetched her bag and jacket.

'Where are you off to?' Boyd said.

'I need a shower and food. Is my car back yet?'

'It's in the yard. Will I drive you?' He half stood from his chair. She put a hand on his shoulder. He sat back down.

'No, I'm fine, Boyd. Give McKeown a hand with Lily's investigation.'

'Sure thing.'

'I'll be back in an hour.'

As she walked out of the office, down the corridor and out to the yard, she couldn't help feeling a sense of intense loneliness settling on her shoulders. As Chloe might say, would she ever get her shit together?

The house was unnaturally silent when Lottie entered. In the kitchen, there was no sign of any attempt having been made to cook dinner. Breakfast dishes were piled up in the sink. The cereal box and milk carton were still on the table.

'They never learn,' she said, and put the milk back in the refrigerator. She noticed Louis' buggy folded up at the back door.

'Katie? Chloe?' she yelled. 'Are you here? Sean?'

Nothing.

She thought she heard a sound upstairs. She flew up the steps and paused outside Sean's room, out of breath. He was talking to someone. She turned the handle. His door was locked.

'Sean Parker, open the door this instant.'

His footsteps plodded across the floor and the door opened. 'What are you doing home?'

'What are you doing in there with the door locked?'

'It's my room. I can lock it if I like. What do you want, Mam? I'm busy.'

Over his shoulder she saw his computer monitor with a screen saver and his PlayStation on pause in the middle of a FIFA game.

'I was wondering where everyone has got to.'

'The girls took Louis into town to get stuff for their escape to New York.'

'But his buggy is downstairs,' she said. What stuff could they need? she wondered.

'They went in Granny's car.'

'Really? Was Leo with them?'

'Suppose so.'

'Was he or not?'

'I don't know, Mam. Can I go back to my game now?'

'Who are you playing with?' She took a step into his lair. Clothes were scattered on the floor and his bed was unmade. He could do with opening a window to let fresh air circulate.

He rolled his eyes because he knew she hated that gesture. 'Like you even care.'

She caught his arm and stared into his blue eyes, so like his father's. 'Sean, I do care, so much it breaks my heart. Listen, I want you to know you can talk to me. You don't have to be calling round to Boyd, complaining.'

'Is that what he told you?'

'No, but—'

'And I thought he liked me. You're all the same.'

'Who?'

'Adults. Just thinking of yourselves. And the girls, too. Never even asked me if I wanted to go with them.'

'They said they did ask you.' So Katie had lied, to placate her. 'But you don't want to go. Do you?' She held her breath. She couldn't allow him anyhow. He was only fifteen.

'That's beside the point. They could have asked me. It's like I'm invisible in this house.'

Lottie couldn't help the laugh that broke from her throat.

'What's so funny?' Sean squinted at her, confusion knotting his brow.

'Oh Sean, I feel invisible all the time.'

'Then you know what it's like. Can I get back to my game now?'

'How was school today?'

'Boring.'

She turned to leave. 'Open the window and bring your dirty clothes down to the washing machine. I'll put on a wash before I go back to work.'

'You have to go back?' The tall fifteen-year-old looked at her like the little boy he was at heart.

'I'm running multiple murder investigations and an eight-year-old girl is missing. So yes, I'm sorry, but I have to go back.'

'I understand.'

'I'll cook something for you before I leave.'

'It's okay. Katie said she was going to pick up stuff for dinner on her way home.'

'Great.' Lottie racked her brain trying to remember if there was anything she could rustle up for herself.

'Make sure you eat too,' he said.

She smiled and ruffled his hair.

He pulled away from her. 'Mam?'

'What?'

'You should take a shower before you go back to work. You smell.'

Water drummed on her head as Lottie tried to expunge the image invading her brain of her half-brother shopping with her daughters, grandson and mother. A half-brother who'd lived all of his life across the Atlantic Ocean. She knew feck all about him. As she lathered shampoo into her hair, she resolved to find out what she could. He was edging sideways into her family's life and she felt a niggle at the base of her skull over that.

After rinsing the shampoo from her hair, she scrambled around for conditioner and found the bottle empty. Typical. Her skin felt coarse and harsh. From the wind and bad weather? From neglect?

Her fingers scaled the ridges left by unknown fingers on her throat. Someone had tried to kill her! She stopped, hands in mid-air, water streaming down her body. No, if he'd wanted to kill her, he could have. He'd only wanted to stop her moving further into the forest. Why? Had he needed time to hide something? To make something vanish? Something from the lookout? Or had he just wanted to frighten her? She shivered with the idea of what could have happened if he'd wanted to stop her permanently. Her family; her children. How would they cope without her?

She watched the water run free of suds at her feet. Switching off the shower, she leaned her head against the glass panel. She barely had time to relish the moment of silence before she heard the front door open and the sound of her daughters' laughter and squeals of delight from little Louis. She smiled as her heart filled with love for her family.

Then she heard a male voice following them into her home. Leo fucking Belfield. She definitely had to do more research on him.

CHAPTER FIFTY-ONE

Showered, but still feeling unrefreshed, Lottie dressed quickly in the cleanest jeans and long-sleeved T-shirt she could find on the floor of her bedroom. Katie's idea of getting something for dinner had reached the giddy heights of a Chinese takeaway. A scowl in Leo's direction and he got the message. She stood at the door until Rose's car had disappeared down the estate. Stuffing prawn crackers in her mouth, she left her children to their illicit feast and headed back into work.

Standing in front of her team, she stared at the victims' photographs. And the one of Lily, long fair hair framing a smiling face. Guilt wormed its way through her body as she thought of the lack of headway they'd made on finding her.

'Okay,' she said, 'first off, Detective McKeown has no leads on the wedding dress found on Fiona. Both her original dress and Cara Dunne's were bought locally. He has circulated a picture of the dress through the media. It might lead us to the killer.' She took a deep breath.

'Now, Christy Clarke. Aged fifty-six. Separated father of one. Pig farmer and garage owner in the village of Ballydoon. His body was found yesterday afternoon at his closed-down garage. Cause of death, bullet wound to the head. The preliminary post-mortem results report that no gunshot residue was found on the victim's hands. It is safe to assume, therefore, that Christy Clarke was murdered. Who wanted him dead, and why? If we can nail down the *why*, we should find the *who*.'

McKeown said, 'Is his murder linked to the Dunne and Heffernan investigations?'

'No evidence to suggest it so far. No hair removed that the pathologist can see, and none of Fiona's hair found on his person.'

'Any eyewitnesses? Anyone hear anything?'

'No one has come forward so far, but Beth Clarke says that when she arrived at the garage, Colin Kavanagh was leaving. When I spoke to Kavanagh last night, he refused to account for his whereabouts and answered no comment to my questions. Beth says he claimed that he owns all of Christy's property, including the garage.' She flicked through a file. 'Has he been formally interviewed yet?'

'He's waiting for his solicitor,' McKeown said, then laughed when no one else did. 'Sorry, bad joke.'

'This is no time for messing.' She scowled at him. 'Sergeant Boyd and I saw Kavanagh leaving the local priest's house earlier today. Surely someone can haul his arse in here for a few questions. We need to eliminate him if he is innocent of any wrongdoing.' She didn't believe this for a second. If Beth was to be believed, Kavanagh had fleeced Christy Clarke.

McKeown said, 'Colin Kavanagh represented some of the mid-player drug gang leaders during his time in Dublin.'

'There could be a criminal element involved in Christy's death. Have you sourced any further information on the stolen cars discovered in the garage?'

'I've contacted the relevant garda stations in Dublin and I'm waiting for replies.'

'Keep on it,' Lottie said. 'The fact that Clarke had stolen property on his premises might be a clue as to why he was killed.' As she spoke, she turned over in her head what Beth had said about the solicitor. 'I need someone to look into Christy's finances and carry out a search on his property folios. Find out what he has in the bank, what he owes, who he owes and what he owns.' Gosh, but she missed Detective Maria Lynch for this kind of work.

'I'll do it,' Boyd volunteered.

'Great. Thanks.' She was grateful he'd offered. Otherwise she'd have had to allocate it to McKeown, which was a bit unfair as he was also working on the dash-cam footage in relation to Lily's case. Resources stretched to the limit. Nothing new there, she thought. 'Has Eve Clarke been in yet for her interview?'

'She's not at her flat,' Kirby said.

'Where the hell is she?' Lottie paced two steps and stopped at the wall. 'Find her and get her here.'

Boyd said, 'Shouldn't we interview Clarke's daughter, Beth?'

'We *have* interviewed her.' Lottie dug her nails into the palms of her hands, adding to the ridges already there from frustration about previous cases that had gone around in circles.

'Not formally,' Boyd countered.

'Okay. Bring her in.' She sincerely hoped Beth had not been involved in the death of her father. But she couldn't discount anything at this stage.

'Now let's move on to Robert Brady. Anything back from forensics on the belt used to strangle Cara Dunne?'

'We've got a result,' Kirby said. 'Robert Brady's DNA is a match to the DNA from the belt found in Cara's apartment. His fingerprints are all over the belt, along with some partials from Cara but no one else.'

Lottie gave him a thumbs-up. 'Great, but Brady was already dead, so how could his belt have been used in Cara's murder?'

'Someone took it from his body or possessions?' Kirby offered.

'Have you located his van?'

'It was found at the rear of the caravan park at Doon Lake. Full to the gills with tools and stuff. SOCOs are going through it.'

'Beth mentioned he was living in it.'

'It's possible. There's so much stuff in it. I'll see if I can find anything further on his living arrangements.'

'Okay. We might also need to exhume Brady's body for another autopsy.'

'This is my fault,' McKeown said. 'After all, I worked Brady's suicide.'

'You didn't highlight anything suspicious in your report.' Lottie twisted her head to stare at him.

'There wasn't anything suspicious about it,' he said indignantly.

'I'm not accusing you!' She balled her hands into fists, trying to keep the exasperation from her voice. 'I'm only saying.'

'Until the pathologist informed us about the lock of hair found on his body – weeks later, I might add – his death was a cut-and-dried suicide.'

She wondered if the *cut-and-dried* comment had been intentional. 'I know Kirby has gone over it, but I want you to review the case file with fresh eyes. See who was interviewed at the time and talk to them again.'

'Okay.' McKeown ran his hand over his head. 'I'm flat out, though. Not enough minutes in the day.'

Lottie said, 'We're all stretched. Any update on Lily Heffernan?'

'There's still no word.' he said. 'Every teacher, caretaker, parent and child has been interviewed twice. All the after-school club staff and kids, and the dance tutors and dancers too. Every business with CCTV has had it checked, but we've found nothing suspicious. The lads are still looking at the dash-cam footage, but the kid seems to have disappeared into thin air.'

'Interview Trevor Toner and Giles Bannon again. And Shelly Forde. They have to have seen something.'

'Right. This will be the third time.'

'I don't care. Keep interviewing and keep searching. And the other kids and their parents, talk to them. Again.'

'No one remembers a thing. It was mayhem that evening, what with the market on the street and traffic diversions.'

'You're telling me that a car couldn't have got close to the dance school for someone to snatch the child?'

'No, I'm not, but we've found nothing. All the apartments and businesses on Gaol Street have been checked.'

'What about the stallholders?'

'No one saw anything.'

'And the theatre where Lily was rehearsing, has that been searched again?'

'From top to bottom.'

Lottie sat on the edge of a table, staring up at the photos on the board. 'A child does not just vanish like that.'

But she knew deep in her heart that that was not true. And for the first time since she'd discovered the little girl was missing, she thought Lily might be dead. She bent down to pick up her bag and noticed her hands were white and trembling. It was as if an icicle had slithered through her blood.

Boyd stood at the printer and pressed the button. It shrieked a warning.

'Needs paper,' Lottie said, sitting on the nearest chair. The meeting had eroded the last fragment of energy from her. She needed to sleep and eat. Soon.

He opened a fresh ream and fed paper into the machine. 'SOCOs sent Lily's toothbrush for DNA analysis.'

'Okay.'

'To have it on file so that if anything or anyone turns up, we can use it for identification purposes.'

Lottie gripped her elbows to quell the shiver. They had to find Lily. Alive.

'Here's the thing,' Boyd said, jabbing the print button again. 'McGlynn fast-tracked it through the system. Checked it against Fiona's DNA.'

'And?'

'It's a match all right.'

'But …?'

'But it also threw up an interesting thing on Lily's father.'

'Colin Kavanagh?' Lottie said. 'He should be on the system for elimination purposes due to his work.'

'He is, and it was run against his DNA profile.' Boyd waved the piece of paper he'd printed off. 'Colin Kavanagh is not Lily's father.'

'What the hell? Show me.' She grabbed the page and scanned the technical data. 'Holy shit.'

Boyd sat on the edge of his desk. 'So who is going to tell him?'

*

He sat and watched her sleep. So angelic. Silent. Unlike the tantrum he'd witnessed not an hour ago. Rubbing his hands together, he tried to think of a way out. He was in a bind. What to do with her now that he had her?

Moving closer to the cot bed, he unwound his fingers from each other and clasped them behind his back as he leaned over her. He needed to see the mist of her breath in the cool air, to hear the soft sound of her breathing. Watching the shallow rise and dip of her flat chest, he was satisfied.

He hadn't meant to slap her, to strike out at her, but she would not shut up. Screaming for her mother. He knew no one could hear, but that did not douse his frustration. He thought children should be submissive and willing to learn from him. Willing to see sense. Willing to let him take the lead. But Lily was different. She was Fiona's child. She was supposed to be compliant and dutiful, not disrespectful and rude. She had to be punished. But should it be by his hand or not?

Exhaling, he turned and left her to her dreams.

There was somewhere he had to be.

He locked the door, pocketed the key and made his way outside.

CHAPTER FIFTY-TWO

Beth had been unable to get rid of Ryan. She hadn't the nerve to be rude to him. He'd sat at the table watching his tea turn cold. She'd made him coffee and he'd sipped it for a second before watching that go cold also. They'd talked a little. Very little.

Eventually she'd said, 'Ryan, I've stuff to organise. You know, for Dad's funeral.'

'Don't let me stop you.'

'Why don't you go home? I'm sure Zoe and the boys miss you.'

'Zoe is better off without me.'

'Don't say that.'

'Look, Beth, you do what you've got to do. I just want peace and quiet.'

'Do you want to have a shower or a bath?'

'I'm fine, thanks. But here, put this with the story you're writing.' He took an SD card out of his pocket and laid it on the table. 'You can upload them to your laptop and put them on a USB stick.'

'The photos?' she said, picking it up.

'Yes.'

She sat in the silence. His head drooped and he laid it on his folded arms on the table. Only when she heard the soft purr of his snores did she feel brave enough to move. To stand up. Take one step at a time out of the kitchen.

Quietly she climbed the stairs and sat on her bed wondering why Ryan was so grubby. Mud and leaves were stuck in his hair and dirt cramped his usually pristine fingernails. At work, he was a stickler for hygiene. Was this what grief did to you? She hoped not. Her father's death had not had time to settle with her. She doubted it ever would.

When her mother had left them, had she grieved back then? She remembered the last night, so clearly it was like looking through glass. Christy roaring at Eve in their bedroom.

'Get out of my house!'

'You can keep your fucking house. I'll get a bigger and fancier one in the sunshine, not this godforsaken dark, wet hole of a village.'

'Oh, your fancy man is a millionaire now, is he?' Christy laughed manically.

'Shut the fuck up.' Eve slammed one drawer and opened another.

'Are you going to make me?' He leaned against the door as she stuffed clothes into an old suitcase with broken wheels.

'You are impossible to live with, Christy Clarke.'

'Silage smells. Slurry smells. You knew that when you married me.'

'I'm not talking about that and well you know it.' Eve sat on the suitcase to squash the clothes down. Her legs were bare and her shoes were soft leather. Beth had loved how her mother always dressed well, even when Dad said money was tight.

'Eve. I'm sorry. Give me a chance. Think of Beth.'

'Fuck you and her.' Eve jumped up and slapped him full on the face. Christy never wavered, and as if realising what she'd done, she sat back down on the suitcase, pulled her knees to her chest and sobbed. 'Oh God, I didn't mean that. I love Beth.'

'Fine way of showing it.'

'I'm coming back for her.'

'Sure you are.'

Eve stood, pulled an orange cashmere coat on over her shoulders and lifted the heavy case. Christy stood to one side to let her pass.

Beth cowered at her bedroom door, waiting for her dad to stop her mother, or for her mother to come for her, at least to say goodbye. But Eve walked down the stairs and out the door without a backward glance. And with the soft click of the door closing, the house lost all its colour.

That was what Beth thought now as she put Ryan's SD card into her box in the wardrobe. There'd been little colour in her life since the day her mother had left. She'd swallowed the shame, sucked it up as her dad had advised. But it had torn her heart in two.

She sat back on the bed and picked at the plastic popper on the hem of her duvet. Opened and shut it; opened and shut. She glanced out the window. Raining hard now. The sound beating like the thrum of fingers on an out-of-tune piano. As loud as a truck engine. The only thing she could hear.

Kneeling up on her bed, she pressed her face to the cold glass. Save for the rain, there was silence. No sound from the pigs. The quiet was unsettling. Something was wrong. Very wrong.

Jumping from the bed, she ran from her room and down the stairs, skidding past the sleeping Ryan and out to the yard. The rain drenched her in seconds. She rushed into the shed. Empty. Nothing. Not one pig or suckling. Sliding through the shitty straw, she checked each pen. All devoid of life. Kavanagh had already started to strip the farm.

Dad would go apeshit.

Then she remembered.

Her father was gone. Everything was gone.

She fell to her knees and cried.

*

She didn't know how long she'd been kneeling on the urine- and excrement-stained ground when the sound of an engine roused her from her trance. She left the shed and glanced around the yard. Her car was gone.

'Ryan?'

Shivering uncontrollably in her rain-soaked clothes, she crashed into the kitchen. No sign of him.

'Where are you?' She shouted up the stairs before running out the back door again. He was gone. Why? Where? And he'd taken her car. Damn him.

'Ryan!' She yelled at the bulbous night sky while rainwater trickled down her face and neck and lodged in a damp pool between her breasts. She felt like a little child alone in the world, with nothing and no one to comfort her. She missed her friend. Missed the cool-headed wisdom, telling her to get up off her arse and sort things out. To confront Colin Kavanagh and demand what was rightfully hers.

She smiled through her tears. Even though he was no longer around, she still heard his voice. He was right. She should go straight to Kavanagh and have it out with him.

She took her phone from her jeans pocket to phone him. It was saturated and lifeless. She'd just have to fetch her jacket and walk. Now that she was full of renewed motivation, she was not going to let anything stop her: not the rain or the lack of a car; not even the pitch blackness of the countryside.

At the back door, she paused. Alert now.

Holding a hand to her brow, she scanned her surroundings, her vision reaching the abbey lights in the distance.

Her mother had walked away from it all. She would not.

CHAPTER FIFTY-THREE

The gardaí eventually located Colin Kavanagh at his home. He agreed to come to the station and was directed into the interview room. He divested himself of his jacket, looking around for somewhere to hang it.

Lottie smiled sweetly, with a forced effort. 'You can put it on the back of your chair.'

'And pick up fleas? No thanks.'

'Give it here.' She took the expensive-looking coat and handed it to a passing guard to look after.

Boyd carried out the introductions for the recording.

'You're waiving your right to a solicitor, is that correct?' Lottie said, sitting down.

'I *am* a solicitor,' Kavanagh said haughtily. As if she didn't know already. 'I'm here voluntarily. Get on with it. I'm extremely busy searching for my daughter, seeing as you lot can't get your finger out.'

'I'll talk about Lily in a few minutes. First I want you to account for your whereabouts yesterday afternoon.'

'You're talking about Christy Clarke again, aren't you?'

'I am.'

'The answer is still the same. No comment.'

'We believe you were at Mr Clarke's garage a short time before his body was found. What were you doing there?'

'No comment.'

'Have you a key to Mr Clarke's premises?'

'No comment.'

'Why did Christy call to your home on the day of his murder?'

'No …' Kavanagh stared at her. 'Murder?'

'Yes.'

He recovered. 'No comment.'

'This is ridiculous.' Lottie slammed the table even though she had warned herself not to get angry. 'I could be out looking for your daughter, but instead I'm wasting my time in here with you. If you have nothing to hide, why don't you tell me what you were doing in Clarke's Garage?'

'Do you have evidence that I was inside the building?'

Lottie chewed on her cheek for a moment. He was as slimy and slithery as the imaginary worm crawling in her stomach.

'You don't even have evidence I was outside it.'

'I have an eyewitness.'

'Reliable?'

'Yes.'

'Are you sure about that?' He leaned into the hard back of the chair, stretched his hands above his head. Lottie smelled the woody scent of whatever he'd sprayed his body with. It wasn't unpleasant, but still her stomach flipped.

'I'm sure,' she said.

'How is Beth doing? Must have been an awful shock, finding her father dead.'

She stared at him. Kavanagh knew it was Beth who had told her about his presence at the garage. 'Why did you harass her? In her own home!'

'Is that what she said? I never harassed that young lady. She's just like her mother –unstable. I wouldn't believe a word out of her mouth if I was you.'

'Unstable? How would you know what her mental health is like?'

'Christy confided in me. After Eve left him, and I know it sounds like a cliché, he was a broken man. He drank hard for a while, his business went down the sewer and he neglected his daughter.'

'What has that got to do with anything?'

'Christy was broken in every sense of the word. Not a penny left. He'd borrowed left, right and centre trying to make that pig farm work. He lost all his friends over it. I dug him out of that particular hole on numerous occasions until finally he signed his worthless property over to me. One less worry, he told me.'

'I can't understand why you would help him out in the first place. What was he to you?'

'A friend. At one time. Then …'

'Then what?'

'Nothing.'

'Why take everything from a poverty-stricken man?'

Kavanagh laughed, his white hair rippling on his head like a startled stream. 'Poverty-stricken? Not quite.'

'What do you mean?'

'I don't really want to speak ill of the dead, as they say, but Christy Clarke had made deals with the devil himself. And you know how those turn out. You end up burned.'

'What are you talking about?'

'You saw those cars in his garage. I'm sure by now you know they're stolen property.'

'Are you saying Christy was involved with criminals?'

'I won't insult your intelligence by feigning surprise at your question. You know. I know. Everyone knows.'

'Knows what?'

'That Christy Clarke dealt with criminals. Using his garage as a safe house until the cars could be moved on.'

'Have you proof of this?'

'Proof? The cars, Inspector. They're still sitting in that dusty showroom. Surely you're not blind?'

'No, I'm not, but there's no proof that Christy was involved in anything illegal.' Lottie smiled. 'Why would *you* get involved with him if you knew about these alleged activities?'

'What?'

'You heard me.'

'You're one sly bitch.' Kavanagh stood, his chair clattering into the wall. He leaned on the table with both hands. Eyed Boyd, then Lottie. 'This interview is terminated.'

'Sit down, sir,' Boyd said. 'The interview will be terminated when we say so.'

'I refuse to listen to any more of your insinuations.' He took a deep breath. Lottie was sure he was going to leave, but he surprised her and sat.

'I don't need to insinuate anything,' she said. 'Acting Superintendent David McMahon was involved in the Drugs and Organised Crime Bureau before he came here. And let me tell you, he is very interested in this case.'

Kavanagh shrugged. 'So what?'

'Why don't you come clean now, before your dirty linen is hung on the line for all to see?'

'I have nothing to worry about.' Kavanagh folded his arms defiantly, but Lottie thought she caught a hint of uncertainty lurking at the corner of his eyes.

'Father Michael Curran,' she said, shifting direction. 'Tell me about him.'

'Why in God's name are you dragging the parish priest into this?' He unfolded his arms and placed his hands on the table, palms up. 'Typical Irish cop. If in doubt, blame the poor priest.'

'You visited him this morning but left at speed. Why?'

'Lily, of course. I was asking him to include my little girl in his prayers. I thought maybe a little divine intervention might help.'

'How long have you known Father Curran?'

Kavanagh removed his hands from the table and placed them on his lap. 'Since I arrived to live in Ballydoon, possibly.'

'Nine or ten years?'

'I suppose so.'

'Tell me about Robert Brady.' She wanted to keep firing names at him, watching for his reaction. Anything at this stage would help.

'Who?' He looked genuinely stumped, and she hoped her changing direction was wrong-footing him.

'The young man who worked on your house.'

'I don't know him.'

'You must remember him. He was found hanging from a tree near your property two weeks ago. The men who discovered him ran to your house to raise the alarm. You called the emergency services. And I believe he worked on the rebuild of your home.'

'Oh, I didn't make the connection. I honestly don't remember anything about him.' Kavanagh looked at her from beneath his white eyebrows.

She eyed him, trying to make up her mind. Time to pull out her ace card and see how his castle crumbled.

'What do you think has happened to Lily?'

'I don't know. Maybe some bad bastard saw an opportunity when her mother wasn't there to collect her.'

'Mm,' Lottie said.

'What do you mean by that?'

'Did you ever wonder why Fiona didn't give Lily your surname?'

Kavanagh shifted on the chair and looked at a point in the corner of the room. She had to stop herself from turning to see what he was concentrating on. Probably a cobweb.

He said, 'Fiona was headstrong when it came to Lily. She wouldn't let me have much to do with the child. Overprotective. Wouldn't even let me buy her an iPad or a phone. Afraid of online stalkers. Jesus, the child is eight! Fiona smothered her.'

'I'd call that love.'

'I suppose *you* would, but there was something else. I don't know what you'd call it.'

'Possessiveness?'

'Maybe.'

'But she allowed you access to Lily even after you'd split up. Why?'

'I was the child's father. I was entitled.'

'Were you, though?'

'Entitled? Of course. I revised our legal agreement. It was ready for her to sign, the day before her wedding. Only she never … she didn't …'

'She didn't live to sign it.'

'That's correct.'

'Someone killed her first.'

He glared at her. 'I had nothing to do with Fiona's death.'

'So you say.'

'I do.'

Lottie felt it was the right moment. 'Why did you need a legal agreement if Fiona was okay with you having access?'

'I don't trust Ryan Slevin. He could've turned Fiona against me, and then I'd have lost all right to see Lily. It was an assurance to keep my daughter in my life.'

'But she wasn't, was she?'

'Ah for Christ's sake. What are you on about now?' He tugged at the hair above his ears, exasperation lacing his words.

'Lily wasn't your daughter.' Lottie sat forward. Watching to see what Kavanagh's face would tell her.

'What?' He scrunched his eyes, brows knitting. 'What are you trying to say?'

'We have Lily's DNA, from her toothbrush. Forensics ran it through the database.'

'Go on.' The only muscle he moved was his mouth. His expression frozen.

'Lily is not your daughter, Mr Kavanagh.'

Lottie pulled back into her chair, waiting for Kavanagh to spring across the table at her. Instead, his head slumped into his hands and his shoulders rocked.

'Are you okay?' Boyd said. 'Will I fetch you some water, or a coffee?'

'Colin?' Lottie said gently, unsure if she had made the right call or not. 'Did you know about this?'

He shook his head, silent except for muffled sobs.

'Fiona never mentioned anything to you? Never gave you any idea?'

Kavanagh raised his head. 'Why would she tell me? I was paying her to raise *our* daughter.'

'If she had told you, would it have made any difference to you?'

Once again, his eyes found the spot on the wall. She thought he had slipped into a trance, he was silent so long.

At last he spoke. 'I always suspected it, you know. That she wasn't telling me the truth.'

'Do you know who the father is?'

'I'm not sure, but I have my suspicions.'

'Care to share them with me?'

'If you know I'm not Lily's father, I'm sure you already know who is. Are you going to enlighten me?'

'Not at the moment.' She didn't know the identity of the child's father. They'd only run Lily's DNA against Kavanagh and Fiona. But she would follow up.

He stood. 'It changes nothing, you know.'

'In what way?' Lottie stood too, suddenly feeling sorry for the man in front of her. A man into whose heart she'd just stuck a knife. Metaphorically speaking.

'I still love Lily. I've made appeals on television and offered a reward. I want to find her. Help me do that. Please.'

'You know that reward offer brings us more difficulties. We are doing everything we can. I'd appreciate it if you could tell us anything you know that might help us.'

'All I know is that I lost Fiona a long time before she died, but I don't intend to lose Lily.'

'We will need to talk more. About Christy Clarke.'

'Okay. But not right now.'

'Sure.' So far, no evidence had been discovered to link him to Christy Clarke's death. Shit.

'One final thing. Fiona had very few possessions at her home. Do you know where they might be?'

'At Ryan Slevin's blasted cottage, possibly.'

'That was empty.'

'Then I don't know. You saw my house. Lily's room there is full to the brim with toys and clothes for her when she's with me. Other than that, I've no idea.'

'Thanks, Colin.'

'I'd like a word with McMahon now.' Kavanagh moved towards the door.

'Why?'

'You've had no success finding Lily, so I'm going to talk to a man who has more power than you.'

Boyd wound up the formalities for the recording. When Kavanagh left the interview room, Lottie felt as deflated as he had looked.

'We discovered nothing new from all that,' she said. 'But I'm beginning to think Kavanagh introduced Christy to the criminal element. Why else would he buy him out?'

Boyd rose, filed his notes into a folder and put a hand on her arm. 'We will find Lily. And the murderer. I have every faith in you and our team.'

She could feel the heat of his fingers through the sleeve of her cotton T-shirt. She leaned her head against his shoulder, longing to have him soothe her scalp with his long, lean fingers. To have him whisper calming words in her ear. But that wasn't going to happen in a stuffy, overpowering interview room. An arm around her would have done, she thought, but Boyd picked up the recording and wrote the date and time before sealing it.

When she was at the door, he said, 'Why did you tell him?'

'Tell him what?'

'That he wasn't Lily's father.'

'To see if he already knew, and if so, whether he knows the identity of the girl's father.'

'I think he does,' Boyd said, holding the door open for her.

'I think he does too. Call the forensics lab. Tell them to run Lily's DNA through the system. Let's hope we find out before Kavanagh does anything stupid.'

CHAPTER FIFTY-FOUR

While Boyd went to the canteen to fetch fresh coffee, Lottie found McKeown in the office.

'We've found out nothing from Kavanagh,' she said. 'He claims he didn't know Lily wasn't his daughter.'

'Her biological father could have taken her,' McKeown said.

'We need to find out who he is. Boyd is contacting the lab.'

'With regard to Christy Clarke, I think I've uncovered a financial morass,' he said.

Lottie wheeled over a chair and sat down. McKeown was busy tapping his keyboard. He stopped and pointed to the screen.

'I've been looking at the land registry folios.'

'I thought Boyd said he was going to do that.'

'I offered to take some weight off his shoulders,' he said. She scowled at him. He added, 'I'm keeping a close eye on everything to do with Lily at the same time.'

'Go on.'

'Most of Clarke's property, except for the garage, is currently in Colin Kavanagh's name. I couldn't find anything in Beth's name, or her mother, Eve Clarke's.'

'Right. What about the pigs?'

'Nothing on paper, but I heard the stock was removed earlier today to another piggery. On Kavanagh's instructions.'

'The cars in the garage?'

'Clarke's accounts were released from the bank and the tax office. I had a quick look. There's no mention of the sale of cars anywhere. The garage made a loss for years. But about two months ago, there was a cash deposit of fifteen thousand euros. It did little to fill the black hole.'

'Where did that come from?'

'It was a cashier's cheque. I'll follow up with the bank.'

'Any employees?'

'No. Not even a salesman or a mechanic.'

'So it was a front for stolen vehicles. God knows how we'll get to the bottom of that one.'

'Our super might have some inkling of what was going on. I had a word with him. He shut me up immediately. I gather he doesn't want it going public.'

'He's waiting for concrete evidence,' Lottie said. 'The bank statements. Had Clarke any money at all?'

'Up to his neck in debt. Loans left, right and centre.'

'But he had enough to buy and sell pigs?'

'All the farm accounts show little or no expenditure on the pigs. Which leads me to believe he was buying supplies and feedstuff with cash.'

'Cash he got for the stolen cars being housed in his garage.'

She stood up and stretched her muscles as Boyd arrived with the coffees. She took one and sipped it, willing the caffeine to hit the spot.

'We need the Criminal Assets Bureau on this one,' she said. 'I'll see if McMahon knows a reliable detective there. It needs to be looked at quickly.'

'I wish you luck with that,' McKeown said.

Boyd said, 'Do you think Christy Clarke was killed as part of a criminal gang feud?'

Lottie thought for a moment. 'I don't know, but it would make things clear cut. Otherwise it's highly likely he was killed by the person who murdered Cara and Fiona.'

Putting down his coffee, Boyd said, 'Oh, I meant to tell you. Eve Clarke is back at her apartment.'

*

Eve Clarke was not happy to be sitting in front of two detectives in her own apartment. She picked at an invisible spot on the arm of the chair.

'Eve, please look at me.'

Detective Inspector Parker looked like she could do with a good feed to put meat on her bones. Come to think of it, Eve couldn't remember when she herself had last had a square meal.

'Sorry, I was miles away. What was it you wanted to speak to me about?'

'Your husband. Christy Clarke.'

'What about him? I heard he killed himself. Always was a coward, that man.'

'It's been confirmed that he did not take his own life,' Lottie said evenly. 'I didn't know Christy, but from what Beth told me, I don't think he was the kind of man to leave his daughter behind with no answers.'

Eve blinked rapidly. 'And what about me?'

'You were estranged a long time, were you not?'

'That's neither here nor there. What do you want from me?'

'Can you think of anyone who might want to harm him?'

'Everyone he owed money to, probably.'

'Who would that be?'

'Christy couldn't manage to find two matching socks, that's how inept he was at everything. Never stopped him trying to be someone he was not. He always put on the big-man act with the real big men.'

'And who were these real big men?'

Eve snorted. 'Colin Kavanagh, with his fancy car and his converted barn that'd fetch a million or more on the open market. His kind has people willing to fork out cash over and above the market value.'

'Really?' Lottie said, and Eve guessed it was with feigned surprise. 'I thought he was an upstanding citizen.'

'Huh.' Eve snorted. 'That's the impression he portrays. But I know that if you get into a bath with sewage, some of the shit is bound to stick. He's mired up to his white head in it.'

She sat back and watched the inspector intently. She couldn't read the vivid green eyes that were boring into her own. Something was coming, and Eve knew she was not prepared for whatever that might be.

*

'How do you know this?' Lottie kept her gaze fixed on the woman's face, watching for signs that showed truth or lies.

Busying herself lighting a cigarette, Eve lowered her eyes. 'Kept my ear to the ground, and the rumours turned to fact over time.'

'You were abroad for a number of years, though.'

'I picked up more information on the Costa del Sol about criminal activities than the drug squad here. Mark my words, Colin Kavanagh is dirty.'

'Did he kill your husband?'

'If he didn't, I'm certain he was behind it.'

Lottie figured Eve didn't know everything. Time to drop the bombshell. 'Eve, we believe Christy signed all his property over to Colin Kavanagh within the last year.'

'What?' The cigarette clung to Eve's open lips.

'Our investigation turned up evidence that his land and property is now owned by Kavanagh. You won't inherit anything by Christy's death.'

'I wanted nothing from him when I left him. I want nothing from him now.' She laughed sardonically. 'I can't believe you think I killed him.'

'I never said that.' Lottie held her stare. 'Who do you think could have been behind the stolen high-end cars?'

'What are you talking about?'

'We found a number of Mercedes and BMWs in Christy's garage. We believe he was being paid cash for either holding them or selling them on. It's possible this money was used to fund his piggery operation.'

'The fucking pigs. His babies. Never wanted him to get involved in that venture. But Christy never listened to me.'

'Answer the question, Eve.'

Another long drag on the cigarette. Blowing out a circle of smoke, she said, 'Ask Colin Kavanagh. It was his idea. He's behind it all.'

'How do you know so much about Kavanagh?' Lottie studied the woman, who seemed much older than her fifty-odd years, her eyes blinking continuously behind her spectacles.

Eve shifted to the edge of the chair. 'He was one of the reasons Christy threw me out.'

'What do you mean?'

'I had an affair, a disastrous affair, with Colin Kavanagh. Christy found out, and to this day I believe Colin told him about us. Boasting or something.'

'But in that case, why would Christy continue to do business with Kavanagh?'

'He was gullible. He saw me as the one who did wrong, I suppose.'

'So you left alone? You didn't go abroad with a lover? Why didn't you tell Beth the truth?'

'Because I'm as big a coward as Christy. How is Beth holding up?'

'Why don't you contact her? I'm sure she could do with a mother's love right now.'

'My rows with her father were loud and ugly,' Eve said quietly. 'And after I left, I heard Christy was a different man. I tried, but Beth never forgave me for what I did to our family. So I don't blame her for hating me. She's better off without me.'

Lottie sank back in the chair. For once, she was struck dumb.

It was late, and she had to go home, but the interview confirmed one thing she'd already suspected. Colin Kavanagh had a lot more questions to answer.

CHAPTER FIFTY-FIVE

Colin Kavanagh wasn't at home. No one answered the intercom. No lights. Beth wondered what had possessed her to trek so far in the darkness. Maybe it was the madness that possessed one in grief. She'd heard about things people did after a loved one died. Irrational things. As if their minds were possessed and they had no control over their actions. Was that what was going on in her head? She had no idea. And no notion of what to do now that she was miles from civilisation, alone in the solid darkness of night.

Robert Brady had lost his life close by, and she recalled how she'd heard about it. The text. Just like the one that had come to her phone the other day, when Cara Dunne died. She still did not know who her source was, and now, in the startling darkness, she wondered if it had been not someone throwing a newsworthy item her way, but someone who wanted her to witness the aftermath of the deaths. Still, she'd stumbled on her father's body without anyone prompting her.

She walked in the direction of the lake. She'd know the way even if she was blindfolded, and that was what it felt like now. Edging along the grass verge to make sure she stayed on the roadway, she thought of what Zoe had told her about her father borrowing money from Giles. What had he needed it for? All those fancy cars in the garage showroom? Madness, she thought, but she knew he'd been involved in something shady. Maybe if she'd been more of an investigative journalist rather than a small-town reporter, she'd have seen what was right under her nose a lot sooner than she had.

Twisting rainwater from her drenched hair, she walked on and on until she could hear the luring lapping of the water on the stones and pebbles. As she inched around the gate and walked on to the shore, the rain stalled in the sky and the moon glittered through the haze of the night. And then she heard her name being uttered.

Rooted to the spot, she could not breathe.

She swallowed a gulp and made to turn around, but a hand pressed down on her shoulder, stalling her movement. The clouds shifted, and once again Beth was plunged into deepest darkness.

CHAPTER FIFTY-SIX

Lottie yearned for an evening, even one evening, with a glass of wine in her hand and a comforting arm around her shoulders. One of those things she knew she should not have, but maybe the other mightn't be so unattainable.

Eyeing the empty suitcases in the hall, she headed for the sitting room. The light was switched off. Her children and grandson were in bed. She had the room to herself. She tapped Boyd's number on her phone and listened to it ring. Listened to it go to voicemail. She hung up without speaking.

How had it got to this?

She had given him the answer he'd craved and now he was ignoring her. She tried his number again. Same thing.

'Damn you, Boyd.'

She waited ten seconds. Dialled again.

'What the hell, Lottie? I was asleep. What's wrong?'

'I need you,' she said.

'I'm way too tired to talk.'

'Where are you?'

'Why do you want to know?'

'Just asking.'

'Lottie, I'm wrecked. I'll see you tomorrow, okay?'

'It'll have to do, I suppose.'

'Right. Goodnight, Lottie.'

'When are you going to Galway again, if you're not there at the moment?'

'Lottie …'

'Okay,' she said. 'Goodnight.'

She listened to the dial tone before moving to the kitchen, where she found the bottle of wine. Without hesitation, she uncorked it, filled a glass to the brim and toasted the dark kitchen window. 'Fuck you Boyd,' she said, and her heart shattered into minuscule pieces.

*

Cynthia Rhodes sat on the narrow sofa with her laptop on her knee, browsing the online evening news. She watched back over the press conference she'd reported on and decided she was fed up with Ragmullin and its crimes, and sick to the bone of Lottie Parker.

She looked at the red wine in her glass before deciding a bellyful of sediment was not the best recipe for a good night's sleep. She clicked on Google, then with one finger keyed in Colin Kavanagh's name. She'd seen him leaving the garda station earlier, and her suspicious nature fuelled her interest. Granted, his little girl was missing, and his ex-partner had been murdered, but a visit to the station at that hour seemed a little unusual.

She scanned over a list of his cases in the criminal court. Gangland crime was on the rise, evidenced by the trials heard there. Dublin was a mess, and in a perverse way she was content enough to be based in Ragmullin for a few months. Living in a hotel suite wasn't all that bad, and from time to time she had an apartment to visit.

'Are you coming to bed?'

She turned her head and smiled. 'Not until you tell me why Colin Kavanagh, solicitor extraordinaire, was at the station tonight.'

He moved from the room, white boxers accentuating his well-toned abs. She felt a stirring in her abdomen, or maybe it was just the wine reaching her bladder too quickly. Either way, she had to agree he was a handsome man, and idly she wondered why Lottie Parker hadn't swooped on him.

'Kavanagh?' he said, moving to stand behind her. 'I have no idea.'

'I thought you were a cop?'

'I am.' He shrugged. 'Perhaps he was looking for an update on his daughter's disappearance.'

'I'm sure he knows how to use a phone,' she said, and smirked as his fingers traced a line on her collarbone, his face coming close to her ear as he sought out the lobe.

'Why are you researching him online?'

'I've got an itchy nose.'

'Want me to scratch it for you?'

'I'm quite capable of doing that myself, thank you.' She twisted on the sofa and patted the seat beside her. 'Tell me something.'

'If I can.' He sat, throwing his leg over hers, allowing her to run a hand along the inside of his thigh. She squirmed with growing pleasure.

'Tell me about Kavanagh,' she said.

He removed her hand from his leg. 'I know nothing about him.'

'At one time he was the best criminal defence lawyer in Dublin, the focus of the Drugs and Organised Crime unit. I'm sure you know about that, don't you?'

'Yes.'

'Do you know what happened?'

'I'm tired.' He stood. 'Are you coming to bed, or what?'

'Or what,' she laughed. 'In a minute.'

'Cynthia?'

'Yes?'

'Forget about Colin Kavanagh. There's no story there. Come to bed.'

He went into the bedroom, leaving the door slightly ajar. He was wrong; she was certain there was a story there. She just had to find a way to uncover it.

*

The latest doll he'd constructed worried him. It didn't look right. He'd checked the stoop outside, but there had been no more hair left for him. Pity.

He opened a drawer and took out the horsehair. He snipped off enough to redo the doll's head. Then he picked up a strip of white material and cut it into the outline of a miniature dress. He hoped this would turn out better. He ran his hand through his own hair and thought about trimming some off, but abandoned that idea. He'd make do with what he had. He bent over the table and got to work.

*

Lily cried into the rough pillow. She really wanted her mummy. Her tummy hurt. Her head hurt and she missed her teddies.

'Mummy?' she cried. 'Where are you?'

She lifted her head from the pillow. She could hear footsteps overhead. Maybe she shouldn't have shouted out. Maybe the man would come down and slap her for making noise. No, she would have to be quiet.

Sticking her thumb in her mouth like she used to do when she was smaller, Lily twiddled her long hair around her other hand, and eventually, she fell asleep.

*

He needed the hair. Beautiful long black hair.

He closed his eyes and heard the imaginary sound of the snip of scissors. Felt the cuts to his scalp. The memories would never fade. As he grew older, the images grew clearer, the need more insistent.

Opening his eyes, he fingered the steel scissors in his pocket.

First, though, he wanted to play a little.

What was life without some play?

Dull.

CHAPTER FIFTY-SEVEN

Saturday

It was dark. Beth's head hurt like she had the worst hangover ever. She could feel her hair matted to her face and was conscious that her body was dripping with sweat, while at the same time she was shivering, her teeth clattering with the cold.

Where was she?

She tried to retrace her movements in her throbbing brain. Tried to put a hand to the area where the most pain reverberated and found she was unable to move.

What the hell ...? But there was no echo of her words. They stayed inside her head, because her mouth was bound. Tightly. Her hands and feet also. Tied so firmly the blood was unable to flow through her veins, her limbs numb.

She kept her eyes wide open, trying to figure out where she was. A chink of light glinted from one wall. A window? She had no way of knowing.

She sniffed above the gag that was wrapped around her mouth, keeping her words silent in her throat. What could she smell? Varnish. And something else. Sweat. It was so acrid, it had to be male perspiration. She was aware of her own body odour. This was different. Someone else's.

Twisting her head to one side, she felt the cold timber beneath her cheek. Her eyelids drooped, and she had no power to stop sleep invading her sentience. Though she could not see, she was aware that everything blurred, her focus shifting to a deeper darkness.

*

He couldn't do this much longer. He had no idea how to care for a child. She continued to whimper like a sick puppy.

He took her by the hand and led her into the kitchen.

'What would you like?'

'My mummy.'

'To eat. What would you like to eat?'

'Nothing.'

'Eggs?' He took a carton out of the cupboard. 'Scrambled. Kids love scrambled eggs.'

'I want my mummy.' Lily folded her arms on the table and laid her head upon them. Her little shoulders heaved up and down.

She was crying again.

Maybe it was time to get rid of her.

CHAPTER FIFTY-EIGHT

'Oh my God,' Lottie said.

The morning light was way too bright when she opened her eyes. She shielded them with the back of her arm, almost stubbing herself with her elbow. She hadn't drawn the curtains last night. Shit. Turning over in the bed, she saw she was fully dressed, an empty bottle on the pillow beside her and everything in the room swimming.

Her stomach lurched and gurgled, empty except for wine. She needed to pee, but the throb in her head prevented her from moving.

It was all Boyd's fault, though she knew she was the only one to blame. There was no way she could face going into work in this state. She'd have to get Boyd or Kirby to cover for her for a few hours. It was Saturday, so it wasn't too bad.

But it was. She had three murders to investigate, and even more importantly, an eight-year-old girl was still missing. The little girl with the long fair hair and those disconcerting blue eyes. Why were they familiar?

Her head continued to throb, and she shoved the bottle under the pillow. What you don't see and all that. But the evidence was as vivid as the light streaming in her window.

The shower. She had to drag herself under water. It was the only way to quell the dull ache rooted behind her eyes.

There was no way she could let anyone know. But Boyd? He'd know. He always knew. Then again, did he even care any more? The ache moved in an instant from her head to her heart, and she yearned for him to soothe her pain. She needed Boyd. She needed him a lot more than he needed her. And she wondered if she still had time to convince him.

She struggled through her shower and got dressed, feeling a little better. A few mugs of coffee might finish the job and she'd be fit for the office. Louis' shrieks of laughter echoed from Katie's room next to hers.

She listened to the sound of her family bringing the house to life.

The soft pat of footsteps on the stairs.

Chloe yelling, 'Cereal for all? Last one in the kitchen washes the dishes.'

Sean's door opening. 'You know it's Saturday, don't you! Keep the racket down.' The door closing again. He was so like his dad.

More laughter as Katie left her room. 'Piggyback, Louis?'

'Yeah, Mama. Wheee …'

Lottie smiled, filled with warm love for each and every one of them. She wanted to hug them; tell them she would protect them for ever and a day. But she'd let them down so many times in the past, they probably wouldn't believe her. And she was about to lose Katie, Louis and Chloe for the whole of Christmas. Biting her lip, she stifled a wayward sob. No, there was no room in her heart for self-pity, not after last night.

She yawned away her lethargy and squared her shoulders, found a hoodie on the end of the bed and pulled it on, then went downstairs to see her family.

*

The chaos of the kitchen made her head spin again.

'We've started packing, but it's virtually impossible with Louis,' Katie said. 'Could you take him for half an hour, Mam?'

Lottie groaned inwardly, trying not to let it show on her face. 'What about asking your granny?'

'She's gone to Dublin with Leo for an urgent meeting with a solicitor.'

'Really? Wonder what that's about?' On a Saturday too, she thought. Must be something to do with the old house, though she wondered why Rose was involved. Looking at Katie's harried face, she said, 'I could do with a quick walk before work. Where's his coat?'

'Work?' Chloe said. 'It's Saturday!'

'You know how busy I am at the moment,' Lottie pointed out. 'Three murders and a missing child.' She felt her body shiver at the thought that Lily had not been found. It was looking ominous for the little girl.

'Right,' Chloe said, swishing her long hair over her shoulder as she pulled laundry out of the dryer.

'It doesn't matter, Mam,' Katie said. 'I'll ask Sean to watch Louis.'

'I want to bring him.' Lottie turned to Louis, who was sitting on the floor hammering a saucepan with a spoon. 'Now, little man, let's get you ready for a walk.'

She muffled her grandson into his snow suit and strapped him into his stroller.

'Make sure you mind him,' Katie said.

'I will. Didn't I look after you three when you were little?'

Katie stuck a finger on her chin in mock shock. 'You had Dad to help you.'

Lottie flinched. 'We'll be fine, won't we, munchkin?'

'Nana. Nana,' Louis said, a big smile lighting up his face.

'See,' Lottie said. 'He trusts me.' She thought of Lily. Had the child trusted the wrong person?

'Just be careful,' Katie said.

Once outside, Lottie walked briskly, feeling the cold air chafe her face. Louis oohed and aahed the whole way to town. She couldn't help the smile that spread across her face. The murder investigations and Lily's disappearance were weighing heavily on her mind, but with each step her brain felt a little lighter.

The shopping centre was busy with early-morning shoppers, so she headed up Main Street and turned onto Gaol Street. The Christmas market was laid out on both sides of the narrow street, and families crowded around the stalls, in some places three deep. Manoeuvring the stroller from the footpath, she tried to wheel her grandson down the centre of the road.

'Sorry,' she said, as the wheels clipped the ankles of a sour-looking woman. 'Come on, Louis, let's get you a present.'

Chocolate and marshmallow scents wafted towards her, along with the aroma of freshly baked bread. Hand-crafted decorations sparkled and bells rang out in the soft breeze. Her heart felt a little warmer. Since Adam had died, she'd hated Christmas. But here, with her grandson, she sensed the return of a little happiness. Then she remembered that Katie was taking him away from her next week, and her spirits dipped.

'Bell. Bell!' Louis gesticulated with his knitted gloves, a gift from his Great-Granny Rose.

She pulled up beside the stall, unbuckled the child and lifted him into her arms. 'Which one do you like, Louis?'

He pointed to a bright red ceramic bell covered with white snowflakes.

'Hand-painted,' the stallholder said.

'I'll take it, Jean,' Lottie said, reading the woman's name tag and cuddling Louis tightly. 'It will be lovely on the tree.'

'He's a gorgeous little boy. Is he your son?'

Lottie laughed. 'My grandson.'

'He's a cutie. Going to break a few hearts. Aren't you, pet?' Jean wrapped the bell in bubble wrap and slid it into a cardboard box. 'Three euros, please.'

'Thank you.' Lottie handed over the coins.

'Just a minute.' Jean stooped under the bench and brought up a chocolate Santa on a stick. 'My friend Liv makes the most delicious chocolate sweets. You should check out her stall.'

'Great.' Lottie handed Louis the treat before strapping him back into his buggy. He was going to make a right mess, but he was happy and that was all that mattered.

Meandering through the masses, she was mindful of what this scene would have been like when Lily Heffernan went missing from her dance school. The street would have been more crowded than it was this morning, the sky would have been dark and the theatre at the end of the street, with its massive Christmas tree, would have been lit up. If Lily had walked down the theatre steps, she would have been immediately swallowed up by the crowd. As people bustled up against the stroller, Lottie was aware of how easily a child could get lost. Was that what had happened? If so, where was Lily now? No, she was certain the girl had been abducted.

Stopping outside Cafferty's Pub, she noticed a closed-up stall. Glancing down at Louis, she saw his smeared face beaming up at her. She couldn't help but smile.

'I see he likes my Santa.' It was the woman selling chocolate.

'Yes, he does,' Lottie said. 'Can I have half a dozen, please?'

'Sure you can. Do you want them in a box or a paper bag?'

'Paper bag is fine.' Lottie glanced around and saw that every stall was a hive of activity, except for the one opposite Liv's. The shutter was pulled down and bolted. There were no boxes underneath. Deserted and cleared out.

'Liv, can I ask you a question?'

'Fire ahead.'

'How long has that stall been closed?'

'Let me think.' Liv scrunched her eyes. 'I'm sure it's been open most days.'

'Was it open yesterday?'

'Now that you mention it, I don't think it was. I think it closed down on Wednesday.'

'What time?'

'I don't know.'

'Would it have been, say, sometime after four o'clock?'

Liv leaned her head to one side and then shook it. 'I can't be sure. The gardaí were asking questions. About that little girl who went missing.' She inclined her head towards the theatre.

'Who was working on the stall?'

Liv shrugged. 'Don't think he was local. I'd never seen him on the craft trail before.'

'What was he selling?'

'Now you're asking.' Liv grimaced.

'Take your time.' Lottie checked Louis. His face was a mess of chocolate, but he was laughing and shaking the box containing the little bell.

'Dolls. That's what it was. Awful-looking things. I saw something like them one time on holiday. Like voodoo dolls. They were hanging all around his stall. Some on key rings. That's how small they were.'

'And the man ... You said it was a man, didn't you?'

'That's right.'

'What did he look like? Did you speak with him? Did you witness anyone else conversing with him?'

'Are you a guard?' Liv looked around warily.

'Detective Inspector Lottie Parker.'

'I've heard of you. Give me a minute.'

Lottie waited while Liv served another customer. When she turned back, she said, 'From what I could see, he was weathered-looking. Tanned. Like he'd spent a lot of time in the sun or wind.'

'Young or old?'

'I'm not sure. I think he had a hat pulled down over his face and maybe a scarf round his mouth. It's been so cold all week.'

'Could you give a fuller description? If pushed?'

'I'm sorry.' Liv's brown eyes flashed with flecks of hazel, reminding Lottie of Boyd. 'It's been frantic here since the market launched. I'm surprised I remember anything about him at all. If it wasn't for the weird dolls, I don't think I'd have noticed him.'

'And I suppose you didn't see the little girl? Lily Heffernan.'

'No. A guard showed me her photograph, but I didn't recall her. It was pulsing with crowds the day the market opened. Today is going to be even better.'

As Liv went to serve another customer, Lottie noticed that a queue had formed. She released the brake on the stroller and pushed through to the end of the street. The theatre stood across the road, banners outside proclaiming next week's Christmas dance show. *Cinderella*.

She turned back towards Cafferty's, thinking that she really needed to get Louis home and get into work. She had to check if there was any word on Lily's biological father, but first, maybe the barman might know something about the mysterious stallholder.

*

For a Saturday morning, the bar was full, which surprised Lottie. She spotted Kirby sitting at the counter with a newspaper in his hand and a gigantic toasted sandwich in front of him.

'That smells nice,' she said.

'Morning, boss. What brings you here?' He swirled his large backside on the stool. 'Hello, little man. Your granny's starting you young in the pubs, isn't she?'

'Less of the granny,' Lottie said.

'Do you want a coffee?' Kirby offered.

She leaned against a vacant stool. 'No thanks, I've to get into work, as do you. I just walked Louis into town to see the market. Giving the girls time to pack. Did you notice the closed-up stall outside?'

'No. I skirted around the back of them, otherwise I'd end up buying a load of stuff I don't need and can't afford.'

'There's a stall out there that's shuttered. The woman who runs the chocolate stall opposite said the owner hasn't been there for the last two or three days.'

'Oh shit. Around the time Lily went missing?'

'She's not sure. But she remembers him because of the weird little dolls he was selling.'

Darren, the barman, raised his head from where he was loading a glass-washer. 'Weird dolls?'

'Yeah. Do you know anything about him?'

'He had a bowl of soup and a sandwich the other day. Hasn't been in since.'

'What day?'

'I haven't a clue. It's been so busy with the market.'

'Did he say anything? Had he an accent?' Lottie wondered if perhaps she was clinging to straws.

'Wait a tick.' Darren shoved in the tray and switched on the machine, then searched behind the till and produced a brown paper bag. From it he drew out a small bundle the size of a key. 'Would this help?'

'That's one of his dolls?'

'Ugly little bastard, isn't it?'

'Why'd you buy it?'

'Felt sorry for him. His was the only stall where no one was buying anything, and he had bought the soup and sandwich. Quid pro quo?'

Lottie stared at the doll. It was indeed ugly. The hair. She shuddered. It looked almost real.

'Who else has touched this, Darren?'

'Just me. It's been sitting behind the till since.'

'Can you put it back in the bag, please?' She glanced at Kirby, who'd been staring open-mouthed at the hideous-looking item.

'Sure,' Darren said. 'Do you want it?'

'I really don't want that … thing near Louis.' She turned to Kirby. 'Could you take it to the station, please? It might be nothing, but just maybe this stallholder took Lily.'

'That's a long shot.'

'Everything is a long shot until you investigate it. Get it photographed.' She thought for a moment. 'And have the hair analysed.'

'What hair?' Kirby peered into the paper bag.

Louis stared to shout. 'Nana. Home. Nana. Mama.'

'The hair on the doll. It looks kind of real to me.' She pushed the stroller towards the door. 'Today, Kirby.'

'Sure thing.' He moved to hold the door for her.

'And see what else you can find out about that stallholder. Contact the market organisers. I'll be in the office as soon as I can.'

'Will do.'

'Do you know where Boyd is?'

'Haven't seen him yet, boss.' He shrugged half-heartedly.

'Maybe he's gone to Galway,' Lottie said, feeling suddenly intrusive. But she was going to marry him, wasn't she? Though not if he kept up his secrecy.

'I wouldn't know about that,' Kirby said with a blush.

As she pushed the stroller back up the street, zigzagging through the crowd, Lottie wondered why Kirby appeared to know more about Boyd than he was saying, and more than she did. That was what bugged her more than anything. Secrets. She bloody hated them.

'I tried ringing him, but there's no reply.'

Lottie said, 'We need to speak with Ryan Slevin to see if there was a honeymoon planned. First, though, I need a coffee. A proper one.'

She pulled on her coat to fly down to McDonald's for a coffee, and bumped into Boyd on the ground floor.

'What's going on?' she said.

He was holding Ryan Slevin at arm's length. 'He's being an arsehole.'

She shot him a dagger and said to Ryan, 'You're just the man I'm looking for.'

'Good, because I'm looking for you. I want you to organise a search for Beth. I can't find her anywhere.'

'Beth Clarke?'

'Yeah, I went to return her car this morning and she's not at home.'

Lottie led the way to the interview room and ushered Ryan in. Boyd followed.

'Why did you have Beth's car?' she said when they were seated.

'Long story,' Ryan said, 'but I think something might have happened to her, with all the murders. She was very distressed, you know, after her father's death.'

'Did you stop to think maybe she could be with her mother?'

'There's not a chance in hell. Since Eve walked out on her, Beth can't bear to hear her name mentioned.'

'Did you check with your sister?'

He shook his head. 'Beth's not there.'

'Okay, I'll follow it up.' She settled her hands on the desk. 'I'm glad you're here, because I need to ask you some questions.'

CHAPTER FIFTY-NINE

It was another fifteen minutes before she had Louis safely home with her daughters. According to Chloe, Sean had headed off on his bike with a gym bag on his back. Between the lines, Lottie could read that there had been a row among the siblings. She'd have to sort it later. Everything was later.

There was no sign of Boyd when she arrived at the office. Kirby had made it in before her and was busy checking with forensics to get the doll processed as soon as possible.

He finished his call and followed her to the incident room. 'Boss, we got access to Fiona Heffernan's bank account. Listen to this. About two weeks ago, there was a payment to Ryanair and another to an online hotel booking site.'

'Honeymoon?' Lottie wondered where Fiona and Ryan might have been off to.

'That's what I thought. I checked the inventories for her home and Slevin's cottage. No mention of passports. I double-checked the list of what was in her handbag, locker ... everything. Nothing.'

'Nothing?'

'I couldn't find passports for either Fiona or Lily.'

'Maybe they didn't have any?'

'I checked with the passport office, and they do.'

'Did you ask Colin Kavanagh? The documents could be in the house, for safe keeping.'

Ryan shifted on the chair, ran his hand through his beard. Lottie noticed the dirt in his fingernails and his grubby appearance. So different from how he'd looked right before she informed him of Fiona's death. Grief-stricken, she thought, but was he a killer?

Trying to instil some normality into the situation, she said, 'Where were you planning to take Fiona on honeymoon?'

'Honeymoon? We didn't organise one. We had Lily to think of, and then there was all the expense renovating the cottage, and anyway Fiona told me Lily had no passport.' He was talking too fast. Jumbled words just about making sense.

'Lily does have a passport.'

'I didn't know that.'

'You never discussed going abroad on holidays?'

'No. I don't think Fiona had ever been anywhere other than around Ireland.'

'Really?'

'Ask Kavanagh, the prick. He knew her longer than I did.'

'You told me you got on well with Lily. Is that true?'

'It's true. My sister has three boys, I'm used to kids and they're used to me. Lily is a sweet kid.'

'Tell me about Giles Bannon, your brother-in-law.'

Ryan shifted some more on the chair, one eye on the door. Lottie thought he was figuring out a quick escape.

'What do you want to know?'

'Did Giles see much of Lily?'

A tic of confusion caused a tremor in one of his eyes. 'Only when Fiona called over with her. Why?'

'And how was he around Fiona?'

'What are you getting at?' His nostrils flared.

'Answer the questions, Ryan.'

'Am I under arrest or something?' His mouth moved furiously as if he was chewing on gum.

'No.' Not yet, she thought. 'But I need you to help with our enquiries.'

Ryan's phone buzzed somewhere on his person. He patted down his jacket.

'Leave it,' Lottie said. 'I asked you about Giles.'

He gulped. 'Fiona didn't like him. She didn't like being in the house when he was there. Said he gave her the creeps, always staring at her. She wouldn't let Lily visit either, come to think of it.'

'Any visible animosity or rows?'

'No, but Giles was acting odd for the last few months. My sister … Zoe thought maybe he was having an affair. He was rarely home early.'

'And was there any substance to this suspicion?' Boyd said.

Ryan fixed his eyes on a point well above Boyd's head. Chewed on his bottom lip, getting a mouthful of stubble. He picked constantly at the corner of a dirty nail.

'Ryan? Answer the question,' Lottie prompted.

He drew his eyes away from the wall and glanced at them both before directing his answer to Boyd. 'I talked to Beth about it … We knew the signs.'

'What signs?' Lottie cut in.

Ryan gulped again before continuing. 'Beth and I … About a year ago, we had a … thing. You know, a relationship.'

'An affair?'

'Neither of us was married to anyone else, so I wouldn't call it an affair.'

'But you were with Fiona at the time, weren't you?'

'Yeah, yeah. An affair, then. It was short. Nothing spectacular. Just happened through work. Anyway, we knew the signs.'

'What signs?' Lottie felt she was stuck in the middle of a riddle.

'The signs someone displays when they're having an affair. Giles displayed them all.'

'Enlighten me.'

'Leaving the room when he got a phone call or text. Always keeping his phone in his hand or pocket, never leaving it on the table where Zoe could pick it up. Out late every evening, using work as an excuse, even when we knew the theatre was closed. Zoe was in a state.'

'Did you do anything about it?'

'It was Beth's idea. She suggested we spy on him.'

'How did you do that?'

'Well, it was Robert's idea too.'

'Robert? Robert Brady?' Lottie looked at Boyd, who seemed to have lost interest in the conversation. She nudged him with her elbow.

'Yeah,' Ryan said. 'Robert was working on my cottage. Overheard us chatting. He said he didn't think it was an affair. Thought maybe Giles was into something illegal.'

'How did he reach that conclusion?'

'Robert had worked on Colin Kavanagh's house too. Kavanagh had asked Robert to build him a cabin out on the land. Then he'd blacked out all the windows and locked it. Robert was convinced something fishy was going on.'

'How does Giles fit in?'

'Robert said Giles was always in and out of Kavanagh's house when Fiona was at work, and most of the conversations were about Clarke's Garage. That was when Beth came up with the idea.'

Lottie felt her jaw drop. 'The lookout on the hill. You and Beth were the ones who used it.'

Ryan nodded. 'Robert did too. It seemed like a good idea at the time. Now it seems just plain childish. Like we were playing cops and robbers or something.'

'Did you uncover anything with your spying?'

'Yeah. Giles wasn't having an affair. But there was definitely something illegal going on at the garage. Cars being driven in at all hours. Cars being driven out. Most times it was either Giles or Kavanagh who opened the garage doors.'

'Jesus,' Lottie exclaimed. 'And none of the villagers noticed anything?'

Ryan laughed. 'You've seen Ballydoon. Dead as a dodo most of the time. Unless there's something on in the pub, it's like a pauper's wake.'

'So Giles and Kavanagh were involved in criminal activity. What did you do with this information?'

'I wanted to report it, but Beth didn't want to get her father in trouble. She said she would write an article, and when the time was right, she was going to sell it to the highest bidder. But she wanted to be sure Christy was innocent first. She thought they were ripping him off and that he was being used by them.'

'Did you take photographs?'

'Yes. I had them on an SD card. I gave it to Beth.'

'Okay. We'll follow up your allegations and speak with Beth.'

'You'll have to find her first. I think something awful has happened to her.'

'Why do you think that?'

'A couple of days ago, I got a threatening email from an anonymous IP address, telling me to back off. Someone knew what we were at. Maybe that's why Fiona was killed. And now I can't find Beth.'

'Ryan, tell me, why did you have Beth's car?' Lottie wondered how Cara fitted into this scenario. It didn't make sense.

Ryan once again found the point on the wall. 'I had a bit of a mishap yesterday. My car ... I couldn't go back to the cottage for it. I ended up at Beth's house. Like I said, she was inconsolable over her father's death. I needed to get away from her. From all that grief. I had enough of my own. I took her car.'

'What was the mishap?'

'I'm sorry ... I didn't mean to hurt you ...'

'What are you talking about?' Lottie felt a vein in her neck throb as her heart beat faster.

'I'd gone to the forest because I needed to check if we'd left anything behind that might land us in trouble. Especially after Christy ... died.'

'Go on,' Lottie said, trying to keep her tone even.

'I saw you there. I panicked. I don't know what came over me. Honestly, I didn't mean to hurt you. I just wanted to check the lookout before you found it. I'm so sorry. I ...' Ryan buried his head in his hands.

Lottie leaped up, ready to thump him.

Boyd caught her arm. 'I'll deal with this. Go on. Find Giles and Kavanagh. I'll arrest him for assaulting you.'

She opened the door. As she stepped into the corridor, she heard Boyd begin.

'Ryan Slevin, I am arresting you under the Offences against the Person Act. You do not have to say anything but ...'

The sound of his voice muted when she banged the door.

Back in the office, Lottie was still trying to calm down, and still dying for a coffee, when a text pinged on her phone.

Father Joe. She opened it.

Had a word with Sister Augusta. Interesting conversation. Speak with her again.

She replied: *Thank you.*

The phone pinged again almost immediately.

She will throw some light on Father Curran too. Best of luck.

McKeown lifted his head from his iPad. 'I found something,' he said.

'Lily?'

He shook his head. 'Sorry, no. There's a nationwide alert, TV appeals, roadblocks, every paedophile on the register has been visited and houses searched. Kavanagh's reward offer is giving us the usual headaches.'

'Oh God, I don't know what else we can do.' Lottie plonked down on a chair. 'Did Kirby show you the doll?'

'Yes. Gruesome thing. Do you think it has anything to do with the case?'

'Possibly.'

'I have more than a possibility here. About the wedding dress that Fiona Heffernan was wearing.'

'Go on.'

'Remember we thought it might have been custom made or bought online?'

'Yes.'

'We put out the appeal like you said, and I've had a phone call from Shelly Forde. She's the assistant tutor at the dance school.'

'I'm listening.'

'Shelly told me a wedding dress was purchased for next week's dance show, *Cinderella*. She is convinced it's the same as the one in the image we circulated.'

Lottie started towards the door. 'What are we waiting for? We need to interview Shelly.'

'Hold on a minute. I asked her to check if the dress was still at the theatre.'

'And?' Why on earth was he dragging it out? This was a real lead.

'She checked the costume room. It's not there. I asked her if she could find the invoice or receipt. She emailed me immediately with this.'

He thrust his iPad into her hand. She was looking at an online invoice. 'Ragmullin Dance School. Doesn't tell me anything.'

McKeown leaned over and swiped the image to the left. 'This is the receipt. Paid by credit card. See the name?'

'Giles fucking Bannon!'

'Exactly.'

'Where is he now?'

'At the theatre. Shelly says he's doing a war dance because rehearsals are behind schedule or some shit like that.'

'Bring the car to the front. We'll interview him there. Best not to give him time to come up with a tall tale, and I need to speak to him about something else anyway.' At the door, she turned. 'Oh, print all that off and bring it.'

'Already done.' He folded the pages into his pocket.

'Good man.'

As she walked down the corridor, she got a familiar warm feeling. The feeling where she sensed everything was about to fall into place. Maybe.

CHAPTER SIXTY

Giles Bannon led them into his office. He refused to sit. Lottie sat down just to piss him off.

'What's this about?' he said. 'I'm busy. I've a show next week and that prick Trevor Toner is playing silly buggers with me. Those kids are not nearly ready. They have to double up and fill in for Lily Heffernan.' His face slackened. 'I hope she's found soon.'

'Mr Bannon, sit the fuck down,' McKeown said, his voice so soft that it made even Lottie shiver.

She kept her eyes on Bannon. He fidgeted, running fingers up and down his tie. Stuffed the edge of his shirt into his trousers where it had come loose during his tirade. At last, barely able to fit in the tight space behind his desk, he sat.

'Do I need a solicitor?'

'For fuck's sake. Not that chestnut again!' McKeown bellowed.

'Gentlemen.' Lottie glanced from one to the other, her eyes resting on Bannon. He was moving about on the chair as if a colony of ants had invaded it, and rubbing his hands into a knot, while his face was suffused with colour.

'Mr Bannon, tell me about the wedding dress you purchased.'

'The what?' He raised his eyebrows like a cartoon character.

'A wedding dress was purchased online for your upcoming show. I'd like to know where it is.'

He shook his head. 'I've no idea what you're talking about.'

'Show him,' Lottie instructed McKeown. He unfolded the two pages and placed them on the desk.

'That's your credit card, isn't it?' she said.

Bannon opened his spectacle case, but it was empty. He squinted at the first page. 'I don't recall purchasing such a thing. Our costumes are kept in the wardrobe room. I can bring you down to the basement and show you.'

'I'm only interested in this one. According to Shelly, it was needed for the show.'

'Shelly? What's that young hussy saying?'

'This dress was purchased from a company in the UK,' Lottie said. 'Customised from the image on their website.'

'I have no idea what you're talking about. I didn't buy any fucking wedding dress, customised or otherwise. I've an extremely frantic day ahead and I need to be getting on with …' He made to get up, but had unwittingly barricaded himself against his desk.

'Do you want to know why we're interested in this particular dress?'

He flipped his tie idly, as if he had no interest whatsoever. 'Probably something to do with Fiona Heffernan and Cara Dunne, because they were found dead in wedding dresses. That's it! You think I bought this shitty dress and killed them?' His tone rose an octave. 'That's madness!' he screeched. 'I refuse to answer any more of your insinuating questions.' He scrambled around his desk searching for his phone.

'In that case, I have no option but to bring you to the station, where you'll be formally questioned about the murder of Fiona Heffernan.'

'I … I … This is absurd. Do you hear me? It's preposterous.' He reached for his mobile phone and tapped and scrolled frantically.

'You can call your solicitor from the station. Come on.' Lottie felt a surge of superiority.

'Do I have a choice?'

'I can arrest you for impeding our investigation, for starters, slap handcuffs on you, then march you out past all those parents waiting for their kids.'

He grunted. Slipped his phone into his pocket, found his spectacles there and placed them in the case. 'I need to leave instructions for my—'

'Quit the bullshit and come on.' McKeown folded the pages back into his pocket and held the door open.

Eventually Bannon was able to manoeuvre his bulk from behind the desk. As they marched him to the car, McKeown said to Lottie, 'Do you think we should search the costume room? Just in case the dress is still there?'

'It's not there, because we have it in evidence. Trust me.'

'You're the boss,' he said.

'I am for sure,' she said, feeling good for the first time that week.

CHAPTER SIXTY-ONE

Even with the success of the morning, Father Joe's text was still on her mind. Lottie left McKeown keeping Bannon company until his solicitor was located. A team was dispatched to Bannon's house to carry out a search for evidence of criminal activity. Ryan Slevin was in a cell. After swallowing a tepid mug of canteen coffee, Lottie, with Boyd for company, drove out to the abbey in Ballydoon.

There was little evidence of a crime ever having been committed. A wayward piece of crime-scene tape was tangled on a bush, like a child waving its hand for attention. A life lost so suddenly, and they still knew little about what had happened to Fiona on the roof or to her little girl after she'd walked out of her dance rehearsal.

The winding corridors criss-crossed and a multitude of doors cut into the walls as they headed for Sister Augusta's room.

'This is like a maze,' Boyd puffed.

Ignoring his complaints, Lottie pulled up a chair and sat beside the sleeping nun, who looked even closer to death than she had the other day. She wondered if she had previously asked the wrong questions, and hoped she wasn't too late to pose the correct ones now.

'Sister Augusta, it's Lottie Parker. The detective who spoke to you a couple of days ago.'

The nun's eyes opened, and as Lottie waited for them to focus, she scanned the room. Unlike before, she now thought the blue and yellow wallpaper was jaded and stuffy. But whereas there had been nothing on the bedside cabinet then, it now sported a poinsettia plant, snared in plastic wrapping. She fought the urge to free the beautiful red petals.

Sister Augusta said, 'He brought me that.'

'Who did?'

'Michael. Father Curran. Trying to soft-soap me in my dying days.' She waved a bony hand in the air. Her face was as translucent as gossamer, her lips grey.

'Do you need anything?' Lottie was sure the nun was confused. 'You had a visitor but I think it was a younger priest. Father Joe Burke.'

'Ah, now I remember. Good-looking young man.'

'What did you speak about?'

'All business, he was. He'd make a good detective if you're ever stuck.'

Lottie smiled. Sister Augusta was correct on that score. 'What can you tell me about Father Curran that might help us solve the murders?'

'You think that old fart murdered those women? You must be as daft as he is.'

Lottie smiled at the nun's language. 'I didn't say that. We have someone in custody, but we're still trying to tie it all up.'

'Father Curran didn't hurt Cara.'

'How can you be sure?' Lottie felt a tingle of surprise.

'He looked out for her. As if she was his own.'

'Really?' This did not gel with Lottie's impression of Father Curran. 'Was she his daughter?'

'No, nothing like that. He was doing me a favour.'

'Why did you need a favour?' Lottie felt as confused as she thought the old nun must be.

'Cara was my sister Eileen's child. I did my best by her. I did what I could.' Tears filled the dry eyes. 'It was never enough. Cara always wanted more in life. Felt she was entitled to something better to make up for the death of her mother in childbirth.'

'What about her father?'

'Never on the scene. A one-night stand resulted in Cara's birth and the death of my beloved sister.'

'Did you raise Cara?'

'No, I was quite a bit older than Eileen and I was in the convent. I did what I could for the child.'

'What did you do?' Lottie wondered how a nun in a convent could look after a baby.

'I spoke with the bishop, must be thirty-five years ago now. The health board found a suitable family who had already fostered another child. A little boy. Not much difference in age to Cara. Oh, I'm not rightly sure why, but it didn't work out.'

'What went wrong?' She was convinced something had happened, but had it had anything to do with Cara's death?

'I promised that family that I would look out for Cara, and if there was anything untoward, they were to call me. I tried to stay in contact, but they were always evasive. I'm sorry to admit it, but I lost contact with them.'

'Do you know the family name?'

'My brain is not what it used to be. Could have been Brown, or Black. Something to do with colour, anyway. All I recall is Cara's name. She was always a troubled girl. Think I told you that. But she was my sister's child, so …'

Lottie glanced at Boyd, whose face appeared distinctly green. The heat in the room was overpowering, and he looked as if he might keel over. 'Sit down, Boyd.'

'It's very hot,' he said, and sat on the edge of the bed, the rubber sheet creaking beneath him.

'I hate the stuffy air,' Sister Augusta said. 'No one listens …'

'We never found out much about Cara's background, did we?' Lottie said for Boyd's benefit, so that he would concentrate.

'No,' he said, 'it was like a closed shop.'

'I think she always felt hard done by.' Sister Augusta's voice was low and weak. 'When she was a baby, before she was taken away to her foster home, I gave her a gift to carry with her through life. It was the only thing I possessed. A suitcase with my trousseau. My father gave it to me when I joined the convent. I thought it would be a reminder to Cara that when all else fails, there is still a good path to follow. Cara became a teacher, so she found her calling. Though it did nothing to soften her heart, if her visits to me are anything to go by.'

Lottie sensed Boyd's eyes on her. She looked up. He shook his head as if telling her that old ramblings were a waste of time. But there was something hypnotic about the nun's voice, and she was sure there was more to be released from the dying lips.

'Did you give Cara anything else? A piece of jewellery, maybe?'

'I did. A lovely silver cross and chain. Blessed by the Pope, it was.'

'You told me previously that you thought Cara was waiting for you to die. Why was that?'

'She blamed me, you see. For abandoning her as a child. I made the mistake of putting a note in the suitcase, vowing to always look out for her. Then I didn't. She never forgave me for breaking that vow.'

'Why was it so important to her?'

'She told me her life had been lived in a crush of broken vows. The latest being that Steve fellow. He broke her heart, like so many others in her life.'

'Is there anything you can tell me about Father Curran?'

'Ah, Michael. He likes to give the impression he's a contrary old git. But he has a soft heart. Believe me. He helps those who are broken, without making any of it public. Don't judge him too harshly.'

Lottie thought she would judge him any way she wanted to. 'The other day, you said "It's all about the child." I thought it was Lily you were referring to, but it was Cara, wasn't it?'

'God, no, silly woman. It was that other youngster. Lovely bouncy tresses all over her shoulders. Inquisitive she was, too. Always asking probing questions.' Sister Augusta's head sank deeper into the pillow and she began to cough.

'Here, let me help you.' Lottie raised the nun's head and plumped the pillows before holding a glass of water to the parched lips. There was no way she was leaving until she got a name.

'I'm fine. Don't fuss.'

'Who's the child you're referring to?'

'Beautiful young thing, but so full of turmoil. Her heart had been broken. So like Cara in many ways. Both lost their mothers.'

'Sister Augusta, who are you talking about?'

The nun's gaze was piercing. 'Beth Clarke, of course.'

*

The door opened and a stream of daylight blinded her. She felt the cold breeze as he entered.

'I'm going to take off your gag, and if you scream, I'll slit your throat. Might even cut your tongue out.'

Beth nodded in silence and waited while he removed the gag. She was unable to see in the darkness, and stars glittered behind her eyelids from the harshness of the outside light when he'd opened the door. But she was sure he either wore a mask or had a hood pulled down over his face.

He was still talking. Mumbling, as if to himself. 'You just couldn't leave it alone. Always snooping around, poking your nose in. I wanted to help you. To sort things out for you. And I did. I got rid of your old man.'

'You what?' Beth hardly recognised her own voice. It was croaky, and her throat was dry, but this was not the time to ask for water.

'Then again, I didn't really do it for you. I'm on a mission, you see. To fix things. To punish those who let people down. I can't stand people who break their promises. You won't let me down, will you, sweet little Beth?'

She had no idea what he was talking about as she strained her ears to identify his voice. It was there, somewhere at the outer reaches of cognisance, but she couldn't grasp it. Was this the man who'd killed Fiona and Cara, and even her dad? Slithers of fear wormed up her spine and gnawed along her hairline. She thought she might vomit if she didn't get a drink soon. That thought caused her throat to tighten, and she gasped for breath.

'Are you okay? I have some water.'

She heard him moving about and felt his hot flesh as he tipped up her head and held a bottle to her lips. She hoped it wasn't laced with poison. Thirst overrode her fear and she let the tepid liquid linger on her tongue before gulping some more.

'Say thank you,' he said.

'Thanks.'

That voice. She knew she knew him. It was there. His voice attached to an image, flittering about in her brain, like an elusive spider trailing a thread from its web. But it was clouded by the night of terror she'd endured.

'Your father, Christy, wasn't a nice man,' he said. 'You're better off without him. He wouldn't take your mother back. He was a cheat and had dealings with bad men. I know, because Robert told me. He had seen the evidence when he was working on Kavanagh's house. Enough to put Kavanagh away for a very long time.'

'Evidence?' She had begged Robert to tell her. The scoop of a lifetime. But he'd said there was someone else who might benefit from his information, and so she'd had to do her own investigating.

'Yeah.'

'Did you kill Robert too?'

It felt like all the air had been sucked out of the space. She heard his breathing quicken and his foot tap on the floor. Anger reverberated in each tap.

'He took everything from me.'

'What did he take?' If she kept him talking, he'd forget to hurt her. Maybe someone would come. She silently prayed.

'Robert took my heart. I loved him and he fucked with me. Fucked with you too, sweetheart.'

'He was my friend. I don't understand.' And she didn't.

'You're not meant to. It's complicated. But I'm making life simpler for all of us.'

'What do you want from me?'

'Your story.'

'My what?'

'All the stuff you've gathered. I know you were spying.'

'I wasn't spying. You've got it all wrong.'

'Don't tell me I'm wrong.' His voice was sharper, acid dripping from his tongue. 'I know I'm right.'

'Okay,' she said and wondered if there was a way out of this, even though she knew it was futile.

She no longer had the story.

CHAPTER SIXTY-TWO

McKeown placed both hands on the back of the chair, stifled a yawn and leaned in over the young garda's shoulder. He couldn't believe what he was looking at on the screen.

'That's Lily Heffernan!' he said incredulously. 'Can you freeze it and zoom in to the number plate, Ben?'

'It's a taxi dash cam,' Ben said. 'Not great quality.'

As the garda fiddled with the keyboard, the screen pixelating, McKeown picked up the screen shot that had been printed from the footage they were watching. Lily, with a small rucksack on her back, sliding into the open back door of a dark-coloured Avensis. Not being pushed or dragged. Someone she knew, perhaps? He looked at the tall man getting into the driver's seat. Who was he?

When the zoom was clear enough to read the registration, Ben keyed it into the database and waited for the name and address to pop up on the screen.

'Holy fuck!' McKeown said. As he ran from the room, he fumbled in his pocket for his phone and with sweating hands quickly tapped in Lottie's number.

*

The gardaí who were conducting the search at Bannon's house reported that Beth was not there. She was not at her own home either when Lottie and Boyd called after visiting Sister Augusta.

'She could be anywhere,' Boyd said.

'Radio for someone to check with Eve. Beth could be in danger, even though we have Ryan and Giles locked up for now. While we're in the area, let's have a quick word with Father Curran. He might be able to fill us in on some details about Cara, and at the same time help us with regard to Giles Bannon.'

'You think Giles is our man?' Boyd said, pulling up in front of the priest's house.

'Any better ideas at this stage?'

He shook his head. 'I only asked the question.'

'Well, don't ask.'

'I can't see Bannon going to the trouble of dressing a woman in a wedding dress before throwing her from the roof of a building,' Boyd said as he climbed out of the car. 'What's his motive? And why kill Cara too? This doesn't make sense, Lottie.'

Lottie ignored him, and banged the front door with her fist until eventually it was opened.

'What's the fuss?' Father Curran said, stepping outside.

She had to move backwards, and collided with Boyd.

'For fuck's sake,' Boyd muttered. 'Sorry, Father.'

'We need to speak to you.' Lottie went to edge past the priest.

He held his ground. 'I was about to go to my gym.' He attempted a smile, but it died on his face. 'I suppose you'd better come in.'

He brought them to the old-fashioned living room and stood at the unlit fireplace. Lottie remained standing while Boyd sank into an armchair.

'How can I help you?' Father Curran said.

'A few things. What can you tell us about Giles Bannon?'

A streak of confusion knitted the priest's eyes into a frown. 'Giles? Why are you asking about him?'

'He's a person of interest in the murders of Cara Dunne and Fiona Heffernan. We also think he may have abducted Lily.'

'That's absurd.'

Lottie recalled that that was the exact word uttered by Giles earlier. 'We have evidence to suspect him. I'm wondering if you have anything to add, maybe about Colin Kavanagh too, as he seems to be a friend of yours.'

'Stop. Stop. You're jumping all over the place. First you accuse Giles, and now you mention Colin. Make up your mind, woman.'

'I witnessed Colin Kavanagh leaving your property in haste the other day. I have a witness who has implicated Kavanagh, Giles Bannon and Christy Clarke in criminal activity. Care to comment on that?'

'What the …?' the priest started, then clamped his flabby lips together.

'Well?' Lottie prompted.

'I've nothing to say on matters told to me in the sacrament of Confession.'

'Don't give me that speech. I know they were dealing in stolen cars. I'm not concerned with that at the moment. I want to find Lily, and I think Giles and Colin somehow organised her abduction and even the murders. Either together or alone.'

Though the room was chilly, Lottie felt her skin tingle with heat. She unzipped her jacket and rolled up the sleeves. She took a few paces around, running her hand over surfaces, and when she turned back, Father Curran was seated opposite Boyd. Her phone vibrated in her pocket. She ignored it.

'Tell me about Cara,' Boyd said softly.

'A beautiful but damaged human being. Cara wanted everyone to love her, but as I tried to tell her, only Jesus on the Cross loves us unconditionally. She could never understand human frailties.'

'Did she know Robert Brady?'

Lottie wondered where Boyd was going with this.

The priest smiled. 'Another broken soul. Kindred spirits have a way of finding each other in this world.'

'Did you place the chain and cross at the scene of his death?'

'No, but I suspect Cara did. She had one just like it.'

'How did Cara and Robert know each other?'

'Through Fiona, I suppose.' The priest let his eyes wander around the room, avoiding looking at Lottie.

She walked over and sat beside him. 'You can tell us. There's no one left to protect.'

'But there is.'

'Who?' Lottie asked. 'Beth?'

The priest shook his head slowly, bowed, studying the floor.

Lottie's phone rang again. She was about to reject the call when she saw McKeown's name. She answered it and listened intently, then hung up without a word.

'Where is Lily?' she said.

'I've no idea what you're talking about.' Father Curran looked up and folded his arms defiantly.

The pieces were clicking into place. The bank statements. The missing passports. Kavanagh's criminal activities. 'Fiona came to you not about the wedding but to plan an escape. Who was she afraid of? Giles Bannon? Ryan Slevin? Or Colin Kavanagh?'

The priest sighed, blessed himself slowly. 'The poor girls. Both of them. Cara and Fiona. I didn't want to believe he'd harmed them.'

'Who are you talking about? Tell me what happened.' Lottie was glad she had Bannon and Slevin back at the station. All she needed now was to find Lily, then arrest Kavanagh, lock him up and throw away the key.

The priest settled back in his uncomfortable-looking chair, and steepled his fingers as if in prayer. 'It started with Robert. He'd fallen on hard times. He tried to blackmail Colin Kavanagh over something or other. Colin was having none of it. Robert spoke to Fiona and young Beth Clarke. You see, Beth's father was involved too – but you know that.'

'Involved in what?'

'In the shenanigans at the garage. Holding stolen cars, and Colin doctoring the paperwork so they could be shipped to England. Laundered money through the pig farm too.' Father Curran began to cough.

'Will I fetch you some water?' Lottie said through gritted teeth.

'I'll be okay in a minute.'

'Do you think Kavanagh killed Christy Clarke?' she said. 'To keep him quiet?'

'I doubt it. Christy was up to his neck in debt and had signed everything over to Colin at that stage, so why the need to kill him? It doesn't make sense.'

'I'll see what Kavanagh has to say for himself. When we find him. Next port of call, Boyd,' she said.

He nodded, but she could see he wasn't really listening to her. He was staring hard at the priest.

'Father Curran,' he said, 'the day we saw Kavanagh here, was he looking for Lily? Did he think you had the child?'

'Something like that.'

'Why would he think that?'

'He knew Fiona had been to see me.'

'About the wedding?' Lottie volunteered.

'Aye, and other stuff.'

Boyd glared at her. Keeping his voice soft and low, he continued to speak to the priest. 'Fiona asked you to help make arrangements so that she could flee the country.'

Father Curran said nothing.

'Do you have Fiona and Lily's passports and flight tickets?'

Still no reply.

'She asked you to collect Lily that day and hold on to her until she could pick her up.'

Big salty tears flowed one after the other down the priest's face. One nod.

Boyd was on his feet and kneeling in front of him. 'Tell me. Is Lily safe?'

Another nod.

'Is she here?'

Sobs now tore from Father Curran as his head jerked up and down. 'She is here!' Boyd said.

But Lottie had already interpreted the priest's nods. She fled from the room. Into the kitchen. Not a soul.

Up the stairs. Opening doors, shouting Lily's name as she ran.

She tore back to the living room. 'Where is she? Where have you hidden her, you demented old man?'

Father Curran rose slowly, wiping his nose and eyes with his sleeve. 'I couldn't help Cara when she asked me. I thought I could help Fiona. All that Satan stuff I told you, that was just so you'd leave me alone. I was terrified after Fiona died. I didn't know what to do with the child. I knew Fiona wouldn't have wanted Colin to have her. I just … kept her here.'

He moved to the hall, pulled open a door almost invisible under the stairs. He dragged down on a string and a single bulb exploded into light.

Lottie pushed him out of the way and flew down the old wooden stairs.

'Lily? Sweetheart, don't be afraid. You're safe now.'

On the bottom step, she paused. Even with the light, the room was gloomy, but she could make out the three suitcases in a corner and the figure of a child sitting on the floor, arms wrapped around her knees.

'Lily, I've come to take you …' She was about to say *home*, but she had no idea where the child would call home any more. 'You're safe now, honey.'

She heard a soft, pitiful sob.

'I want my mummy.'

CHAPTER SIXTY-THREE

Kirby couldn't shake his anger at how Robert Brady had been let down. He knew McKeown should be the one to feel bad because he'd closed the case too quickly. No further investigation needed. Well, it was needed now, and Kirby sensed he was the one to do it.

He reread Beth Clarke's article and studied the photograph of Doon Forest with the lake in the background. So close to Colin Kavanagh's house. The scene was visible from the hilltop at the back of Ryan's cottage, where they'd been yesterday.

He stuffed the last of a tired sandwich into his mouth and headed to the cells. As he chewed, he concluded the bread was fusty. Too late now. It was in his belly.

The duty sergeant opened the door and Kirby stepped inside the bare room. An ultraviolet light gave everything a blue hue, transforming Slevin into a ghoulish form under its glow. He remained lounging on the narrow bed, one leg hanging off it, the other beneath his body. Kirby gave him a kick to move and sat down beside him.

'Tell me about Robert Brady,' he began.

'What about him?'

'You didn't like him as much as young Beth did, then?'

'He filled her head with lies. Telling her he was going to get enough money that they could hide out in a tropical island, away from pig swill, and he without a euro in his pocket. Fucking queer.'

'Why do you say that?'

'About the island? It's true. He gave her brochures and—'

'About being queer, dickhead. Do you mean he was odd?' Kirby knew what it was like to be classed as odd.

'Robert was as gay as Christmas. Not that I think that has anything to do with anything, other than that he led Beth on. Poor girl believed everything he told her. He was only stringing her along until he got money from Kavanagh. He knew she was good at her job and he used her to snoop for him.'

Kirby digested this, and the sandwich caused his stomach to gurgle in protest. 'Tell me more.'

Ryan sighed, crossing one leg over the other and clutching his ankle. 'There's something I haven't told you. Will you let me off the assault charge if I do?'

'Not my call. But I'll have a chat with the boss.' And fuck you if you think you're getting away with that one. Kirby smiled to himself.

'Right.' Ryan seemed to accept it. 'When Robert was working on my cottage, he told me he'd met this guy.'

'Go on.' A sour taste reached Kirby's mouth, and he wasn't at all sure it was from the sandwich.

'He told his boyfriend the story of Kavanagh's criminal dealings and the papers he'd found that proved Kavanagh was involved in laundering money and doctoring paperwork on stolen cars. The boyfriend blackmailed Kavanagh and got this cabin built for himself on Kavanagh's property. It's behind the house, close to the forest.'

'I can't believe Colin Kavanagh would give in to that kind of pressure.'

'No one can understand Kavanagh and his motives. I'm sure down the line he had plans to extricate himself.'

'Who was the guy?'

'I can be as inquisitive too, so I did a little poking around. It was Trevor Toner.'

Kirby sat up straighter, his throat filled with bile. 'The gobshite dance teacher?'

'Yeah, one and the same. He latched onto Robert, all possessive and a bit too needy, if you ask me.'

'You told Beth about him?'

'I did.'

'You knew he was Lily's dance tutor and you never said anything about his connection to Robert. What type of a lug are you?'

'Yes, but Giles would have had access to Lily at the dance school too. Here's the thing.' Ryan stood up and paced the tiny enclosure before turning to Kirby. 'I saw something in one of my photos of the Christmas market the other day, and it got me thinking.'

'What did you see?'

'These weird little voodoo doll yokes. On a stall.'

Kirby grinned. 'Saw them myself. Awful-looking things. Know anything about them?'

'I know someone who has one on his key ring.'

'Trevor Toner?' Kirby said.

'Yeah, and if that prick has hurt Lily, I'll kill the bastard myself.'

*

McKeown was relieved when Lottie phoned to say she'd found Lily safe and well. But with the day wearing on, he was tired and narked that he still had to babysit Giles Bannon.

Bannon was constantly on his phone. Trying to get through to his solicitor, his face growing redder with each unsuccessful try.

'Look, Giles, why don't I get this interview started? Then you can go home to your wife and kiddies. How does that sound?'

Bannon said nothing. Tapped his phone again.

McKeown leaned against the wall, folded his arms. 'What I don't understand is why you bought the dress on the theatre account. Did you not think we'd trace it to you eventually?'

Bannon looked up. 'Read my lips. I did not buy the fucking dress.'

'Evidence says you did.' Flimsy at best, McKeown thought.

'Show me that invoice again.'

McKeown eased his back from the wall and opened the file on the table. He passed over the invoice he'd printed from his iPad.

Bannon put on his spectacles, his lips moving as he read. He picked up the receipt. Read it too. Stopped. Looked up at McKeown.

'What?' McKeown said, stretching exhaustion from his arms.

'The dress was purchased on the theatre account all right, but I have two company credit cards. This one here ... look at the number; it's not the one I use.'

He took out his wallet and extracted a Visa card. Picking up the card, McKeown compared the number to the receipt. They were different.

'So where is the other card?' he said.

'I don't have it, because it's used specifically by the dance school. The head tutor, to be exact.'

'Shit.'

'Now do you believe me?' Bannon sat back triumphantly, but McKeown was already out the door.

In the corridor, he met Kirby huffing up from the cells.

'Trevor Toner,' they said simultaneously.

*

Lily was placed in the ambulance as Father Curran was whisked away in the back of a squad car.

Lottie and Boyd sat in Brennan's Pub while SOCOs began their work on the priest's house. Gossip was flying in all directions as the village came to life in the watering hole. Because Boyd had looked grey one minute and green the next, she'd insisted they eat before they did another thing. She tore into her soup and sandwich and noticed Boyd hardly touched his.

'At least the child is unharmed,' he said, twirling the spoon around the creamy soup.

'You don't think he did anything to her?' she said between bites of her chicken sandwich.

'No, I tend to believe he thought he was doing the right thing by helping Fiona, and then when she was murdered, he didn't know what to do.' Boyd put down his spoon. 'Lily is fine, Lottie.'

'Physically she seems okay, but the mental trauma will be with her for life. I know what it was like for Sean, and even Katie and Chloe. It'll haunt that child.' Lottie gulped down a sob. Her own children had been through so much over the last few years and yet she continued to sweep it all to one side. No wonder they escaped from her at every opportunity.

'Stop, Lottie,' Boyd said.

'What?'

'Beating yourself up.'

'Shut up, Boyd.' She smiled. 'But why didn't Father Curran admit to Colin Kavanagh that he had Lily?'

'Because he believed Fiona was terrified of Kavanagh and didn't want to put Lily in what he thought might be a dangerous situation.'

'Lily has to be told her mother is dead.'

'Poor kid,' Boyd said. 'Much as I hate to say it, we'd better inform Kavanagh she's been found.'

'Even though he's not her father?'

'Yeah.'

'Okay. We need to bring him in over his criminal activity. I still think he killed Christy Clarke,' Lottie said.

'And we have to locate Beth.'

Boyd went to pay for the food. Lottie's phone rang and she answered.

'Kirby. What's up now?' She listened intently. 'Okay. That's great. You and McKeown head to Toner's apartment. We'll be there soon.' She hung up. 'Boyd, let's give Kavanagh a miss for now. We need to concentrate on Trevor Toner.'

'Why?'

'Because both Bannon and Slevin have separately put him in the frame for the murders.'

She explained the conversation she'd had with Kirby.

'Look, we're in Ballydoon,' Boyd said. 'It will take us five minutes to call to Kavanagh, then we can head back to Ragmullin with him. Okay?'

It wasn't, but she nodded and said, 'Okay.'

CHAPTER SIXTY-FOUR

The gates were unlocked and there was no sign of Kavanagh's car. When no one answered her persistent knocking, Lottie moved to the rear of the house.

'That doesn't look like a car Kavanagh would drive.' She pointed to a battered-looking black Toyota Yaris parked at the back door. She peered through the windows. 'The keys are in the ignition.'

Boyd pressed his nose to the glass. 'Holy fuck, what's that on the key ring?'

Lottie put on protective gloves, opened the door and pulled the keys out. 'It's similar to the voodoo dolls at the market. Call in the registration. Confirm ownership of the vehicle.'

But after Kirby's information, there was no doubt in her mind whose car it was.

She walked across the expansive lawn and came to a stop behind a hedge, from where she had a good view of the cabin with the blacked-out windows.

As Boyd approached, she put a finger to her lips and indicated for him to hunker down beside her.

'Trevor Toner owns the car,' he whispered.

'I know.'

'Do you think he's in there?'

'You go round the back,' she said. 'See if there's another door. I'll wait here.'

'I know you, Lottie. You'll be through that door before I …'

His words faded as the cabin door opened. Toner walked out, hooked a padlock on a chain over the handle and locked it, then started to walk away, juggling the key from one hand to the other. His face was lit up by something akin to glee in the dark December day.

Lottie held her breath and knew Boyd was doing the same. The only sound came from the swans on the lake. Before she knew what she was doing, she'd stood up and burst out into the man's path.

The change in Trevor was instantaneous. His eyes darkened like the sky above his head, and he dropped the key. It distracted her for a moment. He ducked beneath her outstretched arm and ran, leaving nothing in his wake but a whoosh of thin air.

'Stop!' Lottie shouted, and took off after him. 'Check inside the cabin,' she yelled at Boyd as she hurdled a bush and found herself in a field.

Trevor was heading for the forest. Fuckity-fuck, Lottie thought. If he goes in there, I'll never catch him. But still she followed.

The darkness clouded around her. She fought off branches and briars, trampled through ferns, bushes and grass. Her heart was thumping so loudly it drowned out the persistent drip of water from the trees and ferns.

Where the hell had he got to? He couldn't disappear that quickly, could he?

She looked up, expecting him to drop from a tree and strangle her where she stood. Slowly does it, she warned herself, scrambling around trying to find his footprints in the marshy forest floor. A bird cawed and something skittered over her foot. She tried not to yell out as she pushed on deeper and deeper, fearful of the labyrinth swallowing her up.

You've been through worse, she reminded herself.

But she had no idea if he was armed. If he lashed out with a knife, he could kill her instantly. She thought of her children. Of little Louis with his chocolate-smeared smile. She even thought of Rose. What would her family do without her? Survive, most likely. Then an image of Boyd flashed in front of her eyes as she ducked beneath another branch. He would miss her, but maybe he had someone else now. He'd asked her to marry him. She'd said yes, but now he was acting like a dick. She would get him back. Yes!

Adrenaline propelled her faster through the maze. She tore away ferns and branches with her bare hands, without even feeling the cuts to her skin.

A dart of something up ahead caught her eye, and her toe stubbed a gnarled branch on the ground. She toppled head over heels, coming to a stop on top of an abandoned bag of fetid rubbish. The foul odour clogged her throat, obliterating the damp forest smell.

Where was he?

A sound to her right. Ignoring the pain shooting from her foot up through her leg, she crept on hands and knees towards it. The swans. Louder now. Close by. It was brighter, the air lighter. A loud shriek pierced the air. What the hell?

At the edge of the forest, the darkness behind her, she saw him. He was standing knee deep in the inky waters of Doon Lake, shouting at the sky.

Dragging herself upright, she inched forward silently. Trying to hear what he was saying above the crashing water and the boom of her heart.

'Come out, demon woman. The invisible can't haunt me. The dead are dead. And soon I will be too. Come out and face me.'

'I'm here. Come with me, Trevor, we can talk. We can sort this out. No need for anyone else to get hurt.'

His laugh tore into her soul. High-pitched, feral. Like a wild animal. And that was what he looked like as the wind gathered momentum and the waves crashed up around his waist.

'I'm the one who's been hurt.' He moved backwards, deeper into the water.

'Don't, Trevor. Come to me.'

'I was abandoned. Left to rot, to fend and scavenge like a rat.'

'Who abandoned you?' Keep him talking, she told herself.

'Everyone. I was abandoned by my birth mother and fostered. My foster mother ditched me for that bitch Cara. Discarded me like trash. And I was treated the same way by every adult in my life. Abused by teachers who almost scalped me bald and a lunatic foster father who made dolls. Dolls! Dressed them in strips of his wife's wedding dress, and the hair! Oh God, it looked so real.' He laughed, an unnatural wail from his blue lips. 'Well, I eventually gave him the real deal!'

'What did you give him, Trevor?' She tried to take one step forward on the shore for each that he took backwards into the lake.

His voice calmed and he looked through her. 'I saw him at the market peddling his fucking gruesome wares. I don't think he even knew me, or that I was the one who left locks of human hair for him.' He laughed hysterically. 'Why do you think I'm like this? Answer me that? I am a product of the people who surround me.'

Lottie was close to the edge of Lough Doon. The stones and pebbles sending shock waves through her damaged foot. 'I can help you.'

'No, you can't.'

'Why did you kill them? Why Cara? Why Fiona?'

He was silent for a moment. Then, his voice floating on the wind, he said, 'It was Robert. I took him in when he had nowhere to go, then he betrayed me. I loved him and thought he loved me. But he was laughing behind my back. He was going to undo everything I'd achieved, with his scheming. He had to die. Then the others, they broke everything. They had to die too. They were breakers of hearts. Breakers of promises.'

The water, up to his throat.

The water, up to her knees.

'Talk to me, Trevor.' She waded forward. 'Tell me, who broke hearts and promises?'

'Cara left me with my foster father. She broke my heart. Then I saw her in the Railway Hotel with Steve. She ignored me, but I was content enough that they seemed happy. She was a sly bitch, though. Filling my Robert's head with lies and breaking up with Steve.'

'You have it all wrong. Steve broke up with Cara.' Lottie slipped on the stones beneath her feet. Tried to right herself, keeping her eyes fixed on Trevor. His face had filled with uncertainty at her words.

'No. No. You have it wrong. He told me she broke his heart.'

'He lied.'

'Well, she deserved to die.'

'How did you get into her apartment?' Keep him talking, Lottie repeated to herself, as the cold water numbed her flesh.

'It was so easy to slip in and wait there for her. Eve didn't even see me take the key one night when I brought her home. She was blind drunk. I let myself into Cara's apartment while she was at fucking Mass. Then she dressed up in that wedding dress and all I could see was my foster father cutting up the white silk his wife had left behind. It felt good to wrap Robert's belt around Cara's neck.'

'But why Fiona?' Lottie yelled over the rising wind and falling rain.

'She had everything she ever needed with Colin. And what did she do? Buggered off with a two-bit photographer. And I knew she planned to run out on him too. You see, little kids talk to me.'

'Lily?'

'I never touched the kid, if that's what you're thinking. I wouldn't touch a child.'

'We found her. She's safe.'

'I'm glad.'

He'd stopped his retreat. The water was swirling around him. Lottie took another step, the cold seeping into her bones, her teeth chattering.

'Why dress Fiona in the wedding dress?'

'You don't see how it made me feel, do you? Watching Cara waltzing around in hers. I did what I had to do. I was on a high. I couldn't stop myself. I knew after I killed Cara that I had to make Fiona pay in the same way. I got the Cinderella dress and drove to Ballydoon as fast as I could. I couldn't let the buzz fade away.'

Lottie couldn't follow the reasoning of a madman, but she said, 'What did Christy Clarke ever do to cause you to kill him?'

'He was a liar and a cheat. He deserved everything he got. And Beth, too. I kept the best for last. With her beautiful black hair and her inquisitive nose.'

'But she never broke any promises or any hearts.'

'She wouldn't acknowledge her mother. Eve came back for her and Beth blanked her. Beth filled Robert's head with ideas of unmasking Colin's criminal activity just when I had him eating out of my hand. I couldn't let her get away with that. I'm sorry.'

'Sorry for all the murders?' She was ten strides away from him, the water rising as the bottom of the lake dipped away.

'Sorry I couldn't cut off all of her hair, make her feel the humiliation I had to endure, and sorry I couldn't have slit her throat.'

Lottie took another numbing step, struggling against the swirling current of the lake. Swans circled. Long necks ready to pounce, to peck and plunder. No matter what he'd done, she couldn't let Trevor drown.

Then suddenly he was gone.

The water swirled like a sink hole where he'd stood a moment before. The swans bellowed like trumpets, the wind whistled and the rain poured down in fat drops. Trevor Toner had disappeared beneath the demonic waters of Lough Doon.

*

Beth had never been so happy to see anyone as she was to see the detective opening the cabin door and rushing in with the padlock in his hand.

He quickly untied the ropes that bound her. With the door open wide, she could see she was in a dance studio. Or a cabin dressed up to mimic a dance studio. A bar and mirror on one side. A sound system on the other. And a sprung floor beneath her feet. Trevor must have had some hold on Colin Kavanagh to wrangle this out of him, she thought. Another piece to add to her story. The story she hoped to get into the right hands.

'I'm Boyd,' he said. 'Is there a quick way to the other side of the woods?'

'What do you mean?'

'You're from round here. Where is he likely to run?' His voice was high, a little hysterical, she thought.

'Trevor?'

He nodded.

Then she understood. 'This way.'

She walked slowly at first, but found strength in the knowledge that she was free, out in the fresh air. She welcomed the beginning of a shower of rain.

The detective was right behind her.

'I think I know this pathway,' he said, panting. 'I walked it in the dark the other night with my boss.'

When they reached the lakeshore, she saw the detective, Lottie Parker, waist high in the lake, and the top of Trevor's head disappear further out in the water.

Before she knew what was happening, Detective Boyd had ripped off his jacket and shoes and was diving into the depths. Then she saw Lottie Parker go under. Bubbles floated on the surface, and then only the crash of raindrops dotted the choppy water.

She watched, transfixed, her voice lost in terror. They were all going to drown. She knew the currents. They did not. She knew what the lake could do. They did not.

Without thinking of her own safety, she rushed into the lake. The waters were gloomy and dank, but she found the floating hair and grabbed it. Pulling the body close to her chest, she shot up to the surface, gulping down big ugly breaths.

'It's okay, don't panic. Tread water.' She pulled the woman to her chest.

As she turned to face the shore, she saw Detective Boyd break free like a torpedo from the depths, Trevor gripped in his arms.

*

On the stony shore, Lottie lay flat on her back, staring up at the clouds scurrying like frightened rats, dropping their load on her face. She welcomed the freshness. She breathed in the air in desperate gasps. Beth lay in a crumpled heap beside her, Trevor Toner at her feet. Boyd! Where was Boyd? She struggled up on her elbow and twisted to her side. Boyd lay there struggling for breath. She put out her hand and squeezed his. He looked at her and smiled weakly.

CHAPTER SIXTY-FIVE

Three days later

The boat rocked slightly on the canal in the morning breeze.

He'd never known any different. He wasn't blessed, or cursed, with children of his own. His wife had told him foster care was the way to go.

A boy and a girl. Perfect family.

Only it wasn't perfect. She'd broken it up and taken the girl with her. Along the way, he'd heard his wife had died. Never knew what became of the girl. Probably more foster care.

He took the wire and pushed the head on. Then he extracted the small lock of hair from the clear plastic bag. Beautiful. He never asked questions. Never enquired as to where it had been sourced.

Once again the boat rocked, and he listened, thinking someone had stepped onto it, but all was still. The ice had melted, but he had yet to leave. He thought of his market stall, abandoned as soon as he'd latched on to those eyes. A stranger in the street. Only they had not belonged to a stranger. They'd belonged to his foster son, Trevor.

Nurture versus nature. Ah, he never knew the answer to that question. The only thing he was sure of was that Trevor had to be taught a lot of lessons throughout his young life. Plenty of necessary hair snipping. Who did he think he was? Dancing like a pansy. Stupid boy. Not heard of in his day. Needed to be cut out of him.

The man snorted. He paused his work. He was sure it had been his foster son who'd left the hair on the stoop outside. Had Trevor followed him, once he'd recognised him at the market? He grimaced.

The talk of the town was that Trevor was the murderer. Stupid boy. All that pent-up anger. The boy who'd tried to become a man only to become a pansy dancer. He laughed, then stopped suddenly. Was it his fault that Trevor had turned out the way he had? Surely not. He'd only been a firm parent. But he couldn't escape the fact that he had reared a cold-blooded killer.

As he held the long black lock of hair to the light, he wondered if it had come from one of the murder victims. Fiona Heffernan, maybe.

He picked up a piece of wire sheathed in a strip of yellowed silk and wound the hair around the head.

CHAPTER SIXTY-SIX

Cynthia Rhodes walked with an added bounce in her step as the duty sergeant led her to Acting Superintendent David McMahon's office. The envelope in her satchel felt lighter after she'd had a good read of the document inside. Unexpected, to say the least. It was a good scoop, but she owed it to him to tell him before she broadcast anything.

He flushed bright red when she entered the office, and started fussing because there was no chair for her to sit on.

'Don't worry, I'll stand.' She placed the envelope on his desk. 'But I think you'll need to sit to read this.'

'What is it? Why are you here?' He plopped onto his chair, his long legs jigging. She wondered what he'd do if she leaned over and ran her fingers up his thigh like she'd done the other night.

'You wanted me to dig the dirt on Lottie Parker, then you changed your tune. Now I know why.'

'I've no idea what you're talking about.' He was vigorously flicking his fringe, trying to keep it out of his eyes.

'You thought if I burrowed too deep into her life and work, it would reflect badly on you.'

'That's ridiculous. You were upsetting her family every time you doorstepped her. You should have stayed in Dublin, Cynthia.'

'If I'd stayed in Dublin, I'd have missed all the fun. Though I think I'll miss our nights together now. Oh, when you've read that, ring me with a comment, will you? It's going to air tonight. Nine o'clock news. And it doesn't matter if you destroy it. I've got the original.'

'What is it?'

'A story. A good one. It will make Beth Clarke hot property. Might even help keep Ryan Slevin out of jail. Not so sure about you, though, David.'

He was out of the chair and rushing towards her, but she wasn't worried. What could he do to her in a garda station? Not a lot, she thought. Still, she took a step backwards.

He stopped and picked up the envelope from the desk. 'What's in this?'

'You'll see. I'll leave you to read it.'

'Cynthia …'

'Oh, and when Colin Kavanagh surfaces from whatever hole you've hidden him in, tell him I'd like a comment from him also.'

'You're a bitch.'

'But I'm not a criminal. Is that why you took this job, David? To be closer to the action once Kavanagh moved from the city. Did you think the two of you could escape from under the radar of the Drugs and Organised Crime Bureau? Move your dirty business to a village no one cared about?'

'I still don't get it.'

'Oh, you will.' She smiled. At the door, she turned. 'I guess you didn't figure on an enthusiastic young reporter or a serial killer disrupting your operation. Even if Beth originally started snooping because she and Ryan thought Zoe's husband was having an affair. I figure she has Giles Bannon and Robert Brady to thank for her story.'

'Wait, Cynthia, you have it all wrong. I was here to trap Kavanagh, not become involved in anything criminal or—'

'Really?' She patted down a curl at the side of her forehead and straightened her spectacles on her nose. Dropped her smile, too. 'If that's the case, how come my sources tell me Kavanagh took a flight out of Ireland Friday night, unhindered? He's now somewhere in the Costa del fucking Sol. Oh, and there's one lovely photograph in the envelope. You and Colin Kavanagh standing outside Christy Clarke's garage. It's date stamped. Two months ago.'

He stared at her with his mouth hanging open. The envelope dropped from his hand.

'I'll be waiting for that quote.' Cynthia left with an even lighter bounce in her step.

CHAPTER SIXTY-SEVEN

Boyd stood at the door to her office.

'Lottie, I know we have mountains of paperwork, T's to cross and I's to dot, but I need to take the rest of the week off.'

'Bollocks to that,' she said, trying but failing to inject a touch of good nature into her voice. 'Will you get those files ready for court as soon as possible?'

'I'm serious.' He remained standing at the door.

'So am I. Please go and do some work. Oh, the forensic analysis on the doll I got from the barman at Cafferty's is back. Horsehair. And the hair found on Robert's body likely belonged to Trevor Toner.'

She had to finish up everything as quickly as possible today, because tomorrow she had to bring her girls and Louis to the airport. She felt her heart break a little at the thought of that. But for now, she was busy.

'The clothes found piled up in Trevor Toner's flat have been traced to Robert Brady,' Boyd said. 'And the suitcases in Father Curran's house belonged to Fiona and Lily.'

'Poor Fiona. She was the only one who realised Robert had been murdered, and she thought it had been at Kavanagh's hand. That was why she planned her escape, only to fall foul of Trevor. If only she'd talked to someone other than that demented old priest. He should have told us everything sooner.' Lottie shook her head. 'By the way, what about that cashier's cheque in Clarke's account?'

'It came from Giles Bannon,' Boyd said, still lingering at the door. 'He says he was helping Christy out, but McKeown is still digging to prove he was involved in criminality.'

'I think Eve was correct when she said Christy was gullible. Kavanagh and Bannon walked all over him. Only for him to be murdered by a damaged young man. Such a waste of a life.'

'How is Beth doing?'

'Fine. Father Joe is trying to get her to reconcile with her mother. It's what Eve wants.'

Boyd walked further into the office. Stood in front of her desk, lines of seriousness etched into his cheekbones. 'We need to talk, Lottie.'

'If it's about Kirby staying at yours, I'll have a room free in a day or two when the girls leave. He can stay there.'

'Not about Kirby,' Boyd said. 'A serious talk. Let's meet in the Railway Hotel. Say in half an hour.'

He left before she could object.

She got up and closed the door, then tapped her computer awake.

Stared at the DNA results for Lily. The name of the child's father.

She had to get her head around it. Made a phone call. Confirmed his location nine years ago, and Fiona's location back then. Wexford. She tried to recall what she'd read about him when he'd been there. It had come up in a case two years previously. It had to be wrong. But DNA did not lie. She'd sensed a familiarity about Lily's blue eyes and fair hair, and now she knew why.

She would have to tell him.

The string of Christmas lights looped around the shelf behind the bar seemed to be the only nod to the festive season that Lottie could see. She found Boyd sitting in the corner with two mugs and a pot of coffee on the table. Eve Clarke, on a high stool, was nursing what looked like a gin and tonic, deep in conversation with Steve O'Carroll.

'Maybe we should have gone to Cafferty's,' she said.

'Why?'

'To get into the spirit of things.'

'I haven't much time for that,' Boyd said.

'Why not? You used to love the whole Christmas thing and I was the one feeling sorry for myself.'

He laughed quietly, his upturned lips bringing a glow to his eyes that had been lacking for weeks. It was good to have the investigations closed, albeit with a lot of collateral damage. Lottie eyed Eve again, dressed in black to give the impression she was mourning her husband. She wondered if Beth would ever forgive her mother. Not her problem.

She poured the coffee and relaxed on the two-seater, her sore foot resting on a low stool. She felt comforted by Boyd's proximity.

The noise of traffic whooshed into the bar every time the door opened, bringing with it a sting of cold air. She moved closer still. Resisting the urge to put a hand on his arm, she said, 'Boyd, remember the question you asked me weeks ago?'

He turned away, picked up his mug of coffee without bringing it to his mouth. 'About us getting married. Yeah. Lottie, I—'

'You've yet to buy me a ring,' she said.

'What?'

'Boyd. You know I want to marry you. Corny as this sounds, I'm lost without you. I loved Adam and I miss him, but I need to move on. I love you. Getting married will throw up issues at work, but we can get over that. And we've yet to decide where to live. My family is squashed into that rented house, but when I get the money from Leo, we can buy something bigger. For all of us. Sean will be ecstatic. And the girls will be too ...' She let her voice trail off.

Boyd hadn't moved. Hadn't turned to look at her. His face in silhouette a stolid study of stillness.

Silence filled the void between them. It was so real, she sensed she could put out her hand and touch it. It felt like an invisible wall had sprouted and the normal bar sounds had evaporated.

'Mark? What's wrong?' she said at last. 'Have you changed your mind?'

She leaned back, creating a physical distance between them. Had he fallen out of love with her? Were her suspicions real? Shit, this was a mess. She was a fool. She rubbed her eyes with the heels of her hands, trying to erase the blindness of her heart.

'I'm sorry,' he said.

'Don't be fucking sorry!'

She wrapped her arms around her waist so that she didn't land a punch on his jaw, trying to keep the hot flush of anger from exploding. She quickly lost that battle.

'I'm the one who's sorry, for making a total shithead of myself,' she said. 'Go on. Take your fucking week off and see your new ... woman ... friend or whatever. She's welcome to you. I'll manage just fine without you. I've done so since Adam died. I can keep on—'

'Lottie! Why do you assume everything is about you?' Boyd's voice was no longer soft. Instead it was tinged with something she couldn't quite put her finger on. 'Are you really that insecure?'

Fighting the urge to lash out, she clamped her lips shut. Tried to keep her tears locked behind stony eyes. She'd been such a fool to lose her heart to him.

He put down the mug, then turned and unwound her arms from her waist, holding one of her hands in his own.

'I don't want to hurt you, Lottie. I know you've gone through terrible pain and grief in the last few years. You've struggled with so much. Through Adam's illness, his death, raising your three beautiful, disruptive kids …' He paused, and she smiled despite herself. 'You uncovered your tragic family history and now you'll have time to benefit from it, once Leo comes through.'

'Provided he doesn't change his mind.'

'And then there's Rose. No matter how much she annoys you, I know you rely on her. She's your rock, Lottie, don't abandon her.'

'What the hell are you talking about? I don't understand. What are you—'

'Shh. Let me have my say.' He released her hand, took a mouthful of cold coffee.

Her heart pounded in her ears. She was sure Steve and Eve at the bar could hear it too. A prickle of fear pushed goose bumps up on her arms like pimples. A portent of what was to come?

'I haven't been honest with you,' he said.

Here it comes, she thought, her fear replaced with an anger so potent it caused her cheeks to burn. The other-woman story. Don't cry, Lottie. Don't you fucking cry, she warned herself. Fuck! She wanted to cry. To run. To escape. But there was something so sad about Boyd, sitting there clutching a mug of cold coffee, that she couldn't move.

'Go on,' she whispered. 'Tell me. I'm a big girl. I can take it. What's her name?'

'Will you stop for a minute?' He put down the mug and looked at her. 'You've gone through this before and that's what makes this so difficult. Lottie, I love you, I truly do, but …'

There were tears in his eyes. Clinging to his beautiful eyelashes. His thin face with its perfect jawline was trembling. She dared not look away.

'I love you,' he said again, 'but I can't put you through this. It's my battle and I have to do my best to fight it. Alone.'

'I don't understand. You're talking in riddles. You're like scratched vinyl on an old record player.' She wanted to make light of what he was saying, because she suspected it was something so serious she did not want to know it.

He stared into her eyes with such intensity that she blinked, and tears dripped down her face in rhythm with his.

'You have to understand,' he said. 'Those trips to Galway … I don't have another woman. Believe me, that would make this much easier.'

'What then?' She asked the question though she was not sure she wanted to hear the answer.

He moved his head slightly, and she thought he was going to rest it on her shoulder, but instead he turned to face her. Gazed into her eyes and said what he'd come to tell her.

'I was attending a clinic.'

'For your OCD?' She tried to be blasé because she knew with every sinew in her being what he was going to say.

And then he said it.

'Lottie, I've got leukaemia.'

CHAPTER SIXTY-EIGHT

On the shore of Lough Doon, Lottie stood with Father Joe by her side. The water rippled on the surface in December's icy breeze. She looked out as far as the eye could see. All grey, a mirror of the sky above her head, reflecting the dull thud in her heart. Four swans swam close to the shore, whistles breaking from their beaks.

'Those swans are like the Children of Lir,' she said.

He laughed. 'Who?'

'It's folklore. Four children turned into swans and abandoned for nine hundred years, condemned to spend three hundred of them on Lough Doon. They only had music for their voices.'

'Not much fun in that story.'

'I'm devastated, Joe,' she said earnestly.

'Will you shush, woman. You still don't know how bad it is. Boyd doesn't either, not until he has his consultation next week. Don't jump off any bridges yet.'

She smiled and wrapped her scarf tighter around her neck. She looked up at the sky, pleading for divine intervention. Something to give her guidance. She thought she could hear an aeroplane flying somewhere above the clouds. Taking her girls and her grandson to America. Her family. Her responsibility.

'I'd better get home to Sean.'

'Sean will be fine.'

'He loves Boyd. They're soulmates, especially if there's sport or a computer game involved.' She suppressed a sob. 'I still want to marry Boyd.'

'What does he say?'

She shrugged. 'He's gone home to his mother and sister. He doesn't want me at his next consultation. Joe, what if he has to have chemotherapy? I saw what it did to Adam. It will kill him. It will kill me.'

'Stop,' he said, and she thought he sounded just like Boyd. 'It won't kill either of you. You are both strong people. Trust in yourself. You've been through it before. You'll get through it again.'

'It's different. With Adam, I didn't know what we'd be going through. It was the unknown. Now I know how … how horrible it is. How can I find the strength to watch Boyd die?'

She felt the priest's arm move around her shoulder and pull her to his side. 'Boyd might look scrawny and fragile, but he's a champion. Trust, Lottie, trust.'

She smiled at his description of Boyd even as she cried into the still air. She tried to focus through her tears, staring at the swans, their voices now muted by the frantic thud in her chest. 'Oh God, I don't know what to do. I've been broken and hurt so often.'

'Do you truly love him?'

'Yes, even though he irritates the shit out of me at times.'

Father Joe laughed. But it wasn't hearty. She thought it was a sorrowful sound.

'I'm sorry,' she said. 'I've been so selfish. You must be heartbroken over Fiona.'

'Don't be sorry. I only knew her for a short time, all those years ago in Wexford.' He looked wistfully out at the water. 'Thank you for telling me about Lily. I never knew I had a daughter. Fiona just disappeared off to Dublin and I returned to the priesthood after my sabbatical. If I'd known, I'd have been a good father.' He swallowed a sob.

Lottie put her hand on his arm. 'What are you going to do about her?'

'I've no idea yet. One thing I'm sure of is that she will not be abandoned like the Children of Lir.'

'She's in foster care for now. She's with a good family. Have you seen her?'

'No. I don't know what to do or how to do it. But I can't let her grow up in care, no matter how good it is. I never knew my own mother and it haunted me. Lily is my daughter and I want to be in her life.'

'I'll help you all I can.'

'And I'll help you. Come on. I know where I'm taking you.'

'Where?' She felt his hand slip though the crook of her arm.

'Home. You're going to pick up Sean and drive to Galway to be with Boyd.'

As they walked away from the lake, Lottie took one last look over her shoulder.

The swans were swimming away from the shore, gliding gracefully, a trail of diamonds glinting in their wake, until the waters were once again still.

A LETTER FROM PATRICIA

Hello, dear reader,

Sincere thanks to you for reading my seventh novel, *Broken Souls*. If you enjoyed the book and would like to join my mailing list to be kept informed of my new releases, please click here:

www.bookouture.com/patricia-gibney

I'm so grateful to you for sharing your precious time with Lottie Parker, her family and her team. I hope you enjoyed the read and I'd love it if you could follow Lottie throughout the series of novels. To those of you who have already read the first six Lottie Parker books, *The Missing Ones, The Stolen Girls, The Lost Child, No Safe Place, Tell Nobody* and *Final Betrayal*, I thank you for your support and reviews.

I hate asking, but it would be fantastic if you could post a review on Amazon or Goodreads, or indeed, on the site where you purchased the book. It would mean so much to me. And thank you for the reviews received so far.

You can connect with me on my Facebook author page and Twitter. I also have a blog, which I try to keep up to date.

Thanks again, and I hope you will join me for book eight in the series.

Love,
Patricia

         www.patriciagibney.com

         trisha460

         @trisha460

ACKNOWLEDGEMENTS

I can hardly believe that *Broken Souls* is my seventh book in the Lottie Parker series. There is no way I could have achieved all this in two and a half years without the support of many people in my life.

Firstly, to you, my readers, thank you for reading *Broken Souls* and for your continued support for me and my books.

My family are totally behind me in all that I do, and I'm so appreciative of their understanding in giving me the time and space to follow my dream. To Aisling, Orla and Cathal, I am forever grateful. You are beautiful human beings and I am proud to have you as my children. And thank you to my wonderful grandchildren, Daisy and Caitlyn, Shay and Lola, for bringing sunshine into my world. You help keep me grounded.

I have the most supportive agent I could imagine. Ger Nichol of The Book Bureau is one of the best, and I'm so thankful to have her working on my behalf. Thanks to Hannah at The Rights People, and also to Marianne Gunn O'Connor.

Lydia Vassar Smith is my wonderful, patient and insightful editor at Bookouture. Thank you for helping me to bring *Broken Souls* to life.

Thank you to Kim Nash, head of publicity at Bookouture, for all the PR work; for reading my books and sending me tremendous encouragement and support. Special thanks also to Noelle Holten and to those who work directly on my books: Alexandra Holmes,

Leodora Darlington, Alex Crow and Jules Macadam (marketing). I'm also so grateful to Jane Selley for her excellent copyediting skills.

Thank you to all at Sphere, Hachette Ireland and Grand Central Publishing who work on my books.

Michele Moran brings the Lottie Parker series to life in audio format, so thanks to Michele and the team at The Audiobook Producers.

The writing community is very supportive of me and my work. Thank you to all who have listened to me, chatted and advised me, especially my fellow Bookouture authors. To all the book bloggers and reviewers, thank you. You are instrumental in helping readers find my books. Special thanks to Sarah Hardy of By the Letter book review. I am so grateful to every reader who has posted reviews, because you all make a difference.

Once again, I wish to acknowledge the tireless work of libraries and their staff, and also bookstores and local and national media. The highlight of my 2019 year (so far) was being invited by Ryan Tubridy to appear on the iconic Friday-night show *The Late Late Show* along with Liz Nugent and Jo Spain. Thank you, Ryan.

Special thanks to John Quinn for advice. I write crime fiction and seek guidance where necessary, but inaccuracies are all my own. I tend to fictionalise police procedures to help with the pace and the storyline. It is fiction after all!

I am blessed to have good friends, people who 'get' me. Antoinette Hegarty, Jo Kelly, Jackie Walsh, Niamh Brennan and Grainne Daly, thank you for picking me up when I'm down and for all your words of encouragement.

This year my mother celebrates her eightieth birthday; she and my father have been solid rocks behind me all my life. Thank you, Kathleen and William Ward.

Thanks to my mother-in-law, Lily Gibney, and family, who have been in my life since the day I met Aidan.

My siblings are always around; we all live in the same town! It is great to have them close by and I'm appreciative of all their support for me, my children and my work. Thank you, Cathy Thornton, Gerry Ward and Marie Brennan. I dedicate *Broken Souls* to my sister Marie. She reads early drafts of my work and offers invaluable advice. Marie, I want to wish you a very happy retirement after thirty-six years teaching little children. Now you have more time to read and travel.

Finally, and I know I've already mentioned them, but my children, Aisling, Orla and Cathal, are three of the strongest, most polite, respectful people I know. As teenagers, they lost their dad, Aidan, to cancer, and they have gone through a pretty rough time in their lives. Maybe that is why they have grown into such caring, supportive and fine young adults. I am so proud of you and thankful to have you in my life.

All characters in my books are fictional, as is the town of Ragmullin, but real life has strongly influenced my writing. I've always lived in Mullingar, the town of my birth, and I'm so grateful for the support for me and my books that I've received from everyone.

Now I'm off to write book eight in the series!